THE RECKONING

THE UNADJUSTEDS TRILOGY

MARISA NOELLE

This is a work of fiction. Unless otherwise indicated, all the names, characters, businesses, places, events and incidents in this book are either the product of the author's imagination or used in a fictitious manner. Any resemblance to actual persons, living or dead, or actual events is purely coincidental.

Cover art by Fay Lane https://faylane.com/

SECOND EDITION

www.marisanoelle.com

PRAISE FOR THE RECKONING

"Captivating!

"Sensational!"

"A fitting finale!"

"Heart-breaking!"

"#TeamJoe!"

"The author makes very good use of foreshadowing as the momentum builds and the climax beckons. I was reminded of the march of the dead army in Game of Thrones and was intrigued to see how Silver et al would succeed in spite of overwhelming odds against this existential new threat. I was fully engaged with this struggle but confess to feeling a little deflated by the ending." – Whispering Stories (Book Blogger)

"The Reckoning was a very well written, intense, violent and emotional story line that held my attention throughout. Marisa Noelle did a fabulous job giving us an exciting story, wonderful heroine (I loved Silver, as she made a great heroine) and great secondary characters. The ending was exciting, wild and emotional and a fitting finale." – Barn (The Reading Café)

"I really liked this conclusion. The ending was a slap in the face, in a good way. I did not see it coming and had an "Oh WOW!" reaction while I was reading. If you are looking for an action-packed, dystopian series, this is a great one to pick up." – Stephanie (Cover2Cover Blog)

"Noelle is skilled at writing emotion, and this novel is full of heart-wrenching and joyful moments in equal measure. Silver is an incredibly engaging protagonist; complex and wise, fierce and loyal, caring and selfless. However, her flaws and limitations are sensitively portrayed by Noelle – Silver is not just a heroine protecting her friends, she has constant battles within herself, facing demons that threaten to crush her." – Nia (GoodReads Blogger)

"The setting of Noelle's imagined world is unique and vibrant. The threat of the dark figure that hangs over the novel is incredibly effective – the reader desperately wants to turn the pages but can't shake the feeling of lingering tension. The plot builds in intensity, leading to gripping action scenes and moments of heart-stopping revelation." – GoodReads reviewer

"This is a tough review to write. Noelle put us in a pinball machine and tossed us around as she played. I found myself irrationally angry with Matt. He was controlling and stifling. It's no wonder Silver spent a lot of time with Eli. But this is the couple you want to pull together and work out to save the world. They have always done what they needed to get things done. When Matt was at his worse, I was cheering Noelle for writing him so well that I felt such emotion. Overall, an addicting and satisfying read and conclusion to the trilogy." – Energy (GoodReads Blogger)

"Even though I spent most of the book being angry at Silver and Matt, the writing had me caught up in my emotions. For me, this is the mark of a remarkable novel. Marisa made me angry, then she made me cry, and finally, I felt joy." – Kimberley (GoodReads Blogger)

"Like ever, Silver is one amazing heroine. A normal girl, who became more with each fight. It was beautiful to see her grow." – Melissa (Book Reviewer)

"I held my breath to see who would survive." - The Reading Café

"I love the premise: it's not having abilities that make you different, it's choosing not to. It goes really deep into human nature." - Lindsay Roberts (Blogger)

"I blinkin' loved it!" – Amazon Reader.

"The action explodes onto the page with such force that you don't blink, let alone put the book down." - Reviewer

"The characters are excellent and imaginative!" - GoodReads reviewer

"It gave me moments of shock and out-loud gasping." – Amazon reviewer

"The Unadjusteds was a well-written, intense and emotional story that kept my attention from start to finish." – Book blogger

"I devoured this book!" – Amazon reader.

"It reminded me of YA heavyweights like The Hunger Games and Divergent. It would make a superb film!" – Book reviewer

CONTENT WARNINGS

This book contains themes and references that some readers may find distressing, including, but not limited to:

- Violence
- Death or dying
- Blood, gore, graphic injuries
- Mental illness
- Prejudice
- Swears or curses
- Murder
- War
- Virus/Pandemic
- Monsters
- Injury/death to animals
- Traumatic child birth

THE RECKONING PLAYLIST

Radioactive – Imagine Dragons
Boulevard of Broken Dreams – Greenday
Ain't Gonna Stop – Carol Kay
Born Free – Kid Rock
God We Need You Now – Struggle Jennings & Caitlynne
Curtis
Play with Fire – Sam Tinnesz
Broken – Jonah Kagen
Unstoppable – Sia
Be Careful – Tommee Profitt, Laney Jones
Dangerous Woman - Ariana Grande
Gangsta's Paradise – Coolio
My Heart Has Teeth - Deadmau5, Skylar Grey
Sweet Child O' Mine - Jae Hall
Ready or Not – The Fugees
Revenge - Danger Mouse
Leave a Light on - Tom Walker

Watch me Burn - Michele Morrone
Lessons of the Fire - Bishop Briggs
Flames - Donzell Taggart

BOOKS IN THIS SERIES:

OTHER BOOKS BY MARISA NOELLE

The Shadow Keepers

The Unraveling of Luna Forester

The Mermaid Chronicles

Secrets of the Deep (book 1)

Quest for Atlantis (book 2)

Fight for Freedom (book 3)

Ghost pirates (book 4)

Vendetta (book 5)

For Quinn

CHAPTER ONE
SILVER

I scream myself awake. Black lightning bolts shoot from my palms and take chunks out of the plaster.

"Silver!" Matt yells and tackles me back to the bed.

His arms trap me. I fight against him, but I can't move. Why can't I move? I'm stronger than him. Panic runs through me, blurring my vision, making me pant and causing an excruciating pain to tighten in my chest. The black lightning bolts shoot everywhere, but Matt doesn't cower away from them, even when they scorch his hair.

"It's just a dream, Silver," Matt says in my ear. He doesn't let go and eventually I stop struggling.

It takes me a full minute to realize I'm in my bedroom. We've only been living here for a few months and it doesn't feel like home yet. The moon shining through the open curtains allows me to identify the objects in the room. There's a wardrobe with sliding doors, a chest of drawers, two bedside tables bookending the king-size bed. No paintings or pictures, nothing personal. I'm not ready for that. Besides, my lightning bolts would probably destroy anything I put out. But there is Matt. Always Matt. He is my one familiar. My one constant.

He sits up, rubbing his eyes, then fiddles with his scorched hair.

"Maybe you should sleep somewhere else," I say.

He shakes his head. "I'm not going to leave you alone."

"But I could hurt you." I chew on my lip. "I don't want to hurt you."

"You're not going to hurt me." He kisses my cheek. "Do you want to tell me about the dream?" Fatigue lines his voice and I catch an undercurrent of irritation. This isn't the first time I've disturbed his sleep. It happens every night. Sometimes more than once.

Suddenly cold, I pull the covers to my chest. "Maybe it's not a dream."

I inspect his face, looking for clues. Whatever he says next will define my future.

"Silver, of course it's a dream. What you've described to me is impossible. It can't exist. Scientifically, fundamentally, not possible. It's just a *dream*."

"I'm sorry, Matt." I hold his hand.

He tucks my hand into his elbow and lies down next to me. "I know you are. I'm just so damn tired. And you are too." Settling under the covers again, he rests his head on my pillow. "I really hope Deja will help you. We can't go on like this. We're not going to have a house left to live in."

I don't reply, but lie there looking at a foreign ceiling, examining the dark shape of the lamp shade I often think is a

2

mysterious entity hovering above me. My eyes are moist, but I don't reach for Matt. He's already asleep again. How does he do that?

I grab a few acorns from where I left them on my bedside table and circle them in my hands, hoping they'll calm me. I think about my mother in the next room. She may be catatonic, but I'm sure she hears things. She's been that way ever since we rescued her from Earl's mountain over five months ago. I've tried everything I know to heal her, but so far nothing has worked. She has around the clock care, but the nurses don't seem to know what to do either. My dad left after a month to go looking for a woman who is rumored to be able to help in such situations. I've only heard from him once and I worry the journey will be too much for his faulty heart.

Worry.

Worry, worry, worry.

The battle with Earl was months ago, but I can't seem to stop worrying. I lie awake for the rest of the night and pretend I'm asleep when Matt gets up and leaves for work. I smell the soil of the farmland as he tugs on his boots. Then I feel him looking at me, but I don't say anything.

"It's going to be okay, Silver," he whispers, then leaves.

A few minutes later I get dressed in a pair of shorts, a T-shirt and my favorite pink flipflops. My combat boots stand in the corner, there if I need them, but I refuse to wear them. Maybe if I wear flipflops every day nothing bad will happen. I know it's a silly thought, but if I dress for fun, if I refuse to believe in the possibility of new threats, then maybe I'll be left alone.

I leave the house and walk through the streets of Camp

Fortitude. It's a new area developed near the old Central City where President Montoya and her most valuable assets are assigned to live. We reside on the border between suburbia and country. Mostly so we can be near the crops my father genetically engineered to grow quicker. But also so the greatest minds, those with the most strength or power, can be together to shape the future of our country. The old mission team all live here with me. I couldn't be without them.

Although most of the world was wiped out by the virus, the population greatly decreased, there are enough of us to maintain electricity grids and factories. But everything is greatly reduced and we've learned to be careful with our usage. It's not a world I recognize. Sometimes I wonder if the battle with Earl was worth it. Then I mentally slap myself and remind myself that I'm grateful for my friends and family. All of those who are still alive.

Reluctantly, I walk past Paige's house, wishing I could visit. She is heavily pregnant and not having an easy time since Jacob's injury. But I know I'd be procrastinating and I'm not interested in the argument with Matt that would result if I miss the appointment. A few minutes later I find myself outside a more office-like building. It's still a house, but there are slatted blinds in the windows and an official sign on the front door.

After the battle, I expected the panic attacks to subside, to disappear as suddenly as they entered my life. I'm dreaming all the time and I can't tell the difference between a vision and a harmless nightmare. I envisioned my anxiety as salt dissolving in water, hoping it would wash away without any effort. Instead, the salt seems to aggravate the scars I carry, and the panic attacks are becoming increasingly frequent, driving me here, to a therapist's office.

I've never been good at talking about myself, about revealing my inner most fears and the things I don't like about myself, like my anxiety. But I promised Matt I'd try. The memory of the dark circles under his eyes is enough to force me to press the doorbell.

The door opens automatically and I follow the arrows along a small hallway and into a comfortable living area. Stifling a bitter laugh, I scan the room. It's such a cliché. The big wooden desk, the bookshelves lined with self-help books, the two armchairs facing each other for more intimate conversations. It's a throwback to the time before, when the world was normal. But nothing is normal anymore. A vase of cheerful, red tulips is arranged on the windowsill. They're my mother's favorite flower and encourage me to bury my hesitation.

The woman behind the desk rises and offers her hand. "It's nice to meet you, Silver. My name is Deja."

The name surprises me. Deja. Déjà vu. A bit like a vision or an omen. I can't seem to stop reading into things wherever I go.

Although she wears flats, she's an inch or two taller than me. A silk blouse is tucked into a smart pair of trousers and her dark hair is swept into a messy chignon. Like it matters anymore. People work from home when they can and when they can't, no one cares what anyone wears. But in spite of her formal appearance, her smile is warm and reaches her eyes.

I force a smile onto my lips and take the hand. "I'll be

honest, I'm really not sure about this."

She nods. "Neither was I before I started. Experience of trauma led me to a new career. It helped me and now I like to help others." Her words make sense but that's her life, not mine.

I shrug.

"Give it a go. For Matt, at least."

I grit my teeth. I want us to be a normal couple. I don't want to worry about hurting him when I'm dreaming. That's why I'm here. But I don't expect anyone to be able to take my anxiety away. It's who I am.

"He's worried about you."

"I know."

She gestures to one of the armchairs. "Make yourself comfortable."

I sit on the edge of one of the chairs, an old-fashioned green velvet thing, and cross my ankles. "Is this where I pour out my whole life story, or something?"

Deja sits on the chair opposite. "Actually, I thought we could start with a bit of hypnosis. If you're up for it, I'd like to take you back to the dream."

A flush creeps over my skin. My mouth goes dry. The dream. Vision? No, definitely just a dream. I won't let it be anything else. Matt is right; it's too impossible to be real.

"You think you can make it go away?" I ask.

"I'm not promising anything. But I'd like to try." She offers me a reassuring smile.

I follow Deja's instructions. Listening to her soothing

voice, I allow my eyes to close and my thoughts to drift. It's comfy here, safe and warm. Then she takes me back. Back to the dreams I desperately want to forget...

Standing in the valley surrounded by the snow-topped mountains, I admire the way the sunbaked rocks glisten in the evening light. The scattered, leafless trees tremble under the effects of a wintery gust. The cold stings my cheeks and I bury my chin into the top of my jacket.

"*Silver...*"

Turning to face the voice, rough, leathery skin sweeps past my cheek. I startle backward, looking for the attack. Ripping my glove from my hand, I ready my knife and my lightning power. But it's just a bat. A lone bat getting an early start on the night's hunt.

"*Silver...*"

I turn again, closing my eyes against the lowering sun. I'm facing the doorway, the blackhole of my nightmares.

With a rushing flurry of wings, more bats emerge. A handful to begin with, bringing the smell of death. Then a dozen more. Fifty. A hundred. Hundreds quickly become thousands. A tumultuous flow of bats dart and weave around each other, as though trying to evade the last rays of the sun before they are saved by nightfall.

"*Silver...*"

The wind howls, dislodging the last remaining snowflakes from the mountain peaks. The bats are joined by clicking, cackling insects. They fly in a chaotic group of directionless fury, as if controlled by an unseen puppet master.

"*Silver...*"

I cover my ears against the noise of their deafening wings. The stench of wrongness fills my nostrils. There are thousands of them. More. Tensing, I watch the gaping entrance of the cave. But nothing else emerges.

"*Silver...*"

Who is that calling my name? It sounds so familiar.

Shadows loom, larger than the angle of the sun should allow. Night descends. The wind whips my hair. Organizing themselves, the bats and insects join together to form a black wave of power. They come for me, tumbling over each other like the crest of a tidal wave. And they call my name.

"*Silver...*"

Other animals appear within the wave. Dark and terrifying animals: howling wolves, fangs dripping a hungry saliva; growling mountain lions with stalking shoulders; a black bear rears up and emits a tree-cracking roar. They run down the mountain with the thousands of bats and beetles, swarming toward me. A cacophonous clicking noise rises from within them, as though they are an endless mass of rolling glass marbles, knocking into each other, eager to reach me.

Spotting a pair of large eyes, involuntary tremors shudder through my body. Yellow, inhuman, like liquid pools of fire. They appear in the middle of the sky as though they are portals to another dimension. Then comes the hulking mass of the body. It's so black it is indistinguishable from the night and the wave. It moves, absorbing the wave, growing taller, wider, swallowing the night sky.

"*Silver...*"

It calls to me from a mouth too large for its face. A mouth

with no lips. A mouth which distorts into a maniacal grin and emits the most horrifying, hair-raising sound I've ever heard. Black hands decorated with crawling beetles reach for me. Fingers that end in razor-sharp claws grab for me. I crouch and roll away.

But there is nowhere to go.

Everywhere I look, the black wave surrounds me, the yellow eyes loom at me, and those hands, those decay-smelling fingers, creep closer and encircle my neck, my throat, squeezing. I gasp for breath, choking, feeling the air wrung out of me. This is the moment, this is how it's all going to end.

I scream.

"You're safe! Silver, you're safe!" Deja grabs my arms and stares into my eyes. The yellow eyes glare at me. No, not yellow. Deja has brown eyes. "You're safe."

I can't breathe. I cough and splutter and gasp for air. My hands fly to my neck to wrestle the attacker away. Instead, all I find is the chain of my pendant digging into my skin. Releasing the chain, I gulp oxygen down into my sore throat.

"You're safe," Deja says again.

Nodding, I wipe the sweat from my brow. The dream. It's the same every time. Waking from a nightmare should put an end to any feelings of terror – for a normal person. Instead, my heart pounds faster, my chest tightens, and I'm almost flattened by a dizzy spell. Clutching a pillow, I bury it deep in my ribcage, something to soften the burning acid flashing through my chest.

It's a panic attack. I'm having another goddamn panic

attack. I thought I was through with all this crap. Earl is dead. We're safe.

Get over it, Silver.

Cupping my hands over my mouth, I draw in deep, ragged breaths until my heart rate slows and the pain in my chest eases.

"That's it," Deja says.

"I'm so tired." I ache everywhere.

"It's an awful dream. I would be too."

"No, not that. I'm tired of the panic attacks." They're almost daily and have been worsening over the last few weeks. The dream won't leave me alone.

Deja pours a glass of water and hands it to me. "If it's any consolation, I get them too. A lot of people do, considering what we've all been through."

"I know I'm not the only one." Sighing, I put the glass on the table. "But I am the only *ultimate weapon.* I'm the one who possesses all this power, abilities I don't even know yet, thanks to Earl. I'm the one who has to fight for control of the destroyer ability. No one else has to deal with that. I'm the only one who has a catatonic mother who is beyond my help."

"Silver. That's why we're here. But one problem at a time."

I fist a hand. "I don't have time."

Deja smiles patiently, which irritates me. "Why not? Your mom's not going anywhere. Neither are your abilities. And your dream is just a dream. You said yourself you recognized Earl's mountain. Well, you've already defeated him. There's no reason for you to go back."

I close my eyes. "I'm tired of the pain."

Deja holds my hand. "I know. We're going to work together so you can live with the pain."

Unable to speak, I ball my hands in my lap. I wish someone could wave a magic wand and take it all away. Deja explains it doesn't work like that. But there might be another option. Not a magic wand, but something equally effective.

11

CHAPTER TWO
SILVER

AFTER MY THERAPY session I walk home, letting the memory of the dream float through me, trying not to get too caught up in the scary parts. Those yellow eyes are terrifying. I look over my shoulder, expecting to see them peering at me from the sky, or a bush, or a dark streetlight. But there's nothing.

Anxiety brings with it the feeling of being watched and of time running out. I've felt that way for the last three years, and it only gets worse. PTSD I guess. But what if it's not? What if there's something out there?

At home, I kick off my flipflops and trudge up the stairs to my mother's room. She's asleep, her face set in a serene expression. Watching the slow rise and fall of her contented breathing, I pray for the millionth time that she'll wake from her nap, cured, returned to her former self, no longer a prisoner of her own mind. I stand in the doorway watching a beautiful sunset form, allowing the pastel colors to soothe my soul. If only there was an ability that made wishes come true.

But there is something I can change, about myself. I can free myself of panic attacks. It's a simple genetic procedure, one I've resisted before out of a determination to stay pure and unadjusted. Well, I'm the biggest altered of the lot, what does it matter anymore? If there's something that can bring me a little more peace, that can make life a little bit easier, then I'm all for it. Life is too short for obsessive worry and anxiety. There's enough bad stuff in the world to deal with, that I've already dealt with. Surely I deserve a break?

The rule of thumb concerning genetic modifications is if you're taking something away it will generally be approved, but if you are adding or enhancing something it will be rejected. I plan to take something away and I don't have time for lawyers and supreme courts. Ultimately, the decision will come back to me, to my lab, anyway. I am Silver Melody. People sing about me. I saved the world, twice, and now it's time for my reward. Anyone would agree. Wouldn't they?

As I slip out the front door, a sliver of excitement flashes through me. After weeks and months, years even, of longing to be free of fear's tight grip, I'm finally going to be rid of it. Walking through the quiet evening to my lab in the presidential compound, the silence unnerves me. With a mere three million souls left in the entire world, silence is often the prevailing status. The survivors of the virus were divided into camps surrounding Central City according to skills and expertise. Animals have begun to replenish, but it's still so quiet, not even cicadas serenade my walk.

After swiping my card at the entrance, the door opens with a soft *click* and *whoosh*. I make my way to my lab and sit at my workbench. I've researched the procedure countless

13

times before. I know the steps back to front and can perform the modification with my eyes closed.

It only takes a few minutes to prepare. Inhaling, I hold my breath to steady my arm, then inject the treatment into my arm. It was my birthday last week. A belated birthday present. *Happy 17th Birthday, Silver!*

I half expect a blaring alarm to go off, a signal to show the world Silver Melody is in her lab performing illegal modifications and needs to be dealt with. Directly beneath the presidential offices, no less. After a few minutes of holding my breath, compliments of one of my abilities, a shaky laugh escapes my lips. Finally, I'll no longer be weak. I'll no longer doubt myself and I'll no longer have to endure a panic attack. Nobody will be any the wiser. Returning to my small house, I flop on the bed and close my eyes. Sleep comes immediately. Deep, dreamless, restful sleep.

I wake to the sound of clinking china and silverware. Crawling out of bed, I make my way toward the morning noises.

"Morning sleepyhead." Matt kisses my cheek. I smooth his long hair away from his face, trying not to feel guilty over the scorched patch. "It's late, did you have a rough night? I didn't hear you dream again."

"Nope," I mumble, as I slide into a chair at the kitchen table. "For once I slept through the night without a single dream." I pour cereal into a bowl, then milk and take a bite. Realizing my crunching mouthful is the only noise in the room, I look up.

Matt beams at me. "I told you seeing Deja was a good idea. Sounds like it went well."

"Oh, it was nothing to do with Deja." I take another mouthful of cereal.

Matt slides into the chair opposite me. Concern knits his eyebrows together. He is tanned from working in the fields and the skin on his hands has toughened. "What do you mean?" His twenty-four-hour stubble only accents his good looks. I melt a little. He is my world, my rock, the love of my life.

"I'll continue to see Deja. I did feel a lot better after our appointment. But I decided a more permanent solution was necessary." Unable to meet his eyes, I brace myself and wait.

The spoon in his hand pauses in midair. "What do you mean?"

"I took myself off to my lab and expunged anxiety from my DNA," I reply, adding more cereal to my already full bowl. I take another mouthful. Anything to delay the response I know is coming.

Matt's frown deepens. "Why?"

"Because I'm tired of feeling so weak." I explode off my seat and stare at Matt and his damningly beautiful eyes. "I'm tired of not being strong, of falling apart at the worst possible moments. I've had enough of the dreams. I'm terrified I'm going to hurt you. I'm tired of the struggle. I just want to be normal. Are you really going to deny me that?" A kernel of cereal in my bowl pops and fizzes.

"No, of course not." Matt leans back in his chair and holds his hands high. "I thought we'd be able to get through it. Together. I thought with Deja's help...things would calm down."

"It's not enough. I need it to go away *now*, not months

from now." I jab a fingertip at the tabletop to emphasize each word.

"I'm assuming you talked to Francesca? Got permission?" Matt stands to face me. Now I have to look up at him.

"Really, Matt? My father and I are head of the goddamn genetics lab. It was going to circle back to me anyway. I saved everyone a whole lot of time and effort."

"Just because you're head of the lab doesn't mean you can go off performing experiments when you feel like it. That's what..."

I know he's thinking of Earl, he is comparing me to Earl.

Itchiness crawls over my palms and my fingers tingle.

"Okay, okay." Matt attempts to placate me when he sees the outraged expression on my face. He reaches for me and manages to circle his fingers around my wrist. The table starts to shake. The bowls and silverware bounce violently off the table and land in a heap on the floor where they promptly disintegrate into a pile of ash. "Silver!"

"I'm sorry, I'm sorry. I didn't mean to. I'm...frustrated. Why is it so hard for you to understand?" I sink back onto the kitchen chair. My destroyer power has been hard to control lately. The pile of ash at my feet isn't the only result of its appearance in the last week.

"I do understand." I look at him accusingly. "Really. I do. But I'm worried about you. This is so unlike you, going off and performing modifications on a whim."

I cross my arms. "It was hardly a whim."

"You know what I mean. You didn't talk to anyone about it. You didn't talk to *me*." His eyes plead with me. Do I detect a watery hurt in those mesmerizing blues?

"I have spoken to you. We talk every night when I scream you awake and you tell me it's just a dream. We can't keep having the same conversation. I can see how frustrated you are."

"I'm not—"

"You are. And you have every right to be." I grit my teeth against my roiling emotions. "Maybe we should just be grateful this is something that was easily fixed."

"You don't need to be fixed," Matt mutters, jamming his thumbs into his belt loops. "I should have been there with you."

"I can handle it on my own."

"That's what worries me. If it was so easy for you to slope off in the middle of the night and perform this modification, without talking to me, without me knowing you were even contemplating such a step, then I guess I'm a little concerned about what else you might do."

"I'm not going to...why would you think...Matt, that's not fair!" The table shakes again.

"Silver!"

Closing my eyes, I force myself to calm down and will the unnecessary power away.

"Silver." Matt reaches for my hand. "It's a slippery slope. Genetic modifications always start with good intentions. You, of all people, know that. No one sets out trying to rule the world. It's a gradual path."

"Matt, I'm not going to change anything else, I don't need to," I say, shrugging off his touch. "I was taking panic attacks away, not adding some other superhuman ability. Everyone knows I've got enough of those. I've done a lot of

17

good for this world." I pause to collect my thoughts. "I think I deserve a reward, I deserve to be free of this emotional shackle."

Matt searches my face, that slight frown tugging at his eyebrows. "Okay," he says after a while. "Let's drop it. But I think we should tell Francesca."

"No," I say immediately.

"I know it's retrospective, but we can't keep something like this from her. There's paperwork..."

Goddamn Matt with his *i*-dotting and *t*-crossing.

"Matt, *no*." I say it calmly and make sure I'm in control of my emotions. "My anxiety problems are embarrassing. It's private. It's not something I want to tell anyone about, least of all Francesca who has such an oddly high opinion of me. Please understand that."

"It's not odd to have a high opinion of you." Matt squeezes my hand. "Francesca already knows about the panic attacks. Everyone does, Silver. Nobody thinks any less of you. Not so long ago I believe I told you it was one of the things I love most about you. Not that you have panic attacks, but why you do, because you are one of the most caring people on this planet and you are moral and just and fight for everything good and feel deeply for every living soul. I just wish it wasn't so painful for you."

"Well, it won't be anymore."

Sighing, Matt blows his hair out of his eyes. His gaze drops to the floor at the drifting pile of ash. "Okay, Silver, okay. Let's just be careful."

"Matt." I place a hand on his cheek. "I'm not going to change anything else. I promise."

"I know." He grabs a new bowl and pours more cereal for me.

"Good."

"I'm glad things will be easier for you." He hands me a spoon.

We finish breakfast talking about anything but my anxiety. Matt heads to my bedroom to grab a shower and a change of clothes. I tidy the dishes and the pile of ash and then walk to the stairs, intending to check on my mother. Einstein hobbles past me, his ears flat and his tail low.

"What's the matter?" I ask the dog.

My back. It's worse.

"Again? That's three times this week." Kneeling beside the golden retriever, I lay a hand on his flank. A familiar golden luminescence builds in my palms, flows to my fingertips and enters Einstein's body. Within moments he straightens and walks normally again. My healing power is one of my favorite abilities.

You can't keep doing this, Silver.

"Of course I can, I hate to see you in pain." I ruffle Einstein's ears, massaging the area I know he loves. His head becomes heavier in my hand.

No, I mean, there will come a day when there will be nothing you can do.

"Einstein! Don't talk like that. I will always keep healing you. There is no way you are checking out on me."

Silver, I'm an old dog. I've had a good life. You must accept I don't have much time left.

I don't know how to respond, so I remain silent. Ever since I've been able to hear his thoughts it's brought an extraordinary closeness to our relationship. It pains me that he's aging so obviously. I know he won't be around forever, but the thought of him passing is more than I can bear.

Einstein nuzzles my palm, licking at my fingers, then turns away. Sinking to the bottom step, I watch the dog leave through the back door and enter the garden. Maybe I can alter his genetics. Maybe I can extend his life expectancy. Maybe I can reverse the ailment currently bothering him. All I need is a blood sample. I glance up the stairs. Up there is another problem I need to deal with, a bigger problem and I have absolutely no ideas.

"Are you coming?" Matt asks, as he emerges from the bedroom, fresh, clean and smelling of lemons.

"Coming where?" I ask as he starts down the stairs.

"To the fields, to check the growth rate of the crops. Francesca was concerned after we altered their growth rate that the development was going too fast." He runs a hand through his damp hair, straightening the waves.

"I was going to check on my mother. I was going to try...well I don't know what exactly, but something." I push myself to my feet.

"Silver, the nurse will be here soon. Your mother will be in good hands." Matt jogs down the stairs and takes my hand.

"Stop handling me, Matt." I twist out of his grip. "I need to be with my mother right now. Especially with Dad away." I back up the stairs a couple steps. "He's been gone for weeks and we haven't heard from him in days. I can't lose...I can't...I need to be with her."

Matt sighs, then turns on his heel and leaves the house. The front door slams behind him and bounces open again.

Why doesn't he understand? My mother was taken from me, twice. I'm not going to let her out of my sight again. And Dad is traveling around the country looking for a friend of Koko's. A lady with a mystical healing ability who might be able to help. With him gone and my mother silent, I feel constantly on edge.

CHAPTER THREE
SILVER

I'M HALFWAY up the stairs when there's a knock on the front
door. I contemplate continuing on to Mom and ignoring
whoever it is, but my unrelenting sense of duty makes me
turn to the door.

I open the door to find Francesca standing on the porch.
President Francesca Montoya.

"Good morning, Silver." She presses her palms together
and takes a step inside. She wears work trousers and sturdy
boots. Her hair is held in a loose ponytail at the nape of her
neck and her sharp eyes don't miss a trick. With Hispanic
origins, she is classically beautiful, although there is no trace
of an accent. "How are you this morning?"

"Fine, good, thank you President Montoya," I stumble. "I
wasn't expecting you."

"Please, Silver, you know you can call me Francesca
when we're alone." Francesca crosses the threshold and
meets me where I stand in the hall. "I'm here to solicit your
advice."

I glance up the stairs, cursing this new delay separating me from my mother. The nurse arrives, her eyes widen at the presence of the president in my hallway, and then she scurries up the stairs.

"Sure, yeah, I guess."

Francesca passes me and enters the kitchen. She waits. After another glance up the stairs, I follow her into the larger room.

I finally remember my manners. "Coffee? Tea?"

"No thank you, Silver. I won't stay long," Francesca says, as she leans over the kitchen counter, resting on her forearms. Although it's a relaxed pose, there's purpose to her movement. She excels at persuasion and guilt trips. She levels her dark eyes at me, causing heat to flood my cheeks. No one can refuse her after receiving one of her penetrating looks. "I was hoping you could help me with something."

"If I can." I abandon the pretense of making a cup of tea and settle on a stool opposite her.

"It's the crops. The genetically engineered ones. They worked beautifully, but something has gone wrong. They appear to be rotting before they're ready for harvest." My heart thumps in my chest. I thought they were growing too fast. Not this. It can't be this. "The scientists at the barn are struggling. I was hoping you could take a look, see if we might have caused a problem." Francesca leans back and drums her fingernails on the counter as rhythmically as a metronome.

I don't want to face this. I dreamed about failing crops. It leads to everything bad. The thing with the yellow eyes. Whatever it is. The crops can't be dying. "Isn't my dad...?"

"Well, yes, he was helping, but with him away I've come

23

to you." Francesca frowns. "I think we need some help before the crops fail."

Resigned, I nod. "Okay, sure. Yep. I can help." Of course I can help. It's not a disease. It's a side effect of the growth rate. It *has* to be. It *is*. It will be. I *will* fix it.

Francesca readies herself to leave, reaches the kitchen doorway, and then turns back to me. "Aren't you coming?"

"What? Now?"

"Yes, Silver, now."

"I can't, not now." I dare to look away from her, into the house, at the stairs. Low murmurings float down from the second floor. The nurse speaks to my mother in a soothing tone. "I need to be here. With my mother. I need to help my mother."

"Silver," Francesca says gently, retracing her footsteps into the kitchen. "Your mother is in good hands. She will be fine. I need you in the fields, in the lab, solving this problem before all of our crops perish and we find ourselves with no food."

She stares at me. I return her stare with what I hope is equal determination. She waits me out. There is no way I'm going to leave my mother. I want to try healing her again. It will only take a few minutes. I know I can do it. I felt a shift in my healing power yesterday. It might be growing, like the destroyer ability.

My powers last so much longer than they used to. I can use them for a whole day before tiring. The more I practice the quicker my stamina increases. I'm getting stronger. If I keep practicing, I might be strong enough to heal my mother. I must try again, today, now. I'm sure something will happen.

One of Francesca's eyebrows arches.

It's not just about my mother. I don't want to go to the fields to be confronted with a dream that might not be a dream. I had a vision when I was in Earl's mountain. Just one. It started with diseased crops. Then there were snakes and insects, a gathering mass of venomous animals that extinguished our camp. I don't talk about it, but I think about it every day. The similarities between this dream and the reports of failing crops unnerve me. I'm never relaxed in the fields, keeping my eyes open for snakes in the corn.

"I'll come later." I won't be able to avoid it forever, not without explaining my hesitation. There is a kernel of doubt in my mind that Matt's assessment of my dreams is wrong. That it's not PTSD, but a vision. But what am I supposed to do about a black wave of terrifying beasts?

I want to pretend, even if it's only for a day, that there's nothing wrong with the crops. I want to enjoy my new anxiety-free self.

"I need to try something with my mother first." Avoiding her gaze, I stare at my flipflops. One of the yellow daisies is coming unstuck from the pink, plastic strap.

"Okay, Silver." Feeling the weight of her stare, I keep my gaze on my ridiculous flipflops. "But please don't be long." She turns and marches out of the kitchen, along the hall, and out the front door, her boots clip-clopping on the wooden floor.

I sag against the wall as the door closes behind her. I thought she might refuse to leave without me. In the street, I hear her car start and pull away from the curb.

"Okay, Mom, let's get you fixed," I whisper, as I take the stairs two at a time.

I enter my mother's room to find her sitting in a chair with a crocheted blanket draped across her lap, almost as if she's denying the spring morning its pleasantness.

"I'll leave you for some time alone." The nurse finishes straightening the bed and leaves the room.

At the window, I pull the drapes wider and fling the window open. Maybe if she hears normal outside noises she'll be curious enough to emerge from her mental prison. I sigh. Who am I kidding? She's been stuck in this catatonic state for weeks. I slump onto the bed opposite her and sweep my gaze over her frail figure. Her hair, although combed, hangs limply about her face. Dressed in a T-shirt and thin, cotton sweatpants, her hands lie folded in her lap. She stares at a point above my head, rocking, back and forth, ever so slightly. She does it every day. It makes me seasick. Her lips twitch, as if about to speak, but she only ever mutters. A constant murmuring. Prayer-like.

"Mom." I speak in a voice used on the deaf and infirmed. "I'm going to try healing you again."

The rocking pauses, her head tilts. Listening? Can she hear me? Then the rocking recommences and her head returns to its neutral position. Leaning close to her, I place my hands on either side of her head. The healing luminescence flushes over my hands, bringing a pleasant heat that emerges from the middle of my palms and spreads along my fingers. The sight of it always takes my breath away. Sometimes I feel *chosen*.

My mother's hair alights in the same luminescent glow.

Her skin softens, her eyes became a little brighter. A surge of positive energy builds within me. Building, building until the intensity becomes uncomfortable. The warmth of my palms turns hot. Too hot, burning, and the golden glow turns white with heat. Tiny projectiles of electricity dance between my fingertips. I mentally flinch from this new progression of my power but keep my hands on my mother's head. She doesn't seem to notice, until she grabs my wrists and pulls them away from her head.

"No, no, no!" she says firmly.

"Mom?"

Did I reach her? The sparks flicker over my fingers, shining an intense blue color, different from the black lightning. I wait a minute for her unseeing stare to focus on my face. "Mom?"

Nothing. Her eyes cloud over and her hands slip into her lap. She's gone again. And so are the sparks. But it's the first time since I found my mom that I elicited a reaction from her. It has to be a good sign.

Rearranging the blanket on her lap, I glance at my fingers where the blue sparks danced over my nails. That was different. That was something else. But is it a good something?

The power inside feels bigger. It's growing and I don't know where I'll end up when the process is complete. Nor do I care. If I can grow powerful enough to help my mother, then nothing else matters.

After nodding my thanks to the nurse in the kitchen, I leave the house and climb into my jeep. I haven't had a license long. Before the resistance I was escorted to school by armed guard and never needed one. I learned when we got back from the mountain. *Thanks, Matt.* As I turn the engine on, I swat at a mosquito that's flown through the open window. Sawyer says they're all over the city, multiplying in force.

Turning onto the highway, I nudge the jeep in the direction of the farmlands. Fields of wheat flash by, reminding me of my dream. The long stalks sway gently in a soft breeze. Then I notice the black. I shield my eyes against the sun for a better look. The familiar golden-brown color of the wheat is speckled with black spots. It looks familiar, because it was in my dreams. My heart rate picks up, even though I took anxiety out of my DNA. Pushing portentous thoughts out of my head, I swing my attention back to the road. It was just a dream. I won't let it be anything else. Matt told me to let it go.

As I drive, I think about him. My irritation has faded and I miss him. Ever since the battle with Earl, I hate being apart from him. Especially with my Dad gone. He makes me feel safe in a way no one else can. I sigh. Why are we bickering so much, about my mother, about my abilities? I'll have to find a better way of making him understand.

To distract myself I sing old songs from the time before. I let the wind tussle my hair and pretend I'm on a road trip with Matt. How amazing it would be to leave everything behind and just drive. No responsibility. No scars. No dreams. I smile at the thought.

A few minutes later I drive into the lot where a large, red barn stands in competition with the sun, casting long shadows over the baking asphalt. In the distance, Central City hovers on the horizon, the forest beyond that. Memories fill my mind. So many. But they are disjointed and feel like they happened to another person.

Shrugging off the sense of nostalgia, I approach the barn which houses all the farming equipment. At the back, there is also a small lab where the two scientists Dad trained perform genetic modifications on the crops.

Beyond the barn is a smaller outhouse where Matt's three hellcats live. I say Matt's, but they belong to all of us. Commandeered during our fight with President Bear, they are half alive and half robot. Matt reconfigured their programing to be loyal to us. They prowl the fields at night as sentries. Every time I see them go back to their shelter in the morning I shudder. I will never be comfortable with a hellcat in the vicinity.

Relishing the sun on my back, I start down the dirt track leading to the crops. These fields are mostly wheat and corn. Further along there are carrots, potatoes, green beans, turnips, tomatoes, and strawberries. Truckloads have already been harvested. Many fields are waiting to be sowed. As I walk, I grab a stalk of wheat and use my knife to cut it in half. It's covered in the black speckle, diseased. I wrinkle my nose as I catch a faint putrid odor in the air. It comes from the wheat. I wave to Matt and Francesca in a neighboring field, indicating I'm on my way to meet them.

As I progress along the dirt track, Adam spots me from the middle of the field and runs over. He's kept the schoolboy haircut, that much is unchanged, but he's put on a little weight and something around his eyes appears softer. We met Adam on our way to Earl, living in Koko's camp of virus survivors. It was him who gave me the unusual power to see the future in visions and dreams. It wasn't an ability I wanted, but at least there are two of us to share the burden. We have each other to discuss our nightmares, to decide if there is any commonalty and if we need to warn the others.

He bends over when he reaches me. "Hi," he gasps.

"Hi, yourself."

He reaches for my arm, then hesitates. He is nervous about touching me, ever since my reaction when I took his ability.

"It's okay." I grab his hand and tuck it under my arm.

His face turns serious and he looks over his shoulder. "I had a dream last night."

I brace myself. Please don't let him mention the mountain and a black wave with maniacal beasts. Or the failing crops. It's too sunny for morbid thoughts. And an eleven-year-old child with a dirt-smeared shirt and bruised shins shouldn't be allowed to have visions of the future.

"There was a helicopter and it crashed into the fields. Everything was burning," Adam says, standing straight. "The whole city. The whole camp. Everything was in flames. Nothing survived." He shivers, but there isn't a cloud in the sky.

"I'm sure it was just a dream, Adam." I smile. "I had a dream too, but there was no fire."

He nods, a curt movement, taking in my words. "Phew. Sometimes I forget what it's like to have normal dreams."

I chuckle and sock his shoulder.

"At the end of it all," Adam says, plucking a stalk of wild grass from the edge of the path. "It felt like something was coming. Something big and mean. Something with yellow eyes."

Pausing in the middle of the dirt track, a chill sinks into my bones. Something with yellow eyes. A creature. A monster. For a brief moment, the prickling grip of fear washes over me. Then I shake it off.

"I'm sure it's nothing." I pat Adam's hand, ignoring the ball of dread in my stomach. "There's no point worrying unnecessarily."

But I too have the urge to look over my shoulder, suddenly sure when I turn there will be the yellow-eyed monster of my dream.

31

CHAPTER FOUR

ELI

Sleeping in his small cabin at the edge of the farmland, Eli dreams. It begins pleasantly enough. In his dream, he is lying on the bow of a boat, a yacht, a luxury forty-footer. The sea is calm and smooth, not a ripple to disturb its perfect surface. The sun shines fiercely, making him reach for his tube of sunscreen. A bottle of beer rests by his head. This is the life.

Pulling his sunglasses over his eyes, he tucks a soft beach towel under his head and relaxes into the clean-smelling fabric. It is sunset yellow. A gentle and soothing color that settles the flicker of unease he carries.

He turns his head at a sudden noise. A dull *thud* followed by a soft scraping, as though the boat rubbed against something. Eli rises to a knee and peers over the side of the boat. He blanches. Something has gone wrong.

There is nothing there. Nothing. No other boats, no harbor, no people walking along the boardwalk bustling from souvenir shop to ice cream parlor. No smell of hotdogs on the breeze. He's sure he tied the knot securely. There isn't even a rope. How odd.

Eli scans the horizon. It's all just blue, blue, blue. He looks the other way to be met with the same wall of color. Panic swells in his stomach. Short, shallow breaths tighten his chest. All he can smell is salt. Looking for a landmark, he pivots in rapid circles. Where the hell is he?

THE MIDDLE OF THE OCEAN!

Then he realizes something even worse. He doesn't know how to operate the boat.

Eli springs to his feet and scurries to the hatch leading to the control room. He pulls on the handle. Locked. He searches his swim shorts for a key. Nothing. Not only is he drifting alone in the middle of the ocean without knowing how to pilot the damn boat, but he can't get to the controls even if he could figure out how to operate the massive vessel. His situation can't possibly get any worse.

A crack of thunder explodes above his head and a sudden stampede of dark, menacing clouds swarm across the sky. Of course, it can get worse, it can *always* get worse.

Rain drills into his bare flesh like thousands of tiny needles. Water bounces off the surface of the boat and rebounds at least a foot into the air. The sky darkens. The ocean turns a stormy gray. And the waves begin. Small enough at first, gently rocking the boat, like a fairground ride he remembers when he was a kid, the one that came every year to the small town where he grew up. But then they crash onto the boat, threatening to topple it, building to such a height that they reach the guardrails and wash over the hull.

The water is cold, freezing, causing goosebumps to form

over his skin and his teeth to clatter against each other violently. Eli loses his footing and goes down on his hip, hard. He grabs for the rope guardrail. But the boat is rocking all over the place. The fairground ride has turned bad. This isn't fun anymore.

With the next crack of thunder comes a flash of lightning and a wave so large that Eli is sure he's about to be washed away. He grabs for the rope again, grits his teeth, and determines not to be beaten. Looking at the black sky, within the darkest of the storm clouds, he swears he sees two yellow eyes staring down at him.

He wakes. In his cabin on the edge of the farmland. Eli lies there unmoving on his bed and stares at the ceiling, waiting for the dream to recede, waiting for reality to return, waiting for his heartrate to slow.

The cabin shakes, as if it's situated on a fault line and a tremor has run underground. But there are no earthquakes around here.

He sits up slowly and swivels his feet to the floor. He is wet. But it isn't the ocean spray that covers his skin in a thin, glistening layer; it's his own sweat. Running his fingers through his damp hair, he smells the ocean, salt. How odd.

Eli attempts to shrug off the dream while he dresses, brushes his teeth, and eats a small breakfast of a buttered roll, but his mood remains somber. He swears he can still smell the ocean wafting through his small home. A headache lands. It pounds at the base of his skull like a drunk in lock-up demanding to be released. He squints against the painfully bright sun streaking through his front window.

Popping a couple of painkillers into his mouth, he

wonders if the headaches are a side effect of the things Earl did to him. He told Silver he refused to follow Earl into the madness of genetic mutations – and that is true, for the most part - but that didn't stop Earl from experimenting on him. There are powers inside him, difficult to control.

Back in the mountain, if something went wrong, Earl fixed it, often bringing Eli back from the brink of death. As a result, Eli possesses more powers than Earl, genetic mutations considered failed that Eli now must now find a way to contain. He tries to bottle them, to push them away, but the harder he attempts to blot the existence of his abilities from his consciousness, the more powerful they become. Silver is not the most powerful altered at Camp Fortitude.

Eli doesn't want to end up like Earl. He was a crazy screwball at the end there. If Eli examines his abilities, if he uncovers and tests them, then what's to stop him ending up like Earl? Better to bury them, forget he has them. Be normal. Settle down.

The headache continues to throb. Every pulse of pain brings the sensation of clawing fingers as if there's a skeletal hand in his head trying to scrape out his brains. Scratch, scratch, scratch, a bit here, a bit there. It isn't an entirely unpleasant sensation and reminds him of the satisfaction he experienced when he was a kid and picked his scabs. Flacking off the crusty cover brought such a sweet pain.

The dishes on the rack above the sink rattle and Eli curses Earl once again. The occasional juddering that shakes his cabin is a result of his attempts to clamp down on all that he is. Control. He must control it. If he can't do that, who is he? Who will he become?

He hasn't dealt with it yet. Earl. And everything that happened. He doesn't want to deal with it. Ever. Any time he thinks of Earl and the things he did, he pushes it away and instead evokes his mother's face in his mind's eye. She was beautiful, right until the moment she died. He prefers to think about how gentle she was, about her lopsided smile that warmed his insides, and her long summer skirts which floated around her ankles. Everything a woman should be.

Eli paces in his small cabin, breathing deep, pushing the nightmare and thoughts of Earl away. He flexes and fists his hands, performs a serious of squats and sit ups. Exercise helps. It exorcizes his demons, allows the control to come, allows him to prepare. His guard must come up and stay up. He can't afford for anyone to discover his secret.

But he craves companionship, something deeper, a purpose to his life, a point to his freedom. Something beyond the monotony of planting seeds. Dig, plant, cover, repeat. On and on. Day after day. He won't complain. It's better than the mountain, which still features heavily in his dreams. At least, he thinks they're dreams.

Eli reaches for his sunglasses, wipes them with his T-shirt when he notices they are speckled with water, and then catches a glimpse of Delta in the fields, planting seeds. His heart flips inside his chest. Like an idiot, he stands there, alone in his cabin, smiling at her as if she can see him.

Something deeper. That's not so much to wish for, is it? But how can he get close to her if he has to keep the most important part of himself a secret?

His smile falters. It won't stop him trying. He'll figure out a way. Maybe when Silver's father gets back he'll be able to help him. Confidentially.

Eli stares at Delta through his window, imagining a ridiculous future. Her hair is cropped short and her delicate hands are covered in mud. She wears long-sleeves, even in this heat. Her pale skin could do with a little color.

She catches his eye and waves, beckoning him to join her. His heart thuds against his ribs and his mouth runs dry. Maybe the future he imagines isn't so ridiculous. Although he is an orphan now, he might find love again. He winces at the thought that he might need love. He and his mom got along fine without his dad. Love is *not* all you need, it does not make the world go around, and it certainly doesn't put food on the table. Genetics does that. The unadjusteds do that. Silver Melody does that. Now there is a woman worth admiring. All that power at the tip of her fingers. Formidable. Strong. Powerful. How he longed to feel powerful when his dad was around, but his dad had a knack of draining all the strength and fights right out of him.

Leaving the cabin, Eli walks into the fields. It's hot already and the sun beats down on his neck. But he doesn't mind. The sun rarely shone where he grew up and he relishes the feeling of being warm. Delta watches him and he can't tell if she's blushing or if she's already hot from the sun. He likes it when she blushes. It makes him feel like he belongs, that bad things won't always happen to him, and he too can rejoice in female attention.

After grabbing a packet of seeds, Eli ventures to the other end of the field, on the same row Delta works along, but the opposite end. A subtler approach might put her at ease.

Pretty soon they'll meet in the middle. Then they'll talk and he'll listen to her sweet, sweet voice.

Eli bends and digs a finger into the moist earth. The loamy scent of rich soil fills his nostrils. He feels the fertility of the earth between his fingers, as though the soil has been waiting for all of time for Eli to come along and pour his seeds into its waiting mouth and be nourished and tended to perfection.

The circle of life fascinates him; baby to adult, acorn to oak tree, seed to crop. It never ends, even when the earth is scarred by fire or tornado or earthquake or meteorite, as in the time of the dinosaurs, the circle of life persists. Energy is never destroyed, only ever transformed. There will always be life. He takes reassurance from that.

He glances at Delta. She's watching him. With her hand at hip level she sends a half wave in his direction. His heart soars, out of proportion to her small gesture.

After an hour of planting and no sign of the headache abating, Eli retreats to the corner of the field to the only available patch of shade. An old camping table with dozens of water flasks is erected beneath a towering oak, which Adam regularly climbs. Sometimes he hangs out there all day. Eli gulps the refreshing liquid, spilling it over his face and chest.

"It's hot work." Matt leans against the trunk of the tree, sipping on his own canteen and fondling an acorn between two fingers.

"Indeed," Eli replies, rubbing his thumb and forefinger across his forehead. Why won't the headache go away?

"You okay?" Matt asks, taking a step closer.

"Yeah. I think so." Eli dribbles water onto the back of his

neck. "Bad dream. Well, nightmare. Landed me with a killer headache. Pain killers don't seem to be working."

Scratch, scratch, scratch.

"You've had more than one? Headache?"

Matt took him under his wing when he arrived. Showed him the store where he got clothes and food and campaigned to have him assigned to Camp Fortitude, even though he has no special skills or experience with technology, has never been an asset to President Montoya. Perhaps she wanted to keep an eye on him.

Matt put him to work in the fields and then showed him the vacant cabin. Although wary that Matt wanted to keep him close for less aimable reasons, Eli accepted the cabin. He had nowhere else to go. After he cleaned away the puddle of green goo adhered to the floor, he made it his own.

"Yeah, a few," Eli replies.

"I'll get Silver for you. Maybe she can help." Matt turns and jogs to the neighboring field where Silver is in discussion with President Montoya.

"I don't need...please don't worry..." Eli calls after him. It's too late. Matt is already out of earshot.

He examines Silver in the distance. There's something about her that makes him nervous. An emotion he's unused to. He's never been nervous around people, girls, before. Yes, he supposes, she's beautiful and all, but it's more than that. She was the one who discovered him tied up in the mountain. She saved him. Saved his life. Freed him from Earl. Not merely by untying his bonds, but by killing Earl too. Earl Landry. He wouldn't be winning any person of the year awards now. Eli didn't bother to mark his grave, let alone mourn him.

Silver welcomed him, unquestioningly, without the wary look in her eyes that Matt wears. Eli will always be grateful for that. She also has the power to be his undoing. He must be careful around her. He doesn't know the extent of the powers she possesses. Might she have the power to discover who he really is, or what powers he contains?

He is aware of the speculation among her friends. Because he is related to Earl, might he share his philosophies? He's given up trying to convince them one way or the other. They'll see in time that he only wants peace. Which is why he can't reveal his powers. To anyone. They'll never understand.

He'll die before he'll let this opportunity at a new life escape his grasp. He is determined. That is one quality he and Earl do share.

Eli turns his attention back to the furrowed line he was planting halfway across the field. The rest of the field remains untouched, waiting. They'll have to get the farm machines. Delta approaches the halfway mark.

Without warning, a small furrowed row appears beyond the pre-existing rows, in the unplowed region of the field. As he watches, the line grows, longer and longer, all by itself, paralleling the one Delta works.

Odd.

Unless there's a new machine which can plow fields from underneath the ground? No. He's pretty sure technology hasn't advanced that far.

Another line appears next to the first. This new row

streaks across the field, almost quicker than he can watch. It's completed in seconds. He blinks three times in rapid succession, trying to dispel the obvious visual hallucination. When Eli looks again the new rows remain. The headache behind his eyes throbs a little harder. It feels like he's butting his head against a brick wall, from the inside.

One more line appears, a third row, trailing the length of the field. When it reaches the halfway mark, it slows and peters out. With his hand on his hips, Eli watches the strange visual illusions take place. He shakes his head, vigorously, even though it makes his head hurt more. The hallucination, if that's what it is, remains. Odd, odd, odd. Unless...

Eli turns as Silver and Matt approach. As she nears, he spots the concerned frown on her brow. Aw shucks. She is worried, about him. Tingly feelings warm his insides.

"Matt said you had a bad headache. We're not exactly near a doctor around here. Can I help?" Silver offers her hand. It's already glowing. She healed him once before and he remembers how good it felt. Like he'd been filled with maple syrup.

"If it's not too much trouble," Eli replies, pushing his shoulders back.

"Of course not." She smiles, and her skin shines, radiating angelic goodness.

Silver places her hand on his head. It's cool, refreshing. Eli leans into the touch, closing his eyes, enjoying the feel of her skin on his, despite Matt's scrutinizing look. The pounding abates, slightly. One lone clawed finger continues to scratch deep within his brain.

"That's weird," Silver says.

"What's weird?" Matt asks.

"It's not working. My healing power is being blocked. I can feel it leave my fingertips but it won't penetrate Eli's head."

Eli snaps his eyes open to find them both staring at him. "Um, don't worry about it. It's feeling a little better now anyway," he lies. *Scratch, scratch.*

Silver tilts her head, staring at him. He can almost hear the cogs inside her brain working. "Unless something is going on with my powers. Like this morning..." She and Matt exchange a worried look.

"Really, it's fine." Eli waves her off. He must get rid of her before she starts to suspect something.

"Or perhaps it's an effect of what you've been through. Maybe Earl did something to you...?" Now she looks all concerned again.

"I'm not sure. Maybe. I can't remember all of it," he lies, again.

"You were in captivity a long time. That'll take a toll on anyone," Matt says. His expression softens. Maybe Eli imagined the wariness.

Silver gives his shoulder a gentle squeeze. "Have you experienced any other symptoms?"

"Uhhh, well..." Eli glances at the three new crop lines, "unless you count seeing three new rows dug with invisible fingers before my eyes in a matter of seconds normal, then yeah, I'd say that counts as a symptom."

Matt and Silver exchange another look. Silver glances at the rows behind Eli and shrugs. "Looks the same to me."

"It might be some hallucinations. From the headaches. Visual disturbance," Matt says.

"That's probably it," Eli replies. *Go, get out of here before you discover something else about me that doesn't add up. Before you peer into my brain and realize I'm not who I say I am, and perhaps see the source of whatever is scratching the coils of gray matter deep inside there somewhere.*

Scratch.

But this time the right spot is scratched and Eli sighs in almost-ecstasy.

"Maybe take it easy today," Matt says, wiping his brow with the back of his hand. "Go lie down, get some rest."

"Maybe," Eli replies. "I'll see how I go. I really want to help." Which is true. The more he immerses himself in a normal society, in a normal life, the busier he can make himself. If he's busy he can distract himself from the headaches, the strange dreams - the boat nightmare wasn't the first dream that woke him in a cold sweat - and the odd visual hallucinations that could be a manifestation of an ability and a crack in his control.

Scratch, scratch.

"Okay," Matt says. "I'm going to go back and look at the irrigation system, see if it can be fixed so we can stop heaving buckets of water everywhere."

Silver gives him a brief kiss on the lips. Eli pictures the velvety softness of her lips, the way they might brush against his skin, ever so tenderly, the way they'll leave a tingle on his cheek, his own lips. Delta is cute and pretty and attractive in her own way and the type of girl he expects himself to be with, like a warm apple pie, but Silver is on a different plane entirely. She's a firecracker of power and emotion and dazzling beauty, the kind of girl he doesn't dare dream about being with in his wildest imaginings. But he can't help his mind wandering.

Stop it! She's not interested in you.

Eli turns his back on Silver and approaches his planting row where Delta squats in the sun. She is the person he should be with.

"Feel better," Silver calls after him.

He turns around. She is waiting for him to reply. "Thanks."

Scratch. Scratch.

CHAPTER FIVE
SILVER

Glad for a respite in the shade of the tree, I watch Eli walk to the middle of the field, still rubbing his head. He's obviously still in pain. Why can't I heal him? Are my powers beginning to fail me? Are they changing, adapting? Into what? Too many questions and too few answers. Sighing, I turn to the red barn. At least things with Matt are better.

I stop by the small lab in the far corner of the barn and speak to one of the scientists, showing him how to adapt the genetics of the crops he's currently examining. We decide to slow the rate of growth a little in an effort to deter the disease growing in all of the fields, no matter what the crop. It might not have anything to do with genetics. It could be bad luck, a normal infestation. One step at a time.

I refuse to think about my dreams, what comes after the crop failures. It's too outlandish, too wild, too fantastical to be true. I tell myself that every day. And yet, I can't stop looking over my shoulder. Even though I expunged anxiety from my DNA, a nervous anticipation hovers. Life is too good to be true. As much as I want it, I've stopped believing in peace. I'm so used to living with anxiety it's become an ingrained habit. But at least I didn't dream last night.

Keeping my gaze averted from the fields with their mysterious disease, I walk back to my car. Next on my list is Paige. She's in the last trimester of her pregnancy and feeling wholly uncomfortable, telling anyone who will listen how much her back aches. She refuses to stay in the new hospital where the doctors can monitor her unusual baby and so receives regular, daily checks from one of the doctors who resides in Camp Fortitude and from myself if I'm not decimating something to ash.

Craving a breeze in the heat of the scorching sun, I climb into my jeep, roll down the windows, and drive back to the residence area of the camp. Paige and Jacob, along with Jacob's mother, live a few houses along from my own, and next to them lives Koko and Adam. She moved her surviving population east to join us, Francesca, and the other refuges of the world.

I pull into the driveway and Erica flutters onto the porch to greet me. Her damaged wing hangs crooked and is a permanent reminder of our battle with Earl. Her lavender hair is long and loose and covered by Sean's Stetson. She never takes it off. A permanent memorial.

"You're not going to try anything are you?" Her arms are crossed, her most common stance these days.

"Hi, Silver, how are you? I'm okay Erica, thanks, although my mom's still catatonic, my Dad's been gone for weeks, the crops are starting to fail, Matt and I are arguing, and I had a weird dream the other night, but thanks for asking." I slam the jeep door.

"Sorry." The intensity in her violet eyes fade. "I don't want Jacob forced into anything he doesn't want."

"I know, you're a bit like a Pitbull with a bone," I reply. Erica and I don't have the easiest of relationships, and her fairy wings used to represent everything I hated about altereds, but much of that is in the past. "I'm not going to heal him unless he asks. And I'm here to check on Paige, not Jacob."

During the battle with Earl on the mountain, Jacob was injured. He took a blow to the back of the neck and lost his ability to walk. Now he spends his days in a wheelchair, sometimes racing Megan down the street, but refuses to talk about me healing him. He believes it's his punishment for being a nanite junkie before, for contributing to the problem. I hate the attitude he has and worry it will rub off on Megan. She is Matt's youngest sister and has been in a wheelchair since she was five, after a bad car wreck. The regeneration nanites were unpredictable for kids so she never took one, and when she came of a safe age, had no interest in it.

"The crops? What's wrong with the crops? You and Matt? You guys don't argue. And what kind of dream?" My words finally sink in.

"Don't worry about it. I think we've solved the problem, with the crops anyway. Matt and I will be okay. The dream doesn't bear worrying about. My mother I'm not so sure." I march up the porch steps and place my hand on the fly screen.

"I'm sorry, Silver."

"Thanks." I let the fly screen swing closed again, then turn around. "Erica? At least let me help you, let me heal your wing."

Erica lost half the wing in a battle with a fire-breathing dragon and has so far refused to be healed out of a misplaced show of loyalty to Jacob. Seeing it all burned and withered is a constant reminder of what we went through. One I'd rather do without.

Most of the mission team put their abilities to good use with the farming, security, and policing. Carter and Mason, the bulks, are the head of our new police force and are training others. Bulks can grow up to nine feet tall, have impenetrable skin and a strength to rival a bull. In the time before, the bulk nanite was a popular choice for football players and soldiers. But it was expensive, and the highest class of nanite. Not just anyone would be approved. Now, Mason and Carter use their strength to help with the crops when a heavy machine or such needs to be moved from one area to another. Sawyer, one of the original mission team members who was homeless before the resistance, is working his way through the city with his pyrokinetic fireballs. He's clearing the puddles of green human remains littering the sidewalks, homes, and buildings. His second job is transporting gallons of water with his telekinesis to irrigate the crops. If Erica's wings were healed, she might find a focus.

Erica's lips thin. Two circles of pink bloom on her cheeks. She nods. "That would be great. It hurts like a bitch."

Laying a hand on her damaged wing, the healing power flows into my palms. The glowing luminescence travels the length of my fingers and casts Erica's damaged wing in a

48

bright, golden hue. The charred, brown area of the wing retreats and is replaced by a healthy pearlescent color. Then the wing grows until it's complete once again. Her eyes brighten and she flutters the new wing. It moves through all the colors of the rainbow, an interesting quirk unique to her.

"Thanks, Silver." Her hand floats to her chest.

"It's the least I can do."

I'm glad it worked. After not being able to cure Eli, I'm worried there's something off with my abilities. Maybe it's not me, maybe it's Eli. Maybe Earl did something to him. Something he doesn't remember or doesn't want to talk about it. I understand that. I can't imagine what he must have been subjected to when he was held prisoner in Earl's mountain, by his own father, even though he'd never been a part of Eli's life.

"I wish you could heal Carter as easily," Erica says, sagging against the wall of the house. "I never see him without a bottle anymore. If he doesn't get it together Francesca will take him off active duty."

I chew on my bottom lip. "I wish the emotional stuff could be as easy to heal. We could all use a bit of that."

Erica offers me a fragile smile. "I'm not surprised you're having nightmares, we all are. We've all been through so much."

I lay a hand on her arm. "You can't fix everyone."

She looks at me, her eyes brightening. "I know. I just wish I could."

She slips into a porch chair and I squeeze her shoulder as I hold open the fly screen again. "Keep me posted. About Carter. Let me know if it gets really bad."

She nods.

I enter the house and I wait for my eyes to adjust to the gloom.

"In here, Silver," Paige calls from an adjoining room.

I walk into the living room. Paige lies on a floral couch, a mountain of pillows supporting her pregnant bulk and a thick blanket draped over her lap, despite the warmth of the day. Her dark hair cascades over the pillows and her emerald eyes are dazzlingly bright, revealing the depth of her worry and fatigue.

"Do you want me to open the curtains?" I ask.

"No, thanks. I'm finding the need to hibernate and wallow in my dark cave." Paige smiles, and caresses her round stomach.

Lifting her legs, I sink into the couch and place them over my lap. "How are you feeling?" Using a pinch of my healing glow, I rub her swollen feet.

"Big," she laughs. "Ah, that feels nice." She leans her head back and closes her eyes.

I let the silence stretch on, glad to note the contented look on Paige's face. It's an expression I rarely see anymore. Tinkering noises float through from the kitchen. The smell of onions on the stove makes my stomach grumble. They were harvested recently and a flicker of pride flames inside me. We can do this. We *are* doing this. The crops will not die, not when they smell this good.

"How is he?" I ask, keeping my voice low.

"The same." Paige opens her eyes, her face now tight. "I don't know what I'm going to do. He's got this ridiculous idea that he deserves to be paralyzed. Like it's a punishment or something. You've heard him." She sighs. "But he doesn't get that it's not about good or bad, punishment or reward. Look at Megan!"

Megan says her disability makes her stronger, that it doesn't define her, that it's a part of her now and changed the way she views life. She won't give any of that up. There's a small part of me, when I look at her, that thinks how easy it would be to give her back the ability to walk with a simple touch of my hand. But then I note the smile on her face and the color in her cheeks and the way she holds court over all her friends, and I know she's right. She doesn't need to be healed, like it's a magical wand that makes everything better. It isn't.

I shake my head, seeing how much wiser Megan is than me. I took myself off to my lab to rid myself of anxiety, thinking it would solve all my problems. Of course it won't. I should take a leaf out of Megan's book.

"Megan is different," I say. "And Claus."

"Not helping." Paige frowns at me. "I can't help him when he won't talk to me about it. The baby is almost here and I don't know how I'm going to cope looking after the both of them. Thank God for Elizabeth." Paige refers to Jacob's mother who moved in with them when we got back from the mountains.

"I do agree with you." I cover her hand with mine. "Jacob is choosing to stay this way for the wrong reasons. But only he can make that choice. Do you want me to talk to him again?" I hate seeing my best friend so miserable, especially when the answer is so simple.

"If you could clobber him over the head with a frying pan

that might do the trick. But yes, please talk to him, convince him to be healed." The desperation in her voice has me rising to my feet and marching to the kitchen.

When I enter the kitchen, Elizabeth stands at the sink washing dishes. Jacob sits at the table wearing a stained sweatshirt and building a tower of playing cards.

"Oh, Silver. I didn't know you were here," Elizabeth says, turning from the sink and removing the rubber gloves from her hands. She offers me a fragile smile as she blots the soap bubbles out of her long, dark hair and turns the heat down from the onions. It's from her that Jacob inherited his Eastern looks; the wideset eyes, the dark hair and skin such a rich shade of brown I can't stop picturing how beautiful his son is going to be. Paige's eyes, Jacob's skin...stunning. "Look, Jacob, look who's here." Her tone is laden with meaning.

"I can hear, Mother," Jacob says, his steely gaze swivels toward me. "Don't come any closer, Silver." I take Jacob's hand and hold firmly. When he tries to pull away, I add a pinch of bulk power. "Don't touch me!"

"Jacob," I say calmly, refusing to let go. "I'm not going to heal you, not unless you ask."

His shoulders slump and he allows me to hold onto his hand.

"I just want you to listen," I say.

Elizabeth puts the clean dishes in a cabinet and then closes the door, the small draft created knocking over Jacob's card tower.

"Great," he mutters.

"Jacob," Elizabeth says as she stirs the onions, "please let Silver heal you. *Please.*"

"That's not going to happen, is it, Silver?"

Jacob spends his days in a wheelchair wheeling himself from one room to the next, building towers of playing cards or sitting in the garden for hours with a pair of binoculars documenting bird species left in the world, but no one cares. Thoughts of survival and cleaning the city are the paramount ideas occupying most people's minds. Occasionally, he allows Megan to entice him outside so she can show him how to adapt to the chair. He'll only go if they can race, and he has to win, or he comes home even grumpier.

"Jacob." Releasing his hand, I lower myself into one of the wooden chairs. "I know you don't feel you deserve to be healed. I understand. We all feel guilty about something. We all feel there is some huge deed in our past we can never be forgiven for. I get it. Really, I do. But I think you're doing this for the wrong reasons. I think you're being selfish."

He startles. "That's not fair."

"Isn't it?" I stare at him. "You're not doing this as a way to hold on to an identity or a strength you might otherwise lose. You're doing it to punish yourself, and at the same time, you're punishing Paige." I check my anger. I want to convince him I'm right, not start an argument.

He glares at me, his skin blotchy. "I don't see you hassling Megan like this."

I purse my lips, trying to find a new way into his mind. We've had this conversation numerous times and he remains obstinate. "You know why. She chose to stay that way for different reasons. Your reasons are..." I sigh. "They make disability a bad thing, they make it a punishment, they make it something to be feared. You don't need to do that to yourself."

He frowns. "That's not what I'm trying to do."

"Do you want Megan to think less of herself, that she did something wrong to make herself end up in a wheelchair?"

Jacob blanches, stares at me, pain whisking through his dark eyes. "I never...I don't want..." he shakes his head and his eyes moisten. "Of course I don't want her to feel that." He looks at the floor where his pile of playing cards has scattered under the table. "But I can't." He says it softly, but there's no doubt, no hesitation. It's an absolute refusal.

"Have it your way, for now," I say, jabbing a finger on the table. "But this isn't the end of it."

I leave the kitchen. I leave Elizabeth hissing at her son and go back to the living room. Paige looks at me hopefully.

"I'm sorry." I shake my head. "I talked. He listened. No joy."

She sighs. "Thank you, Silver."

"I'll keep working on him."

Irritation streaks down the length of my limbs and before I can stop it, a china pot on the windowsill turns to a pile of ash.

"Powers still a bit whacky?" Paige smiles, but it doesn't reach her eyes.

"Something like that," I mutter.

"I never liked that pot anyway."

Cursing myself, I tiptoe to the window and brush the ash into the front yard. My anger flares. My best friend is in pain. Jacob is doing this to her.

Back on Earl's mountain, she killed her own mother for

him, to save him. Every time she looks at him in his chair she's reminded of what she did. And she would do it again, without hesitation. But it would help if he were healed, if he were walking around with a smile on his face, then it might seem a little more worth it. But this stubborn, cantankerous refusal to even consider it? I'm sorely tempted to do what Paige once asked. To heal him in his sleep, when he's unaware, against his wishes.

She only asked the once, right after the injury occurred. I refused and she never asked again. But I see it in her eyes. She wants me to. I want me to. But I can't go against someone's wishes. That mentality is what brought about the rebellion and the war with the altereds. If I give into that desire, however altruistic my motives might be, I'm no better than Earl.

The furniture in the room vibrates, a picture frame falls from an end table. Gritting my teeth, I will the destroyer power back into its metaphorical bottle. I'm not sure what I've done with the cork, it doesn't seem to be working anymore. I need an industrial sized padlock, but I don't know where to find one.

"Silver? Are you okay?"

"I'm fine." I flop down next to her.

She snorts. "You just took out a pot and sent an earthquake through my house. I really don't think you're okay."

I flush and struggle for words.

"Just because I'm pregnant doesn't mean I'm stupid." She waits.

I run my pendant up and down its chain. "I've been having dreams."

She searches my face. "Anything we need to worry about?"

I avoid her gaze and look out the window. "I don't know. I just don't know."

"Silver, you know you can tell me anything."

"I know." I sigh. "Matt thinks it's PTSD. And I do too, mostly. The things I dream are too impossible to be real. So it has to be."

"But there's a little part of you that wonders?"

"Exactly," I say.

Shifting her stomach out the way, she hugs me. "Give it time."

"What if we don't have time?"

"Silver, your dreams have never let us down before. If it is a vision, I'll help you figure it out. And if it's not, maybe try some sleeping pills."

I hug her again, so thankful to have her in my life. "I need to get to the farms, but before I go, let's try a little healing on you."

I lay a hand on Paige's forehead. I can't help with any emotional suffering, but maybe I can soothe her dreams, as well as the backache, indigestion, and shortness of breath. The healing luminescence covers my hands and sinks into Paige's skin. The brief treatment is almost complete when black bolts of electricity flash over my hands. They leap from fingertip to fingertip. I jump away from Paige and cradle my hands close to my chest, unsure what will happen next.

"What is that?" Paige asks.

The electricity crackles and fizzes, as if talking to me. Mesmerized, I stare at my hands as the bolts grow and shrink, hiss and spit. With a final, larger burst the lightning leaps from my fingers and to Paige's forehead, skimming over her skin and swirling in a chaotic circle above her head.

Frozen, she stares at it. "Silver?"

Rooted, I tuck my hands into my pockets and pray the lightning doesn't destroy the entire house. After a minute, the bolts crackle and die out, disappearing from the air. What the...?

"Silver? What was that?"

"One of my other problems."

"A new power?"

I back away from her in case of another eruption and examine her body for injury. "Not a new one. It's the destroyer power getting bigger. All my powers are growing. And thanks to Earl, I have no idea what some of them are."

Slowly, Paige places her feet on the floor. "It's okay. You didn't hurt me."

"But I could." I turn and run out of the house.

I want to help the community, my friends, Paige, my mom. I can't do that if something dark and dangerous erupts out of me at any given moment. I need to understand my abilities. All of my abilities, once and for all. I need to test and catalog, and I need help to do it. There's only one person who might have witnessed Earl's powers. Eli. I need Eli's help.

✕✕✕✕✕

That night, a different dream comes. It's one I've experienced only once before, as a vision back at Earl's mountain, but it's the one that haunts me.

I am alone. More than that, I feel lonely. Bereft, as though the world has abandoned me. A sadness wells inside me as hope drains out of my limbs. I stand in the cornfield, alone, everything silent, listening to the cicadas sing and the wind rustle through the field. The ache of sadness becomes a heavy pressure, unbearable, and I clamp my hands over my ears to blot out the unfeeling world. Quickly, I snatch my hands back. I can't shut off my senses. It's coming, and I must be prepared.

Overhead, the sun is strong, sizzling the air all round me and causing sweat to pool at the small of my back. The fierce light reveals the extent of disease in the field. A disturbing blackness coats the stalks and leaves and creates shadows where there shouldn't be any.

I turn in a circle. I am still alone. Am I expecting someone? Where are all my friends? A shadow passes over the sun and a crow caws from a nearby tree. The only tree to offer shade in the vicinity. The large oak tree that's familiar and comforting. The one Adam climbs while we work. I shield my eyes to look at the sky. A huge flock of birds flies in a circle above my head. Ants scamper across my feet and a snake slithers through the corn.

I hear hissing and scuttling and skittering and I grit my teeth. The birds swoop closer. A black horse neighs from a nearby field. The snake produces friends. All black, all menacing. The ants grow and sting my exposed flesh. The animals gather together, an army, targeting me. There are scorpions and tarantulas. Black panthers and mountain lions. Midnight stallions and scuttling centipedes. The sky clouds over and I am thrust into darkness. Behind all the animals is another force. Something I can't see, something big, something strong. And I am alone. There is nothing I can do.

Electricity dances over my fingers. But it isn't strong enough. I will it to attack, but I have no target. Until the animals close in on me. A wave. A tidal wave of noise and malicious intent. The black clouds loom closer, swarming closer to earth, and within their depths appear two large yellow eyes.

Pushed to my knees, I raise my palms skyward, hoping my powers will work without me directing it. A mysterious blue light appears. And then everything turns dark.

CHAPTER SIX

ELI

THE HEADACHE GNAWS at his skull. But before Eli abandons the field, he approaches Delta. He can't let the day be a complete waste. Even though the heat of summer presses down on the field, she wears a long-sleeved shirt, the sleeves engulfing her slim fingers. White. To protect her delicate skin. It is as pure as silk and as white as cream and he longs to brings his lips to it.

"Hey," he says, with a hand pressed to his brow to shield himself from the sun's glare.

She blushes. A line of sweat appears along her top lip, deliciously sweet, provocative. A fluttering sensation fills his stomach.

"Hey yourself," she replies, her gaze roaming his body.

He steps closer so they're a mere couple of feet apart. Despite the fact she's been working in the fields for over three hours, he can only smell soap rolling off her skin. He wants to taste it, but that would be rude.

"Another headache?" she asks, pushing her hair behind

her ears. Now Eli can see a portion of her neck, a patch of skin he desperately wants to press his lips to.

He manages a small nod without shaking his brain around. "Yeah."

She removes a flask and a cloth from a small bag strapped to her side. After whirling her free hand in the air, she pours water onto the cloth and offers it to him. Taking it, he realizes it's ice cold and oh so soothing against the pain in his head.

"That is a remarkable ability you have there," Eli says.

Delta laughs, a delicate sound reminding him of falling snow. "It does have it's fun side. I'll have to make you a popsicle one day. What's your favorite flavor?"

The cold cloth on his head allows Eli the space to think, and he recalls the frozen treats he enjoyed during his childhood. "Cherry, or cola, I think. You?"

"Lemon," she replies without hesitation. "I've always found it the most refreshing on a hot day."

Her favorite popsicle flavor is lemon. Eli tucks the information into a corner of his brain that isn't being scratched for another time.

There is a gentle pressure on his arm and he looks down to see Delta's slim fingers touching him. He smiles.

"Let's get you back to your cabin," she says.

"As much as I want to help, I think this headache has beaten me today."

"Let me help you." She tucks an arm into his, as if she might be capable of steadying him. He pretends to lean on her, enjoying the proximity, but he worries he would crush her delicate frame if he truly did need her support.

Delta kicks open the door of the cabin and helps him to

his bed. He lies on the mattress and she fluffs the pillow for him, placing it gently under his head. After refreshing the cold cloth, she sits on the edge of the bed, arranging it over his eyes. His pulse throbs, not so much with the headache, but with how her proximity kicks up his heartrate. He's not sure he can take it. There is a small space between them that's filled with electricity. He wants to pull her down next to him and kiss her, but he's not sure his head can take it.

The shelf above the sink rattles and a tin cup falls to the floor.

Delta half rises. "What was that?"

"What was what?" Eli pretends innocence. "I can't see anything with the cloth over my eyes."

She settles again, but he can sense her frown. "Maybe nothing."

The smell of her closeness overwhelms him.

"Do you want me to stay? Until you fall asleep? I always used to like it when my mom did that."

Eli smiles. There's nothing he wants more, but he won't be able to sleep with her around. He can't tell her to leave either. "That would be nice."

Neither of them talk. Eli listens to the small sounds of her shifting weight, her delicate sighs, and the gentle ruffle as she fixes his single sheet. After a few minutes, she strokes his head and he almost melts under her touch. Maybe she's using some of her ability. She can turn any solid into its liquid or gas form. So he could be melting. Or maybe it's him, like the shaking shelf.

He allows more time to pass before he pretends he's asleep so he can deal with the headache. She plants a kiss on his cheek, a hot touch next to the cold of the cloth, and leaves the cabin. It is perhaps a small, trivial thing, but to Eli, to feel cared for is a certain type of heaven.

Nausea rises into his throat as he grits his teeth against the pain of the headache. It's getting worse. His vision swims and he curls into a fetal position. He rubs his forehead and temples.

Scratch, scratch.

He grabs more painkillers from the crate he uses as a bedside table. If only Silver's healing had worked. And why didn't it? Is there something in his head that's impenetrable and incurable? Does he have a tumor? But no, Silver would have been able to cure that. It's something else.

Scratch.

It's the sweet spot again, the one that makes him sigh in a combination of relief and bliss.

Eli tosses and turns in his small bed. The wooden walls of the cabin close in on him and the heat of the day builds, making him sweat, maybe hallucinate, until he is sure he is back on the storm-tossed boat of his dream. The dishes he left in the sink float in the air, along with the sponge, tea-towel and a stale roll he left on the counter. They position themselves in a circle above his head and rotate in a haphazard orbit as though riding an invisible carousal. But hold on, this isn't a hallucination, this isn't wonky vision, this is actually happening.

A coffee mug and butter knife join the other flying objects. They circle his head one more time and then collapse on the floor in a heap, a breakfast plate cracking down its middle. This is not a hallucination, but more likely one of his abilities manifesting itself. Telekinesis. One of the tamer powers Earl gave them both. Was he also responsible for the invisibly dug rows appearing in the unplowed field? In the few weeks he's been here, in Camp Fortitude, he's not manifested a single unique event. Until now. Why now? Maybe he's shoved the metaphorical cork in the metaphorical bottle too deep and now it's about to explode. A grim thought.

Telekinesis. Silver has it. Sawyer too. How much easier it would be to plow the field with his mind. But not if the headaches are the result. Or exposure. Or that weird look on Erica's face the other day suggesting she thought he was "losing it."

Perhaps the headaches are the result of using power. That makes sense. Silver always complains there are limits to her abilities and that each new one she acquires brings pain. Perhaps he is using powers and doesn't even realize it. He can't begin to list the number of abilities he possesses, so it wouldn't surprise him if things happen unexpectedly, whether he wants them to or not. But if he doesn't get the cork back in the bottle, then everyone will know. They will assume he is as bad as his father and cast him out, with nowhere to go. That can't happen.

The lies are getting harder to keep straight. But it will be worth it. For a second chance. To become his own person, to delete the Landry name from his bloodline.

After plumping his pillow a little higher, Eli lies back on his bed and contemplates the enormity of the situation before him. He so desperately wants to belong to this new world. He also finds the power strangely compelling. Can he have both?

With the cold, damp cloth draped over his forehead, Eli wrestles with these thoughts for the rest of the afternoon.

Closing his eyes against the un-curtained window, he realizes the headache has abated somewhat. The pain is more of a memory. But he continues to feel the probing, those scratching fingers digging deep within his brain, sifting through his coils of gray matter, searching. For what?

Scratch, scratch.

If his headache continues to improve, Eli will tend the fields tomorrow. Tend the fields and develop his blossoming relationship with Delta. The only downside is President Montoya. She has traded her suit for a pair of shorts and a shovel and is actually tending the fields herself. Lead by example and all that. She's watching him, a look in her eye that contains more wariness than Matt's. Why can't everyone leave him alone?

Interfering bitch. She's always around, prying, checking, asking questions - where he came from, what his life was like, does he have information about Earl - like she's got nothing better to do. Before he was allowed to live in the cabin, he spent hours in an interview room in the presidential compound, answering questions, telling his "story." President Montoya asked the questions. Also present were a therapist and some security guy called Claus. The questions were designed to catch him out. But he hasn't done anything wrong. Apart from the obvious white lies. Does the president know he is lying? Perhaps he possesses a power within somewhere that will shut her up once and for all.

The headache comes back to knock on his skull, once, twice, and then vanishes like a whispering wind.

CHAPTER SEVEN
SILVER

I TRY AGAIN to heal my mother. Bolts of white electricity leave my fingertips and dance across her face. They fill the immediate space between us. Like mischievous sprites made entirely of light, they bend and flicker and produce a beautiful show. Mesmerized, I can only watch.

My mother remains asleep, a smile on her face, but stays in her catatonic condition. My healing power has grown, is still growing, and I sense there is more to come. Perhaps then it will be powerful enough to heal her. I must understand this power and what it can do. Test its new boundaries, which seem limitless.

Today, I will elicit Eli's help. He may have picked up more information than he realized while he lived in Earl's mountain. Maybe he can tell me why I'm so much stronger.

Feeling a thread of hope, I leave my mother with the nurse and rush downstairs to where Matt is waiting in the jeep. We travel the short distance to the fields and Matt parks outside the red barn. I hop out of the jeep and head to the path leading to Eli's cabin.

"Silver?" Matt calls after me. "Where are you going?" He pauses in the unloading of equipment and waits for me to return.

I step back toward him. "I need to talk to Eli," I say, unable to meet his eyes. I can't maintain a lie when staring into those piercing blues, so I pick a spot on the bridge of his nose.

"Oh, okay. To see if he's feeling better?"

"Yes!" I agree, a little too quickly. "Exactly. I want to make sure the headaches are gone." Truth be told I forgot all about Eli's mysterious headache.

"Okay," Matt says. "But don't be long, I know the scientists are eager to see if your tampering yesterday has shown the desired effects."

"Yes boss." I chuck him a mock salute as I turn back down the path.

"Silver! Don't be like that—" But I'm too far along the path to hear his words.

I put distance between us before my lie can catch up with me. I can't tell Matt the truth. He believes we're living in a time of peace and powers are unnecessary, he won't understand me wanting to get to the bottom of the abilities I possess. He thinks I should forget about them. But how can I? My emotions affect my abilities. I can't let them fly all over the place the moment I'm having a bad day. I tell myself I'm doing this for everyone else. For everyone's safety. I remember when I burned Lyla's leg and singed her hair. I can't live with myself if I do worse.

I head down a dirt path bisecting one of the fields, my boots kicking up dust, the sun already uncomfortably hot. Insects buzz in the undergrowth and I cast my glance warily at the ground, looking for the snakes of my dream. Last night I woke screaming, shaking, and sweating. Matt was unable to console me and I spent the rest of the night staring out my window at the moon's progression, wondering why the night holds such terrors for me. Having the dream again has put me on edge.

I shake it off. If it was a vision, it doesn't mean it's the future. The dreams Adam and I share are open to change, are affected by choices and new situations. They change all the time. The future doesn't have to be black.

Before I reach Eli's cabin, I come across Claus leaning against a fence that borders the main field.

"Oh, Silver, there you are." He taps the dirt path with his cane and makes his way to me.

After hanging his cane on a fencepost, he takes his time examining me. I've known Claus for years. He trained me in karate all the way to black belt and beyond, and yet his silent gazes always make me uncomfortable. It's like he can see into my soul. But he possesses no abilities.

Impatient to get to Eli, I push a smile onto my lips, hoping this won't take long.

"I have a message from your father," Claus says. "It arrived at the presidential building in the middle of the night."

Hope ratchets up my heartrate. I hope Dad has found the person he's looking for. My healing abilities aren't yet strong enough to help my mother. Maybe they never will be.

"It's not the news you were looking for," Claus says, resting both hands on the top of his cane.

My hope crashes around my feet and a black mood engulfs me.

"He hasn't found her yet. But he has a new lead," Claus says. "He's traveling further north."

North. What about his heart? All the traveling, all the worrying, will it be too much for him? The virus is still out there. Yes, he's vaccinated, but viruses mutate and I have no idea if he's safe. But there's nothing I can do. I drop my head into my hands and rake my fingers through my hair trying to ignore the intensive tingling in my fingertips.

"Breathe, Silver," Claus says.

The words irritate me. I hate that someone still needs to tell me to relax. But if I don't and my powers hurt someone...I sigh.

Claus leans over the fence, one of his hands twiddling his mustache. "Perhaps you should stop by my house later and train with Evan and me."

I nod, even though I have so little time for karate at the moment. But Claus' instructions go beyond mere fighting. Most of his lessons are about life, meditation, accepting things we can't change. All the bumper stickers I used to see on cars aren't mere platitudes. They do mean something, and Claus has brought that meaning home to me. But I'm too agitated to relax. I need my guard up.

"I'm serious, Silver. You need to take time for you too."

"I know," I say. "I have something important to do right now. I'll stop by later."

He searches my face. "This, too, will pass."

I dip my chin. "I hope so."

I leave him at the fence and hurry down the path. As I approach Eli's cabin, the front door swings open and he emerges into the morning sunlight. He wears a pair of army combat trousers with a belt dangling loosely from the loops and no shirt. His chest is sculpted to perfection, his eight-pack rippling with every intake of breath. My eyes roll over his body. I have no complaints about Matt's body, but this, this is something else. This is straight out of an air-brushed movie. But it's real. *Stop drooling, Silver!*

"Morning, Silver," Eli says around his toothbrush. He spits the paste into a coffee cup and steps toward me.

"Uh...morning," I stammer. "How's your head?"

"Much better. Thank you. Maybe your treatment worked after all, just a little delayed." He places the coffee cup inside the cabin and pulls the belt closed on his trousers. He wears a beaming smile and I find myself staring at his lips. "What can I do you for?"

"I could use your help," I say. "If you're up for it."

He turns his attention from his belt and looks at me, catching me staring. "Okay."

Heat floods my cheeks. I look away from his chest and concentrate on why I'm here. My mother. My abilities. Getting control. Preparing for an apocalypse, just in case.

"I'm not sure how to ask this, but..." It occurs to me Eli might not want to help, he might not want anything further to do with abilities and power, let alone see me exhibit the same powers responsible for his torture.

"Spit it out." He smiles, revealing perfect teeth. At least his father didn't damage those.

70

I bend a knee and stick my hands in the back pockets of my shorts, wishing I had some acorns with me. I think clearer when I hold a few acorns. "I need to know what Earl's abilities are. All of his abilities. I mean, the physical ones are pretty obvious; the venom-spitting fangs, the changing bulk, the impressive strength, the morphing into other species, I can *see* what they are. I saw him, I saw what he could do. It's the mental ones I don't know about which might produce a key to helping my mother. She's still catatonic. I need to help her. Until she's back to normal I'm not sure I can think about much else." My words come out in a rush, fearful he might refuse.

Eli looks me up and down, a small frown puckering the middle of his brow. Then he glances at the middle of the field where people are gathering to commence the day's work, Delta, Sawyer, Carter, Mason, Matt, and other new members of Camp Fortitude. The bulks pull an old plow, the engine having rusted; it's up to them until a new machine can be located. "Okay, Silver. I'll help. If something good can come from those awful powers," he pauses. "Then I'll help."

Relief drops my shoulders a couple inches. Then I feel a rush of excitement. I know Eli will be able to help me. I will find something to help my mother, and I will determine the scope of my abilities. All of them. It's not something I've ever allowed myself to do before. Now, I get to finally understand who I am.

Eli throws on a T-shirt and sneakers and together we walk away from the fields. Ignoring my friends working with the crops, I lead him quickly along the path, almost jogging, until we're hidden from view.

He chuckles. "What's the hurry?"

We approach a small thicket of trees which will hide my desertion. "I want to get to the bottom of it, that's all."

Slowing my pace, I let my fingers skim the tops of the tall wildflowers, sometimes plucking a flower and shedding its petals as we walk. In the shade of the forest, insects buzz and I'm glad of the temperature drop. After a few minutes we emerge into the backyard of an abandoned farmhouse. A simple wooden structure, the red paint peeling from the cladding. It shields us from the fields and watchful eyes, and we'll have privacy to test my powers.

Eli leans against a rotting fence post and crosses one foot over the other. "So, where do we start?"

"I don't know." I sit on an old tactor tire, staying in the shade of the bordering trees. A frayed rope trails from its girth. It used to be a tire swing. This would have a been a peaceful place once, living in the middle of the fields, surrounded by trees and animals, swinging on the tire underneath a huge beech tree. It's still peaceful. I discovered it a few weeks ago when I was walking alone. Now I consider it my private sanctuary. And I've invited Eli in. "One of the things that's freaking me out is I can use two powers at the same time, and my stamina lasts longer. Much, much longer. I spent a whole day with my wings last week. I've never been able to do that before. I'm used to fatiguing quickly, the power draining before I can be useful. But now I'm getting stronger."

Eli is still leaning against the fence, a couple yards away, his hands in his pockets. "How do you feel about that?"

No one has asked me that before. Thinking, I run a hand through my hair, lifting it away from my neck. "I feel..." I cock my head. "Curious. Excited. Terrified. Hopeful. Guilty."

Eli raises both eyebrows. "Guilty?"

I shrug. "The battle is over. We're rebuilding. I don't need my abilities. Most of them, anyway. And yet, I don't feel ready to shove them away. So, yeah, guilty. Everyone expects me to forget about everything inside me, like I can flick a switch. But it doesn't work that way."

"It doesn't?" Eli asks. Concern rests in his pupils. It touches me.

"No. It doesn't. Unlike the others, except maybe Erica and her wings, my abilities are tied to my emotions. Especially my black lightning and healing power. I'm not always in control of my emotions, and so I'm not always in control of my abilities. So no, I can't just flick a switch."

Eli rubs his sneaker in the dirt, darkening the white leather. "That makes sense."

"It does?"

"Of course. I'd want to know too, if I were you. And you can't be expected to contain something if you don't know how to contain it."

I launch to my feet. "Exactly!" I pace a small area in front of me. "Why can't other people understand that?"

"Seems pretty basic to me. Who doesn't understand that? Are your friends giving you a hard time?"

Matt. But that's not entirely fair. He sees things differently. But the lens he uses to view life affects me and how I feel. In truth, I haven't told anyone else how I'm feeling. Paige has her own issues with the pregnancy and Jacob. Erica, well, she's appointed herself protector of all lost souls and I don't want to be added to her list. The bulks are busy in the fields and Carter, who I spoke to a lot on the last mission, keeps an unapproachable look on his face and a bottle of something in his pocket. I need to check on him. He goes home each day and stays alone, drinking, until he passes out. He hasn't been able to put his brother's death behind him. Dad isn't here. Mom can't hear me. Sawyer and Lyla are too caught up in their own relationship. Which leaves Koko or Claus. But I can't talk to them either. I wouldn't be able to take their scrutinizing looks, their suspicion that I don't *want* to give my abilities up.

Eli walks closer, plants a hand on my shoulder, and I stop pacing. "Why don't you show me what you can do? I've never seen you in action. Only the aftermath."

I try on a smile. He's telling me it's okay to use my powers. Is that what I needed to hear? It *is* okay to use my powers.

Building up to a demonstration, I glance at the old tire swing on the ground. It makes a great seat, but it's in the middle of the yard. It's going to get in the way. With one ability I burn the rope, then I hoist the tire into the air, holding it there with telekinesis, before I let it fall and roll away. Simultaneously, I produce the wings of a blue macaw – one of my favorite abilities - and with a third ability, that of a flea, I jump to the roof of the farmhouse.

Eli's eyes shine. "That's impressive."

"Yeah," I agree. "But it's not going to help my mother."

"What do you think will help?" Eli asks when I jump back to the ground.

"Something to do with my healing ability. It's growing." I've only admitted this to Paige, because she's the one person who won't look at me differently. "The more obvious demonstration is the destroyer power, the healer ability's ying."

Before I can wipe the sweat from the nape of my neck or alter my stance, a black bolt of lightning shoots out of my fingertips and disintegrates the now resting tire into a pile of ash with a fiery flourish. It's like the grand finale of a magician's show. But this isn't an illusion.

Eli leaps back. "Jesus!"

I've had little time to get used to the physical presence of the black lightning. While we were on the mission to find Earl, when the power first manifested, it started small, was totally out of control and I was terrified of hurting someone. I still am. Especially now I have so much to worry about. Now the power is bigger, stretches further, is more destructive and continues to whisper at me, begging me to use it. I won't give in to it, not unless I need it. But seeing it work, out in the open, testing its reach, fills me with a new sense of wonder.

"I know," I say quietly. "It's the destroyer ability. Every healer possesses it. For everything light in the universe there must be something equally dark."

"You sound like a philosophy textbook."

"Even so, I've found it to be true. My healing power is growing too."

Eli plants his feet wide and places a hand on his hip. "Show me."

"Do you trust me?" I ask, looking into his brown eyes.

75

"Yes," Eli says, nodding. "You saved my life. You saved *me*."

Swiftly, I step closer to Eli. With the knife I keep tethered to my belt, I slice across his palm. He flinches, but doesn't complain. I bring my fingers to his palm. He flinches again. The white, electricity bolts appear immediately and leap from my fingertips onto Eli's palm. We become cocooned in a golden aura and a comfortable warmth surrounds us. The wound disappears, drawing the spilled blood back into his palm.

Eli flexes his hand a couple times. "That didn't happen the last time you healed me. What were those...things? It was like mini lightning, without the electrocution part."

"I know. Its growing, or its Earl's," I say.

"Earl didn't have anything like that." Eli stares at his palm.

"You're sure?"

"I'm sure."

"Okay. So, it's not Earl. It's me. Hopefully, when the power has finished transitioning, I'll be able to reach my mother. But in the meantime, I need to know if there's anything else in me that can help." I pace back and forth on the dirt ground again, wishing I'd brought a canteen of water with me. "I can feel things, urges, gurgling around inside, but I'm not sure how to express them. I'm not sure I should." I shudder at a memory of Earl, the devil personified, with powers I don't want anything to do with.

"So, let's figure it out," Eli says. He stands strong, his hands on his hips, his gaze never leaving my face. There is strength and solidarity in his eyes. "Right now."

With my lower lip trembling, I nod. This is what I'm here for. Guilt washes over me. Matt will be furious. But I don't need Matt right now. The thought of what I house inside my body is terrifying, and now I don't have to discover its secrets on my own.

Eli put his hands on my waist and turns me to face the empty, overgrown backyard. Grass towers over a foot tall and dandelions grow in yellow clumps. The drone of a bee sounds as it flies from flower to flower. A rusty slide lies on its side near the tree that supported the tire swing. In its past life it may have been red. "Feel the power. Feel it bubbling around inside you. Can you isolate a single one?"

My stomach rolls, as though a hand has entered my body and is slowly trying to mix all my insides together. Uncomfortable, but bearable. The feeling moves to my chest, like I've drunk a can of soda too quickly. "I can feel...*something*."

"Grab onto it. Let it fill you up. Let it come." The excitement in Eli's voice makes me smile and I feel the pressure of his hands on my waist.

Closing my eyes, I concentrate on the sensations. The bubbling continues and spreads to my arms, my neck, onto my face. It's coming. It's almost here. And then it crests, like I'm riding a tall wave. Snapping my eyes open, I focus on the abandoned house. When I closed my eyes the house was behind me. Looking at my feet, I realize I now stand at the far end of yard, the long grass tickling the backs of my calves.

"Holy crap!" Eli's hands still rest on my hips. "I can teleport much further! With passengers!"

"So it seems." Eli smiles at me. It is a warm, rich smile

that gives me the confidence I need to continue. "That was quite a ride." He rubs his forehead.

"Headache back?"

"A little. It's okay. Not as bad."

"Teleportation – check." Although I already gained the ability from Jacob, I've never been able to teleport more than a few feet before. Let alone with another person. Maybe I won't have to drive to the fields anymore. "Do you know any others?"

"Telekinesis? I know he had telekinesis and pyrokinesis."

"Got them both," I say, ticking them off on my fingers.

"Mind pushing, communicating with animals, and telepathy are the mental ones I know about."

"Really?"

"Yeah, it was impossible to keep a secret around him."

"What a nightmare."

Hearing people's thoughts. It's marginally better than seeing the future. I can read Matt's expression well enough already, and I don't want to pry into his private thoughts. Not when he's mad at me. But when he's feeling loving, it might be fun to know what he's thinking.

"Anything else?" I ask

Eli chuckles. "That isn't enough for you?"

I purse my lips, then say, "I need to know."

"I don't know. I think you're scary enough already." He pokes my side.

I laugh. "Only if you get on my bad side."

Eli holds his hands up. "I'll be good!"

We laugh together. It feels good. I haven't allowed myself to laugh, not while my mother remains in her mental prison.

"I know there are more. We'll have to experiment," I say. "Until we get to the bottom of them all."

"Okay."

Feeling a tiny bit embarrassed, I look at my feet. I'm worried about asking too much of him. "You'll help?"

His presence comforts me. I don't even know him that well, but I feel...connected somehow. There's something about him that eases the rushing of thoughts in my head, that holds my worry over my mother at bay.

"Of course," he says.

He'll help. He understands. Eli is easy to be around, easy to look at, easy to talk to. He might even make this process fun. Relief seeps into me and I feel exhausted, as though the old fatigue of using abilities has come back.

Eli and I spend the day testing my abilities. The telepathy is the most disconcerting. He allows me to read his thoughts. They touch on his headache, which is still there, move to how he'd like to furnish his cabin, then to girls. Specifically romance. I'm surprised. There's no one particular in mind, but he craves...passion. His thoughts land on me. He finds me beautiful. I try hard not to smile. I have never felt beautiful before and it's nice to know someone thinks of me that way. He is wary of Francesca.

I push deeper, but a mental wall goes up, and I can no longer see his thoughts.

He coughs. "I think the telepathy depends on the willingness of the subject."

"You think I'm beautiful?" I touch his hand, the one I sliced.

He blushes. "Have you looked in a mirror?"

"Thank you, Eli." I kiss his cheek. "Then I couldn't read you anymore. Did you pull back? Put up a wall?"

"Some things are private."

CHAPTER EIGHT

SILVER

WHEN I ARRIVE HOME that afternoon, I find Francesca standing on my front porch directing a nurse and two orderlies. One of them wheels my mother out of the house and into a waiting ambulance.

"What's going on?" I ask. "What's happened?"

"Silver, she's fine. There's no emergency." Francesca faces me. "With your father's trip extended, the nurse has suggested we take her to the hospital where she'll get the help she needs."

"But I... you can't...I need to..." I move close to my mother and away from Francesca's shriveling look. "She wants to be here. I want her to be here."

"Silver." Francesca marches up to me and places her hands on my shoulders. I narrow my eyes at her and she removes her hands. "There is nothing more you can do for her. I've seen you try. You can't reach her. She needs to be in a hospital where she can receive the best possible care. It's too much for you." Her tone is firm, non-negotiable.

"You have no right. That's not your decision." I cross my arms over my chest.

"Silver." Matt comes out of the house. "She's right. Your mom needs help that you can't give her."

I shoot him an accusatory look. He, of all people, should realize how much I need to be with my mother and that I can't bear to be separated from her ever again, whether I'm actually capable of helping her or not.

"Silver, I'm sorry...I just..."

I stare him down. An apology isn't going to change the current circumstances.

"It's okay, Matt." Francesca raises a hand. "She can hear the rest."

I swallow, trying to work saliva into my dry mouth. She sometimes has that effect on me. I want to do as she asks, I want to help, but she keeps asking for the impossible.

"Silver, the other fact of the matter is, you are distracted." A stony expression takes over her face.

"But that's not true! I came to the fields. I did as you asked," I cry. I resist the urge to stomp my foot on the ground.

"Silver, we need your help. The situation with the crops is more serious than I previously thought. They are dying, all of them. We need your expertise, your *focused* expertise. I don't think you'll give your full attention to the situation until the issue of your mother is taken out of your hands."

"The crops are not dying!" They can't die. They're not allowed to die. Because then my dreams will be true. It's a mistake. Francesca doesn't know what she's talking about. But that's not the point.

The point is I need my mother and she needs me. Anger

consumes me and I don't trust myself to speak. This is unacceptable. I'm the best chance my mother has.

Without warning, the windows panes vibrate in their sashes. A roof tile falls from above and lands at my feet, then is immediately reduced to a pile of ash. Matt lays a restraining hand on my arm. I swallow my anger.

"I can't have her taken away from me again," I plead, as I watched my mother being loaded into the ambulance. I make a half-hearted attempt to follow her. But it's futile. Francesca simply won't allow her to stay. I glare at Matt again. Why has he allowed this to happen? Why isn't he standing up for me?

"Silver," Francesca says gently, all the firmness gone from her voice now my mother is safely ensconced in the ambulance and pulling away from my house. "I will make it my utmost priority that she receives the best treatment available. Catatonia is not a new disorder. It's been around for decades. Margaret will have access to those professionals who know the most about this condition."

"Like Deja," I say.

Francesca nods. "Yes. Like Deja and a whole team of others."

"That's not her field of expertise."

"She is very experienced," Francesca says.

I squeeze an acorn in my pocket with a bulk fist, smashing it to a pulp. "We can wait for my father. He's away looking for Koko's old friend. A lady who can see into people's minds and understand what's trapping them there. She's out there somewhere. We just have to be patient. You know that. Why can't we wait for him?"

"Are you being patient, Silver?" Francesca's lips

compress. "He's been looking for months already. She may not even be alive. We have to take care of Margaret with the means we have access to, not rely on hopes and wishes."

Tears prickle and spill onto my cheeks.

Matt slinks to my side and puts an arm around my shoulder. I remain rigid.

"This is for the best," Francesca says.

Slowly, I shake my head.

"Your healing hasn't helped, Silver, and I know the hospital staff will work hard with your mother. Please have a little faith in me," Francesca says.

"I don't have faith in anything," I mutter.

Matt's touch turns into a placating squeeze. Francesca frowns. "Have you been to see Deja yet?"

I blanch, feeling sucker punched. How does Francesca know I sought help?

"For all the good it did." I'm tempted to tell her about taking anxiety away from my DNA, but I don't need any more trouble right now. I'm not that stupid.

Her lips thin, and her features soften. "These things take time, Silver. You've been through a lot."

I sigh and swipe at the reaming tears on my cheek. She doesn't insult me with a pat to the arm or any other trite gesture. She gives me a curt nod, then retreats down the porch steps and into her car. She rolls down the window. "Oh, and Silver? We will be seeing you at the farm lab tomorrow." It isn't a question.

"I wished you would have warned me," I snap at Matt as soon as Francesca's car disappears. "Then I could have been prepared. I could have taken Mom somewhere else." I thrust a finger into the middle of his chest.

"To what end, Silver?" Matt's hands jerk. "Your mom needs help. Real help. And we need you."

"I don't care. I'm trying to give her the best help I can." My black lightning power flares on my fingers and destroys one of the porch steps before I'm able to suck it back down. "And Matt? Don't ambush me like that again."

I try to push past him into the house, but he catches my wrist. "I'm sorry for that. I didn't know it was happening until a couple of hours ago. But Silver?" He tugs me closer. "It's the best thing for her. For both of you."

"Hmm," I say, staring at the floor, at my feet and then at the point where the ambulance disappeared with my mother, anywhere but at Matt's blue eyes, because then my resolve will melt and I'll crumple and the depression will come. That feeling of utter uselessness, the feeling that even though I'm the strongest person in the world, the most capable when it comes to abilities, I can't do anything to help my mother.

"Silver, it's going to be okay." Matt places one finger under my chin and lifts my face. He kisses my cheek, then the other, my nose. My resolve to stay mad at him, at Francesca, at the world and the injustice of it all blows away like a dandelion on the wind. I tense for the next wave of emotions. The emotions that will cripple me and send me running to my bedroom to hide under the covers forever. I feel nothing building, no wave of despair, no uncomfortable tightness in my chest, no swimming vision. Nothing is shaking or being reduced to ash. A small miracle. There's only quiet and the feeling of Matt's arms around me.

"Francesca told me because she was worried about your destroyer power." Matt lowers his voice, his eyes shifting around the desolate neighborhood as if he's afraid we're being watched. "I think she wanted me around to help...control you, I guess."

I look up in surprise.

Francesca is scared of me.

CHAPTER NINE
SILVER

WALKING into the kitchen to grab a drink, I realize I'm not alone. Deja sits on a stool at the small island making notes on a pad of paper, her long hair tied into a low knot and trailing over her shoulder. She puts her pen down and smiles at me.

I frown. "Did we have an appointment? I didn't think therapists made house calls."

Matt comes in behind me. "Francesca thought it would be a good idea for Deja to be here. In case..."

"In case I got angry? You got that right."

Deja removes a pair of reading glasses from her nose and slides off the stool. "I wanted to reassure you that your mother will be well taken care of."

Turning my back, I grab a glass from the cupboard. Bypassing the tap, I go for the half empty bottle of red wine Dad left on the counter before he left. It's probably stale, but I don't care. I take a gulp. "Have you treated catatonia before?"

She presses her lips together. "Matt, maybe we could talk alone."

Matt nods, briefly touches the small of my back, and leaves.

"He's worried about you. Try not to be too hard on him."

I can't keep the sarcasm from my voice. "Did you say you were here for me? Or Matt?"

Deja places her hands on the countertop. "I understand you're angry."

"Damn straight." I take another gulp of wine. The alcohol swims in my stomach and makes it gurgle. But I don't care. It feels warm and cozy.

"Have you had the dream again?"

"This is private, right? I mean, you can't go telling anyone about our conversations, can you?"

"No, I can't, Silver. Anything you say to me is between you and me."

"Good." I put my glass on the table. Under the effects of my misplaced power, it teeters, then settles. Deja watches it until it settles. "I slept well after seeing you. Right after I took out the gene for anxiety from my DNA." I don't mention the dream I had last night, or that I spent half the night awake thinking about it.

Deja taps her pen against her lips. "And you did that right after we spoke?"

I nod.

"Why?"

"Because I'm tired of it. I need a break. And I don't need to explain that to anyone. Least of all you."

"And yet, you told me about it." Deja scribbles a note on

her pad. If I want to, I can search her mind for her thoughts, but I hold back. "You're angry, Silver."

"No shit."

"What are you going to do about it?"

"Find a way to fix my mother."

Deja appraises me with calculating brown eyes. "Let me know how that works out for you."

I return her stare.

"I'll leave you alone tonight, you need to adjust to your Mom's absence. But we should talk again. Soon. Especially if you have another dream."

"Once I've found a way to fix my mother, I'll have plenty of time to talk about my *feelings*."

Deja clicks the lid on her pen, grabs her notepad, and packs her bag. She walks out of the kitchen backward, as if waiting for me to say something to hold her back. I don't. At the front door, she looks back at me. "Look after yourself, Silver. There's a lot of people here who care about you. Don't forget that. My door is always open."

Whatever. The fly screen crumples and disappears in a cloud of ash. Deja hurries away, stumbling over the missing porch step, and jogs down the street. She doesn't stop until she rounds the corner. She's scared of me too. Good.

I avoid Matt for the rest of the afternoon and sit in the small garden in the shade. There's a few plastic chairs and a table scattered around the untended grass. I manage to cut the lawn with my abilities, scorching a large patch in the middle. Whatever.

The sound of someone clearing their throat pulls my

attention to the garden gate. Claus stands there, leaning on his cane.

"Silver."

I don't say anything. If this is another intervention, I'm going to lose my shit. I'm about to launch myself off the table when he holds up a hand.

"I know you're angry."

I march up to him. "Did you know about my mom?"

"I just found out. I thought I'd better check on you."

"I don't want to talk about it."

He smooths his mustache. I can feel his eyes on me, boring into me, weighing me up. Am I disappointing him? The thought burns.

"Have you got your knife?"

I pat my belt where my knife rests. I never take it off. I can't. It's become part of me. Even though I don't need it. My abilities are more powerful than any knife. But it was a gift from Claus and it saved my life more than once, before I knew about my powers.

He opens the garden gate for me. "Come on then."

I meet him at the gate. He leads me along the path trailing the back of my house, through a few scattered trees, and into a meadow. It's where Einstein likes to walk. The dog is curled in a ball in the grass, watching me.

Claus points to a thick oak tree, its trunk already scarred from my throwing sessions. "*Suro.*" Throw. He always reverts to Japanese during a training session. Although he was originally German, he spent many years studying karate in Japan.

I remove my knife, taking a moment to run my fingers over the gnarled green cord of the hilt. The blade has three Vshaped indents and is wickedly sharp. I narrow my focus on the distant tree and release. The knife sails across the meadow, over Einstein, and skims the edge of the tree.

I stamp my foot and curse, feeling angry tears form again.

"You can do this," Claus says. "Concentrate. It's just you, the knife and the tree."

Using my speed, I retrieve my knife, but walk back at a more human speed as Einstein joins me. He sits next to Claus to watch, encouragement in his thoughts.

Exhaling, I hold my lungs still. I stare at the tree, but all I can see is my mother's face. Francesca. Matt. Paige. Jacob. Erica. Carter. All my friends. All their problems. Lightning tingles on my fingers. "I can't do this." I lower my arm.

Claus doesn't say anything, just watches me.

After a minute, I push the tension out of my fingers and raise my knife. My thoughts feel like walls closing in, distracting me. I try to push them away but can't get past them. I close my eyes. I know where the tree is. I breathe and listen to the sound of my heart, to the birds in the trees, to the insects in the grass. I throw.

I hear the whizz of the blade as it flies through the air. When I open my eyes, I see I've scored a direct hit on the tree. I *can* do this.

"Better," Claus says. "Again."

I spend the next two hours with Claus and Einstein in the meadow. Claus doesn't speak, but stands there silently watching. Most of the time I hit the tree. Other times the blade goes sailing past when my thoughts intrude. My anger doesn't go away. Claus is patient, but he's backing a losing horse.

When it gets dark, I turn around and march back to my house. I take a shower to cool off. While I'm washing my hair, Matt slides the door open and climbs in behind me. I want to yell at him, to punch his chest, to accuse him of betrayal. But I can't do that. I love him.

Instead, I collapse in his arms and cry. I rest my head against his shoulder and let the water pound my back and I cry. He doesn't say anything, just holds me and rubs my back.

Eventually, his gentle caress eases my anger and arouses desire in me. I kiss him, hard and deep. I'm tired of anger. Tired of fear. I need something else. We have sex in the shower and for the first time in hours the ball of rage dissipates.

When we're dry and dressed, we walk to the community hall for movie night. I hope the movie will distract me enough from my thoughts that my fingers aren't constantly sparking with the black lightning power.

I push open the door to the community hall and smell a mingled array of popcorn, wood polish and a fainter hint of sweat. Part of me is afraid to face my friends. I couldn't heal my mother and now she's been taken away. I have failed.

I swallow the thought and tell myself I deserve a night off from worry.

Inside, people buzz about the area in small groups, sharing snacks and drinks and catching up on the day's work. The movie itself is over six months old, the last thing released before the whole world dissolved into an apocalyptic nightmare. There won't be any new movies made any time soon.

Gathering drinks, Lyla joins me. She wears a blue sundress with a long cardigan and her hair is tied casually in an off-kilter ponytail. I can't look at her hair without remembering the time I singed it off. "Hi, Silver."

"Hey, you here with Sawyer?" I ask.

"Yup." She gestures at the fold-away seating where Sawyer and Matt are talking. Matt laughs and ruffles Sawyer on the top of his head, sending his curls bouncing in all directions. Sawyer chucks Matt on the shoulder and turns to walk away. Matt shoots out a leg, making Sawyer trip over his own feet.

Lyla's cheeks color. "What the hell does he think he's doing?"

Sawyer turns, gives Matt a warning glance and continues on his path to Mason and Carter.

"He's your older brother," I say. "He's protecting you."

Lyla's color deepens. "He's acting more like a dad than my actual dad is."

"You're growing up. It's something he can't control." Maybe now he'll understand how I feel.

"Well, he needs to get the hell over it." Lyla frowns. "I'm not having him treat Sawyer like that."

I flick her ponytail over her shoulder. "He's always protected you, especially on mission, and he can't stand that it might not be his job anymore." It's the first time Matt has seen one of his younger sisters engage in a romantic relationship. Sawyer is a good guy. They're friends, good friends. He's been on both previous missions with us. This is Matt's overprotective older brother thing. I hope he knows when to draw the line.

She gapes at me. "That's *never* been his job."

I grimace. "You know how he is."

93

"For f—"

"Come on, the movie's about to start, let's get our seats."

"If it's okay with you, Silver, I'm going to sit with Sawyer, far away from you and Matt."

I laugh. "Not a bad idea."

I walk to Matt and settle myself in a seat beside him. On my other side are Paige and Jacob, then Jacob's mother. I kiss Paige's cheek as the lights dim. She hugs me back and tells me she's sorry about my mom.

"Just because I'm pregnant doesn't mean you can't tell me stuff," she says. I don't miss the reprimand in her voice.

"You've got enough to worry about." My eyes skirt to Jacob in his wheelchair. "I don't want to burden you with my crap."

"Like it or not, your crap *is* my crap." She emphasizes her point by poking the palm of my hand.

She's right, but I worry our friendship will change. She has a baby coming, which will create new demands on her. Of course I'll be involved and I'll help her with whatever she needs, but she's entering a stage of life I have no experience with. Or maybe I'm overthinking it. I'm prone to withdrawal when life gets tough.

As the movie begins, I have the urge to look over my shoulder. Eli stands at the back of the room. I make out his tall shape in the darkened hall. He's with someone. They're holding hands. A pull of tension twinges in my stomach and I force my shoulders away from my ears.

"Who's that?" I mouth to Paige and nod over my shoulder.

Paige follows my gaze. "I don't know, it's too dark." She shrugs and turns her attention forward.

I glance at the back of the hall again. Who is she? I didn't realize Eli had ventured into the world of romance, I thought he was taking things slowly, getting used to a life of freedom again. But of course he wants comfort from the arms of a woman, anyone would. To know there is someone else in the world who has your back, who's your biggest supporter, who will nurse you through all the nightmares of this terror-ridden world, of course he wants it. Like I have with Matt.

I tear my eyes away from the dark shape of the woman who's captured Eli's heart, whoever she is, and center them on the wall ahead. The opening credits roll. Matt reaches for my hand.

The movie is a thriller, an action bang, bang, beat 'em up, body count kind of movie. It's okay, if I don't think too closely about what it's really like to witness someone's brains blown out in front of me.

There's minimal rustling or whispering from the audience, until near the end when a scream rips through the air. At first, I think it's a reaction to the particularly tense culmination of events on the big screen. But then someone pauses the movie and the scream comes again.

Lyla. She stands rigid, screaming into cupped hands, her eyes wide. Someone flicks the lights on. Matt and I rush over. Sawyer lies on the ground, fitting. His eyes roll into the back of his head, a sickly, oozing foam pours out of his mouth. Veins in his head and arms throb and bulge bright red under his clammy skin.

"Silver! Do something!" Lyla yells.

Dropping to my knees, I place a hand on Sawyer's chest. His body is fire hot. I almost pull my hand away from the shock of the sudden heat. Matt kneels and cradles his shaking head, moving chairs out of the way, giving Sawyer space. Erica wraps her arms around Lyla, holding her back.

The healing glow covers my hands and radiates into the room. The little sparkling white bolts find their way into Sawyer's body and within a few moments he is still. His eyes close and his breathing deepens. After a few more seconds I sense I'm no longer needed and remove my hand. Sawyer opens his eyes and looks around the room, at the crowd hovering over him.

"What happened?" he asks, sitting up. "Is the movie over? Did I fall off my chair?" He frowns as he looks from the scattered chairs to the floor.

"You're okay!" Lyla throws herself at his chest.

"Whoa! I guess it's my lucky night!" Sawyer chuckles.

"Don't even think about it," Matt says, wagging a finger.

"Oh shush. Let them have their moment." I pull Matt away from the scene as Lyla and Sawyer look to enact something a little more advanced than PG friendly.

"What happened?" Paige threads her arm through mine. With the other arm she supports her lower back. My friends crowd around, but I note Eli is missing.

"Mosquito," Sawyer answers, when Lyla agrees to climb off his lap. "Bit me yesterday when I was in the city cleaning up. It must have been infected. It must have given me the virus. I wondered why I was feeling off. Thought it was the heat. Why do I have such sucky luck with bugs?" He rolls his eyes and puffs his hair out of his face. During the last mission he was bitten and succumbed to the virus then too. "Thank you, Silver."

"No problem," I say, frowning. I wish Dad was here. Something isn't right. "But it can't be the same virus. That's the first thing I did when we got back remember? I altered your DNA so you'd be immune."

"What else could it be?" Paige asks, her hands cradling her belly.

"A mutation. Mosquitoes don't have a long life span. This is the result of generations of breeding," Matt says.

Lyla's hand flies to her mouth. "Are we all at risk?"

The crowd stills as they wait for my response. How to explain the different paths of viruses. Some of them jump species and will always be in our world. Others burn themselves out, mutating their genetic code until they end up eradicating themselves. Others can only exist in humans and die out when we isolate or vaccinate. There are countless possibilities. This deadly virus was genetically engineered and its trajectory is unpredictable. Although it is acting more like a normal virus now, there's no telling how it might evolve.

Jacob wheels himself to me. "I thought we were over the risk of the virus."

I sigh. "Dad made a vaccine, unprecedentedly quickly. But we don't know the efficacy of that vaccine, we don't know how long it will last."

"Then how do we know if we're safe..." Sawyer trails off.

"Time will tell." I look at my friends, their faces tight and their frowns deep. "This virus can jump species and it's mutated. The vaccine should keep you all safe from several generations of evolution, but Dad's been looking at new vaccines too, altering the ingredients as the virus mutates. He plans on announcing a vaccination program when he gets back."

Jacob makes as if to stand, then realizes he can't. "Is there anything we can do?"

I shake my head. "You're all protected from mutated strains, at least for the next year or so until the virus mutates a few more times. But Sawyer's DNA was always a little different. His vaccine didn't work the first time around. I had to alter his DNA manually to make him resistant to the original virus. He's not protected against mutant strains."

"Fantastic," Sawyer mutters. "Bring on the insect repellent."

Paige cradles her stomach. "What about the baby?"

The baby will be protected by your immune system," I reply. "And we'll vaccinate him as soon as we can."

She nods, but her emerald eyes darken and she lays a hand on Jacob's arm.

Erica turns to Paige and places a hand on her stomach too. "Nothing is going to hurt this little guy. I'll make sure of it."

I wish she could protect the rest of us too.

"Me too." Carter raises his flask. His eyes are bloodshot and he staggers into Mason, who holds him upright. "Gotta protect the next generation."

He takes a long pull on the flask. When he's done, the flask slips from his hands and Mason catches it, tucking it into a pocket. He hauls Carter out of the room. Looking over his shoulder, he gives me a look. He's not a man of many words, but he'll never let a friend down. He'll keep an eye on Carter. I wish there was something I could do to heal his pain.

The memory of William's death flashes in my mind. Dangling from the broken bridge, fingers slipping from my tentative grasp, my inability to save him as he plummeted to his death. Carter's twin brother. Dead. Because of me.

Everyone labelled it an accident. But Paige was there. She saw what I did. I didn't transition fast enough, I didn't make the right decisions. I should have saved him. I have done this to Carter.

When the door slams shut, I turn back to Sawyer. "Come find me tomorrow and we'll make your DNA virus-resistant to this new strain."

"And what about the strain after that? And the one after that?" he asks. "You might not be around to save me next time."

CHAPTER TEN
SILVER

When I wake the next morning, Matt's side of the bed is empty. He left early to work on the irrigation system and add enhancements to his security system. So far he's rigged camera surveillance and a communication system to talk to the other camps. Although we've managed to keep the electricity grids on, cell phone and internet networks are a whole other beast we haven't yet approached. Matt and Francesca talk about setting booby traps, but it's too dangerous with the kids running around the streets. Besides, to quote his words, we live in peace now anyway.

Ignoring the empty silence from the bedroom along the hall, I throw on clothes, grab a tin of peaches, and march out the door to my lab to meet Sawyer.

When he arrives, he plonks himself on a stool opposite me. He takes a sip of coffee from a travel mug and extends his arm, ready to be poked and probed. "Let's get it over with."

Withdrawing his blood, I put it through my computer

analysis. I note the antibodies to the original virus. I also see antibodies for the newer strain.

"You're good," I say.

"Say what?"

"I don't need to do anything. You already have the appropriate antibodies for the new strain. I guess when the mosquito first bit you, the virus entered your system. You didn't become symptomatic for a few hours, giving your body enough time to start developing anti-bodies."

"But I still got sick..."

"Yes. The virus multiplies exponentially. Your antibodies do not. They got overwhelmed. But you have enough now, in your blood, to protect you if you're ever bitten again."

"Good. Being pricked by needles isn't my favorite thing to do first thing in the morning." Sawyer takes another sip of his coffee, grimaces, then throws a small fireball into it to warm it. "But what do I do if I'm bitten again? Infected with a different strain?"

"Dad will stay on top of it. We'll keep updating the vaccine so you're protected."

Sawyer glances around the room, as if looking for bugs that might suddenly jump him and bite him. "But you're Dad's not around, and he's not always going to be."

"I know it's scary, but I'm not going to let anything happen to you."

He gives me a tight-lipped smile. "I lived on the streets for a long time, Silver. If there's one thing I learned it's that you can't control life, no matter how much you want to."

Sawyer was homeless before our first mission. He came

upon the telekinesis nanite by chance and used it to hustle card games and win money. He also became a food hoarder.

"You're right," I say. "I'm sorry. You're going to have to be careful. You've got some great abilities, they should be useful if anything tries to get too close to you."

He removes a can of insect repellent from his pocket, shoots me his lopsided grin and proceeds to spray it all over himself, liberally. "Lyla's gonna love my new smell!"

In no hurry to move on, Sawyer sips at his coffee while I sterilize the equipment I used to take his blood. He eats my tin of peaches.

"Was everything okay with you and Matt last night?" I ask.

"Ah, Matty boy." He shrugs. "Yeah, I get it. We're buddies, it's his sister. He lays it on a bit thick sometimes though, you know?"

I turn off my monitor and slide off my stool. "I know. I'm sorry. I'm trying to get him to go easy on you."

"I appreciate that. I mean, I can handle it, but I know it bothers Lyla."

Standing, he grabs his thermos of coffee and sprays the repellant again. Choking on the fumes, he takes a couple of backward steps and gave his curls a good run-through with the fingers of one hand, causing a dusty cloud of repellent to rise from his hair. He splutters and gags. Compliments of the ability to hold my breath for over half an hour, I refrain from breathing for a few minutes.

"Think maybe I went a little heavy on the dosage." He coughs again.

I laugh. "Maybe you should try the roll-on version next time."

"Thanks for your help, Silver." Sawyer makes it to the door, then turns. "By the way, how's things with the crops? I know Francesca is worried."

I join him at the door. "We have five warehouses stocked full of rescued dry goods. If the crops fail. We'll be okay. We'll figure it out."

"You sure?"

"I'm on it, Sawyer. You don't need to hoard anything."

He blushes. "Okay. Good. That makes me feel better."

I return home to swap my sweatshirt for a T-shirt. Air conditioning is no longer permitted and the day is heating up. On my way out of the house intending to visit my mother, I pass Einstein lying on the porch, whimpering.

"Again?" I ask.

It would seem so.

I lay a hand on his flank and let my healing power do its work. But I'm worried. These treatments are becoming frequent, almost daily.

Where are you going? Einstein asks as I slip my feet into my flipflops.

"To see my mother. I want to make sure she's settled in okay. Then I'm going to find Eli and continue cataloging my abilities," I reply.

Can I come? He wags his tail and pushes his head under my hand for a pat.

"Sure."

When we arrive at the hospital Einstein follows me through the automatic doors of the main entrance. It's not as fancy as the hospitals we used to have. Purpose built with a ton of portacabins so it can be contained within the new residential zones, but it still has all the necessary equipment, along with a few doctors and nurses. I stop at reception to enquire after my mother's whereabouts and we wind our way through the maze of hallways until we arrive at my mother's room.

My mother sits in a chair gazing out the window at the half dead city beyond. She isn't really seeing what's there. She's watching her own private images circle around her head.

The room is okay. Standard hospital green with a few prints of landscapes framed and hung on the walls. Someone thought to put fresh flowers in a vase by the side of her bed. I make a mental note to bring more of her personal belongings from home. Either that or I'll break her out of here and we'll go away together. Far away where no one can tell us what to do. I'm still bristling that I had no say in this decision.

"Hi, Mom." I try for a cheerful tone.

Einstein approaches her and lays his head in her lap. His soulful brown eyes would melt any soul. No reaction.

Crouching in front of her, I peer into her face. I wish I knew what was going on in her brain. I try the telepath ability but can't read anything but static. A few images, but they change too fast for me to make sense of. The only one I can grab onto is a carousel moving so quickly it makes me dizzy.

For once my mother is still and doesn't whisper to herself. Perhaps it's an improvement. I wrap my hands around her folded ones. Frowning, I concentrate and will my strengthening powers to help my mother. The healing power rises quickly and fully. The golden light extends to my arms, face and neck and little frizzes of dancing electricity cover my mother's hands too. When a bruise on her wrist disappears, I know the power is working. Abruptly, she raises our hands in the air so they are level with our chests and stares at me. Einstein wags his tail.

"Silver, I'm not ready yet." She drops her hands to her lap and averts her gaze. Then comes the rocking and the whispering.

"Mom? *Mom*? Please come back," I beg.

It's no use. She's retreated once again. Why isn't she ready? What's going on in there? What is she so afraid of?

I sit with her for the morning, listening to the clock tick above the bed and footsteps come and go in the hallway beyond. Once or twice a nurse enters to check her vitals, administer medication, or bring food. I catch sight of Deja in the hallway reading notes on a clipboard and dare her to enter the room. She gets the message and leaves us in peace. I read to my mother from an out-of-date gossip magazine. Perhaps the sound of my voice will bring her back to me. I want to try again but I'm afraid. She warned me not to. I don't want to push too hard if she isn't ready. But when will she be ready?

In the early afternoon Einstein and I make our way back to my jeep, onto the highway and to the farmland. I'm aware I've not reported to the lab, as Francesca asked. Well, she didn't ask, it was an order wasn't it? But I have no intention of going to the lab and looking at the crops. Not today anyway. Today, Eli and I are going to investigate my powers again.

And perhaps I'll find out who he was holding hands with at the movie night.

Parking the jeep in the shade of the red barn, I find the track leading to Eli's cabin. Einstein chomps at the bugs in the weeds as we walk.

Gross, when he manages to catch a cricket.

The sound of fluttering wings warns me of Erica's approach. I turn and wait for her to land.

She leaps to the ground without a sound and nestles one foot behind the other. She touches the continuous membrane of her wings. "It's so nice to be able to use them again."

I smile. "No one's giving you a hard time about them?"

She frowns. "My wings? Why would they?"

I keep my voice as neutral as possible. "Matt doesn't think I should be using powers."

Her button nose wrinkles. "But everyone is using their abilities. To help."

"That's what I said." I look away. I hadn't intended to confide in Erica, let alone dredge it all up again. "Don't worry about it. It's a me and Matt thing."

"He always has been a little black and white." Erica bends to pet Einstein, who rolls onto his back to expose his belly. "I know we haven't always been close, but I'm here if you want to talk. I know Paige is your person, but she doesn't need any more burdens right now."

I bristle, quashing the urge to respond to her unsubtle reprimand. "Was there something you wanted?"

Her violet eyes narrow as she stares down the dirt track. "I was worried about Eli. He's been complaining about a lot of headaches. I know you're friends with him and I wondered what you thought?"

"Appreciate the heads up. I was going to check on him now."

She takes Sean's Stetson off her head and fingers its leather ribbon. "Maybe he needs a doctor. A real one."

"Erica." I inject some gentleness into my voice. For all our past differences I have a lot of respect for her. There are times when I feel close to her. But not right now. "Maybe stop worrying about everyone else. Re-adjustment is hard. Maybe you need to find a purpose."

"What's wrong with helping others?" Her cheeks hollow as a challenge sets in her eyes. Erica will never stop helping others. But is it altruistic or is it to relieve the guilt she carries over her best friend's death? She pushed her into taking a nanite and she died. Erica took up archery in her honor, and got damn good at it too, but does it actually help her?

"Nothing," I say finally.

"It's not like there are any archery or cheerleading competitions going on right now," she snaps. Her wings turn an acid green, a color I was once familiar with. She's mad at me.

"I know."

"Joe would understand." She lets the name dangle between us. Joe had been special to both of us. An ex-pro football player, a bulk, who injured his knee and joined the resistance. Before Matt and I got together, we had a thing, and Erica was in love with him and it all got messy.

I sigh. "What do you want me to say?"

Her lips press tight and the watery look in her eyes disappears. "Nothing." She leaps into the sky and her wings carry her away.

Gritting my teeth, I continue along the path with Einstein beside me. Before I can knock on the cabin door, it opens and Eli stands there, a canteen of water in one hand, condensation dripping down his fingers, and a smile on his face. "Afternoon. Was wondering where you were."

Einstein turns in a circle and paws at the ground. *He smells bad.*

"Einstein!" I chide. "That's not nice."

I turn back to Eli who's raised an arm and is sniffing his armpit. "Well, I know the shower's been on the brink as it's connected to the irrigation system, but I thought I was managing okay with my bucket of water." With an enticing smile hovering on his lips, he shrugs.

"You are! You smell great!" Oh my goodness, did I just say that? "Fine. I mean you smell fine." I try again. But it's too late to stop the blush rising on my cheeks.

I scowl at Einstein.

He smells like the lab, Earl's lab.

I kneel before the dog, partly to hide my embarrassment and partly to reassure him, and whisper in his ear. "I'm not surprised. I'm sure he endured unspeakable acts in the mountain. I'm sure the after-effects are lingering. That's what you smell."

Einstein whines and turns away. He isn't interested in continuing the conversation.

Now that my blush has abated, I face Eli once more. "Sorry about that. You ready?" I glance over my shoulder. We're at the edge of the crop fields, I've spent too much time here already and I don't want Francesca or Matt to notice me before I can get away.

"Let's go." Eli steps out of his cabin and leads the way to the abandoned farmhouse.

As we walk along the narrow path, I watch the rise and fall of his broad shoulders as he ducks under branches and picks his way around stinging nettles.

"Did you enjoy the movie?" I ask.

"It was okay, I don't usually go in for that sort of thing."

"Is that why you left?"

He holds a branch out of the way for me. Then smiles. "You noticed, huh?" Heat rises on my neck. "I was getting another headache."

"Again?"

Eli nods. "S'okay. Not as bad. The flashing lights were getting to me is all."

"You missed all the drama, with Sawyer," I say.

"I heard. Bitten by an infected mosquito."

"Yup."

"He was lucky you were there. The way I hear it, the virus wipes out in a matter of hours."

"It's scarily quick," I say. "Lyla was freaking out."

"Anyone would, seeing someone they love like that," Eli says, falling into step behind me.

His tenderness surprises me. Perhaps beneath the toned abs and biceps that rival a bulk's, there's a sensitive soul under there. But then I know that, he is sympathetic to my needs when Matt isn't. He's helping me.

Emerging from the shade and into the abandoned farmyard, Eli squints into the sun. He pulls his sunglasses down from where they are resting on top of his head. "I was thinking we could try meditating. All those relaxation exercises Jacob used to teach? It might help focus your mind and bring an isolated ability to the surface."

"It's worth a try," I say, placing my own canteen of water on the ground.

Einstein retreats to the shade of the house, growls, then remains quiet.

"Here." Eli gestures to the ground under the shade of the large beech tree where the tire swing used to hang. "Let's lie down."

Stretching out on the prickly grass, I close my eyes. I sense Eli lying next to me. He is close. Close enough that the skin on my arm tingles.

"What does Jacob do now?" he whispers.

"Deep, slow breathing," I whisper back, not wanting to break the hushed, peaceful spell that has fallen over us.

"Okay, in, one, two, three, out, one, two, three," he says softly. "That kind of thing?"

"Yes." My body melts into the ground. Blades of grass tickle my feet. Filtered sunlight warms my skin. In the distance, I hear my friends calling to each other in the fields. "Just like that."

I drift away from it all, my mind closing in on itself, aware only of my deep, measured breathing and the feel of Eli's arm touching mine.

Listening to his voice, tension in my limbs drains away. I breathe deeply, allowing my body to relax, waiting for an ability to make itself known. Feeling feather-light, as though I'm drifting lazily on a soft summer breeze, I release my mind and body. I drift up and down and around and around, ever so gently. Higher and higher, up and up. Lighter than air, like a helium balloon, I feel as though I can simply float away. How nice would that be?

"Silver," Eli says. His voice comes from far away.

"Hmm?" I reply, too happy in my detached moment to care much about anything or to listen.

"Silver? Open your eyes. Please don't panic though." I pinpoint his voice to be somewhere below me.

CHAPTER ELEVEN
SILVER

Opening my eyes, I find myself staring at the sky. Well, that's okay. Nothing to worry about here. When I closed them, I was staring at the sky, but through the green branches of the tree. Confused, I put my hands beside me, intending to push myself into a sitting position. There's no ground. I look down. Eli is somewhere below me. I'm floating above the roof of the farmhouse and still drifting upwards.

"Holy...!" I exclaim and fall back to earth, slowing my fall with telekinesis at the last moment. I land on my butt. "Ouch!"

"Are you okay?" Eli is at my side in an instant. Einstein wanders over and, licking my face, expresses his concerns too.

"I'm okay." I push myself to my feet and rub my sore butt.

"That was something," Eli says.

"But was it a new something?" I think aloud. "Or was it my flying ability?"

"I thought you needed your wings to fly?"

"You're right. I do. It must be a new ability," I say.

"Levitation," Eli says. He uncaps his canteen and offers me a sip.

"Damn." Gulping at the canteen, the water dribbles over my chin.

"Damn – good, or damn – bad?" Eli asks.

"Both, I guess. Levitation's great and all but I was hoping for something else." I sigh as Einstein curls into a ball at my feet.

Eli touches my arm. "We'll find it, Silver. We'll get there."

Where his fingers meet my bare skin a tingle of such intensity ignites that I think I'm acquiring a new ability. But Eli doesn't have abilities. Perhaps there's another power inside trying to make itself known. Or maybe I have to admit to myself his good looks and well-honed body are having more of an impression on me than I want them to. I waver. Should I have enlisted Eli's help? Perhaps I'm embarking on a dangerous game. But his information is valuable. He observed Earl for eighteen months. I need the knowledge inside his head.

This is not good, Einstein growls.

Has he sensed my inner conflict? "What's the matter?"

It's that smell, his smell. It's much stronger.

I turn to Eli who's moved to the shade of the tree and is resting his head in his hands.

"I think it's another headache," I say to Einstein. "Whatever Earl did to him has left him with these crushing headaches. Maybe you can smell his pain." I pat Einstein back into a lying position. He snorts, turns his head, and rests it on his paws.

Leaving the dog in the sun, I walk over to Eli. "Can I help?"

He smiles, but pain shines in his pupils. "I'm not sure, but you're welcome to try."

Laying my hand on his head, the healing power immediately emerges and shines its beautiful golden light. Feeling a shift within his head, I think it's going to work. But then an accosting image of the menacing yellow eyes comes to me and a gate, a wall, a steel door even, shuts itself firmly and kicks my power out of Eli's body.

Before I can react, before the hairs on my arms rise in response to the image of the yellow eyes of my nightmare, a second image pierces my brain. A troll with a spear decked in armor standing guard by the steel door, much like the doors in the prison where I killed Bear. But this door is the entrance into Eli's mind and the troll will not allow me to pass. Why not? I remove my hand. The image of the yellow eyes chills my skin and makes my throat dry out. Why did I see that when I tried to heal Eli? Are my dreams hounding me in my waking hours now too?

"I'm sorry," I say. "I told you my powers are out of whack."

"Not your fault." Eli glances at me, the pain making his brown eyes darken. "It does feel a little better." He digs up clumps of grass. His mouth opens, as if to speak, then closes again.

"What is it, Eli?"

Eli stares at me, through me, into me. "Can I trust you, Silver?" He waits.

"After all you've done for me?" I sit next to him, breaking the eye contact. "Of course."

"It's more than the headaches," he says. "I think there might be something else going on in me. Something...something...*scary*." Maybe it isn't pain I see in his eyes. Maybe it's fear.

"We'll figure it out," I echo his earlier words.

Eli shakes his head. "It's the nightmares too. They seem so real. And the visions that happen when I'm awake."

I remember his hallucination. "Like the crop rows being dug?"

"Exactly. I could swear..." Eli nods and then massages his temples. He takes a sip of water. "In the dreams, it feels like I'm missing something. Like there's something off stage I can't see. Every time I turn to look, it's gone. But I know it's important. I feel desperate to discover it, like the most urgent of yearnings. It's primal, almost sexual." He coughs. "But I'm not alone. I mean, in the dream I'm always physically alone, in the middle of the storm-tossed ocean on a boat, or in the middle of a desert with nothing to see for miles, but I can feel a presence. I'm not *really* alone. But I can't figure out what it is. Who it is. Or where it is. But I know I have to find it."

"When Earl touched me, he gave me all of his abilities and I haven't figured them all out yet. I'm sure the trauma you suffered under his...kidnapping has affected you in ways you haven't anticipated."

"It's more than that." Scanning the yard, he frowns.

"Did he experiment on you? Can you remember? Maybe you do have abilities."

"No!" Eli shakes his head and his hands fist.

"It's okay if you do. I'm here to help."

He stands. "I'm not like him. I'm nothing like him. I won't be." His eyes meet mine. "I'm not him, Silver."

"I know that," I say. "He probably made it so you wouldn't remember." Nothing was impossible for Earl in terms of science, he was the master of genetic modification, but he also possessed no moral bounds to constrain his ideas either. "If I were you, I'd take one day at a time and concentrate on recovering from the trauma of being held hostage for eighteen months. The rest will come. The dreams, if they're important, will become clearer over time."

"I could say the same to you." He smiles wryly. "But we all know you won't take a moment's rest until you've figured out your powers and your mother is cured."

"That's true," I say. "That's absolutely true."

Rising to his feet, Eli digs painkillers out of his pocket and swallows them. "I'd love to see more of your destroyer power. I've heard so much about it, will you show me?" He offers me a hand.

I look from Eli to the empty fields beyond the farmhouse and to the forest beyond the fields. "I wouldn't mind seeing how much it's grown myself," I reply, taking his hand and allowing him to pull me to my feet. "Keep your eyes on the tree line out there." I gesture to the forest at least two miles away. The same forest I ran through with my father. Can I make it?

Narrowing my eyes, I focus all of my power at those trees. The black lightning covers my hands. Raising my palms above my head, I aim them at the tree line. Black streaks shoot from my fingers and travel the distance to the tree line

116

in a second. Less than a second. Ten trees simultaneously catch fire and then disintegrate. It all happens in the briefest of moments.

"Awesome!" Eli jumps up and down. "That was totally awesome!" He claps.

Shocked, I stumble into Eli. I didn't think my power could travel that far. The black lightning doesn't always appear. Sometimes the power makes things around me vibrate, like the bowls and silverware I disintegrated during breakfast the other morning, and the screen door. And sometimes, like the forest here, there are black streaks of lightning, like I've rocked up to a movie set with my own bag of special effects.

The lightning power twitches on my fingers, wanting more, begging to be released again. It takes all my willpower to shove it away deep inside. I feel it knocking around in there, wanting to come out.

"Yeah," I say. "That was something else."

〉〈〉〈〉〈

After leaving Eli at his cabin, I drive home with Einstein who remains oddly quiet, refusing to engage in conversation and insisting his back is not hurting when I enquire. When I walk through the front door the lights are dim and soft music plays from the living room. Entering the kitchen, I find the table laid with the best china. It's stuff we've never used, reclaimed from a fancy department store from before the resistance. We've been saving it to celebrate when my mother is cured. There must be another reason why it's out. A vase of roses forms a center piece and flickering candles are placed around the room.

"What's going on?" I ask Matt as he turns from chopping and slicing and assembling various items of food on the kitchen worktop.

"Tonight, it's all about you and me." He smiles warmly. "We haven't been getting enough time alone together. We've both been stressed and we need some time to unwind and talk."

"You've been stressed?" I thought it was just me.

He gives me a look that says I should know better. "I'm worried about you." His voice is gentle, and I accept his concern comes from a good place. "About your mom. The crops... I don't need to spell it all out."

I nod and accept a glass of chilled, white wine Matt places in my hands. "This is nice."

He turns back to the counter and the chopping and slicing and assembling. "Where were you today?"

Sinking into one of the leather kitchen chairs, I sip at the cool wine and attempt to ignore Matt's question.

"Silver?" Matt pauses in the act of chopping a carrot, stirs something delicious smelling on the stove and levels his bright blue eyes at me.

Turning from his intense gaze, I straighten my shoulders and prepare for an interrogation. "I went to see my mother. I don't like her not living here with me. I wanted to make sure she was okay in her new surroundings." I take another sip of wine, relishing the warm glow it lights in my stomach. Before, I was too young to drink. There isn't a drinking age anymore.

"Oh. And was she?"

"Yes, she seemed okay." I don't have the energy to tell him about the few words she spoke. There's no point sharing the information with Matt until I have a better idea of what's going on. "I need to take her some personal effects. To make it seem a bit more familiar."

"Great. Let me know if you need any help." His face is so tender it makes my chest hurt.

There's no more interrogation. No questions about why I didn't turn up at the barn lab. I relax. Maybe I'm not giving Matt enough credit. He loves me, he's concerned about me, he wants to make sure I'm okay. I wince against the sudden wave of guilt. Perhaps I should reveal what I'm doing with Eli.

"Here." Matt places a steaming bowl of pasta in front of me, the onions and bacon enveloping my senses until I salivate.

"Where did all this come from?"

Matt smiles. "I traded in one of my tokens for the deep freezer food. There's loads of goodies in there."

"S'good," I manage around a mouthful.

"Easy there," Matt says, watching me shovel food into my mouth.

"I forgot to eat lunch," I say. "I'm starving."

"Lyla came to help in the fields today." Matt tops up my wine and takes a sip of his. "She seemed particularly...bouncy."

"More than normal?" I laugh.

"Yes, I'd say she seemed...happy. It was nice to see. We've been through so much, not many people smile anymore."

I think of the way Eli and I laughed together in the yard. It's true. Laughter is a rare commodity.

"Sawyer might have something to do with it," I say.

Matt's eyes narrow. "He better not hurt her—"

"He won't." I place a hand over Matt's. "He loves her."

Matt eats pasta and dabs his lips with a cloth napkin. His eyes dance in the candlelight. "Well, if he loves her anything like the amount I love you, then I guess that's okay." He grimaces. "I can't get my head around the two of them...you know...actually...." He blushes.

"Why do you want to be picturing things like that?" I laugh.

"We have three million people left in the world. We need to repopulate. And not that I think Sawyer and Lyla should be part of that...but eventually...they'll have to and mentally I just can't go there..."

I smile. "Stop worrying about Lyla. And repopulation. It will happen when it happens."

A frown flickers across his face. "We need to help it. Eventually we'll have kids, you and I, and then —"

"Kids?" *Kids?* The word flies out of my mouth before I have a chance to clamp a hand over my lips.

He tilts his head. His frown deepens. "Of course. I mean, what's the point unless we're going to have kids?"

I can't move. I'm glued to my chair. "How about love? That's the fucking point. You can't put an end goal on a relationship."

"That's not what I—"

"Isn't it?"

Matt's shoulders sink. "I don't understand. I'm sorry if I upset you. I thought eventually we'd have kids..."

"I'm tired of feeling railroaded into decisions that aren't my own. You don't get what you want, because *you* want it. There's two of us in this relationship, Matt."

"Yes, of course, I...but isn't that what everyone wants, Silver? Kids? Don't you want kids?"

I'm about to break his heart. I dip my chin. "No. I don't want kids, Matt. I shouldn't have kids." I meet his eyes. His face is crumpling. I'm worried he might cry. But I can't spare his feelings when it comes to the one area of my life I'm certain about. "I will not subject a child to my genetics. God knows how it would turn out." Anger bubbles inside, along with a few other things I can't identify. I take my frustration out on the napkin in my lap, twisting it one way with tight fists and then back the other way. Misjudging my own strength, I manage to tear the thick cloth in two.

"I thought you might have changed your mind by now, given the circumstances," Matt says. "I thought you would have realized how much you have to offer."

"Matt, if we have a kid it's probably going to exhibit some kind of ability, right?" I jab my finger at the tabletop.

"I suppose."

"Paige and Jacob are having a kid. There are a small handful of people left here who still have abilities, but add us all together and it makes a large percentage of the total population now that we don't have much of a population. Abilities will be passed down, irrelevant of and resistant to the cure. Future generations will have abilities, maybe a lot of them. Isn't that what we fought against? That no one should have that kind of power over anyone else?" Let's see him argue his way out of this one, him and his advanced intelligence.

"I would hope..." Matt takes my hand and rubs his thumb over my palm. "That we learned our lesson. I would hope we are wiser to the future, *potential* problems and that the safety laws we've put in place would prevent a world dominated by altereds ever happening again. Silver, it's not about the abilities, the powers, the showy displays, it's a mentality thing. It's about how you decide to live your life."

"Don't be so naive."

He stares across the table, across the roses and candlelight at me. His eyes are softer in the flickering light, muted, but I can see the pain in them. The pain of my potential, or probable, refusal to give him what he wants. We are at an impasse. Neither of us willing to yield. But why do I feel like I'm the one in the wrong?

"Silver, I don't see my future without children."

The dishes vibrate. The cupboard doors open and close a few times. A single burst of black lightning shoots out of my right palm and disintegrates one of the roses in the vase. Matt snatches his hand away and gives me a *get-control-of-yourself* look. Squeezing the acorns in my pocket, I try to pretend this conversation isn't happening.

"I'm not asking for this now, Silver." His voice turns husky. "I want you to think about it for our future. Contemplate the possibility. *Please*. For me."

"Okay," I say, wiping a hand across my forehead. I've fought enough battles for one day and I've run out of counter arguments. I'm not going to have kids, but he needs some kind of gesture. "I'll think about it. But that's it." I jab my fork in his direction. "I'm just thinking about it."

"Thank you, Silver, that's all I ask." Matt stands and removes two plates from the fridge. Dessert. Chocolate torte. It's been in the freezer for six months, waiting for a special occasion. Taking a bite, I find the chocolate thick, bitter and it gets stuck in my throat.

"I meant this to be a romantic dinner, a chance to catch up," Matt says, after he finishes his own slice. "I'm sorry for bombarding you."

"S'okay." Picking up the plates, I take them to the sink. I squeeze the washing up liquid onto the sponge and begin to methodically wash the dishes. Matt approaches me from behind and rests his hands on my waist. He kisses my neck and nibbles on my ear lobes. He moves his hand under my shirt and draws lazy circles over my stomach, ever so slowly arcing higher.

Reaching a hand forward, Matt turns off the tap, then pivots me to face him. His lips find mine, his hands are all over my body. His touch melts my bitterness and I'm carried away on the sensations.

Suddenly it's not Matt's face I hold in my mind, but Eli's. Eli and his strong jaw and impossibly defined eight-pack. His silky dark hair, and the way tenderness leaks into his voice when he talks. Embarrassed at the intrusion, I shake the image of Eli's impressive body out of my mind. I open my eyes and concentrate on Matt.

"Silver?" Matt says around a kiss.

"Hmm?" My hands find the bottom of his T-shirt. I pull it up and over his head.

"You said you went to see your mother today," he pauses, kissing my jawline. "Erica said she saw you in the fields."

Tensing against him, my hands stop dead in the middle of Matt's back. Is it time to come clean about testing my abilities? Noticing my hesitation, Matt's lips pause over a throbbing vein in my neck. He drops his hands and takes a step back.

"Silver?" A note of alarm creeps into his voice.

Leaning against the sink, I clench the counter in both hands. "I went to see Eli. Eli lives in the fields."

"To check on his headaches?"

And here it is. "Not because of his headaches. Because he can help me." I pull my T-shirt straight and toy with my pendant.

Matt shoves his hands in his pockets. "With what?"

"With my abilities." I hold up a hand as Matt starts to protest. "He knows what most of Earl's abilities were. He was around the altereds for eighteen months. He's helped me isolate some of the new powers so I can learn what they are and what they do."

"But why do you even need to know what they are? You already have enough abilities to help society get back on its feet. We're in a time of peace." His words come out clipped and hard and his face colors. "Unless you can uncover something that will raise the dead and restore the country to its former glory - and I think that's highly doubtful - there's no point."

I take a moment to focus my destroyer power away from my twitching fingers. "I'm trying to find something to help my mother. I want to see if there is anything in me that can cure her."

Matt rolls his eyes. "Earl is not going to have anything benevolent. All of his abilities were for the purpose of causing harm." He points an angry finger at me. Matt has never pointed an angry finger at me before. "You don't need to be experimenting with them."

"I have to know," I say. "I have to make sure. No stone unturned and all that." And there's something alluring about all these new powers I'm discovering. But I'll never admit that to Matt.

"That's why you weren't at the lab today," Matt says under his breath. "Silver, has it occurred to you what will happen if the crops die and we have no food?"

Trying to stay calm, I grip the lip of the counter at my back. "I know you need my help with the crops. I need my mother. I'm losing time. I can't explain it, but I feel an urgency to her treatment." I try to ignore the thunderous look on his face. "What's a few days? Give me a few days with Eli and my mother and I'll come and help with the crops."

"No! Crops first, then you can spend all the time you want with your mother. Let the doctors do their jobs. And as far as you testing your powers, that's gotta stop. You promised me you wouldn't change anything else."

"I haven't changed anything else!" I yell. "I'm only trying to catalog what's already there."

"And being seduced by it at the same time!" Matt stiffens and gestures to the pile of ash the rose became. "You said you were afraid of turning into some insane power-crazy thing."

He raises his eyes to mine and I brace myself for his next words. "Now I'm afraid of it too."

Another black flash of power erupts from my hand and scorches what's left of the roses in the vase along with the table they're resting on.

See? Matt's expression says it all too clearly.

She's losing it, if she hasn't lost it already. Of all the pig-headed, stubborn-assed, singled-minded things to have an obsessive attitude about, her goddamn powers. Why aren't I enough for her? Do I not make her happy anymore? I wish she would stop already, come back to me, come back to the sweet, innocent, trusting person she used to be and forget about all the abilities.

His thoughts rush at me.

Oh, Matt! My heart aches for him and the misguided faith he has in me. Used to have in me. I didn't realize my telepathic ability was activated. I turn if off before I hear more. I can't reply. The tears will fall then and he will see. I can't let him see.

He's right, in a way. I do feel a powerful urge to use my powers. It makes me happy. But I'm not going insane, I'm not turning into a power-crazy thing. Can't he see that? Concentrating, I quiet down all the powers within me that are fighting for their chance to shine.

"Slippery slope, Silver! It's a slippery slope and you are charging down it!" Matt shouts. He grabs his T-shirt, turns on his heel and marches out of the room.

CHAPTER TWELVE
ELI

ELI STARES out the square cabin window while he waits for Silver. He taps an unusual rhythm against his tin coffee mug, which is complemented by an edgy wriggling of his toes. He goes through the events of yesterday, trying to keep all the lies straight in his head.

Okay, okay, maybe they aren't all lies. He does have horrible headaches and he is experiencing crazy dreams and he does feel a level of urgency in them. It's like one of those computer games where he has to complete each level in a certain time, those games he used to spend his pocket money on in the arcade strips when his mother allowed it. Well, he's running out of time and he isn't anywhere near the end of the level. He has Earl's powers. And then some. He's pretty sure he knows what most of them are, but a few remain a mystery.

He drinks coffee from the mug, not caring that it's cold or that the caffeine will agitate his burgeoning anxiety. Yesterday he had the opportunity to tell Silver everything. But he didn't. She said she'd be supportive if he possessed abilities, but Eli suspects if she was confronted with the truth she'd feel differently. He's seen it happen before. Like the way people looked at Earl. Even Carmen, who could get any animal to do her bidding and was Earl's oldest friend, was scared of him. Only too happy to run off to that town in Utah and get as far from the mountain as she could. Much to her detriment. Erica killed her, and Silver let it happen. Carmen was nice to him.

Putting the coffee cup and toothbrush down, he dips his head. He will never admit he carries all the powers of their defeated nemesis. People would exclude him. They would look at him in fear. They might drag him to the oak tree and hang him there for all to see. That will not be his future.

Eli holds his head in his hands as he sinks to his single bed. The pain has morphed into something he feels able to live with, although there are times when it grabs a hold of him a little too tightly. But at least the scratching comes soon after, soothing away the pulsing aches.

Since he started experimenting with his abilities the headaches have abated somewhat. Not completely, but enough to take the edge off.

The other day he ignited a tumbleweed with his mind. It was an ugly heap of a bush that got tangled near his cabin, an eye sore. Merely by wishing it engulfed in flames, it happened. It startled him, but also brought a tug of satisfaction. More recently came the crop rows dug with so little effort. It happened without him realizing it. None of the back ache, none of the grueling work under the hot sun. How easy it can be if he embraces these powers.

The teleportation ability yesterday wasn't Silver at all. It was him. Or at least she

wasn't the only one in control of the experience. The power churned inside him, excited by the proximity of Silver's strength, eager and desperate to consume his body, to be used, to be exercised. He teleported too, right there along with her, making her believe it was her power which teleported them both.

There are lots of different abilities waiting to make themselves known and they all want their shot at experimentation, they all want to prove themselves. But here he is, talking like a crazy person, as if his abilities possess a mind of their own. That *is* crazy, right?

Eli lies on his back and bends his knees, staring at the cobwebs on the ceiling. He imagines himself and Silver together. They would make a formidable force. They experience life the same way. Together they would be indestructible. A team. Like Batman and Robin. But equals. Oh, yes. They are equals. He will tell her the truth. In time. When he can be sure of her reaction.

In the meantime, he will help her discover her abilities. It's the highlight of his day. She has released something inside him. Curiosity. Belonging. Strength. Power. A connection to something bigger than him. Maybe he isn't as big a freak as he feared.

She will be helping him too, in ways he didn't anticipate. Perhaps she will help him understand the urgent whisperings he feels uttered at the back of his mind. They come with the scratching. Whispers and urges and desires enter his mind in a needful manner, opening new doors of possibility, showing him different paths. They are all...interesting.

He was relieved to discover a mind-blocking power. Otherwise he wouldn't be able to spend any time with Silver. He only realized it when his thoughts started to float to her. The mortifying one about how beautiful she is. As she read his mind, his mind rebelled, clawing his thoughts back from traveling into her. He clamped down and closed the steel door on his mind. Put a troll by the door to guard it, just in case.

She can't cure him and he assumes it's because of this blocking power. It is the most important ability he possesses. He can't have her reading his thoughts if she ever feels so inclined. She would never forgive him. All those lies.

The dog was almost his undoing. He heard its thoughts; that he smelled bad. At first, he believed perhaps he was little lax with the showers. Although the plumbing was reinstated for most of the town, it doesn't extend to his cabin and he's made do with a bucket from the well. But there was a strange expression on the dog's face - if dogs can have expressions - and he knew the dog was wary of him. He reacted to the dog's thoughts before Silver communicated them. A serious mistake. But she didn't notice. He must be more careful.

What he's supposed to smell of he isn't sure. Dogs sense cancer and other illnesses in people, right? Maybe the headaches are a sign of something more untoward. But Silver would have healed him. It can't be that. Unless Earl screwed up his DNA so perversely that anything is possible. That's probably what the mutt smelled. All the same, it makes the dog dangerous. He can't have that. He can't let his chances at a new life be jeopardized by an overgrown stuffed animal that happens to be able to communicate with humans. Never.

Eli rolls onto his side as the scratching fingers soothe him. He imagines a tantalizing future of acceptance and power. He merely needs to listen to the whispers, appreciate the scratching, respect his abilities, then this future might be his.

He closes his eyes and immediately sees the yellow eyes. They come to him in all his dreams and are now part of his nightly routine. Eli swears he's seen them somewhere before. But where? In his latest dream, he no longer ran, afraid, from the unusual entity. He faced the yellow eyes and tried to fathom the power they possess.

"Knock, knock." Delta's voice breaks into his thoughts.

Eli rises and opens the door. "Hi, Delta."

She wears an oversized football jersey, shorts, and sandals. She's removed her arms from the sleeves and has them folded inside the jersey somewhere. Adorable.

"I'm here, like you asked. I hope that's okay?"

What is she talking about?

"You know, after movie night, you asked me to drop by?" Delta says, backing toward the door. "It you're busy than I'll go..." She puts her arms back in her sleeves and wraps one hand around the opposite elbow. Her eyes skitter all over the place. How deliciously sweet.

"No, no it's fine, I forgot...please, come in." Reaching for her folded arm, he tugs her deeper into the cabin.

It's easier than he thought, charming Delta. Her fierce, resolute demeanor may have worked for her when she was battling altereds and it was all a matter of life and death, but with him, it crumbles away like the bottom of a cheesecake.

The slightest pressure in the right place; whispers in her ear, a hand at the small of her back, two fingers stroking a rogue hair away from her face, and oops, an accidental grazing of his fingers on her thigh. In his arms, her guard drops, her emotions run raw, and she looks at him with adoration. She succumbs to his every desire. They left the movie night early. It didn't take much. Back in his cabin, she was surprising. Uninhibited. He's looking forward to a repeat performance.

Eli scans the fields as he shuts the cabin door, noting Silver's jeep pulling into the lot. He wants to learn more about Silver's powers, especially the destroyer ability. It isn't an ability he possesses himself, and he's curious. Okay, more than curious. She'll be along in a minute. He'll have to get rid of Delta after all.

CHAPTER THIRTEEN
SILVER

ADAM WAVES to me from the middle of a field. He's sitting on Mason's shoulders and directing Carter where to move the plow. Carter's red hair blazes in the sunshine and I spot a new tattoo on Mason's skin. One of the lines of the freedom song is printed across his shoulders.

I am free. And I won't back down.

I haven't sung the song in months, but the words are held tightly inside. I think of them now, wondering if we might have another battle to face.

When you hear the lone wolf howling,
When sky comes crashing through.
With all the hellhounds growling,
If it ends, just me and you...
Just close your eyes and breathe in deep,

Look to the new sun's sky.
Because our voice is freedom,
And they will hear us cry.

I wave back to Adam, but don't venture closer. I don't want to talk to him right now. He's a sweet kid and all, but I'm not ready to compare notes on dreams or visions. Instead, I continue along the dirt path to Eli's cabin, regretting my decision to wear my plastic flipflops as seeds and prickles get caught between my toes.

"Hey," Eli says, opening the door before I have a chance to knock.

"Hey yourself," I reply.

"No dog today?"

"Thought it best to leave him at home today."

"Whew." His shoulders drop a couple inches and he leans against the frame of the door.

"Not a dog fan?"

"Haven't been around them all that much. Especially ones that can communicate. But I put on extra deodorant, just in case. Didn't want to offend his high-falutin' nose."

I chuckle.

Eli's smiles. "I had an idea."

"Just the one?"

"Ha, ha. But it's a good one." Laughing, he reaches for a shirt and pulls it over his head. "Sawyer showed me where he's been cleaning up the human remains with his pyrokinesis in the old city. I thought it would be a safe area to test your destroyer ability."

"My destroyer ability? I was hoping to find something to help my mom, not concentrate on a destructive ability."

"I know, but hear me out."

"Okay..."

"It's the opposite of your healing ability, right?"

I nod.

"And the healing power is growing?"

"Yep."

"Maybe if we concentrated on growing the destroyer ability, perhaps the healing power will grow along with it and then maybe it will be strong enough to help your mother." Eli looks at me expectantly.

It's a fantastic idea. Without my dad or news of the lady he's looking for, I have no other options.

"Plus, I get the impression you've been having trouble controlling it. You need to practice. Especially if it's getting stronger. You don't want to hurt anyone," Eli says, his voice equal parts warmth and sympathy.

That convinces me. There's been enough death in this world for several lifetimes. I don't want people to come to fear me because I can't control my own abilities. The look on both Francesca and Deja's faces when my black lightning erupted with my messy emotions, although satisfying at the time, is enough to reinstate my determination that I get control over my abilities. Once and for all. I don't want people to be scared of me. I want respect and understanding. I won't use my abilities to intimidate. "You talked me into it. Let's go."

"Oh, and before we go." Eli reaches into the cabin. "Here,

this will quench our thirst." He produces two orange popsicles

"Where'd you find these?" I ask, bringing the refreshing treat to my lips.

"Compliments of Delta."

Of course. Delta has the unique ability to turn any liquid into its solid or gaseous state. Which means she can turn water to ice, Kool-Aid to popsicles. With our sunglasses shielding our eyes and orange juice dribbling down our chins, we follow the path to my jeep. I ignore the speckled blackness growing on the corn stalks, telling myself that's a problem for another day. I drive away from the farmland and into the abandoned city. As I drive, the wind blows our hair and we grin at each other. Life almost feels normal.

"How *is* your mom?" Eli asks, as we wind our way through the empty, potholed streets. Towering gray edifices surround us. Glass windows reflect the sun, chasing shadows into the drains. Trashcans overflow. Puddles of green goo dot the sidewalks and roads. The stench of the old and decayed makes me wrinkle my nose. This city, the place I used to live, feels like another lifetime ago.

I sigh. "The same, I took her some of her belongings this morning, not that it makes a difference."

"It's important to be around the familiar, it'll help," Eli says. "When I was in the mountain, I really wanted Mr Snuffles."

I raise an eyebrow. "Mr. Snuffles?"

Eli grins sheepishly. He was my favorite toy when I was a kid. A rabbit. I gave him up years ago, but when I was in the mountain, I missed him."

I smile. "Wouldn't it be nice if teddy bears could solve all our problems?" Or guitars. I haven't played my guitar for months. Although I craved the feel of its strings under my fingers when I was on the last mission, I can't bring myself to play. It no longer calms me.

I sigh and pull at the ends of my hair. The wind tosses it into my face. I'm no longer enjoying the drive.

"What else?" Eli asks.

"Paige," I say. "She's my best friend and now she's in the hospital too. She was feeling so uncomfortable she finally agreed to let the doctors take care of her. Which is a good thing, I guess. But the closer the due date gets the more nervous I feel."

"She'll be fine, once the baby is born."

I hope so. What I'm not telling Eli, and I won't because it's private to Paige, is she checked herself into the hospital because her belly was emitting strange blue lights and it freaked her out. There's no premise for this kind of pregnancy. No one, with any confidence, can predict how it's all going to turn out. She resides a few rooms down from my mother, trying to get the rest she needs and leaving Elizabeth the gargantuan task of arguing with her disgruntled son.

Eli and I arrive at the vacant high-rises, now the home of crows and pigeons and other stray animals. I pull the car to the side of the road. When we got back from the mountain, I came here once. To say goodbye and put it all behind me. I walked the streets, visited my apartment block, running a finger through all the dust that collected in the penthouse. Dad's lab was still a wreck, destroyed, the way we left it. Then I moved on. Tried to, anyway.

Being back now doesn't unearth the plethora of emotions I expected. There are hints of a sweet sadness, a forlorn nostalgia. But I don't want to live here again. I don't want to turn back the clock. I have moved on.

"You okay?" Eli asks. Again, I'm touched by the concern in his voice.

"I am."

We jump out of the jeep and walk through the deserted streets, shrouded in the buildings' shadows. There are no puddles of green goo. Sawyer has been through this part already. But trash whisks through the streets, creating a raw skittering sound that grates on my nerves. Potholes litter the sidewalks and shattered glass from the high buildings covers the asphalt. It's a ghost city.

"It's so empty. So quiet." Eli edges closer to me.

"I can't believe I used to live here."

We wander for a bit longer, soaking up the lonely atmosphere, listening to the ghosts whisper about what used to be.

After a while, Eli points to a tower block, an old office building, five-hundred yards away. "How about that one over there?"

I turn to the gray, miserable building and focus my power, the black sparks already dancing across my fingers. I'll be doing the city a favor, it's an ugly building, a scar on the skyline.

A vibration pulses through my feet. The building trembles, then collapses in on itself, level after level. A gray cloud of dust and debris rise high into the sky. The sound reaches my ears, great crunching exploding sounds; shattering glass and slamming concrete. *Faster. Make it faster.*

"That's it!" Eli smiles triumphantly.

Erupting from my hands, a continuous stream of jagged black electricity streaks its way to the building and vanquishes it out of existence in an uninspiring flash of nothingness. The building is no longer there. There is no rubble either. The concrete is reduced to fine ash particles now hovering in the breathless air.

"That was...wow...I don't have the words."

"That's the biggest thing I've ever taken down," I say. The power is back in its bottle. I didn't even have to force it. I didn't have to think about it. "Maybe I should take down all the buildings before they become a cesspit of disease and infection." I glance at the open space where the office building stood and is now replaced with a shaft of harsh sunshine.

"Another!" Eli claps his hands.

"You think?" The destruction of one building in the middle of the old city might go unnoticed, but two, more?

"You need to explore the limits," Eli says.

A very good point. "Okay."

Destroying the building felt as though I was finally using a muscle that's been cramped and underused. Exercising my mental power in the way it should be, the way it wants to be, the way I yearn to do it, is a relief. I allow myself to test the limits, and I'm not afraid. It's my emotions that sometimes make the power difficult to control, during arguments, disagreements. But right now, I'm on top of the world. I feel...*content*. I have this.

Scanning the city for my next target, I spot a building I want to erase from the skyline. My old apartment building, from the time before the resistance, when President Bear lavished every luxury upon my parents, until he didn't anymore and placed us under armed guard instead. The penthouse apartment is full of mixed emotions. I've already said goodbye to it.

It stands on the outskirts of the city, not far from where the forest begins, but I think I can make it. The growing power strains and stretches as though it's an elastic band pulled tight and is finally allowed to fly. The apartment building, along with the one next to it, disappears. They puff away, no sign of a crumbled breezeblock or sliver of glass. No dangerous falling rubble, no loud thunderous noises. It turns to ash and disappears. Two more shafts of sunlight are revealed, as if I'm bringing light back to the city. The evidence of my previous life is expunged forever. I'm mildly disappointed. Without the noise, without the destruction, without the exploding rubble, the experience feels anti-climactic.

"That's the most unimpressive - albeit safest - demolition I've ever seen." Eli says, humor twitching at the corners of his lips.

"Hey!" I poke his side.

"You don't have a tickle power, do you?" Laughing, he grabs my finger.

I search inside and tickle him with my telekinesis until he begs for mercy.

When our laughter fades, I scan the city once more. "I was going for just the one building."

"But look at that," Eli says, splaying his hands. "Look what you can do." He gets it. He gets *me*. He understands. "I think your healing power will be growing nicely now too."

"Let's hope." I cross my fingers on both hands.

Eli stares at the gap in the skyline, his eyes taking it all in. "Did you see what you did? What else are you capable of?"

The question is rhetorical. While I *am* looking for something to help my mother, it isn't *all* about my mother. I allow a slow smile of satisfaction to creep onto my lips.

When the sun lowers and the sky is lit with a pastel rainbow, I return Eli to his cabin and make my way home. After eating a simple dinner, I settle myself on the couch to wait for Matt. Any minute now. He'll want to know why I wasn't at the fields today. I can explain. I will make him understand.

Switching on the lamp beside the couch, I realize I've been sitting in the dark for over an hour. Where is Matt? I lean my head back against the pillows and close my eyes. Sleep tugs at my eyelids and I'm taken to a world where unimaginable creatures with fangs and claws and snarling mouths roam and they all have yellow eyes. Something whispers to me through the dream. An alluring sound, a voice that wants to play. It sounds like ice. A familiar voice. It's the voice I heard on the mountain before I killed Earl. But there's nothing left on the mountain. We destroyed all the altereds and monstrous creatures. We burned everything inside. There's nothing left, and yet I can't shake the feeling I missed something.

"What are you doing?" Matt's voice wakes me from my dream.

Opening my eyes, I find myself hovering in the air, my

nose two inches from the white ceiling. My levitation power. Turning upright in the air, I bang my head on the ceiling. "Ouch!"

"Why are you up there? How are you up there?" Matt asks, tapping a foot on the floor.

"I think it's a new power. One of Earl's. Although I'm not sure why it's happening when I'm asleep." I drift back to the ground. At least my landing is gentler this time. But I brace myself anyway, the tone in Matt's voice is enough to put me on guard.

Matt leans against the door frame, arms crossed, eyes narrow. "This is getting out of hand."

"I can't help what's happening when I'm asleep!"

"No, you can't," Matt says. "But I wonder if it would have happened if you hadn't been exploring your abilities with such intensity?"

"I don't know, Matt." I sigh. "I imagine they would have popped out anyway at one point or another."

"Not if you turned it all off. Not if you don't go looking for it."

"I'll never be able to use an ability effectively, when it's needed, if I don't know it's there," I say, coming to meet him under the wide threshold. "I can't do that. I can't just leave it all."

"Yes, you can. It's actually very easy. You just need to decide." His eyes fix on me, those mesmerizing bright blue eyes that burn a fire in my soul. But I won't back down.

It's an impossible situation. I'll never stop trying to find something that might help my mother. I'll never stop exploring my powers. I don't want any surprises at inopportune moments. And, I have to admit, bringing down the building today felt good. It was a bonus.

Besides all that, Matt has missed the part about me needing my abilities. The part of me afraid of my dreams. The part of me that can't talk about it because it will open the box of dread. That tiny niggle of doubt which wonders if the yellow eyes are real.

"Perhaps I should tell Eli to stay away from you. I know what you two did today. Everyone knows. Sawyer was there, he watched you demolish those buildings."

"I'm not going to stop," I say. "Please try to understand, Matt. *Please*." I want to step closer to him, to touch him, to make him see with my hands what I can't with words. But his rigid stance dispels any illusion that he'll welcome my touch.

"I have tried. I don't get it. It's dangerous, Silver, and you have too much power to become...an altered. You are no longer limited and can use your abilities for as long as you want. We don't need another Earl on our hands."

Did he just call me an altered? That's a low blow. I'm nothing like that evil, narcissistic, demented scientist. I'm tempted to use my telepathy to peer into his thoughts to see if he means it. But what if he does?

"Notice how nothing is shaking?" I say, with barely controlled anger. "Nothing vibrating? Nothing reduced to ash? No black electricity on my fingers? It's because using the power, exploring all my abilities is helping me gain control over the destroyer ability. I'm learning to contain it. Even when I'm mad." I glare at him.

Matt scans the room, but his hard expression doesn't change.

"And why is it okay for everyone else to use their abilities? Carter and Mason turning bulk in the fields, Sawyer hoisting water with his mind, and Delta's making popsicles with her ability for God's sake? I don't see you getting all up in their faces."

"They are trying to help," Matt says slowly.

"What is the point of having all these abilities if I can't put them to use? It's not like you turn off your intelligence."

"I can't turn it off." One of Matt's eyebrows rises. "And I'm not running about demolishing buildings for fun. What if someone had been inside one of those buildings?"

"They weren't."

"How would you even know?"

"I—"

"You have too many abilities, you have too much power. You could be very, very dangerous."

I don't respond. I can't. I don't know what to say. When did he lose his faith in me?

"You think I'm dangerous?" I whisper.

"Not right now." He forms a fist and taps the side of the door frame. "But you could be. You're one of the most determined individuals I know, and when you get an idea in your head..." He sighs and slinks into one of the armchairs.

"Silver, again, it's not about the abilities, it's the mentality." He picks at dirt on his work trousers with an uncut fingernail. "And going around destroying buildings..." Cutting himself off, he seems to give up on the whole argument. His face sags, his cheeks are devoid of color, and he wipes at an eye with the back of his hand.

"*Again*, Matt," I echo sarcastically. "It's helping me control the destroyer power. And there might be something inside me that can help my mom."

A long silence hangs between us. Will he ever understand?

"Why did Erica take her nanite pill?" he asks, his tone calmer.

"She wanted butterfly wings. Stupid popularity stunt."

"Stupid. But harmless."

"I guess."

"And Jacob to further his career, Paige to control her parents, Joe to save his parents money—"

"Matt—"

He holds up a hand. "Let me finish. It all started harmlessly enough. But Erica effectively murdered her best friend. Jacob became a nanite junkie, Paige lost her parents to the dark side, and Joe blew his knee out, destroying his football career and spiraling his family into poverty."

"I get it, Matt. I was there. During the resistance. I fought right alongside you, with Erica and Jacob and Paige and Joe. I *get* it."

"Do you?" Matt doesn't wait for an answer. He doesn't expect one, not one he wants to hear. His thoughts fly from his mind, like darts, circling me, faster and faster. They are loud and angry and so numerous that I'm momentarily crushed by the despair behind them all. His bewilderment and frustration floods out of his mind, so I clamp down on the telepathic power before I hear more.

Matt stands, walks away from me, and paces a circuit of the living room. His face reflects a range of emotions, the most poignant of all seems to be regret, and then he circles back to me. But not before he sets his face in impassive neutrality.

"The panic attacks? What about those?" he asks.

"I'm not getting those either." I have zero regrets on that front.

"Oh, Silver." He reaches for me, but his hand doesn't connect and drifts back to his side. So it's going to be like that. "I'm very, very worried." He shoves his hands in his pockets and examines my face. "When is it going to stop?"

"When I've found something to cure my mother and learned about everything inside me."

He nods, a slight movement. He expected as much. Regret washes over his face again and lingers there. "Francesca's gonna have a fit if you don't show at the lab tomorrow. She was storming the fields today as it was. You need to be there. I expect she might detain you or something if you don't step up."

"Okay, okay." I attempt to soften my tone. "I'll fix the crops first."

"Good, that's my, Silver," Matt says, his shoulders sagging. "And when are you going to talk to Deja again?"

Never. "I don't know."

We stare at each other. I want him to touch me. I want him to comfort me. Maybe he wishes the same. The small, physical gap between us seems so wide. As wide as a valley we once crossed with a churning white-water river below.

146

A hard lump rises in my throat. "Are we going to be okay?"

"We'll get there." A fragile smile wobbles on his lips. Exhaustion makes his eyes shine. *I hope.* The last is uttered in his head, not meant for me to hear, but I do. "But, no more buildings, okay?"

"Okay." I'll find another way to make sense of my destroyer ability.

CHAPTER FOURTEEN
SILVER

THE NEXT MORNING, as Matt and I drive to the lab in the red barn, Einstein sticks his head out the back window and lets the wind massage his ears. His tongue lolls out the side of his mouth and Matt and I both laugh. We lock gazes, a thousand words communicated in one look. We need to get through this rough patch.

The tires bump over the uneven ground as Matt pulls into a space. I note heaps of corn, harvested early, their stalks dark and unnatural. My stomach flips. Matt looks at the diseased crops, then at me.

"I'll fix it," I say.

He nods, then leads Einstein to the fields as I walk through the wide barn doors. As I head for the small rooms at the back, the smell of stored hay and farm equipment fills the air. I used to wrinkle my nose at it, but now I've grown accustomed to it.

"What's the problem?" I ask one of the two scientists in the small lab. Countertops run across two walls. Wide windows line the back wall, letting in strong shafts of light, but the air in here is cool. The floor is boarded and swept clean, but I smell the earth underneath. There's a large table in the center, heaped with seeds, grains and fully harvested crops, all dismal looking, all showing signs of disease. I didn't realize it had gotten this bad.

The male scientist, Edgar, has a graying comb-over which emphasizes the shiny baldness of his head, and a kind smile. The other, Greta, is a woman, younger, but crow's feet decorate her eyes and deep lines cross her forehead. She's too young for such signs of age. Although her hair is dark, she possesses a white swatch of coarser hair at the halfway point between her temple and her middle parting. It's striking.

"The crops are failing faster and faster," Edgar replies, his smile vanishing. He leans over a microscope, gray tufts of hair coming loose. "And the seeds are infected by the same disease that's killing the crops." Straightening, he fiddles with some of the slides and seeds on the worktop in front of him. "Look."

I close an eye and examine the seeds. His observation is correct. Their molecular structure has changed.

"Where are they coming from, the seeds?" I ask.

"From a grain store up north. We've brought in more from another location but it's the same with them," Koko says, as she enters the room and embraces me. She's shed her thick parka and snow boots. Now she wears a pair of shorts and a T-shirt. Her dark hair is contained in a ponytail and her weather-beaten face is kind and warm. She is one of my favorite people and gave us room and board during the last mission. We returned her hospitality by bringing a massacre to her town square, an event I struggle to leave behind. "It's good to see you. It's been a while."

"And you," I say. "Any ideas what's causing the problem?"

Edgar looks at me. "I was hoping you could tell us."

Sliding into a stool at the workbench, I prepare for the work ahead. "I need to examine the DNA of the seeds."

"I thought you'd say that," Edgar says. "I've prepared a sample for you. The computer analysis was finished a few minutes ago." He hands me a printout with the relevant analysis report.

It's as I expected, but I'm not sure what to make of it. "I've seen this before. Recently. It's the virus. The new mutated version. The same one Sawyer had in his system."

Koko blanches and runs a hand across her brow. "But the virus didn't attack plants, just animals, us. Viruses don't leap across species divides like that."

"Until now," I say. "It's rare, but not impossible. Especially with Earl behind its genetic code. But if the seeds are infected too..." A flicker of alarm sparks in my stomach. If the virus entered the DNA of the crops...this could go on for generations. I thought Francesca was exaggerating the situation, but I'm wrong.

Edgar's mouth drops open. "So it's everywhere."

"I guess. But it can't hurt you." I hand him back the printout. "Everyone alive today has either been vaccinated or is immune. The virus hasn't mutated enough for your vaccine not to work."

"Whew," Koko says, her eyebrows rising.

"I wonder if..." I look from Koko to the two scientists. I want to try one of my abilities, but will they approve? I'm struggling to judge people's reactions when it comes to the use of my powers. But Mason and Carter are still bulks and Sawyer uses his telekinesis. "If you don't mind, I'd like to try something?"

"Please, we're out of ideas," Greta says.

Taking a handful of seeds from a hessian sack, I roll them around my palm, feeling their grainy hardness. They are smaller than the acorns I often keep in my pocket, but equally soothing. My healing power kicks in and its warm glow covers my hands. The seeds shine in the golden luminescence. They wouldn't glow if they didn't need healing.

"Thank goodness for you, Silver." Koko smiles. "Try the rest."

"You sure? I've been getting a lot of flak for using my abilities lately."

"Silver, if you use your abilities for the good of others then there's nothing wrong with that," Koko says. Why does no one else understand? "I know having the destroyer ability is a heavy burden." It was Koko who first explained what the ability was. "Weigh your decisions carefully. Perhaps run them by a friend, or Matt, to make sure you're thinking straight."

"Thank you, Koko," I say, feeling encouraged.

Matt's interrogation the previous night left me doubting myself and my intentions. He made me question my instincts. Now I know I'm doing the right thing. I lay my hand on the seeds in the hessian sack. White lightning dances over the seeds like an elaborate game of leapfrog. The whole sack glows majestically like it's filled with Rumpelstiltskin's woven gold.

When the treatment is complete, I return to the small group. "You can carry on altering the genetics to accelerate the growth rate."

"You need to heal the crops next," Koko says, gesturing for me to follow her out of the barn. "If you think your abilities can extend that far? If you don't tire too quickly?"

I shake my head. "Stamina and scope don't seem to be a problem anymore."

Koko's eyebrows lift for a second time. "What's that about?"

I tilt my head as I walk beside her. "I assume it's something I got from Earl. Some kind of stamina thing. I never tire any more. I don't even sleep as much."

Koko places a gentle pressure on the small of my back. "Just be careful. You don't yet know what kind of toll it might take on you in other ways. I know it scares you to have access to such a wide range of abilities, but I've always been impressed with how well you handle it. Just don't expect too much of yourself. You *can* take breaks."

I smile at her. It's good to know she's on my side.

We walk along the dirt track to the fields. Entering the first field, I find Francesca at the water table blotting the back of her neck with a rag. Ants crawl up the trunk of the single oak tree and I spot a squirrel leaping in its higher branches.

"I'm glad you decided to join us. Hopefully, it's not too late. Have you found the problem?" Francesca asks, her words clipped.

The irritation in her tone annoys me. "It wasn't a genetics problem."

"Silver used her healing ability to rid the seeds of the disease," Koko says, throwing her arms around me like a prized trophy. She manages to elicit a smile from my lips. "She needs to do the same with the crops."

Francesca glances across the fields. "Will there never be an end to the genetic revolution?"

"I think we'll be living with the repercussions for some time," Koko replies.

Francesca blots her face, dampening the hair at her temples. "Silver, would you please heal the crops?"

"For the record," I say. I want to get a point in here. "You're okay with me using my abilities if it helps *you*?" I know I'm being rude. I've never spoken to the president so pointedly before. I don't care.

"I never said you couldn't use them." Francesca drops the rag and stares at me. "But I wanted them focused in the right direction, where they can help everyone, not just you. Do you see the distinction?"

I'm tempted to *not* heal the crops. I'm tempted to make her beg. I'm the one who holds the power. I'm the one who decides whether people live or die. It's all in my hands, this moment, the power, the glory, it's all up to me. Francesca *needs* me and my abilities. Matt needs my abilities. Everyone does. I take a second to revel in the feeling of being needed, of being the only one who can help.

Before, on the missions, when I felt that level of responsibility, I would have a panic attack and be accosted with violent images of death and doom. This time, no panic attack, no images of impending death and doom, just an over-whelming sense of confidence with a dash of glee which makes me want to giggle inappropriately. I take another moment to enjoy the fact that expunging anxiety from my DNA actually worked.

"Silver." Koko breaks into my thoughts, her tone patient. "Heal the crops."

"Okay, okay," I say, and focus on the wheatfield I'm standing in.

"And, Silver? Don't talk to me like that again," Francesca warns, her eyes flashing.

Ignoring the president, I enfold my fingers around a lone stalk of wheat. I'll try one to begin with. The power builds quickly. It feels bigger, as though it's trying to expand past the confines of my body. But it's a good feeling, a stretching, as though every muscle is being thoroughly kneaded. I open my eyes to find the entire field awash in a golden glow. The brilliant hue pales until it reaches a white so bright and pure, I can barely keep my eyes open.

Koko gasps. "Oh my goodness!"

"Silver, is this you?" Matt stands behind me. I feel his closeness, his breath tickling my neck. His pinky finger brushes against mine. "This is amazing."

Francesca remains quiet. Others gather behind me; Erica, Eli, Sawyer, Mason, Carter and Lyla all stand, mouths hanging open.

I didn't think I'd be able to alter the entire field with one touch. Then I realize it's not just this field basking in a saintly light, but all the fields as far as I can see. Perhaps beyond the fields and into the city and forest? How far is my power reaching?

Without warning, the light extinguishes and leaves us standing amid a field of perfectly healthy wheat stalks. My power worked. My power has grown, more than I ever imagined it could. I smile.

"The crops are cured!" someone remarks.

"We'll have food!" another exclaims.

"Well done. Look what can happen if you practice. That was quite something," Eli whispers in my ear.

He's right. This was possible because I practiced, because I let go of my black and white leash and was willing to push the boundaries a little. I've achieved so much, and with Eli's help and more practice I'm sure I can achieve more.

"You're welcome," I say to Francesca, portraying my own warning in my voice and eyes. "And now, if you don't mind, I'm going to see about my mother." Without waiting for a response, I turn and march through the fields to my jeep.

Matt runs after me. "Silver, wait."

"What for?"

"Thank you."

I laugh. "You don't need to thank me for doing something good. It's my job."

He frowns, but reaches for my hand, and doesn't let go when I try to shrug him off.

"It's a good thing you've done."

I try to read his expression, but for the first time in our friendship I'm uncertain of his thoughts. "I thought you'd disapprove."

"Why would I...?" He pulls me closer, wrapping his arms around me. "I'm tired of worrying about you. I love you."

"I love you too." But suddenly that doesn't seem enough anymore. "I need to check on my mom."

He nods, and lets me go.

When I arrive at the hospital and place my powerful hands against my mother's head, there's no response. The dancing white sparks refuse to penetrate my mother's body. According to them, there's nothing left to heal. There isn't a sound from her. I tuck my maybe not so powerful hands behind my back.

I can't tolerate the medicinal, green walls of the small hospital room any longer. The air is thick with inactivity and I can't bear to see my mother in this helpless, unresponsive state. The weight of my failure hangs around my shoulders as I remember how she used to be; how her laugh was as rich and thick as maple syrup, how her smile could light up my world and make me forget about my troubles, how her slightest of touches could banish pain to a faraway place and how, when she put her arms around me, it was the only place I ever felt like being. If she was here now, she would know how to handle the situation with Matt. She would make it all seem so simple. A tear escapes. It takes me by surprise and I quickly wipe it away.

Leaving my mother's room, I walk down the hallway to Paige's. She watches a TV screen, engrossed in a sitcom from the time before about a gay couple with an adopted daughter and all of the complications that entails. A smile twitches at her lips.

"Hey," she says, when she sees me in the doorway. "What's up?"

I can't unleash my problems on her. She has enough to worry about. She is smiling at me, but I see the effort in her eyes, and that her skin is pale and her face strained.

"Nothing," I reply, setting my face into a neutral pose. "Just checking on you. Do you need anything?"

She taps the bed beside her. "Come sit."

Approaching the bed, I shuffle up next to Paige. Her enormous bulk spans most of the space. Placing my hand gently on her protruding belly, I feel the baby kick.

This time her smile reaches her emerald eyes. "Oof, that was a big one."

I sit with Paige, feeling the baby kick, and I attempt to ignore any depressing thoughts concerning my mother. Paige laughs at the comedy show while I wonder if I'll ever have a conversation with my mother again. I want her to tell me she loves me. I want her to tell me everything is going to be okay.

"Is everything going to be okay?" I ask Paige.

She turns from the TV to look at me. "What do you mean?"

I struggle with what to tell her. "I'm trying to do the right thing."

She smiles. "Of course you are." The smile slips away. "Sometimes people do the wrong things for the right reasons."

I shake my head. "This isn't that."

She rolls onto her side and props her head on an elbow. "Why don't you tell me what it is?"

"Have I ever given you any reason to be afraid of me?"

She searches my face. "No. Of course not. But I understand why some people might be."

I do a double take. "You do?"

She hesitates. I can tell she's trying to figure out what to say.

I stand. "I'm just me. The *ultimate weapon* who's supposed to save everyone. I killed Bear. I killed Earl. And now I want to be left alone. Is that so much to ask?"

"Of course not." A single green feather floats between us. I love collecting Paige's feathers. She's rarely produced her wings during the last few months, but I know she is longing to fly again. "But think about what you said. You think of yourself as the ultimate weapon. You did kill Bear, and Earl. You have a lot of power, Silver, and some people are afraid of that."

"But people should know I'd never—"

"I know that. Matt knows that." Paige squeezes my hand.

I shake my head. "No, he doesn't."

Sitting, she takes my other hand and holds them both. "You never asked for your abilities. But you have them. And it's your job, like it or not, to deal with them. To help people, but to put people at ease too."

"It's too much."

"I agree." Paige rubs my fingernail with the pad of her thumb. "But it is what it is. With great power comes great responsibility."

I once quoted those lines to her when I first discovered my abilities. They're from my favorite superhero movie. Now she's throwing them in my face.

I drop her hands. "You sound like a fortune cookie."

Her fingers twitch in her lap. "I thought it would make you smile."

"I don't think anything could make me smile."

"Don't be like that."

"Like what?" Damn her and her eternal optimism. "I never asked for any of this. You're supposed to be my best friend. You're supposed to tell me what I want to hear."

"That's not fair."

"None of it's fair."

She reaches for me. "I love you. You know that."

"And I love you. But I guess there are some battles only I can fight." I turn and march away from her, still holding her green feather.

"Silver, please come back."

I don't. I keep walking. Are people afraid of me or not? Do they want to use me or want me to go away? I don't know who I am anymore. I don't know who I want to be. I remember when Paige and I used to fly together. Her green wings and my blue ones. I loved flying with her, discovering her world. I felt so free.

I wander to the hot car lot and sit in my jeep. I don't bother turning on the ignition, where will I go? They don't need me in the fields anymore, the crops are fixed. And my healing power, I have to admit, is not going to help my mother. It's bigger than it's ever been and still she remains in a catatonic state. There's nothing more I can do.

There is nothing more I can do.

The black lightning power tingles on my fingers.

"No," I whisper. "Not now." The black sparks of electricity wink out. I lean my head against the steering wheel.

I'll have to wait for Dad to return with the special woman. It's all I have left. I cling to my last hope as a little black streak shoots the smallest of holes through my windscreen.

I contemplate going home, but I don't feel like sitting there all alone. Pressing the start button, I make a decision. I will return to the fields, but I won't go near the crops. I'll visit Eli. It's such an obvious answer, I don't know why I avoided the idea. I still need to catalog my new abilities, and it might take my mind off everything else.

CHAPTER FIFTEEN
ELI

MATT STANDS IN THE DOORWAY, blocking the sun, and preventing Eli from leaving his cabin. "Eli."

Irritation spikes. "Matt."

Matt looks past him, into the gloomy cabin, as if searching for something.

"Can I help you with something?" Eli has nothing to hide, nothing physical anyway, but he still has the urge to step out of his cabin and shut the door.

Matt sighs. "I hope." All the air pours out of him and he crumples a little, resembling a half-empty sack of potatoes. "I don't have any right to tell you who to spend time with..."

Eli knows what's coming. He settles in for the ride.

"Spit it out," Eli says, resisting the urge to smile.

"I need you to give Silver some space. She's going through some stuff right now—"

"With her mother," Eli says.

Surprise flashes across Matt's face. "Yes."

"She told me."

"Did she?" Matt frowns. "Of course she did," he whispers to himself.

The guy looks decidedly uncomfortable now, with his hands in his pockets and his shoulders all hunched and his pride hanging by a thread.

"I don't want her experimenting with her powers right now." Matt loses the hesitation and levels a pointed look in Eli's direction. The fierceness in Matt's eyes takes him aback a little and he finds himself with his back pressed against the cabin door. "She's in a delicate emotional state and I'm asking you to stop encouraging her experimentation with her powers. Can you do that?"

"Matt," he says. "Silver is her own person—"

"Don't I know it," Matt mutters, and barks out a laugh. It falls flat, leaving an awkwardness hanging in the air.

"I can't stop her doing what she wants to do, but I can be there for her and nudge her in the right direction." *Which might not be the same direction you're hoping for.*

"I guess that's all I can ask." Matt offers his hand.

Eli takes the offered hand, a little reluctantly, and not before Matt notices the hesitation.

"Is everything okay, Eli?"

"Yes, all good."

"The headaches?"

"Not so bad," he replies. It's the truth.

Matt stands there, as if plucking for another conversational straw, but they don't have much in common. They've already exhausted the one topic they do share an interest in.

Eli senses he wants to say something else, about Silver, press his point somehow, but he backs away with merely a frown and an abrupt pivot.

A little while later, after Eli becomes resolute in his decision to stay out of Silver's decision-making process, he senses her approaching. He's been expecting her. When she exhibited all that power in the fields, he knew she'd want more, and she needs him to do it. She's wrestling with a righteous inner conflict, one he struggled with for a time too. But the power will always win, he realizes that now, nothing else can top experiencing all those abilities.

"Hey." Eli opens the cabin door to reveal Silver, standing in shadow, backlit by the descending sun, her face pinched in worry, her eyes bright with emotion. He stifles an inappropriate gasp. Her beauty always catches him by surprise.

She splutters something incomprehensible, shakes both hands as if she's trying to stem tears and starts again. "I need..." she chews on her bottom lip a little, reaches for that musical note pendant of hers and runs it up and down its chain. "I need you," she says simply, and Eli's whole world lights up like Christmas morning.

"Anything," he says, stepping out of his cabin and steering her in the direction of the abandoned farmhouse.

Wanting to avoid any scrutinizing eyes, he tugs Silver along the path quicker than usual. He pushes branches out of her way and puts a hand on her back to hurry her along. How delicious it is to be touching her, to be so close to all the power.

"What's the matter?" she asks when she catches him

glancing over his shoulders at the last workers leaving the fields for the day.

"Matt, he was here...and..."

She swivels to face him and comes to a stop. "He was here? At your cabin? Why?"

He considers his response and decides on the truth. It might work to his advantage. "He wants me to give you space."

Fingers twitching, she stumbles back a step. Bewilderment is a passing expression across her face. Then she throws her shoulders back and her eyes darken. Not so silver anymore. More charcoal.

"I can't believe he would...who the *hell* does he think he is?"

"I guess he doesn't think I'm a good influence on you. He wants me to keep my distance." He braces himself for a display of anger. Despite the murderous look in her eyes, she maintains her control. Nothing is reduced to ash.

"He said that? He told you to stay away from me?"

"Not in so many words."

They walk in silence for a few moments, picking their way through the long, wild grass. "I told him you were capable of making your own decisions."

A grateful look mellows the anger in her eyes. "You did?"

"Of course. But it does put me in an awkward position. He wasn't exactly happy with my response, but I'm not about to stand in your way, especially when I believe in what you're doing. And now I feel like I'm stuck in the middle a little." Maybe that isn't such a bad place to be. If he drives the wedge a little deeper, maybe she'll set those silver eyes on him and there will be something more than friendship behind her look. Together, they would be unrivalled.

She clenches her teeth. "I see." He can tell she wants to let loose on something. Eli reaches for her hand and sends good, calm thoughts to her brain with his telepathy power. It's a risk, but one he's willing to take. She's probably too emotional to notice.

After a few minutes her shoulders drop an inch or two and her lips relax into a fragile smile. It worked. She's calming down. He tugs her along the path again, pleased with the even rhythm of her breathing. When they arrive at the farmyard, Silver gazes at the back of the yard, her eyes resting on the pile of ash that was once a tire. She seems to struggle with a decision.

"He wants kids." Laughing bitterly, she stands in the middle of the yard. Eli approaches carefully and stands close behind her. His breath moves the fine hair on the nape of her neck.

"Seriously? Are you...?"

"No! *God* no. But eventually. It's what he wants." She leans back, not against him, but her hair tickles his face and if he leans forward his lips would be at her ear. "I can't imagine anything worse."

"You and I are two people who should never have children," he says.

She turns to face him and cocks a surprised eyebrow.

He laughs. "I didn't mean together!" Although the thought isn't far from his mind. Not the baby part, but the practicing bit of it. "I meant with your genetics, and my psychotic family, neither of us should pass on our DNA."

"Thank you!" she says, with a little flourish of her hands. "Thank you! Finally, someone who gets it."

"I do." He offers her his best disarming smile, the one he's been practicing in the square mirror hanging above his sink. "And Matt can't force you to have kids. He needs to know your feelings are as valid as his."

Her eyes turn watery. "Thank you, again." She wraps her arms around his neck, almost throwing them both backward. She apologizes and takes a step back. "And he keeps giving me a hard time about using the abilities, ridding myself of anxiety. *You.*" Her chin juts in a defiant gesture. He wants to kiss it.

"Give him time," he says, his hand still on her waist. "He needs time to get used to the new you. He didn't envision a world where people still have genetically enhanced abilities, where they are still needed. It's not what he expected after the revolution, so he needs time to see things from your point of view. Be patient. He'll get there."

"You think?"

"Yeah. And if he doesn't, then that's that." He can't believe he's actually suggesting it.

She cocks her head, considering. "Then that would be that."

"I do feel slightly guilty. He's asked me to give you space...and now I feel like I'm doing the exact opposite." He takes a step away from her to show he's willing.

"I know." She sighs. A sound so delicate and soft he feels

he can almost touch it. "I'm sorry our problems have put you in that position."

Eli licks his lips as he stares at her. It's impossible to tear his gaze away. "I want to be supportive of you, Silver, but I need to tread carefully. He's intimidating. He was one of the leaders of the resistance, the head of two mission teams and he's a respected member of the community. I don't want to mess with that. He has a lot of power." But Eli has his own abilities. So does Silver. She looks like she might cry. "Give him some time," he says, and sends calming thoughts to her through the air.

How much time? Eli hears the thought in her head.

"I take it you couldn't heal your mother?" he asks, as he gestures for her to sit next to him under a tree.

Silver shakes her head, smothers a sob, and puts the heels of her hands in her eyes. "It's not going to work. No matter how big the power grows, it's not enough." She leans her head against his shoulder.

The action surprises him. After a brief hesitation he puts his arm around her and pulls her closer. It feels right. It feels warm and comfortable and *right*.

"Then we'll wait for your father and this mysterious lady to arrive and everything will be okay," he says.

"Really?"

"Really. Your mom is going to get better. I promise."

He can't promise anything of the kind, but he can't stand the downtrodden look on her face. A look of such utter misery that he wants to promise her the world, the universe, anything, to see her smile again. He likes it when she's happy. Or angry. Either will do because then she experiments with her powers. Then she radiates a golden light and her hair flies around her face and those silver eyes glow like limestone in a mysterious cave. Then, she is perfect.

"I'm sorry to dump on you," Silver says, pulling herself together. She throws her shoulders back and combs her fingers through her hair.

They spend the afternoon lying on the grass, in the shade of the tree, talking. They let the topic of Matt and her mother float away and drift from one conversation to the next; the battle with Earl in the mountains, fixing the crops, Lyla and Sawyer's relationship, and then they circle back to Matt and her mother. She takes on the problems of the world, but who is there to help Silver when she needs it?

"And Francesca, she took my mother away."

"Why did you let her?" Eli asks.

"What choice did I have?"

"You're the most powerful person on this planet. You didn't have to let her."

She chews on her fingernails. "Because I don't want to be that kind of person. I don't want to use my powers that way. That would make me no better than..."

"...Earl," Eli finishes.

Those silver eyes settle on him. "Yes."

"If I were you, I couldn't have stood by and done nothing." He will never allow anyone to take control over his life ever again. No one. Ever. "She shouldn't be able to tell you how to care for your mother."

"It wasn't really about my mother," Silver says. "It was about getting her out of the way."

Eli scoops a handful of earth at his feet and lets it fall through his fingers. "Still..."

"You don't like her much, Francesca, do you?" Silver wiggles her toes. A plastic flower on her flipflops falls off. Eli picks it up and sticks it back on, making sure it stays there with the compliments of one of his abilities. As his fingers graze her toes, she smiles at him.

"She gave me quite a grilling when I first arrived here." He lifts his head and watches the clouds scudding across the sky.

But that isn't all of it, is it? If he's truthful with himself, he doesn't like her. She doesn't approve of abilities. She was the leader of the resistance who organized the uprising against the altereds. While Silver became an awesomely powerful creature, and the rest of the mission team took back their abilities, Francesca remained Francesca. She prefers to get things done without the aid of genetic enhancements. Now Eli has abilities of his own. A lot of them. He suspects Francesca will not approve of having another person around with power.

He has embraced his powers. It began with the little things; reheating his coffee cup with his mind, moving water from the well to his cabin without having to work the pump, using bulk strength to hoist sacks of seeds, and digging more crop rows with his mind. The little things became bigger things. And more fun. Perhaps these powers are his reward for all the evil things Earl put him through.

"She's harmless really," Silver says, playing with the strap of her flipflop. "As long as you don't push her too far."

"She already looks at me suspiciously. Because of who I am."

Maybe she's right to be suspicious. The back of his mind houses a niggling fear. What if he becomes a power-crazy monster like Earl? He isn't as troubled about using his abilities as Silver, but, as a consequence, he's more in danger of losing himself. He doesn't want that to happen. But is will alone enough? For now, Eli is pretty sure he can refuse the seduction of dark powers.

"Give her time. She'll come to see you're nothing like him." She smiles her twinkling smile. "I'll vouch for you."

That's all the reassurance he needs.

Einstein appears around the corner of the house. Eli frowns and is tempted to send him some choice thoughts with his mind, but he resists the urge and watches the dog's slow approach.

You shouldn't be here.

Eli pretends not to hear, pretends he can't understand, and instead hums a soft tune under his breath. Silver's freedom song.

"Don't you start," Silver says to the dog. "Go back to Matt, I'm busy here."

The dog hesitates, directs one brief glance in Eli's direction, whines a little and then backs away.

Stupid dog.

"Sorry about that," Silver says. "Matt must have sent him to check on me." A pained expression flitters across her face.

Eli squeezes her hand.

"Shall we?" she asks, getting to her feet. "I want to try something." A glint forms in her eyes, vanquishing her previous pained expression. She is ready to play with her powers.

Silver turns her back on the farmhouse and focuses her gaze on the woods beyond. Eli waits. He swats a fly buzzing insistently around his nose. *Bzzz. Bzzz.* He stomps on it with his mind and the fly drops to the ground. He glances at Silver to make sure she didn't notice. She's too busy squinting into the middle distance, the effort of whatever power she's trying to evoke sending a bead of sweat from her hairline down her temple. Subconsciously, she wipes it away.

"Damn..." she mutters.

Eli shifts his weight between his feet, giving her time, and turns in a slow circle. Shock lances through him. The farmhouse is gone.

"Uh, Silver?" He taps her on the shoulder. "Silver, turn around."

She spins on her foot and sees the great big pile of ash the farmhouse has become. He can make out the distant figures of Delta, Matt, and Sawyer in the fields beyond.

"Put it back!" The farmhouse is a shield from prying eyes. "You need to put it back!" She'll be in a whole truck load of trouble with the powers that be if...*when* this is discovered.

"I don't know if I can! I wasn't trying to..." White lightning dances across her fingers, scurries over her palms and up her arms. Her hair stands on end as if she's attached to the mains electricity. Sparks streak across her pupils.

And then the farmhouse re-materializes before his eyes. It springs into re-existence like one of those kiddie pop-up tents.

"That's...That's..." *Impressive.* It's so impressive he wishes he too possessed the healing-slash-destroying ability.

With a bit more emphasis on the destroyer side of things. He doesn't need the re-materializing bit.

"That's new!" She giggles, black and white lightning continues to dance around her hands.

He gained a whole new respect for Silver when she demolished the buildings, but now he feels a flicker of fear. She is more powerful than he realized.

CHAPTER SIXTEEN

SILVER

ARRIVING HOME after midnight and wanting to avoid another confrontation with Matt, I make a beeline for the couch in the living room. What a night! Eli and I discovered a new power. Or an extension of an already existing power, I'm not sure which. After making the farmhouse disappear and reappear, I experimented with half the trees in the woods by making them vanish and return, like a flickering hologram. Despite the obvious destruction of the destroyer power, it's the most like God I've felt. I imagine what it would feel like to create the earth in seven days. An ocean here, a river there, a mountain a bit yonder, but no, not there, take it out again and oh, put it there, much better. *Wow.*

I was tempted, for the briefest of moments, just a nanosecond, to make Eli disappear and reappear, but I don't know what would happen to something alive. Would he come back in the same way? I won't do that to a friend. A surprising good friend who's so easy to talk to. I fall asleep with a smile on my face.

The sound of the doorbell pierces my dream. Rubbing a crick in my neck, I realize it's morning. "Coming!"

Lyla stands on the front porch below the missing step I haven't fixed yet. She carries a basket of muffins and I can't help drooling when I smell them. "Mom made them with the wheat you cured."

"Come in," I say, taking the basket. The muffins are still warm. She follows me into the living room and settles into an armchair. I unwrap one of the muffins, crumbs going everywhere. "What's up?"

"That's kind of what I wanted to ask you." She leans forward in the chair, her arms resting on her thighs. She has the same bright blue eyes as Matt, and staring at me, they feel like sniper sightings.

"What are we talking about here?" There are so many things going on in my life that aren't anywhere near the realm of okay.

"You and Matt. He slept at home last night, with us." She shifts in the chair.

I didn't realize. I didn't bother to check my bedroom. But I thought he said he was tired of worrying about me.

"I drop the uneaten muffin into the basket at my feet.

The slightest of frowns wrinkles the smooth space between her eyebrows and her lips twist. "He's really upset."

I quash the growl rumbling in my throat and raise a stern eyebrow. "So am I."

She raises a hand. "I'm not here to get you all pissed off."

"I don't need people interfering in my life."

"But you're my friend. You're like a sister to me. I hate to see you in pain. I hate to see you fighting with my brother."

I grip the hilt of my knife on my belt. Its corded grip brings me reassurance. Maybe I should meet with Claus again. "I didn't think anyone had noticed."

"Of course people noticed." She inches forward until she's balanced on the edge of her chair, leaning closer. "Silver, he loves you, he needs you. Can you work it out?"

Exhaling an exasperated sigh, I contemplate going for the bottle of wine still lurking around the kitchen. I don't want to have this conversation. "Why doesn't he come and talk to me? Why has he sent you? This is ridiculous!"

Lyla pulls at the collar of her shirt. "He doesn't know I'm here. Matt told me how he feels, I want to understand what you feel, Silver."

"Just because your relationship is running perfectly does not mean you need to solve mine!"

Her hands grip the armrests. "Silver, I go to my parents with my problems. Or you. Everyone comes to you. Who do you go to? Matt, right? And now you're fighting. Paige is in the hospital. I don't want you to feel alone."

I look at her, some of the tension wilting out of me. "When did you get so wise?"

She shrugs. "It's this world we live in."

Staring out the window I let my thoughts wander. I didn't leave things with Paige in a great place the last time I saw her. I owe her a visit. I miss her. Ever since she became pregnant and Jacob got injured, I haven't spent as much time with her. To be expected, but I want her back. I'm a better person when she's in my life.

"I want to help my mother."

"I know," Lyla says. "We all do."

"He doesn't get it." I keep my attention fixed on the window, away from Lyla's concerned face that's starting to irritate me. "He thinks I should sit back and do nothing. He thinks I'm turning into an altered."

"You did take away your anxiety problems."

"He told you?" Half rising from my chair, I round on her.

"Easy, Silver. He's just worried."

I narrow my eyes. "It's the least I deserve."

"I agree."

"I need to understand my powers, all the new ones. I want to make sure I don't hurt anyone inadvertently."

"That makes sense," Lyla says, pulling absently on her ponytail. She of all people knows what it feels like to be hurt by my powers.

I blanch. "It does?" I was sure another member of the Lawson family was here to judge.

"I think so. It sounds okay to me." Lyla shrugs. "Matt's a little rigid sometimes. He's afraid of genetic abilities. Things didn't turn out so well the last time they were around and he's afraid what will happen this time."

"I know all that, Lyla."

"But he's also incredibly grateful to them. He'd be brain damaged if your parents hadn't helped him. As a result, he has increased intelligence. He wrestles with that."

I slump back into the chair. "So did I. When I first discovered my abilities. He was the one who told me it didn't change anything."

Lyla smiles. "My brother is stubborn."

I roll my eyes. "Don't I know it. But I'm not Earl and I'm not President Bear. I'm me. Why doesn't he get that?"

Her tone turns serious again. "Because he knows you'll do anything to cure your mother and he's worried you'll cross lines in the process."

Hmm. Some lines are meant to be crossed.

"I almost took a nanite, before the resistance." Her features turn wistful. "I was dancing so much and I reached a plateau. I wasn't going to progress anymore without *something*."

"You are so good."

"Thanks." She tilts her head. "Not that there's much of a call for it these days. I managed to recruit all of five people to put on my play." She rolls her eyes. "But anyway, what I was trying to say was I didn't care about the nanites, or what I might take. I knew I couldn't stop dancing. I couldn't give it up. I was about to cross that line."

"So what if you have a pair of wings or need a little extra muscle to perform?" I ask. "It's harmless."

"You've changed your tune."

I look at her. "We've all changed. It isn't one way or the other anymore. Life is messy. It's gray. It's a mixing pot of morality."

"Maybe."

"Definitely."

"But where do we draw the line?" she asks.

I lift a shoulder. "I'm not sure I can answer that. But I'm going to keep looking until I find something to help my mom."

Lyla stands and hugs me. I remain stiff at first. I'm not used to Lyla being tender and affectionate, but maybe her relationship with Sawyer has mellowed her.

"Things with Matt will work out," she says. "It's you and Matt."

I hope so.

Lyla is right. I'm beginning to feel very, very alone. Thank God for Eli.

After Lyla leaves, I eat one of the muffins on the way to the hospital. I might not be able to heal my mother, but I can still spend time with her. Her presence is clarifying, as though in her motherly wisdom, without her having to utter a single syllable, she'll reveal the correct path. I hope, in turn, my presence might be comforting to her, if she's in any way aware of me.

Sinking into the uncomfortable hospital chair, I settle myself in. There's no place else I have to be. Listening to the soft rise and fall of her breath as she sleeps, I wonder what she's dreaming about.

The door opens and I squint against the sudden intrusion of light.

Erica appears. "There you are." Beating her delicate wings, which are a soothing shade of baby blue, she flies into the room. "I've been looking for you."

Here we go again.

"Still got your wings out?" I say.

"I can't turn it off." Erica lands gently on the ground, removes the Stetson and runs a finger over the stiff material. "Ever since you healed me, I've been unable to fold them away. They're out here for good I guess."

Some people have all the luck.

"What's up?" I prepare myself for an order from Francesca, or a rehash of our conversation from the other day.

"At the risk of pissing you off again, I think we need to do something about Eli." Erica closes the door behind her. "He's acting weird."

"I was with him yesterday afternoon. He was fine."

"Did he say anything about the headaches?"

"He said they're getting better."

Erica's wings remain unfolded, fluctuating between a pale pink and a soft yellow. "There's something else going on. He's been talking to himself, in the fields. He was turning around and around in circles, muttering to himself, generally acting as far from normal as you can get. Then he said something about yellow eyes. The look in his eyes when he said it...it was creepy." She shivers.

Yellow eyes? *Yellow eyes?* Sweat prickles my palms and the hairs on the nape of my neck spring to attention. What are the chances of Adam, Eli and I all having dreams about yellow eyes? Could it be a coincidence? My instinct tells me not. But what's the alternative? They can't be real. I can't go down that road again.

"I'm sure it's stress. He was a prisoner for a long time. He needs to rest," I say, blotting my slick palms on my shorts.

Tilting her head, Erica watches my mother. "It seems more than that."

"How so?" I ask.

Erica toes the floor. "I'm worried he's going to...snap, or something."

"Half the population experienced nervous breakdowns. Is Eli not allowed to too? After I killed the hellbirds I had the worst panic attack of my life. If you'd seen me then...he'll be fine."

"I'm not so sure. The way he looked this morning—"

I erupt from my chair. "Why can't people just leave him alone?"

Her wings turn to a thunderous purple, darker than her eyes. "I'm only trying to help."

"Are you?" I cross my arms over my chest. "Or are you sticking your nose in where it's not wanted? Again?"

Her arms straighten by her side, ending in tight fists. "What are you talking about?"

"Joe. Jacob. Killing Carmen." I snap the words out, regretting them as soon as they leave my mouth. "I'm sorry, Erica, I didn't mean..." But she's already out the door.

Then she pivots around and faces me. "You need to get your shit together. I don't know what's eating you, but you've got to stop going around looking like you're about to explode. And I'm only saying that because I care." Then she leaves.

I sit in the gloom with my mother and lower my head between my knees. I think about the yellow eyes. Actually, I try not to, but the image of a black beast with fangs and claws and looming yellow irises refuses to be ignored. If Erica knew what I've been dreaming about, she wouldn't give me such a hard time.

CHAPTER SEVENTEEN

ELI

ELI WAKES from the dream with the yellow eyes—it was the one on the yacht again—and feels tainted. Covered in sweat, he casts his gaze around the small cabin to see everything covered in a yellow glow. The same yellow as the eyes. Blinking rapidly, his eyes adjust and his heartrate slows. The yellow sheen is just a trick of his complicated mind.

But Evil touched him. Evil with a capital E reached down with one of its dark claws - or perhaps up considering Evil surely lives beneath the ground where all things dark and needful exist - and touched him, tainted him with its malevolent brush.

Eli tries to shrug off the sentiment as he goes about refreshing himself, but it sticks to him harder than feathers on tar. It lingers at the base of his skull and it takes all of his resistance not to turn and scream and run with his tail tucked between his legs, so to speak, into the woods where he might collapse in a pile of incoherent nothingness, never to be heard from again. What a frightening image.

Breathing deeply, Eli uses his mental skills to bring feelings of calm to his body. After a few moments, he can still sense the tainted evil hovering and whispering false promises, but he's calmer, more accepting of its existence.

It came with the scratching, the evilness. When those fingers probe his brain they bring whispers and promises of power, but also death. He doesn't know how to stop the fingers, but he knows they're not just a metaphor. Not anymore.

Eli walks behind his cabin to the outside tap where he now collects water. Matt finally fixed the irrigation system and Eli doesn't have to pretend to heave buckets of water to his cabin anymore. Instead, he turns the tap with his mind and waits for the bucket to fill.

A moment later *The Dog*—as Eli now thinks of him—comes sniffing its way around the corner, stops when it notices him and tries to stare him down. Well, two can play that game. Eli returns the stare with a little added something extra causing The Dog to whine, take to the floor and expose its belly. That's more like it. There's the respect he deserves.

It was The Dog who alerted everyone to his odd behavior in the fields. The fingers probed his brain right in the middle of the day and brought him visions of such clarity he thought he'd teleported to a whole new world. He walked around marveling at all he saw, until he realized it was only a vision, or a dream or...something, and everyone was looking at him weird. Apparently he spoke about yellow eyes. Then The Dog fetched the fairy girl and a crowd gathered and he was sent home.

The probing fingers belong to the yellow eyes. They

revealed that much to him. They are full of power and knowledge. What kind of creature possesses yellow eyes like that?

Before Eli lifts the bucket with his mind, he urges The Dog to leave. It immediately rises to its four doggie feet, about turns and scampers away. Better. He can't have him around when he's practicing his powers. He needs privacy for that. Having The Dog report on his every move would be disastrous. Especially now Matt is wary of him.

Although Matt doesn't know about the destruction and re-materialization of the red barn, he is aware he and Silver are still spending time together. Matt threw him a look, a I-thought-we-talked-about-this look that made it clear he's let Matt down and is no longer considered an ally when it comes to the topic of correcting Silver's misguided decisions.

But what Matt doesn't understand is he's going to lose Silver if he doesn't stop trying to control her. He'll let Matt figure that out, maybe when it's too late and the wedge between them is buried so deep extracting it will be like trying to pull Excalibur from the rock, if you aren't King Arthur.

As Eli has been sent away from the fields, he has nothing to do but practice his powers. He's found one which excites him. He is, with the appropriate attention, able to recall any moment in his past with perfect clarity. It only applies to his memories since his release from the mountain, but there are plenty to keep him satisfied. Most of them contain his time with Silver. He relives the moment she fell into his side seeking comfort a thousand times. Every detail of her face is etched into his brain; her soft, long hair which always seems to fly about her face in a tangle of disarray, evoking in him a wanton feeling. And those eyes. They are the merest of blues, the dullest of metals, but oh how they shimmer. The way she leaked those few, angry tears which made her seem more alive, more...*more*. And then there's her body. Eli is glad he's alone when he thinks about her body. His body is responding in unpredictable ways, surprising ways. But would she ever feel that way about him? She's with Matt. But they're having problems. If Matt is going to deepen the wedge all on his own then it might be possible to...

But what about Delta? Eli heaves the bucket of water into his cabin with a little mental help and ponders the creature that is Delta. A few dates in, they could be considered a thing. She makes his heart race and he makes her tongue-tied. That's the way it's supposed to be. It's all so adorably, predictably sweet.

He is caught between two women. The one he wants to be with, and the one the yellow eyes want him to pursue. The elusive whispers echo in the back of his mind, spilling their secrets, pushing him toward Silver.

Looking into the mirror, he pushes a razor against his stubbly chin, and lets thoughts of Silver dull Delta's image. He craves her presence. But what he wants, what he really longs for - if he truly admits it to himself - is her power.

He wants her power.

No, not quite.

He wants to consume her power.

He wants to consume her.

The tainted evil sensation he thought had almost disappeared returns and sends a pulsation through his body, coiling around his insides and squeezing a fraction too tight.

The scratching fingers crawl through his brain and almost make his head turn without Eli having any say in the matter. Images of Paige's unborn baby come to mind, images of a chortling infant emitting a magical blue light.

He's only met Paige once, has barely even considered what her baby might be like, although he's heard stories about the protective blue bubble. Is the baby going to possess a powerful blue light? How can he know that? That's when the metaphorical light bulb flashes.

A-ha!

Not only are those probing fingers showing him images of what might come to pass, but they are pushing him onto a different path, showing him different possibilities if he decides to follow. His resistance to use his powers made his head ache with agonizing fire. He remembers feeling deter-mined to keep his abilities locked tight. Was that only last week? But how easily he let go of it all. Because of the whis-pers in his mind, urging him on, telling him it is okay.

Eli cuts his cheek with the razor as a sliver of trepidation slices into him. He feels the foreignness in his brain, like a dark shadow, but can do little to exorcize it. It's gaining control over him, his thoughts, his feelings. The yellow eyes. The probing fingers. What do they want? He's not sure if he cares.

Eli thinks over the conflicting emotions he's experienced during the last month. Does he truly hate Einstein? Glancing out his window, he spots the golden retriever jumping about in the wheat, biting the heads off the stalks and then running to Matt when he calls. He doesn't hate Einstein, but he's afraid the dog might expose him. No, that isn't right.

He leans into the probing fingers, opening the connection wider. Now he can see.

Eli isn't afraid, but whoever is trying to gain access to his mind *is* afraid. He can feel the connection now. It's a two-way thing.

Without warning, Eli sees the mountain in his mind's eye, the snow still capping the peaks and a gathering of wild animals at its base. Is it Eli or this other entity who craves Silver's presence, her power, the baby's power?

Glancing out his window again, Eli watches his friends working in the fields. Does it even matter, about the power, who wants it? Perhaps they both do. Eli smiles to himself. He has an inkling his place in this new world as loner-who-lives-at-the-edge-of-the-field is far from determined. The tables are about to turn in his favor.

Sensing Delta's approach, he tries to smother the connection with the other thing, the entity which doesn't seem quite so tainted anymore. He focuses his attention on the girl *Eli* wants to be with. Why is he referring to himself in the third person?

Opening the door for Delta, he welcomes her into the cabin. This is better. If Silver were to ever cast her eye in his favor, it would be messy, there would be a fallout involving the entire community. But Delta? Delta is the one he should be with. It will be much easier. She is sweet and gentle and so infatuated with him.

She peers up at him from under her fringe. "Hey. I missed you." Wrapping an arm around his bare torso, she rakes her fingers across his back.

Kissing her cheek, Eli feels the connection to the entity

break. Disappointingly, the image of the wild Californian mountains and the unusual gathering of prey and predator at its base disappears from his mind. But he's in control of his thoughts and his body once again. He kisses Delta, a fully focused, deep kiss he throws himself into without those claws searching through is brain. Shutting the door, he leads her further into the cabin, to the bedroom, onto the bed. A last image of Silver ripples through his mind before he dismisses it and concentrates all of his efforts on Delta and what is about to happen.

CHAPTER EIGHTEEN
SILVER

THE DIM LIGHTING in my mother's room matches my gloomy mood perfectly. There's nowhere for me to go and nothing for me to do. Everyone is mad at me. Okay, well, maybe not everyone, but I want to wallow in self-pity for a while. I need to hide away with my thoughts. It's my process. Give me a few days to collect myself, pick myself up and try again. And, dear God, Dad better be back with this mysterious lady or I might retreat into a magical land of my own creation and look for my mother that way.

Lyla seems to understand. Perhaps she can talk some sense into her brother. I want to talk to Paige, to apologize for my abrupt departure the other day. I hate thinking of her mad at me. But after a day of sneezing and coughing, the worried doctors put her in isolation. Sometimes I walk by her room and watch her sleeping. One time she wakes and I blow on the window and scrawl the words *I'm sorry*. Her eyelids fall closed. I'm not sure she sees the message. Another time I catch a blue light seeping under the doorway and into the hallway. The baby.

Uneasy about the pulsing blue light, I remember my last dream. The crops were no longer dying, but the yellow eyes remained. Staring at me from a dark sky. Animals gathered around Earl's snowy mountain. Scuttling, whinnying, bucking, and writhing. They crawled and skittered over one another. They growled and bit. More and more gathered under a full moon. Then they marched as a unit, away from the mountain, across the land. A black wave formed at their backs, pushing them on, destroying everything in its wake. Underneath it all was a thread of blue light. Like the baby's.

The animals are monsters of the worst kinds of genetic chimeras. The black wave is made of insects and...something else. I can't define it. I have no idea what the dream means. I can't make any sense of it.

Keeping it quiet eats away at me. But I can't bring myself to voice my fears. Not until I know more, if it really is a threat. Erica said Eli mentioned the yellow eyes. Maybe he can help.

Thinking of him eases the tension coiled in my shoulders. My thoughts continue down a more inappropriate path. Unnervingly inappropriate. I don't want these feelings, but I don't know how to stop them. But no one has ever understood me so completely. I can't walk away from that.

Leaving the hospital, I make my way to Eli's cabin. My head is a mess with Matt and my mom and Paige and the yellow eyes. He will understand. He'll make it better.

Strolling along the moonlit path to Eli's cabin, I dangle my fingers in the healed wheat as I walk. The smell of freshly plowed earth hangs in the air and the moon illuminates rows and rows of healthy crops. Crickets chirp and fall silent as I approach. For me, their insistent song is the sound of summer. It's the first time I've heard them since the virus and the sound transports me to a time when life was simpler. When I didn't have such responsibility. When I was free.

Matt's hellcats stalk the perimeter of the farmland. I make one out returning for its inspection of the barn and nearby fields. Its mechanical red eyes glow unnaturally and it emits a rumbling growl. Why did Matt have to make them growl? Shuddering, I wait for it to pass me before I move on. Its fur brushes my legs, bringing flashbacks of Bear's death. So much blood.

Once it's past, I can move again and I continue along the path. My heart lifts as I approach Eli's cabin. I want to carry the feeling of contentedness with me forever. Standing outside Eli's door, I gather myself. I raise my hand to knock but then stop myself, fist raised, experiencing a sudden urge to peer in his window. The moon gives me enough light to see into Eli's home, all the way to his bedroom where I spot his legs tangled in a mess of sheets. But it isn't just his legs. Someone is there with him. Someone else is asleep in his bed. Pressing my face to the glass, I can't make out the other person. Is it the same person he took to movie night? A pang of jealousy shoots through me so fiercely that I know I'm in trouble. I can't allow myself to feel this way. I simply have to turn it off. I love *Matt*. But does he still love me?

Walking quietly away from the cabin, not back to my jeep as I intended, but deeper into the fields, a deep, seething anger grows inside me. The list of my woes seems dauntingly enormous. And now there is this, this betrayal. I thought Eli and I had a special relationship. I thought we shared stuff. I bared my soul to him when no one else would listen. I told him things I told no one else. And he has told me nothing.

I thought he was mine.

I laugh at my own stupid naivety. We never expressed any romantic intentions. He is perfectly entitled to pursue his own personal relationships. I foolishly believed I was the most important person in his life. I wanted to believe that, because he's the one person who supports the use of my powers. He never looks at me differently. There's never fear in his eyes. Surely that means something?

Away from the cabin, I pick up my pace and stomp through the fields, not caring about the noise I make. The wheat flattens under my feet.

If I'm as important to Eli as he is to me, he would have told me about her, whoever she is, as I told him about my problems with Matt. My knee buckles and I fall, my hands sinking into the parched earth.

I rise slowly. Wiping the dirt from my hands, I stand under the twinkling, mocking stars and look at the fields and forest. All my anger and frustration charges to the surface. I march to the center of a cornfield and decimate it to ash.

I didn't mean to do it. I thought I had control over the destroyer power. Suddenly, I don't care. I want to use the power and so I do. I destroy another field. The relief is palpable. It's like diving into deliciously cool water on the hottest day of summer. Reveling in the feeling, I allow myself to be. I don't try to shove the power into a box as everyone, including myself, expects of me. I let it be and I finally accept it's part of me. The power streaks through the fields, illuminating the sky, and takes with it my feelings of anger and betrayal.

The light display is mesmerizing. As another field turns dark, the lightning dances from fence to field to tree and back to my hands. The whole sky is alight with my power. Like an electric storm. I've never seen anything so beautiful.

As my mood lifts, I lower my hands. With my fury sated, I retrace my steps through the empty fields and return to my jeep. Eli is leaning against the driver's door.

I'm not angry anymore. I'm not jealous. Those emotions evaporated when I used my power. But I'm glad he's here.

"Was that you?" Eli gestures to the empty cornfield.

"I guess." I glance at the fields, taking in the devastation I've caused. I've destroyed three fields of corn. "Who are you with?" I turn my attention back to Eli. "Are you seeing someone?"

He stiffens. "It's none of your business." He pushes away from the jeep, and me.

"No, I guess not. I thought that—"

"You thought what?" Eli scowls. Anger, or something like it, twists his lips into a vicious sneer. Why is he angry?

"I thought we were friends. I thought we were shar-ing...our lives," I say quietly.

"Haven't I given you enough? I've been supporting you when no one else has, when people asked me not to inter-fere..." His voice drips with hostility.

"Matt—"

"Yes, Matt. I've supported you even though it hasn't won me any popularity points. And I *have* shared a great deal with you, about Earl, about what I've been through..." he is shouting now. "...that isn't enough for you? You have to invade my private life too?"

"I didn't realize my presence was such an intrusion in your life," I reply as icily as I can manage. "And I thought I was part of your *private* life."

Eli leans back against the car and crosses his arms. He stares at the fields and then at his hands. He holds a wheat stalk and rotates it in his fingers.

"I'm sorry." He sighs. His voice softens into one I recognize. "I didn't mean that." Dropping the wheat, he moves his hands over his temples in a circular motion, massaging. "You *are* part of my private life. You are. You're right. I have another headache. It's making me cranky." Reaching for my hand, he pulls me closer.

"Just a little." I dare to lighten the tone, relieved whatever made him snap at me is now gone.

"It's making me say things I don't mean."

"You sure that's all?" I ask.

"I'm sure," he says. "I'm sorry, again."

"S'okay. We all have our moments." I gesture to the ruined fields.

Eli considers. "I guess you should fix that."

"Maybe." *Maybe.* Maybe if someone asks me nicely rather than making demands on me all the time.

He pushes himself off the car and taps his forehead. "I'm going to go take care of this before I snap at you again."

"Goodnight, Eli," I say, climbing into my jeep.

Eli waves, tucks his thumbs through his belt loops and retreats along the path to his cabin. I forgot to ask him about the yellow eyes.

Matt and I stand by the water table, me sitting on the wooden bench, him pacing an angry line into the ground. It's hot again, but at least I'm sitting in the shade of the tree.

"Don't think because they're the most distant fields I haven't noticed, Silver," he hisses. "The corn was almost ready for harvesting. No one else has realized yet so I suggest you fix it before they do. You can heal it, right?"

"I..." I forgot about the cornfields. I intended to put it back. When I calmed down.

"Not so much of a slippery slope is it? More of a freefall?"

"Matt!"

"What?"

I refuse to let my anger take over, no matter how much his last statement hurt. "I thought you said you were going to stop worrying about me."

He stops pacing and sighs. "I will never stop worrying about you. I love you."

"Do you?"

He runs a finger across his lips. "What's that supposed to mean?"

I shrug. There are too many emotions inside me. I don't know what to feel anymore. I don't know when to feel.

"Why are you pushing me away?" he asks.

"I thought it was you who was pushing me away," I reply.

"We've always done things together."

When I first discovered my abilities, it was Matt who ran after me and cradled me in his arms. Before we were together. He told me it didn't change anything. That I was

194

still the same person. What happened to me, happened to him too. Except I don't feel like that person anymore.

"Silver, I'm trying here."

"So am I."

"Silver, Matt," Erica calls, fluttering in our direction. "We're here to talk about Eli."

"Isn't this whole thing a little heavy-handed?" I say to her, forcibly lowering my shoulders. "Going behind his back and all."

"We're here because we care." She glares at me and then turns to gather the rest of the group. We convene under the oak tree, the discussion about the decimated cornfields and our bumpy relationship to be had another time.

Paige approaches me, her green wings spread wide.

"You're here," I say, glad my best friend is out of a bed, but unsure of how we left things.

She flaps her wings. "Flying is easier than walking at the moment. Thought I could use a little air and see what all the fuss is about with Eli."

"You're feeling better?"

She tucks a strand of hair behind her ear. "The cold has passed."

I nudge her elbow. She nudges back. I smile. She plucks a feather from her wing and places it behind my ear. "That's better."

I escort her to one of the wooden benches and sit next to her. Her wings arc high, shading us both.

"It might be some kind of post-traumatic stress reaction," Lyla says. She's talking about Eli and the strange turn he experienced in the fields the other day. "I mean, it still exists, right?"

"Of course it still exists," I say. "I'm a walking case study."

"Silver..." Matt shoots me a sympathetic look, but doesn't continue.

I set my jaw and face my friends. "There will always be trauma and people will always have to deal with it. It's got nothing to do with genetics."

"I think it's more than that," Erica says, using the Stetson to create a breeze at her neck. "There's something strange going on with him."

"We're all a little strange," Adam says from a few feet away. He's playing fetch with Einstein, picking up a stick and throwing it for him tirelessly. It takes Einstein a long time to retrieve it, but Adam is unfazed.

Paige smiles, stroking her belly. She took care of Adam on the last mission and has a soft spot for him. "I don't know Eli at all, but Adam is right, we are all a little strange."

"Strange how?" Sawyer says to Erica.

Delta wears an odd look on her face, opens her mouth to say something, then falls quiet.

"Turning in random circles, grabbing his head like it was in a vice, talking to...no one. That's not normal behavior." Erica plants her hands on her hips. "And what does he mean by yellow eyes?"

At the mention of the yellow eyes, Adam stops playing fetch with Einstein and stands, as if waiting for an imminent attack. A line of sweat forms on his top lip and his face turns as gray as my piles of ash. Keeping an eye on him, I drift away from the group. Paige follows me, perhaps also sensing his unease.

Carter shrugs. "Who cares about someone else's crazy dreams? I don't. Not unless they come from Silver or Adam." He gives me a brief look, then takes a long glug from the bottle hanging between his fingers. "Maybe he got injected with something back in the mountains. When William and I were in the compounds during the resistance we were experimented on. It was nasty. Horrifying. You never knew if they were about to inject something into you that was going to kill you on the spot, turn you green, or something else. Our imaginations were endless. Genetic expressions are infinite. Maybe Earl did something to him."

"We should get Deja to have a look at him," Erica says.

Adam turns to face me, stiff as a frozen water warrior. His gaze flits between me and Paige. Einstein barks once, twice, trying to re-engage him in the game of fetch. Adam's face crumples. I scramble to get to him before he starts to spout about dreams, premonitions, and yellow eyes. Catching his eye, I press a finger to my lips. Paige frowns.

Matt places a foot on one of the benches. "He seems way too fascinated in powers. Who has abilities and who doesn't, and he seems to want to spend time with those who do." He sweeps a hand through his hair and gives me a pointed look.

"That's not true," I say as I near Adam.

"I actually agree with Silver," Erica says, not looking at me. Her wings are acid blue. She's still mad at me. "I have powers and he doesn't seek my company."

"Nor me," Sawyer says. "I haven't spent much time with

the guy either. And my powers are pretty kickass." He produces a fireball in his hand.

"Less heat, more ice," Lyla says.

I reach Adam and lay a hand on his shoulder. Paige's wings arc high, shielding us from the rest of the group.

"I thought it was just a dream," Adam whispers. No one else hears, so occupied in discussing Eli.

"What was just a dream?" Paige asks.

Stepping in front of Paige, I crouch to meet Adam's level. "It's okay."

"I had a dream about yellow eyes. Now they're in Eli's dream too. That's not coincidence. That's something else. Something is coming." His bottom lip quivers as he speaks.

I told him about the diseased crops, but I never mentioned my own dreams concerning the yellow eyes. It's too much for a boy of eleven. It's too much for anyone.

Paige puts a hand on my shoulder. Sweat beads on her forehead. "Maybe we should tell the others."

I straighten to face her. "Please, Paige, you haven't been around. Let me handle it."

Her wings straighten, lowering to parallel her arms. "Handle what, exactly?"

Ignoring her question, I chew on my lip and look at Adam. Neither Adam nor Eli mentioned a voice. Am I alone in that? Through every dream I have, whether it's about the crops or the yellow eyes, the menacing voice calls to me. It tries to disguise itself as alluring, enticing, and my curiosity is piqued. But I know enough to recognize the danger in its whispering taunts. It's the same voice I heard on the mountain. The same voice I tried to destroy in the lab. It's the reason I burned the entire bunker. But still it persists in my dreams. I'm sure it belongs to the yellow eyes.

"Adam," I say gently, offering him water from a canteen. "It's just a dream. Eli was in the mountain for eighteen months. He was witness to a lot of creepy things. Creepy things with yellow eyes. They probably aren't even the same yellow eyes you've seen. Your dreams are filled with horrifying images. Some of them are real; the hellcats and hellhounds. Some of them are not. Some are from the past, some from the future. There's nothing to worry about. Its far more likely something is wrong with Eli than the yellow eyes are real."

That's a good explanation. He seems to buy it because his lower lip stops trembling, and he leans into my arms. His features slacken and he unfists his hands.

Paige wraps her fingers around my wrist and whispers in my ear, "What's going on, Silver?"

"Nothing is going on."

She scans my face. "But maybe if we told people—"

"No, Paige." My voice rises. "No. Everything is fine. The dreams are never accurate. Everything is *fine*."

"Silver, I don't think we should keep this—"

"Paige," I hiss. "Please, stop. The yellow eyes can't be real."

"Can't?"

I turn away from her questioning look. I don't have the answers she wants.

"Well, what do we *do*?" Lyla asks, bringing me back to the topic of Eli.

"Let's keep an eye on him and see how he goes." Sawyer

summarizes the conversation I turned my back to. He bites into his oversized sandwich and is rewarded with a mayonnaise beard.

"Hmm," Erica says, still fluttering above us like a moth fascinated by a flame. "A *close* eye on him."

"Gee, Sawyer," Matt says. "You gotta a little something right there." Matt points at his chin. "A little to the left, a little more." Following Matt's directions, Sawyer manages to smear the mayonnaise all over his face. Everyone laughs. Lyla scowls at her brother.

Adam pulls on my hand. "Are you sure?" he whispers.

I nudge his shoulder with mine, eliciting a small smile.

I can't bring myself to return his smile. "Of course I'm sure."

I feel Paige's eyes on me, her doubt. She pulls me aside. "I know things have been hard lately. And I know I'm not the first one to face up when there's trouble. I mean, look at me, I took the wings nanite so I could literally fly away from my problems. But, Silver, God dammit, don't hide things from me."

"I'm not," I lie to my best friend.

CHAPTER NINETEEN

ELI

Before the workers arrive in the fields, Eli walks to the abandoned farmhouse. He has time to practice. Silver is currently in her house, tucked into her cocoon of a duvet, with her wild hair all over the place and wearing only a singlet and white panties. It's a strong image and it comes to him clearly. White. Pure. There's something about that color, something that makes her seem achingly innocent and untouched, something that makes him want to devour her when she wears it. But he's getting carried away. He didn't come here to imagine Silver like that, or to recall any other memories. He came here to practice his powers. Alone.

With the sun on his back, Eli stands in the same spot Silver did when she vanquished the farmhouse. He doesn't possess the destroyer ability, but he wonders if he could unearth anything remotely as powerful. Cycling through his abilities, he casts his mind back to the other night when he almost bit her head off, metaphorically speaking of course. She caught him during a bad moment. He was enjoying some time alone with Delta, the channel to the entity for once silent. But when Silver used her power to destroy the fields, the creature felt it and woke Eli, demanded he get involved. Eli momentarily rebelled, so comfortable was he in his bed, limbs entwined with the sweet Delta, but the entity insisted and landed Eli with the largest headache yet. He was grumpy and annoyed at first. Then he saw the result of the destruction she caused and he could sense the entity smiling along with him.

Standing on what they now joke of as 'the power spot,' the spot where Silver decimated ten trees in an instant, Eli stares at the ground, gathering himself. Raising his eyes to the distant tree line, he concentrates on the powers bubbling inside, all vying for attention.

Staring at the trees, Eli winks out of existence and looks at feet that are no longer there. Invisible. He's having fun with that one. For the most part. Apart from when he eavesdropped on the conversation the group had at lunch yesterday, about him, about an intervention. So, he hasn't been welcomed with open arms. They know he stands apart. He'll never be one of them.

He expected as much. He's never belonged to any group. The bruised feeling he carried in his chest made it easier to give in to the whispering fingers. They talked about him as though he's a problem. Mostly, it was Erica and Matt. Matt's reaction wasn't a surprise, but Erica? She might become an irritant. And then they spoke of the yellow eyes. His yellow eyes. How dare they.

The probing fingers come now, scratching and massaging until he throws his head back and sighs.

They show him an image of Eli standing on top of a mountain, snow swirling around his head. Or perhaps he really is there. It's all he can see.

"Isn't it nice?"

It's not even cold. In this vison, Eli is shirtless, but he feels no discomfort. Beneath him a pack of black wolves bay at the rising moon. It crests over his head, making him look like an angel.

"There is power here."

Eli smiles. He has never felt powerful before. Not until recently. He recalls the swim in the January ocean, the one he was challenged to, the one which sent his asthma into overload. His chest seized. Blue and red lights flashed. The rest of the images are unclear.

"You will release yourself from Earl's grip. You will never feel weak again."

The yellow eyes speak to him, and he listens. That powerful brain offers the answers to everything he's ever wanted to know, and then some. The whispers massage the back of his mind, promising wonders of such scale he'd be a fool not to listen to them.

Eli's feet pop back into existence. His smile becomes a grin. Well, if he can't have friends, at least he has Silver and the power.

"The power is yours."

Hearing a faint noise behind him, he turns and is met with what can only be described as a dumbfounded expression on the face of The Dog. The Dog stares at him, unmoving. Eli stands his ground and plants his feet, ready to face off against The Dog. The irritating mutt takes an advancing step and cocks his head suspiciously. It limps forward.

I saw you, I saw you do that.

The Dog's thoughts float into his mind.

"I don't know what you're talking about." Denial usually works well. But it's too late. The Dog already saw him appear from nowhere, now it also knows Eli can hear its thoughts. Stupid. The Dog will be his undoing, unless he stops it.

Invisibility plus reading my thoughts. The Dog thinks smugly. *I wonder what Silver will think about you having abilities and not telling anyone?*

"You can't tell Silver." It doesn't escape Eli that he's pleading with a dog. "You can't tell anyone." Can he possibly save this situation?

Why wouldn't I tell Silver? I knew you smelled bad.

The Dog shuffles closer. Will it attack? Even in such a crippled state? The presence of the yellow eyes appears abruptly in his head, preparing for battle. Strength surges through his muscles offering a clarity of thought he only achieves when tethered to the entity.

"I'm not bad!" Eli says, hands flying to his chest. "I have a father who was evil and experimented on me. I'm trying to escape that."

He holds his hands high in an attempt to ward off the approaching dog and stumbles back a step.

The yellow eyes narrow. *"Stop him."*

Without warning, The Dog shoots backward, faster than Silver's speed ability, and slams into the farmhouse fifty feet behind him. Wood cracks, splinters rain down, and The Dog lands in a contorted heap beneath it all.

Oh no.

"Oh, yes!"

Did he kill The Dog?

Eli creeps closer to the animal. It's alive, whimpering miserably. Big brown eyes look back at him. How will he explain this?

"Finish it."

With no further thought and with the merest flick of a wrist, Eli mentally squeezes The Dog's throat until one last squeaky whimper escapes the canine's mouth.

"This is your future. This is your path to power."

Eli examines his handiwork. He no longer needs to worry about The Dog. He can now think of it as just *the dog*. But oh, what is he going to tell Silver?

"You'll think of something."

A glimmer of guilt settles in his stomach, making him nauseous. Silver is going to be sad and he is the cause.

With fast feet, a faster brain and burst of powers so intense that the whole world turns blurry, Eli moves the dog's body and repairs the broken farmhouse. Scene set.

CHAPTER TWENTY
SILVER

I creep to the beech tree in the backyard of the farmhouse, trying to delay the inevitable moment. My knees buckle a little and then I give into the heartache and kneel beside Einstein. But it isn't him, not really.

"I'm sorry, Silver," Eli says. "I found him here...he must have wandered in..."

Lifting his furry head, I kiss his snout. "He was probably looking for me, to heal him."

I have failed him. Where was I in his hour of need? Off experimenting in the old city with my destroyer ability where he couldn't find me. He came to the one place he thought I might be. And I wasn't there. I wasn't able to heal him, and he died. Why didn't I change his genetics? I promised myself I would expunge all his weakness so he could live longer. I was too busy with my own life, my own stupid problems.

"I'm sorry, Silver." Eli reaches for my shoulder and rubs at it briefly. "I'm sorry."

Standing, I rally against the emotion swelling in my chest

and raise Einstein's limp body into the air with my telekinesis ability. Carrying him in front of me, I shuffle my way along the path. We move around the farmhouse, along the dirt track and into the busy fields. I lay Einstein's body near the water table and fetch Matt.

I find him kneeling in the middle of the field, sunhat pulled low. "You need to come with me." He must hear something in my voice because he rises to his feet immediately and follows without protest.

Leading him to Einstein, we find a small crowd of people gathered around the body. I take his hand. "I'm sorry, Matt." Others move out the way as he approaches. Matt kneels before his beloved dog.

"I knew he was getting old, but I didn't think he'd actually leave," he says.

I put a hand on his shoulder.

Matt buries his face in Einstein's fur. He chokes on a sob. Then he raises his head, wipes his eyes and whispers to the dog. "Goodbye, old friend."

We bury him on the edge of the farmland so he'll always be close by. Chewing on a piece of straw, Matt sits by the rock used to mark the grave, Einstein's name painted in bold black lettering.

"Can we go for a walk, or something?" I ask. He hasn't said a word to me since I brought him the news.

"I'd rather be alone." He pushes away from the fence surrounding the grave.

I take his hand, but he doesn't squeeze back. "But, Matt, we should be together. Please don't go off alone, not like this—"

"Silver, please, let me be," Matt replies without looking at me, still staring at the grave marker.

"Don't shut me out."

He looks up, stares right in my eyes. "I could say the same to you. I know you were in the city again this morning. But this isn't about us right now, Silver. It's about Einstein. And I'd really like to be alone."

He places his sunhat on his head and takes the trail leading deep into the woods. I stare after him, uncertain of our future.

CHAPTER TWENTY-ONE

ELI

ELI LEAVES Silver and Matt and their friends to their grieving. He can't maintain the pretense well enough to endure a drawn-out service for an oversized stuffed animal, even if it is intelligent, even if it can communicate with humans. The dog was nothing but a thorn in his side. Well, a thorn in the side of the yellow eyes, if it even has one. Does it matter whose side the thorn is in?

His thoughts are scattering again, something that's been happening more frequently. He has no control over them or their direction.

Eli returns to the scene of the crime, so to speak. When he reaches the backyard of the farmhouse, he lies on the dry grass and watches the clouds float by in a blue sky. The blueness of the sky reminds him of the dream on the yacht and the never-ending ocean and Eli almost scares himself into a sitting position. But then he remembers he isn't afraid of the dream anymore or the yellow eyes and he relaxes onto the grass again.

A shadow falls across his vision. Eli props himself on elbows and cups a hand over his eyes. Perhaps it's Delta coming to check on him.

"You don't want Delta."

Eli bristles, but doesn't try to argue. The fingers tighten in his head. But it isn't Delta anyway.

"I'm sorry for interrupting you," Lyla says, her blond curls tumbling over her shoulders. They are very nice curls, but not to his taste. Too pert, too exuberant, too *not* Silver.

"That's better."

Eli doesn't say she isn't interrupting. Let her sweat it out.

She shifts her weight to her other foot. "I was wondering if I could recruit you for a play?"

"A play?"

"Yes, we're going to perform at the theater downtown. A musical. I thought it might be good for you."

The yellow eyes laugh.

"Good for me?" Eli has never been in a play. Nor does he want to.

"Yes. I thought it might take your mind off...the headaches and stuff." Lyla moves a hand to indicate his head and face.

"Be careful."

"The headaches and stuff?" Is this part of the intervention? "If it's all the same to you," he replies as politely as he can manage. "I'd rather not. I'm no good at that kind of thing."

She taps a finger against her cheek. "Okay, but think about it. It might help."

He holds back his own laugh. "Goodbye, Lyla."

She frowns. "There's no need to be rude."

"Sorry." He swirls a hand in the air. "I have a headache. Bad dreams."

"About the yellow eyes?" She asks.

"Be more careful. If you want the power, you'll do as I say."

"I don't really have the energy to talk about it."

"Right. Sure. Yeah. Okay. I hope you feel better." She backs away.

He lies back when he hears her crunch through the dry grass and out of the yard. A few moments later another shadow passes over his face.

"Goodness, Lyla, I do have to give you points for persistence." He raises himself into a sitting position.

"Lyla?" It isn't Lyla. It's Silver. Her hair is doing that wild thing he likes and her eyes are bright with fiery emotion. It looks like there's a small whirlwind spinning around her, in the otherwise still as a picture day. A weather power?

"She was here a few minutes ago." Eli shields his eyes from the sun once again. "You okay?"

"Yeah." Silver sits beside him, but she looks mad, like she wants to use her powers, all of them at the same time.

"I remembered a new one," Eli says. "Of Earl's abilities. It's not particularly useful, but—"

"What is it?" she asks.

Eli pauses, delaying the revelation, watching her salivate with the want of it all. She needs the distraction. And he needs her mind focused on something else besides Einstein's death. "He can change the color of things. Touch something and think of a different color."

"Very good."

She touches the grass beneath her and a small patch turns red. Blood red. It matches the color of the farmhouse. Then it turns yellow, brown, purple and the most beautiful shimmering silver. Like her eyes.

"This is fun," she says, and touches his nose.

"Hey." Eli swipes at her hand. "What color is my nose?"

"Blue." She laughs and winks at him. They are back to normal after their rather tense conversation the other night.

"It's good to see you smiling." Eli sweeps a rogue strand of hair from her face.

"It feels good to smile. I need to do it more. I haven't been myself lately." She leans close, her curtain of hair shielding them from the sun.

He returns her smile. "Well, I'm glad I'm the cause."

"Yeah, you and your blue nose!"

She laughs again and Eli seizes the moment. Brushing her hair away from her face again, he lets his fingers dangle in the smooth silkiness. He touches her cheek, draws a lazy circle with his thumb, and cups her jaw in his hand. Decisively, he brings her face to his. He hears her gasp just before his lips meet hers. But she doesn't refuse. She doesn't pull away. She leans deeper into him and kisses him back.

"Yes."

The kiss is long and deep, lingering and exploratory. The heat between them builds spectacularly, igniting feelings in Eli he didn't know he possessed.

"Yesssss."

She pulls away. Remaining silent, she touches his nose to

return it to its normal color, then stares at the spot where he set Einstein's body.

"I'm sorry," Eli says.

"Don't be sorry."

She doesn't reply. Is she thinking of the future of her relationship with Matt? He tries probing her mind but she appears to have her own protective mental wall in place. Glancing at the farmhouse, he spies a wisp of blonde curls bounce around the corner, out of view. Lyla. She remained. And she saw. A thrill courses through Eli. Sparks are going to fly. Matt will come at him. But he welcomes it, especially if it brings him closer to Silver.

"Excellent work."

"I'm sorry?" He tries again, reaching for her, his hand finding a space on her leg above her knee. She doesn't remove it.

"Don't. Be. Sorry."

He lurches away from the voice in his head.

"S'okay," she says finally. "It was bound to happen."

Bound to happen?

"But it can't happen again." She turns the grass red again.

Oh?

"Oh?"

"I love Matt." She turns her silver eyes on him. "I do. I need to make things right with him. I'm sorry."

Oh.

"Try harder."

What is he going to tell Delta?

"Delta is insignificant."

"She is not insignificant!" he yells.

Silver startles. "What are you talking about? Who's not insignificant?"

Eli looks at her. "Sorry, not feeling great." He plays with an acorn that rests between them.

She touches a glowing hand to his. The tension in his neck disappears, the muscles in his back relax, and his shoulders drop an inch or two. But the fingers and whispers remain.

"Better?" She asks.

He nods. But the treatment doesn't last. As soon as he imagines Delta's face receiving the news of his betrayal, all his muscles recoil.

"I should go," she says, but makes no move to rise to her feet.

"I hope this doesn't make things weird between us," Eli says.

"My whole life is a series of awkward, difficult, terrifying moments. This," she holds out her hands to encompass them both. "This is nothing." She smiles and he knows she means it. "But now I have to go."

He watches her leave. When he's sure he's alone, Eli sits up and plays with his powers. It helps him recover from the rejection. Not that it was a surprise. He didn't really think she'd leave Matt, but it was worth a try. Together, they would have been indestructible.

"Try again."

Why do the yellow eyes care so much?

"You need not concern yourself with that."

"If you want me to do your dirty work, then you better damn well tell me what's going on!" He yells at the sky.

There's no hint of the yellow eyes up there, but he feels their stare.

"It's not time."

He throws a fireball at the beech tree and scorches every one of its wilting leaves.

CHAPTER TWENTY-TWO
SILVER

PANIC SWIRLS through me as I run from the farmhouse. What have I done?

My fingers tremble, but the destroyer ability remains contained, for now.

Who have I become?

I don't have answers. I never have. About anything. But I know this is irreparable. If it comes out.

I stop running when I'm halfway home, sink my blade into a tree and try to calm myself. There has to be a way out of this.

Eli and I were the only ones there. No one has to find out about it. I'm sure he won't tell; he doesn't want to risk further issues with Matt. I'm certainly not self-flagellating enough to admit to a mistake of such titan proportions.

In a way, I'm glad Eli kissed me. It proved I'm not imagining the attraction between us. It's mutual. It also showed I do have feelings for him *and* confirmed how much I love

Matt. It's pretty fucked up, but I don't know how else to describe it. I'm attracted to Eli and I love Matt.

I can fix it. I can turn the tap of emotion off. The desire, attraction, whatever you want to call it, I will turn it off and focus on fixing my relationship with Matt. That will be my focus now.

Matt.

There isn't any room in my heart for anyone other than Matt, no matter what the status of our relationship. I wavered momentarily because he's been judgmental, but now I'm back. I will be good and true and honest, apart from the kiss bit, and all the other things a girlfriend is supposed to be. I won't let him shrug me off again. I will get through to him.

I sit on the curb in front of my house watching a line of ants march across the tarmac. With the descending sun on my back, I lament the disused streetlights lining the sidewalk. Streetlights aren't considered an essential use of electricity. When night descends, it's the deepest darkness the world has seen for decades. The shrouding blackness often leaves me feeling isolated. It's the perfect cover for misdeeds. I look for the yellow eyes in the sky. I can't see them, but I sense them watching. They're out there somewhere.

I think about talking things through with Paige. She would know what to do. But I can't face her disappointment when I tell her what I've done. Or not done.

As I sit there trying to understand how I've fallen out with so many people, the loss of Einstein weighs heavily on me. To compound my guilt, Lyla walks out of the Lawson family home.

"Is Matt with you?" I ask as she approaches.

She shakes her head. "He hasn't come back yet. I guess he needed some time." She settles herself beside me on the curb.

"Have you found people for your play?" I ask.

Lyla grimaces. Maybe it will be a one-person performance. She looks at her hands, then her feet, which drum a soft beat on the tarmac. Finally, she looks at me. There is disappointment in her eyes. It must be crushing not to be able to rally interest. The theater and dancing were her whole life before the resistance. "Are we going to talk about it?"

"The play?" I ask. "If you'd like? But Lyla, I said before, I'm no good on stage."

She clears her throat, as if waiting for me to catch up. "No, the great, big, fat elephant in the room."

Einstein. She knows it's my fault. She knows I could have made him better, that I could have prevented his death. "I'm sorry..." I taste tears in the back of my throat.

"It's okay." She puts an arm around me. "Why don't you tell me about it?"

"If I hadn't been so caught up in my own problems..."

"I know, you and Matt have been having trouble..."

"It's not just that..." I hesitate. "I wish I'd saved him before it was too late."

With a blank look on her face, Lyla scratches her temple with a painted, pink fingernail. "Eli?"

"Einstein. I should have saved him," I reply, equally confused. But a slow awareness creeps up my spine. My world is about to implode.

"I'm not talking about Einstein. I'm talking about Eli." Lyla's arm slips from my shoulder and her nostrils flare. I remember when I burned her leg, how angry she was, how long she held her grudge. A shiver runs through me. "The fact that he kissed you, and you let him."

Protestations of denial flitter through my head. Can I plead temporary insanity? Can I feign complete ignorance? Or perhaps I should pretend to be insulted at the mere suggestion. Maybe I could blame it all on Matt. But that's childish, Matt wasn't even there, it's entirely my fault.

"I was mad at Matt," I sigh. "He won't let me in. He doesn't understand me anymore. I don't know how to make him."

"That doesn't mean you stop trying. That doesn't mean you give up and go kissing the next person in line." Lyla's voice pitches.

"I know! I know. I don't know what to do." Wringing my hands, I bite the inside of my cheek until I taste the coppery flavor of blood. "Please don't tell him."

"I won't," she says. I sigh with relief, but she isn't done. "As long as *you* do. If you want it to work, Silver, then you need to come clean, get it all out there and start again."

Easier said than done. Everything comes so easily to Matt; technology, weapons, security. He always knows what to say, in any situation. Morally just, he is so sure what is right and wrong and he's unwavering when it comes to the defense or prosecution of either side. How will I explain to him why I let Eli kiss me, that I didn't stop him, that I *wanted* him to?

She stands. "Talk to him." Then she leaves.

I'm alone again. Maybe it's better that way.

Unable to move from the edge of the curb outside my house, the night falls around me, sequestering me in its shadows. I expect the creatures of the night to appear, maybe the thing with the yellow eyes. Even scarier is the thought of Matt returning. Unsure where to go, I find myself in the quiet car park of the hospital. Standing there on the cooling tarmac, with my stupid flipflops hanging by a thread, I'm unable to move. The thought of my mother's eternal rocking emphasizes my lack of power to help her.

I teleport to the old city and find my high school. It seems like such a long time ago, before the resistance, before the battle with Earl. A lifetime ago. Graffiti decorates the entire right flank of the building. Not pretty graffiti, but ugly tags and fearful messages of doom. Trash and leaves line the path and steps leading to the main entrance and many of the windows are smashed. Perfect setting for a ghost story.

Pushing open the squeaky front door, I walk past the tattered American Flag and weave through the empty hallways. Open locker doors spill their contents onto the ground, and the odd liquid puddle of green remains adhered to the floors, walls, and chairs. I evaporate them with mental fireballs when I come across them. Sawyer hasn't reached this part of the city yet. Walking on, I arrive at the gym where I trained with Claus. A bucket of chalk is overturned and leaves a white trail halfway across the crashmats. The TV faces me from the back of the room, in the position it was used to deliver President Bear's fatal message about the enforced nanite program. That was the last time I was here.

Flying high, I cup my hands around my face and peer out the window. I blanch when I spot a pair of yellow eyes and blink rapidly to clear my vision. They wink at me from the sky, staring, searching, and settle on me. Slowly, they blink, and I imagine the creature they belong to is smiling. I send a fireball toward the sky and the eyes disappear. Just a figment of my imagination. When I look again only the brilliant glow of the full moon and a hopeful glittering of stars are visible.

Guilt floods my betraying heart. I've treated Matt badly. A rising sense of panic makes me nauseous as I consider everything I have to lose. Pulling back from the window, I wonder how I'll ever make it up to him. Lyla is right. He needs to know. Not only because he deserves the truth, but because I'll never be able to continue in our relationship with such a secret. It will eat away at me until I'm no longer able to look into his beautiful blue eyes. I have to tell him, and I'll have to live with the consequences.

I return home to see Matt coming out of his family home. "We need to talk."

He nods and follows me into my house. The house where he used to spend all his nights.

"I have something to tell you and you're not going to like it." Praying for strength, I cradle the musical pendant hanging at my neck and run it up and down its chain a few times.

"Really?" he says quietly. I can't read his tone. "There's more than destroying three field's worth of crops?"

"There's more," I say.

"Christ, Silver, what have you done now?" He deflates onto a kitchen stool and crosses his arms over his chest. Is he interested in working things out, does he even care? But I vowed to try.

My stomach drops, but I don't stop. "It's about Eli."

"What have you two done? Destroyed a building with

people still inside it?" The thunderous expression on his face threatens my resolve to stay honest.

"We...he...I..." Oh crap, this is so much harder than I thought. I have to spit it all out, then deal. "I felt myself becoming attracted to Eli, Matt, because of the problems we've been having and because he understood me."

Matt recoils, as though he's been slapped. He was expecting stories of destruction, new powers, not this.

"We kissed. Earlier today. It was wrong. I realize that now—"

"You realize that *now*?" Two angry red spots appear high on his otherwise bleached cheekbones. "Did it not occur to you to think through the implications of your actions before you embarked down this path?"

I rush on, trying to explain myself before he can interrupt, trying to make him see before he gets all righteous about it.

"I stopped it, I put an end to it. I've realized I don't care for him that way."

"I'm so happy for you. Halleluiah, Silver's had a revelation!" Matt claps his hands together three times with excruciating slowness.

"I love *you*, Matt!" I shout at him. "I love you more than anything in the world. I can't bear to hurt you."

"Well, congratulations, you just did." He stares at me, his blue eyes watery and hurt.

"Matt, please, don't be like this—"

"How did you expect me to react?"

"I..." I look blankly around the room. How *did* I expect him to react? Did I think he was going to forgive such a betrayal and then we could carry on in our merry way? "I'm sorry."

"I'll tell you what I think," he says, standing. "My girl-friend, who I've loved my entire life, who insisted on becoming arrogantly superior because she has powers, who is turning into an altered, who refuses to contemplate having a future with me if it means taking a risk and bearing children into an uncertain world, my girlfriend, who would rather experiment with her powers than help people, who would rather play with some over grown hunk than deal with any of life's issues, with us, and after all we've been through together, kissed another guy. On the day my dog died. How do you expect me to react?" Matt blows his hair out of his eyes and ignores my crestfallen expression. "I'm not all that surprised, Silver. Nothing you do surprises me anymore. And the fact that you have now reduced our entire relationship to a teenaged, angst-filled confused moment...well...I may not be surprised anymore, but I did expect better of you."

"I am not turning into an altered!" I shout at him. *That's* what I choose to focus on?

Kitchen cabinets rattle, crockery falls out of the cupboards, the fridge door opens and closes, three, four, five times and then it reduces to a pile of ash.

"Really?" Matt holds his hands wide to encompass the room, the slamming cabinet doors, the swinging chandelier we never use and everything else moving and shaking and being reduced to ash before our eyes.

"I can't help it!" I yell. "I don't want to lose you. You're everything that's good in my life. I can't lose you. You're all I have left."

"You should have thought of that before!" he yells back, slamming a fist on the table.

The cupboards rattle harder, a couple disappearing into a fine ash cloud. Windows shake in their panes. The black lightning rips into the room, looking for a target. Matt stands, a pained look on his face, waiting it out.

"Are you not afraid of me?" How could he not be? I'm afraid of myself.

"No. Why? Do you want me to be?"

"No," I whisper.

"Do I need to be?"

"No." *No.*

He narrows his eyes. "Are you sure about that?"

I gulp around the lump in my throat and will the cupboards and cabinets and chandelier to stop shaking. After a concerted effort, quiet finally reigns. Matt holds my gaze for a second longer, then turns and leaves the house.

This is not good. Understatement of the year. Understatement of my life. This is so much worse than I dared to fear.

I have lost Matt.

I've lost him. Somehow, in all the scenarios which played in my mind, I didn't think I would. But now, I have to admit, I've lost Matt.

I've lost Matt.

I can't get those three words out of my head. Around and around they go, like a spinning top, making me nauseas, refusing to quiet down.

I've lost Matt.

The cabinets shake again. Everything inside them is ash.

Fighting for control of the power, the cabinets slam, whipping the ash into a whirlwind. I don't want to control it. I want it to grow and feed and become so strong that perhaps it will devour me too. Then I can forget about all the pain I caused. I can forget my own pain. I can drift away and never have to think again.

I've lost Matt.

The pain is unbearable. I can't breathe. I can't breathe, I can't....

Out flashes the powerful blue wings of a macaw and then my body follows suit. I morph into a bird. I've seen Earl do it before. I've seen him change from one species to the next, and I tried to find a way to do it myself. It alluded me until now.

I am a blue macaw. Flying through the house, I knock into the chandelier, then escape out the kitchen door into the world beyond. I ascend quickly, flying over the fields, over the old city. As I fly, fireballs of rage scorch the land beneath. My vision fills with orange and red. I see nothing but fire and pain.

The power is mighty, demanding and all encompassing. As I fly through the city leaving a trail of fireballs, black streaks of power shoot from my talons, decimating anything they strike; buildings, houses, parks, trees, bushes, gardens, signs, and once a lone wolf raising its snout into the cold night, sniffing for its prey. I fly and I destroy. Tucking my head under a wing, my pendant slips off my neck and is lost somewhere to the world below.

I laugh, partly in fear, partly in glee, but mostly trying to exorcize the pain that is buried inside.

When I tire of destroying, I fly aimlessly through the sky, scavenging on meat when the primal need arises. I lose track of how many moons pass. Occasionally I stop to rest. Sometimes I drink from a stream and often I hear other animals in the forest below. I ignore them all. My pain is all-consuming and it takes everything I have not to fly to the moon and never look back.

CHAPTER TWENTY-THREE
SILVER

"Silver, I know that's you." Francesca's voice reaches me.

We are in the woods. I'm still in my bird form. I've been hiding in the woods for three days, or is it three weeks? When I realized I pretty much destroyed the entirety of the old city I wasn't sure how to return home. Or if I wanted to. There's nothing there for me anymore. My mother is unreachable, I haven't heard from my dad for weeks, I lost Matt, I've argued with Paige and Erica, and I'm sure I'll lose the rest of my friends over the inanely stupid decisions I made. I'm not ready to face reality, I'm not ready to see anyone. I'm not ready, dammit!

"Could you come out please, Silver?"

I'm tempted to fly off. Instead, I transition into my human form and accept the clothes Francesca hands me. When I'm dressed I dare to look at her.

"We've got a lot to talk about," she says.

I'd rather not.

"You've caused an enormous amount of destruction." Francesca's lips compress in thinly disguised displeasure.

"Really? I thought I'd done a good job of sanitizing the old city. Nothing left for vagrants to inhabit, nothing left for disease to fester in," I snap. The black lightning tickles my palms.

"Silver, I understand you're upset. I know things have been difficult for you, with your mother, Matt, Einstein, and the demands I've been making on you, but you can't go off half-cocked because something doesn't go your way..."

Half-cocked? There have been more bumps in my life than a mogul-infested black run ski slope. *Half-cocked?*

"...running around, destroying the city, the fields, your old apartment building. Surely you must have memories..."

Yes, bad ones.

"...and the way you've treated everyone, your friends, Paige has been asking for you...

With the mention of my best friend's name something painful clamps over my heart. I haven't checked on her in days.

"...you haven't visited your mother and the lady who is coming...

Oh, Mom.

The weight of the guilt makes the pain unbearable. I'm not ready to feel it yet. I'm not strong enough. I've heard enough. I don't need to come back to this crap. Yes, I know I flew off into the woods. Whether it was avoidance or the need to be alone doesn't make much difference. The end result is the same. But to stand here and listen to Francesca chastise me, tell me off like a grade-schooler. The twitching black lightning bubbles eagerly on my fingers, boiling, and then it erupts.

"...I can't believe you would stoop to...it's not like you, Silver..."

Without warning, Francesca disappears. She was just there, standing three feet from me, spouting a moralistic diatribe about the growing list of my failings in the last month. Where did she go? Has my teleportation power grown to the extent I can teleport someone away? Scanning the woods and fields, I can't see her anywhere. My heart pounds in my chest. Where *is* she?

Then I see it. Gathering at my feet is a small pile of gray ash.

Oh...*no*. No, no, no!

Trying to deny what I've done, I cover my face with my hands. Choking down a sob, I make a thousand wishes, but when I remove my hands from my face, the gray pile of ash is still there and Francesca is still missing. I have reduced Francesca to a pile of gray ash. The black streaks continue to dance across my fingers.

"Oh...no, no, no. *Nooooo!*"

The pile begins to drift and float away on the wind. I panic.

"Shit!"

The ash dissipates in the air. Francesca is about to be lost to a fine summer's breeze. Everyone will know. People will notice if the president of the country goes missing and they'll know it was me. I killed Francesca. I am a murderer.

"*Nooooo.*" Grabbing at the dissipating ash, it coats my hands. I grab and scoop and whimper as the ash drifts further away, sinks into the ground, and dissolves into my sweat-soaked palms.

With a flicker of hope, I recall what happened to the farmhouse. Squeezing my eyes shut, I wish desperately for Francesca to be whole again.

Nothing happens. A dizzy spell accosts me and I retch into the grass, bringing up bile. It coats the pile of gray ash.

"Come back! Please come back!" I pound at the grass with my fists. "I promise I'll be good again."

My hands shake and my throat dries out. I scream at the sky, at the ground, at the trees surrounding me. I am not this person. I am not a murderer.

"*Please*, Francesca."

I pray to a god I don't believe in. I offer Satan my soul. And still she remains a pile of ash. I stare at it. A clump of grayness coated with my stomach bile. That is all that remains of President Francesca Montoya.

Pushing myself to my feet, I turn my back on the ash pile and walk a few paces away. I dry my eyes with the backs of my hands, smearing a bit of Francesca across my cheeks.

What can I do?

I breathe. Slowly. In and out. Deeply. Several times. My hands continue to shake, but my core gains a new strength.

Don't rush it.

I have to get control over my emotions. Why do I find it so hard?

I breathe. And breathe. And suck in the clear air. I think of Matt, my parents, my friends, how much I love them. Then I think of Francesca, of all she has done for our country.

"What about the crops?" She demands. "You destroyed three fields of corn which were almost ready to harvest..."

I open my eyes and turn to face her. Thank God! She's back. Even if she's still raving at me.

In that moment I'm humbled. I nearly killed Francesca, the president of our country, because I was pissed off. Matt is right. I'm arrogant. I don't care about anyone else's problems except my own. I thought mine were more important, bigger.

The heat of shame flushes my cheeks. I've been monumentally stupid. I've been selfish and single-minded and unwilling to see a different point of view. My parents, if they knew what I did, would be disappointed. That's what burns. That's what rescues me from jumping down a path I can't return from. Because I could have killed Francesca, I could have left her as a pile of ash, and I could have walked away. But that isn't me, and the disappointment of my parents, of Matt, of my friends, would crush me.

"...ouch." She pauses in her lecture to rub a hand across her forehead. "Where's that come from?"

"Are you okay?" Did I not put her back together well enough?

"A stabbing pain across my forehead. Ow." Francesca's knees buckle.

Approaching her, I rest a golden palm on her head. She rises seconds later, healed and complete once again.

"Thanks." She looks me up and down. "Anyway..."

"I'm sorry," I say

"I know you are."

"I'll fix the crops."

"Yes, you will, and that's just for starters." One of her

eyebrows arches. Then she sighs and her shoulders drop. "I feel responsible. I should have guided you. I should have realized how much you were dealing with. And I'm sorry for that. I'm sorry I let you down. But, Silver, it's time to come back to us now."

"I...I...I..." Emotion clogs my throat. It appears I'm not going to be hung, drawn and quartered. Francesca isn't about to throw me in lock-up for the rest of my life. I'm grateful. She's far more understanding than I've given her credit for. But how will I face Matt? "I can't go back there. I can't face—"

"You can and you will." That eyebrow again.

My pulse pounds at my temples. "What will I say?"

"You'll say you're sorry." Francesca throws an arm around me and draws me into her side. She marches me through the woods, into her waiting 4x4, and onto the farmland. If she knew what I did to her...

She points to the empty fields. "The crops first please."

Kneeling in the decimated field, I dig my fingers into the rich soil, feeling the gnarly hardness of seeds. Life waits. Using my unusual restoration power, I return the crops I destroyed to their former glory. I surprise myself a little when the seeds begin to bud. The shoots grow toward the sun and within seconds I'm standing amid six-foot stalks of corn. I didn't know I was capable of that. It's beautiful to watch.

"Thank you, Silver."

As Francesca and I approach the central field with the water table under the massive oak tree, a small crowd grows. Has everyone learned of my indiscretions? Is everyone here to witness my humiliating return? But no, as I look beyond the tilted heads, there's an altercation taking place.

"I can't believe you did that to my sister!" Matt swings a fist at Sawyer.

Sawyer has a swollen eye and a ripped shirt. His curls are matted to his head. Matt looks equally disarrayed. Although no bulging eye, his clothes are torn and there is a wildness in his eyes.

"It was a misunderstanding!" Sawyer shouts. "Will you stay out of it?"

"She's my *sister*." Matt throws a jab at Sawyer's jaw.

"I love her!" Sawyer dodges Matt's right hook.

"You're not allowed to love her. Look what you did to her!"

"Cut it out!" Lyla screams louder than them both. Those who are still working in the fields stop and stare as Lyla's words carry easily on the breeze. "Everything is okay!"

Apparently, I've missed a huge ordeal while I was hiding in the woods.

"Matt, Sawyer and I are fine. It was just a misunderstanding." Storm clouds scud across Lyla's bright blue eyes. "But really, this fight!" She throws her hands toward the filthy pair, "is so not about me." She walks between them, separating them with her arms and throws a glance in my direction.

Cue my entrance. "I'm sorry!" I call into the fray. This isn't about Lyla. This is about me. And Matt, and our complete ineptitude to handle our problems privately, without involving our friends.

"I'm sorry," I say again. All eyes swivel in my direction. Carter salutes me, his bottle oddly missing. Maybe he's on his own road to recovery. Erica flutters a little closer, her wings turning acid green. She holds grudges longer than Lyla. Adam runs to me and wraps his arms around me. Delta sits on the fence bordering the field.

Claus is there, sitting at the table, his cane held between his legs. He doesn't smile, but there's warmth in his eyes. I can't bare to return his gaze.

"Everyone, I'm sorry about my actions, I'm sorry about the crops, I'm sorry I haven't been acting like me."

I gave into my anger and I ran away. Like a coward. Because life got hard. It wasn't until Francesca found me and I almost deleted her out of existence that I saw I needed to make things right. I'm capable of causing terror. Matt may be right about that. My frustration with my mother's lack of recovery had deepened my already fragile sense of self, and no matter how much I practiced the powers, no matter how much they grew, if I came to believe my mother was truly unreachable, then there would be nothing I could do to stop the black streaks emerging and no one would be safe.

It's time to reconvene my place among society, among my friends, if they'll still have me, rather than become the object of their terror. That isn't a life I want.

Mason tips me a salute. "S'okay, Silver."

"It's not okay. Matt was right. I was turning into an altered."

Ironically, it's Matt who leaps to my defense. "You're not—"

"I was." I raise my hand. "Just because I have power doesn't mean I get to use it whenever I feel like it. I thought I was doing the right thing. Or maybe they were the wrong things for the right reasons." I think of Paige's words and smile. "Whatever. We are where we are now, and I'm sorry for my part in it all. I'm sorry if I caused anyone pain."

"Thanks, Silver," Sawyer says.

Carter winks at me. "Good to have you back."

"I spent a whole week working in that cornfield," Erica says, but she's smiling, her wings fluttering a pleasant sunset orange. I want to hug her, but she's not the huggy type.

Claus stands and shuffles over to me. He puts a hand on my shoulder. "I think you and I need to spend more time together."

I dip my chin. "I think you're right."

"I'm proud of you."

I shake my head. "Don't say that—"

"I'm *proud* of you." He says it louder, firmer, and I don't protest. I look at him, and he holds my gaze. It's going to be okay.

Francesca claps her hands. "Everyone back to work." She shoots me a sideways glance as she leaves with Claus. "I know that was difficult for you."

Matt and Sawyer separate and Lyla marches Sawyer out of the fields. The crowd disperses, leaving Matt and I standing by the water table, alone, but so far apart.

"I've been so worried about you..." Matt takes a step closer. "You've been gone for almost three weeks."

"Was it that long?"

Matt nods, relief washing over his face and softening his hard edges. "I'm sorry," he says, before I have a chance to speak again. "I'm sorry for pushing you so hard. I was too hard on you."

"Just a tad." I brace myself, trying to read the answers in his eyes, but he doesn't give anything away.

"I expected too much of you—"

"Well hang on a minute—"

He ignores my interruption. "When you were gone I had time to think." He fiddles with a stalk of wheat, shredding the spikes with his fingers. "I expected the world of you, Silver. I expected too much. You have so much power and you're the most genuine, caring person I've ever known." Dropping the wheat, he rubs at his jaw. "I know what I would try and do if I had half of your abilities. If my mother was...and if...well, I don't blame you for trying. But I think I built this image of you in my mind, this image of you that was a bit like...well...God-like." Matt smiles sheepishly. "Because you have the power of one, I expected you to act...well...selflessly and without a thought for yourself. But I realize that's not human, it's inhuman, and I was wrong to put that on you. You're not a god. I lost sight of what was important. I think, and Lyla helped spell things out for me, I lost sight of what was important to *you*. And I will never, ever do that again."

I melt a little. My brain turns to mush and my tongue won't work. I stand there and stare at him.

"I get it. Finally. I didn't realize how out of control you felt. That's why you rid yourself of anxiety, it was the only thing you could think to do that would help you readjust after Earl and deal with your mother. The fact that I gave you a hard time about it was unforgivable." He pauses, raking a hand through his hair. His eyes never leave mine. "But the more you experimented, the more scared I got. I was worried you wouldn't be able to control the powers. I wasn't sure what that would do to you, or me, or us."

I hang my head. Everything he says is true. It broke us.

Matt takes my hand. "I, obviously, was not there for you. My priorities won't always be the same as yours, I realize that now, and that's okay. But I promise from now on, I will always try to understand your point of view." He takes my other hand and we stand there, staring at each other.

"I'm sorry too," I say, releasing his hands, unable to bear the familiarity of his touch. "I should have tried to explain to you better, about my mother, about cataloging my abilities...I've never been good at expressing my emotions. And you were right, it did feel good, I did...*do*...enjoy it."

His hands dangle by his sides, his fingers twitching, as if seeking my hand. "But you're over that now?"

"I'm over that now," I say. "For the most part. I like the feel of using my powers, but I wasn't trying to seek the ultimate high or anything like that. I was trying to find something to help my mom and I happened to enjoy the ride that went along with it."

"I can accept that." Matt punctuates his words with a short nod.

"Thank you," I expel quietly.

He smiles, a smile of such welcome and joy and forgiveness that my world feels filled with rainbows once more. Matt looks around the fields at our friends working. He grabs a canteen and takes a swig of water, and then, glancing at Eli's cabin, purses his lips. "Do you know what, Silver? Most of it wasn't even about your powers."

"I'm sorry about Eli. I never wanted to hurt you." I pause,

swallowing the tight feeling in my throat. Unshed tears sting my eyes. I blink them away. I have no right to cry.

He shakes his head. "I knew I was pushing you away... straight into Eli's arms."

"Is it...are we...are we okay?" I caused him so much pain. Even if he can forgive me, I'm not sure I can forgive myself.

Eyes widening, Matt stumbles closer. His voice is gravelly with emotion. "Of course we're okay." And then his arms are around me and I'm finally home. "I love you."

"I love you too."

He raises my chin to meet his face, cupping it in his hand. As his lips meet mine he lifts me into his arms and I wrap my legs around his waist. He holds me and we kiss. I can't describe how right it feels. How much I love him. We could grow roots, like the oak tree we're standing under, and stay here forever

When he pulls away, we smile at each other and hold hands.

I lean my forehead against his. "So what do we do about Eli? Does everyone know about us?"

"No, no one does. Lyla and I thought it'd be better that way. At least until we could find you. Now I guess that you're back, he'll be all over you again and you'll have to come clean with Delta. I don't think anyone's told her yet, either."

"Delta? Why would she care?"

"They were...dating."

My thoughts spin back to movie night. The woman in the shadows. Delta.

"Have you spoken to him?" I ask.

"No. He knows I know and we're keeping a healthy

238

distance." The familiarity of Matt's body, his scent, brings home anew how deeply I love him. "And, Silver?"

"Hmm?" I moan, kissing his collarbone. "No more playing with Eli."

"I know."

I skirt a look over the fields at my friends. Healthy crops stretch for miles. We have built this, together. This is our new world.

"I suppose I should go and heal Sawyer's black eye," I say, catching sight of him with an icepack on his head.

"Aw, let him live with it for a day or two, a reminder of what will happen if he ever hurts my sister."

"Jeez, remind me never to get on your bad side," I say.

"Oh, you have, and you survived okay."

"Even if I am pig-headed, single-minded, and stubborn-assed?"

"Huh?" Matt cocks his head. "How did you know I thought that?"

"I can read thoughts now." A smile twitches on my lips. Matt groans. "Trust me, it's not so fun. I don't use it often. I wasn't in control of the powers then. They kept popping out at odd moments. Peering into your head? That's not something I want to do again!"

"You are by the way," he says.

"What?"

"Pig-headed, single-minded and stubborn-assed. All of it, at the same time."

"Humph," I reply, socking him on the shoulder. "So are you!"

"Ouch!" Matt grabs his shoulder. "Turn off the strength, will you?"

"I didn't...I'm so sorry...I didn't mean to..." But Matt is smiling, a mischievous twinkle in his eye. "Oh! That's *so* bad. This time I will turn it on!" I laugh. A great big all-consuming laugh which medicates the depths of my soul.

"That's better," Matt says, flicking my nose playfully. "But you're right. I've been giving Sawyer a hard time and as we're all in the spirit of reconciliation, I should apologize."

"Good." I reach for the chain at my neck and then remember it isn't there anymore, it fell off my bird neck in my rage through the woods.

"You lost it?"

I nod. "I'm sorry. I don't know where..."

"It's okay."

"It's not okay. That necklace means more to me than—"

Matt kisses me, muting my protests. I lean into him, relishing our renewed closeness. But then a shout pierces the peaceful moment.

"Silver!" The scream is wretched, terrified. Turning to face the voice, I see Elizabeth, Jacob's mother, running through the fields toward me. Her eyes are wide and the tendons on her throat stick out. I'm sure the yellow-eyed monster from my dream is behind her, trailing a path of death, chasing her across the field.

CHAPTER TWENTY-FOUR
SILVER

Elizabeth pumps her arms, her long hair trails behind her and the scream continues to rip out of her mouth. I've never seen her run so fast. "Silver!" Her voice cracks on my name.

Matt and I run to meet her. Panic wells in my chest, but there is nothing behind her. This isn't the yellow eyes.

"It's Paige," she gasps when she reaches us. "The baby's coming. But there's something wrong. There's so much blood."

"Where is she?" I ask.

"At home. There wasn't enough time to get her to the hospital. Please hurry."

"Matt, take her in the car, meet me there."

Teleporting away, I'm outside Paige's front door an instant later. I have no time to collect my thoughts, no time to prepare myself for however bad the situation might be. I push the front door open. On my way up the stairs, I hear another agonizing scream, but this time it's one of pain. Not Paige. Jacob. It turns my blood cold and makes me hesitate.

"No! No! NO!" It's the agonized scream of loss. I've heard it enough times to know it well.

Dashing into the bedroom, I find Jacob sitting in his wheelchair beside Paige. She lies on the bed, pale, motionless, dead, in a puddle of deepening red. Dr Lucas, the camp's obstetrician, stands at the foot of the bed with a gurgling infant in his arms.

"Do something!" Jacob screams.

Blinded by tears, I trip over the carpet and stumble toward the bed. I know I'm too late. Paige isn't Paige. It's just a body, a shell, but I'll try all the same and hope against all hope I can do something.

With my stomach twisting, I kneel beside the bed and rest my golden hands on her head. The little bolts of dancing electricity turn all the colors of the rainbow, a kaleidoscope of goodness. The colors flicker over my palms, over Paige's head and down her body. But they remained on the outside, unable to penetrate her lifeless shell.

"Do something!" Jacob screams again, the color bleached from his skin, his eyes frantic and unfocussed.

Leaving my hand on Paige's head, I will the healing power to stay. With Paige's body cast in the golden glow, I can almost believe she's asleep, that she's lain down for a nap and will arise in a second, refreshed, ready to accept her newborn baby.

"Do something else." Taught tendons rise on Jacob's neck. "Surely there's something else!"

Matt and Elizabeth run into the room. A small crowd

gathers on the street below. No one is talking outside, but I sense their presence and hear their scattered thoughts, their love and hope, not yet knowing it's too late. Matt comes beside me and gently removes my hand from Paige's head.

"No!" Elizabeth yells, her hands gathering the folds of her dress into her fists and twisting them around and around. "*No.*"

Jacob wheels his chair to the window which looks upon the street and stares through a small crack in the curtain, at nothing.

I stay kneeling at Paige's side, but instead of touching her head, I grab her hand and bring it to my lips. "I'm sorry," I cry. The last thing I said to her was a lie. "I'm so sorry."

Matt crumples beside me and he buries his face in my neck, his own tears flowing freely.

The baby cries. Not a loud wail, more of a cheerful, blubbering noise signaling its presence in the world.

"Here." Dr Lucas hands the baby to Elizabeth. "It's a boy." Elizabeth chokes on a sob and the baby reaches out with one, disjointed fist and grabs hold of her long hair, turning her sob into an awkward squeak of joy. I glance at the baby and receive a mental flash of the evil yellow eyes. Shock shudders through me. Why would the baby be thinking about yellow eyes? Do babies think?

"He's so beautiful," Elizabeth says, as she approaches Jacob.

Jacob looks at his son. There is no emotion on his face. There is a brief flicker of indecision and for a second I worry he might turn his back on his son.

"He is. Just like his mother," Jacob whispers, emotion

pooling in his eyes. Reaching for the baby, he holds him close. He kisses his forehead, his nose, and sticks a finger in the palm of the baby's hand, which promptly closes around it. The baby smiles at him. Without warning, a blue light seeps into the room. The baby's skin shines in an unusual blue glow. "Oh," Jacob says, a flash of awe passing over his face. "Oh!" He rises from his wheelchair, able to walk once again.

Jacob rushes with the baby to Paige's side and settles him in the crook of her arm.

"Jacob," I caution.

Paige remains lifeless. The baby continues to chortle, unaware it's lying upon the bosom of his dead mother.

"I thought it was worth a try," Jacob says.

"I'm sorry," Dr Lucas says, splaying his hands.

At Paige's side, with my head resting on her stomach, I clasp her lifeless hand in mine. I stay with her and wish, over and over, that this is all a terrible nightmare, that none of it's true, that I haven't lost my best friend. I cry. My tears are caught by her hair. The warmth leaches out of her too quickly.

Matt and Jacob and the baby remain, for hours it seems, or perhaps it's minutes, until Matt takes my hand and leads me out of the room. Elizabeth places a blanket over Paige's body, and Matt and I steer Jacob down the stairs and into the kitchen.

We sit around the table, mute. I'm afraid to speak. Maybe if I don't say anything, if I don't commit aloud to the fact Paige is dead, then perhaps she won't be. I can pretend it isn't real, at least for the next few hours. I've never wanted anything so desperately. Please?

I need my parents. But my mother remains unreachable and my Dad is still combing the country for the mystical therapist.

Matt gathers four glass tumblers and a bottle of whiskey.

"I didn't realize...I've been so selfish." Jacob breaks the silence and gestures to his now functioning legs. "My son wanted me to walk...and now I can...it's...it's...I don't know what to say."

I squeeze his arm. "We all understand, Jacob."

"I made her last few months miserable. I'm sorry, Paige," he whispers with an upwards glance.

"She knows," I say, as Matt places a shot of whiskey in front of him. "You've got to shake it off. Or the guilt will kill you."

Matt looks at our friend. "It was never about the wheelchair, Jacob. It was about the why. You were punishing yourself. You didn't need to. Your son has shown you how to forgive yourself."

Jacob nods and raises his glass. "Paige's drink." Back in the caves, before we left to kill President Bear, Paige secured a bottle of whisky and passed it around to give us a shot of courage. Now, Jacob brings the glass to his lips. Matt pours for the rest of us.

"His name is Patrick." Jacob strokes the head of his son who sleeps in a baby chair on the table.

Elizabeth enters the kitchen. "Dr Lucas has contacted the medical team. They'll be here soon, to take...Paige away." She slumps into a chair beside me.

I hand her a tumbler of whiskey.

Paige is dead. She is actually dead. My best friend is

dead. She is going to be taken away. I have no words left. I sit in the darkening room, unable to move, unable to express the depth of my misery. The loss echoes hollowly inside my chest. I don't understand. Everything she fought for, and now this.

The four of us sit around the table for hours. The medical team take Paige away and the night ticks on. Matt's parents come and go, change Patrick's diaper and locate a box of formula and some bottles. They replenish the bottle of whisky and plant small bundles of food on the table. All but the whisky remains untouched. Dr Lucas presents us with sedatives, but no one reaches for the small, blue pills. Elizabeth knocks back a couple more shots and excuses herself to bed.

We watch the baby coo and giggle and smile. This is the first day of its life, and yet it is capable of cooing and laughing and smiling. It has power. It healed Jacob. Unsurprisingly, Patrick is a special baby, and with Paige's death, I feel a fierce pang of emotion for this small creature, this tiny human, and I vow to protect him at all costs.

I rest a hand on the baby's head and prepare myself for an onslaught of pain. But there is none. Warmth grows inside me, spreading from my chest and filling my limbs, all the way to my toes and fingers. Reflexively, I smile. Joy fills me, almost quashing my grief. It turns to hope as I realize how special Patrick is.

"You took his powers?" Jacob asks.

I nod.

"What are they?"

"I don't know yet," I say. "But he has more than one."

Matt eases out of his chair and says, "We'll help."

"Anything you need. You won't be raising this baby on your own." I squeeze Jacob's shoulder.

He covers my hand with his own and gently squeezes back. "I know, thanks."

We leave the house as the sun rises, the baby asleep in Jacob's arms. Matt and I return to my house and we climb the stairs to my room. He falls instantly asleep and I cover him with the duvet. I lie with my head propped on a pillow and stare at the ceiling. I am numb. Even though I saw her body, I can't believe Paige is gone. She doesn't feel gone. It feels as though I can walk back over there and she'll answer the door. She'll put the kettle on and we'll drink tea and talk inappropriately about the men in our lives and giggle and hold each other's hands and Patrick will be sleeping in a basket at our feet. Patrick. There *is* Patrick, but no Paige.

I clutch a pillow against the pain in my chest, hoping the softness will ease the tightness. Turning on my side, I close my eyes against the sun. Unexpectedly, sleep comes, but it is not dreamless.

I'm standing outside Earl's mountain. The snow has receded to the tops of the peaks and all around me is granite and earth. Movement shifts around me, hard to train my eye on. I sense the yellow eyes watching me, waiting to make its appearance.

Unseen, it calls to the insects in the mountain. Emerging from the dark tunnel I once ventured down, the creature uncurls and rises to its feet. A thing so black I can't make out its dimensions. Beetles and spiders and cockroaches and centipedes and other such insects click and clatter and scuttle to the hulking dark mass in a sudden rush of needful activity. They climb into it, as though the monster is absorbing their mass, and it grows.

I stare, open-mouthed, at this thing crawling down the mountain. I can't move. I can barely breathe. I've never seen anything like it.

A sea of scurrying rats flows past my ankles to join it, quickly followed by a twisting river of brown mice, a dark cloud of flapping bats, and a slithering mass of black and brown venomous snakes. I'm not bitten, but it's only a question of time.

I hold my knife in one hand, the other comes alive with my dark power. My weapons feel insubstantial against such a great beast. Where are my friends? I can't face this alone.

Larger animals join the growing mass. Wolves, stallions, bears, and mountain lions. They all unite with the creature and became one swarming, slithering, howling, baying entity that's so large in its entirety, it appears as though a black tidal wave has swallowed the mountain.

"*Silver...*" The name dribbles from its salivating lips. Fear prickles my scalp. I can't do this.

"*Silver...*" It repeats my name, like a mantra. Why does it want me? Why can't it leave me alone?

The monster, with its yellow looming eyes. Eyes possessing such fiery depths I'm sure I could fall into them and disappear to the center of the earth. Or perhaps it's a flaming trail leading all the way to the sun. They are eyes of terror, eyes of pain, eyes of murderous intent, and they stare down at me, examine me, and wink.

"*Silver...*" Its rough, gravelly voice spills from a leathery mouth lined with jagged teeth. A black tongue licks those sharp teeth. Licks and licks, absorbing the saliva dripping out of its mouth. My bladder tightens and the stench of darkness fills my nostrils.

From within the black wave of moving beasts and crawling insects, one black hand reaches for me, bringing the reek of wrongness closer. The hand is encrusted in spikes and horns and boils, with claws longer than my arms and sharper than any manmade blade. It stretches out of the wave, closer and closer. The black stallions within the wave neigh and buck. The deafening tornado of insects swirls closer and I lose my footing. Terror strikes deep inside me as the wave blocks out the sun.

The insects climb over each other, their eyes twitching with malicious glee, their wings beating with malevolent eagerness. The wolves and bears and panthers howl and purr and tear at the earth, at each other, all within the black wave. As the wave thunders closer, as those claws slice at me, constantly descending, they become the bars of my own, private prison.

I realize I'm holding the baby. Clutching him to my chest, I duck and roll out of the way. But the animals within the wave continue their single-minded trajectory. Their claws dig into the earth and trap me. The other black hand pries the baby loose from my tight grasp. A blue light shines.

"Silver...."

The mass moves over me, leaving Earl's mountain, to journey east. I can't let them reach Camp Fortitude. But I'm powerless to stop it.

I erupt from the dream and stifle the scream in my throat.

Panting, I touch Matt's shoulder. He's still asleep, but I shake him awake.

"What is it?" He is immediately alert.

"I had a dream."

He rubs his eyes and shuffles closer. "What happened?"

"The mountain..." I start, but I don't now how to describe the horror of the images in my mind.

"We left the mountain..." Matt rubs his temples. It's not fair to put this on him. On any of them. I haven't dreamed about the yellow eyes for over three weeks. Half of me thought the threat had disappeared. But now I know it's real. People need to know. We need to prepare. I think we still have time. "What happened in the dream, Silver?"

"It's the yellow eyes. The black wave of animals. It's coming, Matt. It's really coming. Adam's had a similar dream—"

"Adam too?" Matt winces. "Why didn't you tell me?"

I twist the covers in my hands. "I didn't want to believe it was real. I wasn't ready...it was too big...I'm not powerful enough."

"Shhh." He pulls me into his arms. "It's okay."

"It's not okay. I've put everyone in danger." This will be our biggest fight. I know that. It's why I've been avoiding it. The loss will be great. We won't all make it. Hell, I'm not sure anyone is going to make it.

Matt holds me. "This is my fault. I told you it was PTSD. I told you not to worry about this. *Shit*." He rakes a hand through his hair.

"This is not your fault," I say. "Neither of us wanted to

believe there could be another threat. We wanted to be happy."

He cups my cheek, kisses me. "What do we do?"

"I don't know yet." I feel surprisingly calm. Now I've admitted the threat is real, I can face it. It's trying to push it away that's been eating away at me. "But it wants the baby. Patrick is in danger."

"Why Patrick?"

"He has a lot of power."

Matt tugs the end of my hair. "So do you."

"I don't know if it's enough."

"This isn't all on you. You aren't the only one with power."

I smile at him. Why haven't I learned this yet? We are a team, we will fight this together.

"We have to tell Jacob," Matt stands. His eyes are bloodshot, his clothing rumpled and stubble lines his jaw. "And we'll have to prepare."

"I'm not sure there's anything we can do to prepare." I am scared. Bear and Earl were men. Sociopaths, altereds, but somewhat human. This thing with the yellow eyes is something else entirely. I don't know what it is, let alone how to fight it.

CHAPTER TWENTY-FIVE

ELI

Swiping at his cheek, Eli opens his eyes. Weak, gray light assaults his vision. It takes him a few seconds to figure out where he is. *Not* in his bed where he fell asleep with Delta nestled beside him. He's somewhere else entirely, somewhere wet and cold and squelchy. The smell of damp earth overwhelms his nostrils.

Something stabs at his cheek. Eli raises his hand and grabs a fistful of squirming fur. A rat. A large, brown rat took a chunk out of his cheek. Eli throws the rat in the air and explodes it with his mind on its downward arc. He raises his fingers to his cheek to staunch the oozing blood.

Sitting, Eli squints in the dawn light and surveys his surroundings. He's in an unplowed field beyond his cabin. It must have rained in the night because the mud he sits in is wet and seeping into his trousers. His bare torso is streaked with it. With the unnerving feeling he isn't alone, Eli glances at the overcast sky. Empty.

This isn't the first time he's woken in a strange place. He's been teleporting in his sleep. The yellow eyes have shown him all sorts of places. It has taken him a while to admit his dreams aren't merely dreams. They can't be. They're too real. How else does he explain the smell of the ocean and the damp, salt encrusted clothes after he's had the dream about the yacht? Or the sand in his shoes and the sunburn on his shoulders after the dream in the desert?

But who do the yellow eyes belong to?

"All in good time."

He senses he'll be meeting the creature behind the fiery yellow eyes soon enough.

Rising to his feet, Eli cleans his chest with his mind powers. He wanders away from the field as a light drizzle begins to fall and finds himself on the path to the abandoned farmhouse. *His* farmhouse, as he now thinks of it. Silver doesn't visit him anymore. In fact, he hasn't spoken to her since her return from the woods. She's been too busy grieving over her friend to pay him any attention. Which is okay, he doesn't need her anymore either; he has enough power of his own.

"You will take her power from her, once and for all."

Eli smiles.

The yellow eyes smile. They are good to him.

"Are you ready for the pain to go away?"

"Yes."

"Are you ready to leave Earl behind?"

"Yes."

"Are you ready to belong?"

"Yes."

Eli's attempt to belong at Camp Fortitude has backfired.

Delta is the only one who spends time with him, which might have been enough, if the others didn't call emergency meetings and look at him like he really is Earl's son.

He's ready to belong. He's ready for something else.

Eli turns the corner of his farmhouse and enters the yard. He walks to a particularly grassy patch and settles himself on the damp, wild lawn. Sitting with his elbows resting on his knees, he contemplates his next move. The wild urges within have become impossible to contain. There is so much power.

"It can all be yours. Ours. Together. You will never have to think of Earl again."

So. Much. Power. He grins.

A drizzle falls on his shoulders and washes away the blood from his cheek. He's too tired from his night-time antics to divert the rain to a different path. A black rabbit scampers across the yard. It stops a few feet before him. It's nose twitches, detecting his sent, and it freezes.

"Be afraid, little rabbit, be afraid."

Without moving a muscle, Eli raises the rabbit in the air. It tries to twist out of his mental leash, so he clamps harder. It freezes again. Eli sends a fireball from his mind on a flaming trajectory to the rabbit's brain. The fireball engulfs the rabbit and burns it in an instant, not to a crisp, but nicely enough to enjoy the succulent flesh. He chuckles as he brings the rabbit closer and tears chunks of meat from its roasted body. It's a shame he doesn't have a salt and pepper ability to season it with. Feasting, the juices run past his lips, down his chin, and drip onto his chest.

Behind him, a twig snaps. Eli takes another bite of the juicy flesh before he turns. There's no one there. He thinks to look up. Erica hovers in the air, the expression on her face changing far too quickly for him to guess what she might be feeling or thinking. But she is feeling and thinking something, her wings say it all; they are a virulent orange. Such an unbecoming color.

"I knew it!" She exclaims.

"Well, hello there, Erica, won't you join me for a nice tender piece of roasted rabbit?" Eli pats the ground next to him, noting the bow in her hand and the quiver of arrows strapped to her shoulder.

Erica remains in the air, her lavender hair flying ethereally around her face as her shimmering wings flap. *Flap, flap, flap,* faster and faster, as though she's about to be shot into the sky from a cannon. Perhaps he could arrange that.

Cyan, fuchsia, cyan, fuchsia, the most absurd, repulsive colors for wings, unless you're a parrot. *Flap, flap, flap,* the wings go, fighting against the increasing rain. *Flap, flap, flap.*

Stumbling in the air, she shakes off the raindrops waterlogging her chitinous membranes. Pretty soon she won't be able to use the wings at all. The colors change more rapidly. Eli is aware the colors represent her emotions. Cyan and fuchsia must be fear. He can smell it.

"It really is ever so good," Eli coaxes. "You know, I used to go hunting with my father and my brother, back home, in the Oregon woods. It's been a long time. I miss it. It feels good to be doing the familiar once again, even if the methods are a little different—"

"Father? Brother?" She frowns and her pupils narrow. "I thought you grew up here? I mean, in Central City, with your mom...Earl...Who *are* you?"

Oops. Looks like the secret is out of the bag. Earl isn't his father, but he is a family member.

"I saw you," Erica says, pushing her shoulder back as if she's squaring up for a battle. "Whoever you are. I saw you." *Flap, flap, flap.* Stumble. She releases an arrow from her quiver. Eli isn't afraid of Erica's arrows, no matter how good a shot she claims to be.

"But to be out in the woods, in the weather, just us men...it was exhilarating. The thrill of the kill. I remember bringing down a stag. I had that over my brother at least. I remember lining up the sights, right between the eyes. One moment it was sniffing the air, the next it was on the ground. We ate venison stew for weeks. Ah, the good times." It's the first piece of truth he's spoken for some time.

Erica raises her voice. "I saw you!"

Eli cranes his neck to look at her. "You really want to have this conversation? It might be better for you if we don't."

As Erica fights for her position in the air under the pressure of the pouring rain, Eli places another sliver of meat into his mouth.

"I saw you use powers," Erica says, nocking the arrow. Her ridiculous Stetson falls off her head. "How is that possible? *Who* are you? Who is your father? Who is your brother?"

"Please, one question at a time." Rising, Eli chucks the rabbit bones on the ground and incinerates them with a mental fireball. The flames sizzle under the rain. Erica gasps. "Which one is it you would like me to answer first?" Erica is a bit like the rabbit. But he'll enjoy toying with her first.

With the rain pummeling her wings, she lands on the ground. "You have powers."

It sounds like an accusation. It's beginning to grate a little. "Yes, you said that."

"Explain yourself," Erica says, and has the gall to aim at him.

"No," he replies. "No, I don't think I'll do that." With one flick of his wrist he mentally breaks Erica's neck. The arrow goes wide and buries itself in the farmhouse behind him, not far from where Einstein impacted. Her bow clatters to the ground, bounces once, rolls on its arc twice before finally becoming still. Eli releases his mental grip from Erica's throat and lets her fall to the ground too. With her death, he feels a surge of power. So this is how it's done. This is what the yellow eyes want.

"Get rid of the evidence."

As he raises another fireball, a strangled noise snaps his attention to his rear. He pivots on his heel. Delta stands there in the rain, bare-footed, wearing one of his white shirts. My, isn't she beautiful in her bed-headed disheveled state? Her hands fly to her mouth, tears run down her cheeks, mixing with the rain, and then she doubles over. She rocks herself on her haunches like a little girl who's realized the boogie man is real.

"Now, now," Eli says, striding toward her.

"Oh my God, oh my God..." Eli can barely make out her repetitive whispers.

"There is no God. Only us."

"Only us."

Delta pauses in her childish mutterings and aims a hand in his direction. Tension coils inside Eli's body, as though he's a snake needing to shed an old skin.

"*Stop her!*"

The pressure of Delta's power threatens to burst his ear drums. Goodness. He can't have any of that. Eli shakes himself and the tightness and discomforting pressure fades. He straightens his shoulders and marches toward the cowering girl.

"Why did you have to go and do that?" He towers over her.

"I'm sorry," she cries, her arms over her head.

"*Finish her.*"

Eli stares at this beautiful girl. He shared a bed with her. He's kissed those waiting lips. He's buried his head into the warmth of her skin. He cares for her deeply. But he can't leave a trail of witnesses behind.

"I'm sorry, Delta. Truly, I am." He grabs her throat in a mental grip and strangles the life out of her too. He flings her body next to Erica's. What a waste. What a shame it all has to end.

He'll have to move the bodies. Events are moving forward swiftly and he needs time to prepare.

"*It's almost time.*"

"For what?"

The yellow eyes fall silent.

With his mind, Eli gathers Delta, Erica and her bow and arrows, and hoists them far above his head where they will remain unobserved by the workers entering the fields. He walks them to the woods and arranges their bodies under a tree. Perhaps it will be assumed they stumbled upon a surprise enemy and died in a deadly battle.

He adds a few artistic, post-mortem injuries for good

measure. Or maybe it'll be concluded they fell out of the tree. He looks at Erica's wings, a pale pearlescent in death, with a clouding of gray at the edges. Perhaps not. But it's of no concern to him anymore. They're out of his backyard, so to speak, and the others can assume whatever they like about the circumstances of their death as long as the theories don't involve him. As the rain slows, Eli retraces his steps out of the woods.

Feeling the need to freshen up, Eli brushes a finger over his chest and collects the dried-on residue of the roasted rabbit. He sticks his finger in his mouth and savors the flavors of meat and sweat. It won't do to smell of fire and burned flesh when he appears at the fields. People think he's odd enough already. What would they do if they found out who he really is?

CHAPTER TWENTY-SIX

SILVER

It's been two days since Paige's death and twenty-four hours since the bodies of Erica and Delta were discovered, in the woods, mutilated as though savaged by a wild animal. Adam found them. He had a cryptic dream about their deaths and the location of their bodies. Without his information they probably wouldn't have been discovered.

Three deaths within our ranks in such a short space of time. Delta and Erica's deaths aren't as benign as they look. Somehow, the creature with the yellow eyes is responsible.

We gather in Francesca's house for an emergency meeting. Guards are stationed at the front and back doors. Claus sits on an armchair, his cane by his feet and a walkie talkie crackling at his hip. Mason and Carter keep their bulk power turned on. Francesca stands in front of a disused fireplace, her face drawn and her hands trembling. I've never seen her look scared.

Outside, the sun is high, the air hot, incongruous to an advancing threat. The windows are closed to keep our meeting private and the room quickly builds with a suffocating heat. My friends look at me with bleary eyes and shocked faces.

"We need to do something, *now!*" Jacob's muscles flex. In his arms, the baby cries. Breathing deeply, Jacob calms himself, cradling the gurgling Patrick closer to his chest. Kissing his perfect head, he sniffs his baby smell before handing him to Koko.

"The problem is, we don't know what to do," Matt says wearily. He sits on one of the dining chairs brought into the room for extra seating. He and Claus are the only two seated. Dipping his chin onto cupped hands, he blows a lock of hair out of his face. He's tired. We're all tired. We've been awake for twenty-four hours, ever since the bodies were discovered.

"Whatever killed them, whatever hurt Paige..." Jacob punches one fist into the palm of the other.

"The two are unrelated," Mason says gently. "Paige died of a hemorrhage." He puts a hand on Jacob's shoulder. "Erica and Delta were killed, violently."

Jacob's eyes narrow. "All the same, something's out there, and I'm ready for it."

Since the birth of his son and the miraculous healing of his paralysis, Jacob has rediscovered his old fire. He even asked for his modifications back, which I gave him, knowing what we have to face. Perhaps needing distraction from grief, he's thrown himself into action. Since Patrick's miracle two days ago, the baby hasn't shown any more signs of power.

"We know you are," Francesca says. "And it's appreciated. But before we do anything, we have to determine if there even is a threat."

"There's a threat," I say.

The president looks at me and the doubt disappears from her eyes. She nods, resigned, and smooths her rumpled clothing. "Let's get to it then."

The stuffy air closes around us. Adam sits in a corner, hugged between two walls. Slowly he rises and raises his hand.

"What is it, Adam?" I ask.

"I had a dream last night." He hangs his head. "It wasn't soon enough to help. But I know who killed them."

The atmosphere in the room turns suffocating, but Carter doesn't wait a beat. "Out with it."

"It was Eli," Adam replies.

My stomach churns. Everyone starts talking at once. Why would Eli hurt Delta and Erica? He was in a relationship with Delta. I don't understand.

"He needs to be stopped," Francesca says.

I raise a hand. "Wait." Everyone looks at me. A trickle of sweat wiggles down my spine. My friends are equally hot and weary.

"We know visions are subject to change, they aren't always reliable. Let's take a moment. I haven't had this dream."

Mason clears his throat. "With all due respect, Silver, this is the first time Adam's had a dream about a past event. It's like the dream is filling in the facts we need to move forward. Like more is coming, and we need this knowledge now."

Adam nods along with his words. "That's how it feels."

The walls start closing in around me. Eli and I still

haven't cleared the air. I don't know what that conversation will look like now. If he killed my friends...

"Eli is dangerous," Carter says. His strong bulk shoulders rise above us, offering an image of power. The black wave is stronger than him, stronger than all of us, but I'm grateful for the illusion of strength he presents.

"Whether Adam's dreams are true or not," Francesca says. "We still have a law in this country. No man or woman is condemned without a trial. We will follow the process—"

"But what if he has powers?" Lyla interrupts.

"We will proceed with caution," Francesca says. "I understand there is a threat coming. But we don't want to be caught panicking."

Claus clears his throat. "I think Silver has more information for us."

He knows me so well. He can read my face and emotions. He knows I have something to tell them. My dreams. With the discovery of Erica and Delta's bodies, Matt and I haven't had a chance to tell Francesca about my dreams, the yellow eyes. I can't delay anymore.

Everyone looks at me.

Matt and Adam give me nods of reassurance. Now is the time to reveal what I know. Eli and I share visions of the yellow eyes. I don't know what that means. It's a revelation which will rock everyone.

"I've been having dreams."

A thick silence stifles the heat in the room.

"Which is why Matt introduced you to Deja," Lyla says. "Why you've not been sleeping. Honestly, Silver, it's a wonder you aren't dreaming." She's clinging to the impossible.

"And Adam," Matt says. Several people gasp. Lyla clamps a hand over her mouth. "They've both been having dreams. The content is a little different, but they both involve a monster with yellow eyes."

"Fuck me!" Sawyer kicks a chair.

Blank eyes stare into the middle distance. Mason's shoulders sag as though defeated already. Elizabeth stops fanning the V of her dress and chews on a fingernail instead. Carter lowers himself to a chair.

Collecting myself, I glance at Francesca. I never realized how much I relied on her unflappable stoicism before now. She is pale, but determined, and gestures for me to carry on.

Carter nods at me. "Let's hear it."

"I was hoping it was nothing," I say. "I was hoping I wouldn't have to tell you at all. I wasn't sure there *was* a threat, not until Patrick was born."

"Explain faster," Lyla whispers.

"It's kind of like Patrick is this pure, albeit incredibly powerful, innocent being, and the yellow-eyed monster is his opposite. The monster wants Patrick. And it wants me." Despite having vanquished anxiety from my DNA, panic threatens. A monster is a monster. There is nothing I can take out of my DNA that will make me unafraid of the yellow eyes. "There will be a reckoning."

Mouths hang open. Disbelief settles in everyone's eyes. Adam, hunched at Matt's side, nods his agreement. Jacob draws Patrick close to his chest.

"Why are you only telling us this now?" Lyla asks, her

voice pitching. "You've been dreaming about yellow eyes. The same goddamn eyes Eli is talking about. What the hell does it mean?"

I raise a hand. "I didn't tell you because I didn't think it was real. It made no sense. It was an impossible vision. Then I was in denial. We've been through so much. I was tired of anticipating danger in every dream, trying to interpret every possible threat."

"And now?" Francesca asks.

I look at Claus for reassurance. He twiddles his mustache, thoughtful. He is the only one in the room who doesn't look terrified. He stares back at me and a small measure of confidence finds its way into me.

"I have no words of comfort to offer. I don't know how this monster came to be. All I can tell you is it comes from Earl's mountain. Something he did there created it. I don't know what its powers are or how strong it is. But it is strong, unbelievably so. And it's coming. Soon."

Despair hangs over the group like a heavy raincloud. They digest the information in numb disbelief, or perhaps it's acceptance of the already damned. We've been down this road before, of course we'll have to fight again. It's unlikely our world will ever be simple and carefree again. That was a pipe dream. So much for rainbows and unicorns.

An image of Earl as I last saw him comes to mind. I was the last to see him alive, I killed him. He made himself into the image of the Devil. Who better to portray an image of invincible, dark power? He was all red, reptilian skin and swishing tail, horns on his head and pustules covering his body. He reeked of death. In my dreams, I imagine him sinking sharp fangs into live human flesh and chortling when the screams reach his ears. Then he bathes himself in human blood like he's enacting a sadistic ritual.

I've lost three friends in a week. And we aren't even at war. More of us survived the battle with Earl and his altereds.

Francesca searches my face. "How accurate are your dreams?"

"They're open to interpretation. They can change as we make decisions. It's hard to say," I reply. "But I'm certain about this. It's been the same dream for weeks now. Nothing has changed."

Francesca's lips tighten. "We'd be foolish not to heed your dreams."

Claus gets to his feet. "We need a few action plans. Until we get more clarity on Silver and Adam's dreams, we stay together, in groups. No one goes anywhere alone until we understand the scope of the threat."

Francesca nods her approval. "Let's add a curfew too. No going out after dark. We'll tell the rest of the population there is a wild animal about. There's no point causing a panic until we have more information."

"And someone needs to have a little chat with Eli." Sawyer says, placing his glass back on the table harder than necessary.

"I hate to suggest it." Matt cuts a glance in my direction. "But Silver might be in the best position to do that. If he does have powers, then she can defend herself."

"Okay," I reply, though my stomach roils at the thought. I haven't spoken to Eli since my return from the woods. I've been hoping to avoid him altogether. Now, I don't have a choice.

The baby chooses that moment to wake and release an enormous burp. The group laughs and bends toward the baby to admire him, pat him on the head, or offer an encouraging word.

When I glance at Patrick, he locks eyes with me longer than a baby should be capable of. He smiles and a shimmering blue light radiates from his skin. The entire room is cast in a pale blue light. It gives me an idea.

I pull Matt to a quiet corner. I'm not going to do it alone this time. "Matt, I need your help with something."

He nods, and we slip out of the room and walk back to my house. Walking into the backyard and through the garden gate which leads to rolling fields, he doesn't ask any questions until I stop by a small thicket of trees. I turn to face him.

"I'm feeling oddly nervous," he says.

I smile, trying to reassure him. "I need your help."

He frowns. "You know I'd help you with anything, but did you have to drag me out here to ask?"

"I thought we'd be safe here, away from everyone else."

His frown deepens and he chucks a glance over his shoulder as if the yellow eyes might have already arrived. "Safe?"

I finger the hem of my shirt, suddenly shy, but knowing I need to do this. "There's still a lot of abilities inside me I haven't unearthed. I touched Patrick, and I have the sense he has many, many powers."

"But Paige and Jacob's abilities aren't that complicated..."

I chuckle. "It all started with genetics, but we've moved far beyond that now."

He tilts his head. "What did you have in mind?"

I pluck a leaf from a branch and shred it along its central vein. "When we were on the mission to defeat Earl, you helped me to get control of my black lightning power."

"Until I couldn't anymore." His chin dips.

"All the same, I needed you and you were there."

"I have a feeling I know what you're about to ask."

I muster a smile. "I still have a great number of powers inside me. There might be something which can beat the yellow eyes. But I don't know what it is yet. I need your help to find it."

His hands float to his hips as he mulls over my words.

"I don't want to do this alone anymore. I don't want to do it without you."

He hangs his head and rubs at the back of his neck. My chest lurches as I wait for his response.

"Of course I'll help you, Silver." His soft tone surrounds me with love. "We need you and your powers. We need everyone for this fight. Of course I'll help you."

I hug him and press my face into his shoulder. I resist the urge to cry, and instead kiss his neck, then his lips, whispering my thanks.

He adopts a battle stance and strokes his chin. "Did you have anything in particular in mind?"

"I'm not sure yet. I want to see if I can tap into what the baby gave me."

Matt puts his hands on my waist and swivels me away from the glare of the sun. He pushes my hunched shoulders down. With his voice in my ear, he says, "Remember what your dad always taught you. Deep breaths, in and out."

I push away the threat of the yellow eyes. The death of my best friend. Instead, I concentrate on the moment I'm in. The feel of Matt's touch. The strength of the sun on the back of my neck and the caress of the breeze as it trickles across my face. Powers bubble under the surface. I recognize most of them, can identify the familiar ones surging to the surface. But I push all the known ones away and wait. I breathe and I wait and I feel Matt touching me.

My mind fills with the color blue. This is new and I know I have stumbled across the right power. I push and pull at it, tug and yank. It is flexible, like an elastic band, and unwilling to listen to harsh commands. I relax again and tease it gently until it yields to my will. I'm unsure how to use this power, whatever it is, but sense a circular boundary to it. I poke at it in my mind and it wobbles. It reminds me of an old childhood toy I used to bounce around on in the apartment, a space hopper.

"Anything?" Matt whispers.

"I'm not sure."

After another half hour of prodding the blue ball in my mind, I sigh and lean against Matt. Although I can't discern any difference in the landscape or in an ability I may have used, I'm thoroughly exhausted. It's like the wariness of maxing out my powers when I first got them. I haven't felt that way in months, and now I can barely keep my eyes open. My limbs shake and my eyelids flutter.

He kisses my cheek. "Don't worry, we'll get there."

"But will we get there soon enough?" I mutter, sagging against him.

Suddenly a piercing scream shatters the humid air around us. Elizabeth is running from my garden, arms pumping, screaming my name.

"Silver!"

I pivot to face her. She collapses her hands to her knees and pants for breath. "You have to come quickly. Now, it's Paige. She needs you."

I frown and gently touch her hand, wondering if in her grief she forgot what happened. "Elizabeth. Paige is—"

"Having the baby and there is so much blood! You need to hurry, Silver!" She grabs my hands.

I look at Matt. His eyes are wide and uncomprehending. "Go," he says. "*Go*."

I teleport to Paige's house to find her in her bed, bleeding all over the place, already dead, just like before. Jacob is yelling. Matt and Elizabeth come in behind me. It happens again. Like before. What the hell is going on?

I try to heal her again, but of course nothing happens. Jacob cries. The baby snuffles. I brace myself against the pain of loss.

As Jacob is healed for a second time, I drag Matt out of the room and into the hall. "What the hell?"

His face is pale, the blood vessels on his skin visibly blue. His hands shake. "I don't know. But I think you may have reset time, or something."

"That's impossible." It is impossible. But didn't I just tell him everything had evolved beyond mere genetics? That the yellow eyes and the baby's abilities were something else entirely? But time...travel...how could that be possible? "And what's the point of resetting time if I can't save my best friend?"

"Do it again," Matt says. "Try it again."

My eyes fly wide as I contemplate all the things I could go back and change. I push Jacob's screams to the back of my mind and try to focus on the color blue. I search for it in my mind, but it won't come back, I can't even see it anymore. No! This isn't fair. How dare I lose my best friend twice.

I push and pull and yank and tug until I pant for air and my knees buckle. Matt holds me, telling me to stop, but I can't. I have to save my best friend.

Blood trickles from my nose and I feel the warmth of it in my ears. My chest tightens and it's almost like I'm having a panic attack. But there's pain. Everywhere. A pressure on my lungs, a vice around my limbs. But I don't stop pushing, I can't.

"Silver, stop it, you're hurting yourself." Matt holds me tight, pinning my arms, refusing to let me stand and try again. I collapse against him, barely able to draw breath let alone summon the energy to heal myself.

The world goes dark, and when I wake I'm tucked in my bed. Paige is dead. Erica is dead. Delta is dead. Everything is bad.

Matt is there and he holds me as I cry. "I have to try again."

"No, Silver." He holds my hands, pressing his thumbs into my palms. "You've been unconscious for three days. You almost killed yourself trying."

CHAPTER TWENTY-SEVEN

ELI

THE SCRABBLING fingers scurry around his brain faster than a hamster in a wheel. Eli laughs as the power surges through him. Something connects in his mind. A telepathy unlike any other. He no longer hears the yellow eyes as a voice in his head. The connection is seamless, the images presented vivid and true.

The yellow eyes show him Earl's mountain. There is a black wave. Almost as high as the mountain. Wider than a valley. Thicker than an entire forest of Redwoods. Inside the wave, insects scuttle, mammals bay and whine. Glowing eyes wink.

The wave moves. Away from the mountain.

Eli smiles.

The wave of beasts consumes every living thing in its path, or it kills and leaves carcasses behind. There is no behind anymore. The country stretching out in their wake is a clean slate. Mere soil and rock and fire and ash. That is all.

A hellhound growls, then attacks a wide-eyed stallion.

Snarling dogs compete for alpha position. Pumas stalk prey at the base of the wave. The wave is full of life and energy.

Earl's mountain is no longer. Silver destroyed the lab already, but now there isn't even a peak. Just granite and dust and bones. A new beginning.

In his vision, Eli takes a step closer to the advancing wave. He touches the wall of blackness. Then he understands. His destiny unfolds. Energy. It's all about energy. It can never be destroyed, but when life is altered, when fire burns, energy transforms. After all, that's how he came into existence.

Eli's pain vanishes. All the resentment he harbored. All his dreams and aspirations alter instantly. The wave welcomes his touch and the yellow eyes look on approvingly.

CHAPTER TWENTY-EIGHT
SILVER

I DON'T KNOW whether this weird time power came from the baby or somewhere else. I guess it doesn't matter. Matt won't let me practice it again, and he's right. It almost killed me. Took a long time to recover. I wasn't able to use a single ability for three days. I can't afford to be unprepared when the yellow eyes come. And if it is the baby's power? He's too young to know what to do with it.

Outside my house a storm begins. The first clap of thunder erupts above my head and sends my heart beating double time. The flashes of lightning follow, like clawed hands of a withered, old man. The violent streaks are nothing like the sparks of my powers but illuminate strange shapes in the shadows. Leaning against the door, I catch my breath and listen for unusual sounds hidden beneath the drumming rain. Now that I'm recovered, I'm trying to gather the courage to talk to Eli, to find out what he knows, who he really is, but can't bring myself to go to the farmhouse. If the worst is confirmed about him...

The lights flicker, once, twice and then go out. Feeling oddly shaken, I remain in the partial darkness. I've never liked storms. The thunder reminds me of my irregular heartbeat during a panic attack.

"It's just a storm," Matt says.

"Is it?" A sense of foreboding ripples down my spine.

Matt goes to the closet and fiddles with the fuse box. The lights come back on and chase the unwanted shadows into the corners.

A streak of lightning hits the roof of the empty house opposite ours. The house ignites and a section of the roof caves in. But the fire is quickly doused as it loses its fight against the driving rain.

Matt glances at the ceiling as though fearful our roof will cave in too. Watching the storm, I wonder when the yellow-eyed monster will make itself known. The storm is the perfect cover for an attack.

"I'm better now," I say. "I should talk to Eli."

Matt looks at the ceiling. "I don't want you out there in this storm."

"We've wasted enough time already."

He takes my hand. His touch is clammy. "Wait until morning. Please."

He jumps at the next flash of lightning. I've never seen Matt this scared before.

"Are you okay?" I ask.

He sets his weary eyes on mine. "I..." he shakes his head. "I...I don't know."

Usually it's me who falls apart, who has a panic attack at the worst possible time. I'm not without fear, but I want to get on with it, get passed it, kill whatever needs to be killed.

I kiss Matt and he wraps himself around me. The kiss is deep and hungry and filled with longing. His hands roam my body. He takes his time, caressing me, kissing me, until desire burns inside. I need him closer. Skin on skin.

A loud banging draws my attention away. Someone pounds on the front door. We find a soaked Francesca and Koko standing on the porch.

"She's here. The therapist from the north. Your father has returned with Asatira," Koko announces with a smile on her face in spite of her drenched appearance.

"They're going to meet us at the hospital. We're here to take you there," Francesca says.

My open top jeep will be useless in this weather and I can't teleport all of them. Clamping down on the hope in my heart, I climb into Francesca's bullet-proof 4x4. Koko slides into the driver's seat and battles with the elements.

"Have you managed to talk to Eli?" Francesca asks.

"Silver has been unwell," Matt says,

Francesca turns in her seat to look at me.

"It's a long story," I say, waving off her concern. "Didn't have powers for a while. I've been waiting for them to come back. I was going to find Eli in the morning, after the storm."

Francesca glances out her window as a flash of lightning illuminates the empty road. "Let's heal Margaret first, then we'll pick him up."

At the mention of the word 'heal' the clamp around my heart breaks. Nervous tension jitters through my veins. This is it, the last card to be played. Crossing the fingers on both hands, I mumble a continuous prayer.

If my mother wakes, I can hug her again. She can hug me. Then maybe she'll be able to answer our questions. When I rescued her from the mountain, she spoke to me briefly. Then she took one look at Eli and retreated back into herself. She must know something about him.

Koko picks her way along the deserted streets, tires spraying water higher than the roof of the car. With every flash of lightning and shriek of wind the apocalyptic world beyond the car exposes itself. The water level rises until the roads becomes rivers and the tires struggle to grip the tarmac.

"We're here." Koko pulls into the hospital's undercover parking garage. At least we're safe from the elements for the time being.

The four of us make our way into the shelter of the hospital. Doctors and nurses rush around the hallways, oblivious to the storm outside. Lights flicker as backup generators kick into life.

I spot my father first. He is wet and crumpled and looks five years older. I run into his open arms. "Thank God you're home."

He holds me tight. "I missed you so much."

I take a step back, examining his face for signs of wear and tear. "Are you okay?"

He nods, patting his chest. "The old ticker's got life in it still."

"So much has happened. There's so much to tell you." I press my palm to my own heart.

"All in good time."

"We may not have much of that."

Dad glances at the dark windows. "We have tonight. Let's see what we can do about your mom."

"Here she is." Koko pulls my attention away from my father. She gestures to a short, round lady with black skin and a kind smile. The lady's smile radiates enough light to illuminate the earth for a thousand years. Asatira. *Please help.*

"Koko, how lovely to see you," Asatira says, in a voice an octave higher than it should be.

Introductions are made and when Asatira shakes my hand she clasps it in both of hers and won't let go. She pulls me close until our noses are almost touching and peers into my face. It's impossible to look away. She examines me for what feels like a full minute before she releases my hand and claps hers together decisively. "Just like your father. And so it will be done, Silver. Let's get to work."

She doesn't have any powers. From everything Dad and Koko told me about her, I expected her to. Although she used to be a psychologist in the time before, I figured the rumors around her mystical abilities had something to do with a genetic ability. But I'm wrong. I experienced no pain when I touched her. Whatever power she possesses is natural. Innate.

Matt, Dad and I follow Asatira into my mother's hospital room and wait for instructions. I hold onto Dad's wet sleeve, like a little girl. I can't let him go.

My mother is sleeping. Her eyelids flicker in a dream. Asatira presses the electronic button on the bed and cranks my mother into a sitting position. Mom opens her eyes and stares at the wall. Asatira approaches the side of the bed and places a hand on either side of my mother's head. I squeeze my eyes shut. My heart hammers against my ribs. Dad's faulty heart pounds too and I whisper at him to breathe.

This is the moment. This is the moment when my mother will either be returned to me or she won't.

"Oh, I see," Asatira says cryptically and then remains silent for a further five minutes.

I squeeze Dad's arm, chew on my lip, and tap my foot on the ground. My wet boots squeak against the Lino.

Abruptly, my mother's body jolts upright and she clasps both of Asatira's hands. "Energy can never be created or destroyed, only transferred. Beware of his brother, the brother who is connected to the yellow eyes."

"Mom!" I launch myself at her. But she flops back onto the bed, her head lolling to the side, and appears to fall asleep.

"She's gone again." Asatira removes her hands and looks at the three of us. "What did that mean?"

Dad sighs and slips into a plastic chair. "I have no idea."

"I was hoping you would tell me," I say. "Will she come back?"

"Not yet," Asatira replies.

"Energy can only ever be transferred," Matt says. "It's one of the basic laws of physics. Like when the chemical energy of a stick of dynamite is transferred to kinetic energy during the explosion."

"Why would my mother be citing laws of physics?" I ask,

wondering if it's got anything to do with resetting time. "She's not a physicist, she's a geneticist."

"I have no idea." Matt turns to Asatira. "Is she cured?"

"No, not yet." Asatira's face darkens. "She won't come out until she feels it's safe. It's a self-induced state. One she feels is necessary to protect herself."

"I don't know who's she talking about," I say. This isn't helpful. I look at Dad who rests one hand over his forehead. He's traveled for weeks, for this. I'm desperate to make sense of her words, but they are meaningless. "What brother are we supposed to fear?"

"Earl had a brother," Dad says. "But he's been long dead. They were twins. Died in the ocean when he was seventeen. What was his name...? Earl only mentioned him once, when we were in college." He frowns, then slaps his thigh. "Eli, that's it!"

My world spins and my knees threaten to buckle.

"I don't understand," Matt says, his voice trembling. "How is that even possible?"

Dad looks between our tense faces. "What's going on?"

"Eli," I whisper. "He's here. You didn't meet him before you left. He stayed a few weeks with Koko and by the time he arrived you'd gone looking for Asatira. But he's my age, a little older maybe...I don't understand."

"Energy can never be created or destroyed, only transferred," Asatira says with a wise smile. "I assume when Earl died his energy was transferred to Eli, who returned from the dead."

Matt laughs, a hollow sound. "That's not possible."

Asatira raises an indignant eyebrow. "Oh, I assure you, it is."

"Earl was a scientist, for fuck's sake, not a medium," Matt says. "Ghosts don't come back to life. Ghosts don't exist."

"And time travel shouldn't be possible either," I say to Matt, then look at Dad. "Does this make sense to you?"

Dad shrugs. "I may have been the lead geneticist in the country for a while, but I'm humble enough to admit I don't know everything. I don't know about the existence of God. I don't know about *this*. I suggest we stop concerning ourselves with the hows, and accept it's here. We need to find Eli."

I curse myself for not approaching him earlier. My hand flies for the pendant and grasping empty air, settles on my throat.

"I don't...this can't be..." Shaking his head, Matt looks at me blankly. He likes clear cut black and white data. He doesn't give much credence to the mystical or unexplained. "I don't get it. Is Eli Earl? Is Earl in Eli? What the hell is going on?"

Dad takes a breath. "My guess is when Earl tampered with his genetics, he did it so often he became something else. He released something. An energy. A force. I don't know what to call it. But it brought Eli back, and we don't know who Eli is."

"Released more than one something," I mutter. "He created the yellow eyes." I feel the truth of it. When I searched the mountain for the source of the whispering voice, I thought I'd exterminated it when I destroyed all the genetic monstrosities in the lab. But it continued to call to me, continued to affect my visions. Whatever Earl did changed the boundaries of life and death, good and evil, Heaven and earth.

"But he said he was a hostage," Matt says. "You rescued him from the mountain."

"It was lies," I reply. "All lies. He was never a hostage, never experimented on. He merely stepped into Earl's shoes, and probably took all his powers too."

I'll have to fight the devil again.

"We need to get Eli." Matt's eyes narrow. "Now."

Dad moves to sit next to Mom. He plucks her hand from her lap and holds it. "I'm going to stay here, with Margaret."

Asatira approaches me. "I'll try to work with your mother again. But right now, she needs rest. My presence always exhausts them."

"Thank you for your help," Matt says.

Before we leave, I hug Dad. I don't want to leave him yet, but I have little choice. "I'm glad to have you back."

His mouth sets into a grim line. "We'll face it together this time."

Despite the circumstances, I feel stronger with him here.

In the hallway, Matt relays the information to Francesca.

"You and Silver go to Eli. Detain him. We'll put him in a holding cell in the old genetic jail until we figure out what he's all about." The genetic jail is a jail for altereds from the time before. The jail cell is immune to most of the more benign, less destructive abilities. It might not be strong enough. "I'll get the rest of the mission team and send them to you for backup."

"Now?" I ask.

"Now." Francesca nods, handing me her car keys. "And

Silver?" I turn back. Her eyes flash dangerously. "You do what you have to. Use whatever abilities you have to. Don't hesitate. I won't have this country threatened again. We're at war again and during a war, anything goes."

"Got it," I reply.

If Eli so much as moves a muscle in the wrong direction...

CHAPTER TWENTY-NINE
SILVER

MATT PARKS in the lot of the red barn and jumps out of the car. The rain hasn't stopped. It runs down my nose and the back of my neck. As we start along the path, I spot Matt's gun tucked in the waistband of his jeans. I haven't seen it since Earl's mountain.

"You think you're going to need that?" I ask, as my foot gets stuck in the mud. Tensing my calf muscle, my foot comes out of my boot.

"I hope not. Besides, I've got you, my indestructible girlfriend," Matt replies, pulling my boot free for me.

When we arrive at Eli's cabin, it's empty. The door hangs open on its hinges and a rancid stench wafts into the dampening rain.

"What is that smell?" Matt covers his nose with a sleeve and nudges the door open with his gun.

The floorboards creak as we walk inside and the stench rises to meet us like rush of expanding steam. It's coming from the kitchen. A dead rabbit lies on the counter in an advanced stage of decay. Maggots swarm over its body and its eyes are missing.

"That's disgusting." Matt retches and recoils from the mutilated animal. "He's deranged."

I usher Matt out of the cabin. "Come on, he'll be at the farmhouse. He always is."

"What does he do there all day?"

"That's a good question." Maybe I should have taken longer to consider it.

We make a detour to the small outhouse next to the red barn. Matt opens the door and six pairs of red eyes stare back at us. The hellcats never sleep. They are in a stasis.

"Are you sure about this?" I shudder.

Matt removes the hellcat remote from his pocket. "They're programed to obey. I'm sure."

He presses a few buttons on the remote. The hellcats rise to four legs. The top of their backs meet my shoulder level. The three cats are all male and their manes add bulk to their already powerful frames. Built for speed, strength, and to kill, they often fill my nightmares. Half of their heads are gleaming metal. But their red eyes are the scariest of all.

Matt taps another button and the cats turn invisible. But I can make them out. Knowing where they are, I can spot their shimmering outlines as they move. Adapted with the DNA of a chameleon, like my own genes, they take on the background of wherever they are.

We emerge from the shed, the hellcats flanking our sides. I concentrate on Matt's broad shoulders but feel the warm gusts of breath as the hellcats prowl beside me. I can't get used to the idea they're on our side now.

We creep along the dirt track, our boots squelching in the oozing mud and sloshing in the puddles. Rounding the corner of the farmhouse, we enter the abandoned yard as a scorching fireball streaks across the wild garden and lands in an enormous pile of sticks and logs. The fire ignites and the flames leap high, despite the weather. Matt directs the invisible hellcats to a corner of the yard, where they wait, then pockets the remote.

"That's better." Eli turns to face us. "This storm we've been having, all the rain, I thought it was a little on the cold side for summer." He smiles a smile so charming, so genuine, it's hard to believe we witnessed him using an ability. He acts as if we've known all along. As if it's no big deal.

"What was that about?" Matt uses his gun to point to the blazing bonfire. Then he levels it at Eli's head. The rain drips down Matt's forehead, his nose, and cheeks, and he wipes a hand over his face.

"Oh, come now." Eli takes a step closer.

Matt's voice turns to steel. "That'll do."

"You've come to have a little tête-à-tête, you and Silver. You must have been expecting *something*. You're hardly coming here to hold hands, sit in a circle, and sing Kumbaya." Shirtless, small rivers of rain run down his torso, around his well accentuated muscles.

"I thought you'd try to deny it," I say, feeling my way for the right words.

"We're a little past that now, aren't we? You don't trust me anymore. I can see it in your eyes," Eli says.

"No, no I don't."

"What happened to Erica and Delta?" Matt demands. His gun arm hasn't moved.

"Really? That's what you want to talk about? I hear they were attacked in the woods." Flicking the water out of his dark hair, Eli grins.

"It was you," I say.

Eli's chin dips in the impression of remorse. "I tried to fight it. Really, I did. But I wasn't strong enough."

The black lightning power tingles at my fingertips. "Tell me what you did to my friends!" The rain runs down the back of my neck and into my shirt, pooling in the small of my back. I blink the water out of my eyelashes.

"It wasn't my fault. I wasn't in control. Einstein..." He catches himself and his gaze shifts guiltily.

"Einstein?" Matt chokes out the dog's name and his gun hand wavers. The other hand edges toward the remote in his pocket.

Eli rests his hands on his hips. "Unfortunately, he witnessed me using an ability. He was going to run back to Silver and tell her all about it. I couldn't have that. Not before I was ready."

"Ready for what?" I glance behind me, fearful the yellow-eyed monster is readying to pounce. But there's nothing. The rain pours, bouncing violently off the ground, splashing my boots and trousers.

"He was just a dog," Matt spits. Straightening his gun arm, he marches closer to Eli. With the manic smile curling into a sneer, Eli shoots out a hand. Matt tumbles through the air and lands in a heap fifteen feet away. I hear the crack as the remote breaks apart. The hellcats roar.

"No!" I yell.

Eli turns, trying to make out the source of the roar, but the hellcats remain invisible. "What was that?"

I don't reply. He doesn't deserve to know.

Unharmed, Matt leaps to his feet and marches back to Eli. With anger distorting his features, he holds the gun with a white-knuckle grip.

"Really? Again, Matt?" Eli laughs. The flames leap higher, illuminating something dangerous in Eli's eyes. He is not in control of himself. I don't know how strong he is, I don't know what abilities he possesses. Can I beat him?

Matt stops marching. I hold my sparking fingers high.

"And no, Silver, you're not going to use that on me." Eli holds one hand in my direction and the other in Matt's.

The raindrops fatten, pummeling the three of us, creating rippling puddles in every direction. The wind strengthens, spraying my face with the downpour and causes a chill to gather at the nape of my neck. Or maybe it isn't the rain.

One of the hellcats shakes its head repeatedly, as if its wiring is misfiring. The red eyes in a second dull, then brighten again.

"Did you kill Erica and Delta?" Matt pushes the question through clenched teeth, his gun leveled at Eli's head again.

Eli cocks his head, taking time to consider his answer. "Why yes, I did. Erica discovered who I really am and Delta saw me disposing of Erica. I wasn't ready for people to know."

My mouth drops open. A thousand thoughts run through my head, but I can't speak. Even though we suspected he was the murderer, I'm surprised to hear it confirmed so causally.

As if my two close friends were nothing but annoying flies who could be swatted away without a second thought. My lips burn. Right where he kissed me. I can't believe I ever let him get that close to me.

Streaking from my hands, the black lightning power scorches the earth in swirling patterns and makes the puddles hiss and steam.

Unconcerned, Eli stands still, addressing my display of powers with a mere quirk of his eyebrow. "It was hard, at the time. I knew I was burning bridges. But things are clearer now. The yellow eyes showed me the way."

My anger threatens to erupt. But I must remain calm. I need to focus.

Eli raises his hand higher and I feel an uncomfortable pressure inside. I raise my hands in return.

"Silver!" Matt calls, sifting the ground for the pieces of the remote. "We don't want to kill him. We need him alive. To figure out the yellow eyes."

My face contorts with the strain of controlling the destroyer power. It wants to be free. I want to let it loose to deal with the object of my fury. The thing responsible for the murders of my friends, Einstein. I trusted him once, I considered him one of my closest friends, more. He betrayed me, he took pleasure in it. How blind I was.

Eli throws his head back and giggles into the rain. "There's nothing you can do to stop the yellow eyes! It'll take all the power. The baby's power."

"What are the yellow eyes?" I ask.

Eli stares at me. "The yellow eyes are me. I am the yellow eyes. We are now one. I'm so glad the headaches are gone."

Matt fires. Despite the rain and the wind and the popping bonfire, the crack of the bullet thunders through the air. Birds erupt into the sky. But the bullet has no effect. It bounces off Eli as if he's made of rubber and then ricochets back in Matt's direction.

The hellcats roar again. I make out their shimmering form advancing, one of them still shaking its head.

Matt collapses. Eli remains standing, giggling into the downpour. "It won't work," he says over and over again. "You can't hurt me."

One hellcat snarls, leaps at Eli, but bounces off his force-field. It shakes itself back to its feet and sets its predatory eyes on Matt and me. The other two join the first. They stand in a line, watching us, their eyes intermittently glowing and dimming.

"Here, kitty, kitty, kitty," Eli sings.

Lying in a muddy puddle, Matt clutches his shoulder. I edge to his side. Blood seeps through his fingers.

"It's a forcefield. He has a protection forcefield." Matt clenches his jaw. "The bullet bounced off it." I offer him my healing hand. "No, not yet. Deal with him."

"But we need him alive," I say.

"Not that much. Finish him."

Pushing the black lightning away, I draw on the blue color and it immediately comes to me.

"No, Silver!" Matt calls.

I'm aglow with a blue light and I push at it until it wiggles and wobbles and shudders.

The hellhounds are back in the corner. Matt is standing again and he fires. Despite the rain and the wind and the popping bonfire, the crack of the bullet thunders through the air. Birds erupt into the sky. But the bullet has no effect. It bounces off Eli as if he's made of rubber and then ricochets back in Matt's direction.

Time didn't go back far enough, not like before when it was at least two days. Wiping blood from under my nose. I try again and prod at the blue bubble. A headache pulses at my temples, but I have to stop Eli. I have to try.

"What just happened?" Eli frowns, as if sensing we've been here before.

"Did you kill Erica and Delta?" Matt pushes the question through clenched teeth, his gun leveled at Eli's head again.

"Why yes, I did," Eli replies, frowning at the hellcat with the reflexively shaking head. The hellcat pops in and out of invisibility, its dull metal head flashing shards of firelight. "Erica discovered who I really am and Delta saw me disposing of Erica. I wasn't ready for people to know."

Blood runs from my nose and ears. I feel dizzy, barely able to stand on two feet.

"Stop it, Silver!" Matt screams. He is on the ground again, shot, bleeding.

Turning my back on Matt, I face our new nemesis and push the blue bubble away. It's too hard to control. Raising my palms, I throw the black lightning power at him. His absurd laugh cuts off. He stares at me, tension tightening his cheeks. He doesn't disappear. He doesn't explode into a pile of ash as I intended.

The hellcats growl and their huge forms shimmer into existence, the invisibility wearing off.

"You're stronger than I thought." Eli brings a hand to his face. His fingertips are black, scorched from my power.

"Where did you get your abilities?" I ask, readying my power for another attack. I'm weak from using the blue bubble, but I refuse to let him get away. "Who are you?"

"From my brother. My twin brother," Eli replies, raising his hands once again. This time I can make out the mysterious forcefield. He is surrounded by a bubble, like Paige's bubble when she was pregnant, like my time bubble. But Eli's bubble is transparent and occasionally, it glistens, revealing its circumference. "When he died, I was set free, and everything he had became mine. I didn't want it at first. I wanted to fit in, have a second chance, be friends with all of you." Hurt whirls in his pupils. "But the yellow eyes showed me the error of my ways."

With his hands dangling at his sides, he stands majestically. The rain pours off his bare shoulders, his muscles are tensed for action, and a cold glint flashes in his eyes. Tombstones, eyes like tombstones. Just like Earl's.

"You lied. About everything."

His eyes narrow. "No, I didn't. I've always been Earl's hostage." His face turns thunderous. "Murdered me. Challenged me to a swim in the ocean in January, even though he knew my asthma wouldn't cope."

One of the hellcats attacks Eli, leaps at his head with a wide jaw. Eli laughs as it bounces away, and using telekinesis, tears its head from its body. The other two retreat, but their red eyes stay fixed on Eli.

Within his forcefield, Eli morphs into a vison of Earl as I last saw him. The red pustulating skin, the swishing peaked tail, the madness in his eyes. I take a step back. Eli becomes a hellhound, then a hellcat, snarling and spitting. Well, two can play that game. Drawing on a power I only used once before when I turned into a bird, I transform into my own hellcat. Locking eyes on each other, we snarl and growl. But then he changes into an image I'm not expecting. He grows to a bulk's dimensions. There is a familiar cleft in his chin, a slightly wonky nose, hair the color of corn. Joe.

Startled, I morph back into myself. Every detail is so perfect it's hard to believe it isn't him.

Joe smiles. His warm brown eyes beckon. I take a step toward him.

"Silver! It's not him!" Matt yells.

Shaking the image off, I hit Eli with the black lightning power again. With one palm I aim at the forcefield, with the other I aim at Eli's head. A few strands of his hair catch fire before he teleports away, out of my grasp.

"Where did he go?" Matt asks, fumbling with putting the remote back together.

I hear the click of a button, and both the remaining hellcats swivel in our direction.

"I don't know," I say, readying the black lightning in the direction of the hellcats. "But I think we've got more trouble."

Matt raises his gun. "The remote is broken."

The hellcats attack. Matt shoots his gun, emptying the clip. Bullets punch through the rain, tearing one hellcat apart. I attack the other with my destroyer ability, reducing it to nothing.

"I thought they were on our side," I pant.

Matt lies back in the mud, hands on his temples. "I'm sorry, Silver."

"It's okay," I say, looking over my shoulder for a return of Eli. "Hellcats have always been unpredictable."

Matt scans the yard. "I don't think we'll see Eli again until—"

"Until the yellow-eyed monster arrives." Kneeling by Matt, I place my hand on his shoulder. The warming glow spreads from my fingers and into Matt's shoulder. He sighs as the wound knits together.

"Thank you."

"Anytime," I reply, and kiss him lightly on the lips.

"What did he mean that he is now the yellow eyes?" Matt whispers.

I purse my lips. "Whatever Earl created, however Eli came back, the two things are connected. Like they share a mental link." I offer Matt a hand, then collapse on top of him.

I fall, nose planting the wet earth, the scent of electricity all around me, mingled with the fainter smell of my own blood.

I'm only out for a few minutes, because when I wake the storm is still raging and rain is filling my eye sockets. Matt cradles my head in his hands, crying. "Oh, thank God. Thank God." He holds me against his chest. "Please stop using that power. Please, Silver."

I nod and kiss him. I have a headache and exhaustion makes my limbs heavy, but my nose and ears have stopped bleeding. Matt helps me to my feet.

Sawyer, Mason, and Carter appear in the yard.

"You guys okay?" Carter asks.

Sawyer glances at the raging bonfire and the dead carcasses of two hellcats. "What happened?"

"Francesca sent us," Mason says. "Looks like we missed all the action."

"I'll say," Matt replies, holstering his gun. "We need to gather the others."

On our way out of the yard, I spot something half buried under a scraggly hawthorn bush. When I get close enough to examine the object, my heart lurches. I tug Erica's Stetson out from under the shrub. It's soaked and filthy. Touching the material, I think of her, and Sean. A sob clogs my throat.

With Matt's newly healed arm propping me up, the five of us make our way back along the muddy path to Francesca's car and drive to the presidential compound. Lyla, Koko, and Francesca are already there and a few minutes later we're joined by Jacob and Patrick. He refuses to let the baby out of his sight and uses a sling to hold Patrick at his chest.

After Matt and I change into dry clothes, we settle around the underground conference table. Claus pats my shoulder and Evan gives me a gentle hug. I return their embrace fleetingly, afraid of letting my guard down.

"What happened?" Claus asks. "You look like shit."

I laugh, despite how bruised I feel. Claus never swears and it's the tonic I need. "Things got a little hairier than I expected."

Matt hands me a hot water bottle, a glass of water, and a handful of painkillers, which I dutifully swallow. I don't have the energy to heal myself right now. He sits next to me and doesn't let go of my hand.

It wasn't so long ago that we sat here, about to embark on

a different mission. This time there are a few people missing; Hal, Kyle, Erica, Sean, Paige, William, and Luis. I picture Hal sitting there, straddled over a backward chair, giving me encouraging looks when we realized Earl was holding my mother hostage.

"We all know why we're here." Francesca sits ramrod straight, shifting her serious gaze to each of us. "We have another enemy to face. We have a fight coming our way."

"Eli and the yellow-eyed monster," Matt says, running his fingers through his damp hair. "They're working together. Eli confirmed it. He has abilities. A lot of them."

A rumble of gasps spread through the room.

"What power? What are we dealing with?" Mason asks, flashing his tattoos. Although the black ink is hard to see on his dark skin, he doesn't stop adding to them. They are symbols of everything he fought for, and all the mistakes he made that he refuses to make again.

Matt clears his throat. "I think he has as much power as Silver." He looks at me for agreement.

Carter launches to his feet. "That's not possible."

"Surely not." Sawyer pales. Despite Sawyer's power and his contributions to the last two missions, he's never learned to be brave. I guess it's like me and anxiety. Although my panic attacks no longer reduce me to a quivering wreck, I'm still...scared. Terrified. Just like everyone else.

"Then we're all screwed," Lyla whispers under her breath.

"Is that true, Silver?" Francesca asks, a hand raised to silence the questions.

"Maybe," I reply. "He doesn't have the destroyer ability, but he does have abilities I don't."

"Like what?" Mason asks, pushing his sleeves past his elbows, as if he's getting ready for dirty work.

"Like a force field," I reply. "It's a transparent forcefield and it protects him from other people's abilities. Even my black lightning power. But I think I can wear it down."

"It seems he has an ability to block Silver," Matt says. "He can block her reading his thoughts and taking on his powers."

The room becomes so still I hold my breath in case I disturb the air.

"He's responsible for Erica and Delta. He admitted it." I bite back my anger. "And Einstein."

A squeaky sound erupts from Lyla's throat. Sawyer immediately throws an arm around her.

"The yellow eyes are influencing him," I say. "Somehow they're connected. It's weird. When Eli first arrived he seemed so eager to please, helpful and happy. But as time's gone on, that's changed. I assume his connection to the yellow eyes has grown stronger, that it has more control over him now."

"He's a monster," Mason says.

"It's not his fault," I say. "But that doesn't mean he's not dangerous."

"We'll make it pay." Carter turns bulk, his shadow casting a long line of darkness. Mason stands and follows suit.

"Where is he now?" Sawyer asks.

"We don't know." Matt runs his fingers across the smooth

surface of the polished table. "He teleported away when Silver tried to kill him."

"He'll come back," Lyla whispers with wide eyes. "He'll come back when we're all sleeping."

"That's why we're here," Francesca says. "We'll stay in the compound, under lockdown until the situation resolves itself."

Claus steps out of the shadows. "We can fit about two hundred people in the compound. I have a list of people who might be able to help. They're being collected now. The rest will be evacuated to underground sanctuaries until this is all over."

Leaning back in my chair, I warm my hands on the mug of coffee Matt hands me. Sawyer tears open a packet of cookies, his appetite never assuaged.

We have a plan. Ignoring the rain outside, I force myself to relax. We'll be safe here until we decide our next move.

"There's more information some of you don't know," Matt says. "Eli is Earl's twin. Earl killed him when they were teenagers. Apparently. Who knows what the truth is."

Sawyer does a double take. "Huh?"

Everyone else frowns.

"How is that even possible?" Carter asks. "He's like, thirty years younger."

"Energy is never created or destroyed, only transferred," Matt says, looking at me. "That's what your mother meant."

"I've seen it happen once before, with two sisters," Koko says. "If Eli was hanging around after his alleged murder, not able to move on because he wanted revenge, well, then he would be hanging around in the form in which he died – a seventeen-year-old by the look of him - and when Earl died it would have been all too easy to gather his life energy and make himself mortal again."

"Well, no wonder then," Lyla says. "No wonder he's some crazed, murderous sociopath. They're freaking identical twins!"

"He didn't start out that way," I say. "Really, he didn't." Why am I defending him? It doesn't matter anymore. He's made his choice, and now we all have to live with it.

"If he has all the abilities Earl had..." Mason lets the thought dangle.

More. He has Earl's abilities and more. I fought Earl. We struggled. I thought I was going to die. It wasn't a battle I was in control of and I don't want a repeat performance. Eli has a forcefield and the ability to block me. More. Where did he get them from? From the yellow eyes of course. It all makes sense now.

Fear balloons in my chest as I look at my friends. Do we have enough power between us? Mason and Carter are bulks. Sawyer has telekinesis and pyrokinesis. Lyla can swim under-water with gills. Useless in this situation, unless the rain continues and we find our world submerged. Matt is handy with the bombs and automated weapons. Then there's me and all of my abilities. I miss Paige, Erica, Delta, Kyle...Joe. Can we do this without them?

"I have a new power..." I start, unsure how to describe it.

Matt is on his feet. "No. No you don't."

I look at him. "What if it's all we've got?"

"No," he says. "It almost killed you. Twice."

"Silver?" Francesca asks.

"It's to do with time. I managed to reverse time, or go back, or...I'm not sure what I did."

"Which ended in her bleeding out both her nose and ears and blacking out and having a very thready pulse for three days. No," Matt says. "I'm not going to risk you."

I lean over and kiss his cheek. "I don't want to fight with you. This may be all you have."

"Are you able to practice it?" Francesca asks.

"That's the problem," Matt says. "That's what almost killed her."

"We can't risk you being incapacitated before we need you," Francesca says.

I wish my life didn't boil down to such cold calculations. But she's right. I'm the best chance we have to beat the yellow eyes and I can't take risks.

I'm too weary to argue, so I hold onto Matt's hand and let the others talk.

"What about the yellow eyes?" Lyla asks. "What *is* the creature with the yellow eyes and how is it connected to Eli?"

"It's an entity," I say. "Something Earl made in his lab, by accident. Something born of all the evilness he created." All my dreams come rushing back to me, showing the connections and the truth of the yellow eyes. It was already in the mountain when I killed Earl, but it existed in its infancy. It's been biding its time, preparing, gathering the animals and the black wave, reaching out to Eli's mind. It needs Eli. "It's evolved. And now it wants...me and Patrick, and anything standing in its way."

Jacob holds Patrick a little closer.

"I'm sorry I asked," Lyla mutters.

"So he's been stumbling around talking about yellow eyes because they share a connection?" Mason asks.

"Can he be saved?" Sawyer asks.

"He murdered our friends!" Mason slaps Sawyer on the back of the head. "It's too late for redemption."

I shake my head at Sawyer, confirming Mason's words, but for different reasons.

Koko presses her lips into an unhappy line. "I suspect Eli is too far under the entity's control."

"It *is* too late, and Eli wasn't completely innocent to begin with," Matt says with a pointed look in my direction. Perhaps he's right, Eli wouldn't have lied about his true identity and abilities if he didn't have something to hide.

"Okay, so we stay here and we wait—" Carter says.

"You train. All of you. In the weapons arena. Practice your weapons, practice your abilities," Francesca says. "Carefully." She looks in my direction. "And when it, or they, comes we'll be ready."

"We'll be ready." Matt gets to his feet.

"And we'll make them pay," Jacob says from the corner. Patrick sleeps in his arms, aglow with his special pale blue light. Matt looks at the baby with a curious expression. Is he thinking the same as me?

✕✕✕✕✕

That afternoon the people on Francesca's list arrive at the compound. They include the remaining doctors, nurses, teachers, and scientists across all the camps. It's Francesca's attempt to keep the knowledge of the world safe, just in case.

There are several soldiers and Dad immediately begins turning them into bulks. My mother and Asatira are brought to the medical unit underground.

After taking the civilian population to the underground sanctuaries, the soldiers return to the compound to receive their individual genetic cocktails which will be impervious to the cure. Matt's parents and youngest sister arrive and won't stop holding him until Francesca convinces them to head to the living quarters so Matt and I can prepare.

The mission team and soldiers make their way to the weapons arena, a new addition Francesca added when we were away at the mountain. I hoped we wouldn't need it, but knew we would. It's a large gym-sized room with fire-retardant walls and floor. Along one side, weapons line a wall. Anything from knives and spears to automatic rifles and rocket launchers. It's a formidable array. Bright strip lighting hangs from the ceiling and a couple of benches are stacked at the far end. A water cooler stands in the corner, the only free-standing object, asking for trouble. The room is odorless, apart from the faint smell of sweat.

Francesca assigns a small anteroom for Matt to build his bombs. With furrowed concentration, he cuts wires and connects stacks of explosives. Unsure how to practice my abilities safely, I bring him a cup of coffee. He drinks an incessant amount when he's thinking.

Sawyer throws fireballs with his mind while a couple of soldiers follow him with fire extinguishers. He practices his telekinesis and moves objects, people even, around the large room, testing his limits.

"Put me down!" Lyla shouts from twenty feet above

Sawyer's head. She spins in circles while orbiting Sawyer in a ten-foot radius.

"Sorry," Sawyer says, as he places her gently on the floor. "I wanted to see how fast I could move you."

"I'm think I'm going to throw up." Lyla clutches her stomach and walks in a jagged, diagonal path to a bench along the side of the room. She collapses on the bench, lies on her back, and closes her eyes.

Carter and Mason spar in hand-to-hand combat, bulk to bulk, their strength equally matched. They show the new bulks how to turn their ability on and off and adjust to their new centers of gravity. Jacob practices all his old abilities. Strength, speed, teleportation. He is intimidating. All the time Patrick hangs from his chest.

I leave the arena. Matt catches me at the door. "You're too weak to try anything."

"I know. I'm going get some rest. Then I'm going to see if I can get to the bottom of the rest of my abilities."

He holds onto my arm. "I'm scared. I'm scared of your blue bubble."

"Me too. But, Matt, I'm not going to risk it. You're right, it's too dangerous and unpredictable."

Finally he lets me go and I walk away from him, satisfied in the knowledge I'm no longer lying to him. We are a team, working together. Matt and I forever, unless we can't defeat the yellow eyes.

CHAPTER THIRTY

ELI

THERE IS ONLY one path open to him now. All the bridges are burned.

A coil of nerves snakes in his stomach. Yet again, his future has been thrust upon him. There is no time to backtrack. Not that he wants to, but he'd like more time to prepare. Eli is used to dwelling in the past, thinking over the thing that might have been, harboring burgeoning resentment toward those who wronged him, like Earl.

When he thinks of Earl now, it is merely a name. No more. Not a brother, not blood, not his killer. Merely a name of a person who once lived. The yellow eyes took away the pain.

Eli trudges through the woods, the rain soaking his skin. He barely feels it, but relishes the symbolism. A baptism. Not of fire, but of rain and power. Anticipation replaces the nerves in his stomach, hardening his resolve.

"It is time."

"Yes, it is." He licks his lips.

His bare feet sink into the squelching, muddy path as he marches on. He doesn't know where he's going. When Silver managed to penetrate his forcefield he didn't think about direction, merely escape. No wonder the yellow eyes want her. She is more powerful than *him*. Is she more powerful than the yellow eyes?

He ended up in the woods. Which woods? There are woods and trees and forests everywhere. Hopefully he hasn't teleported clear across the country.

Plowing forward, the mud sucks at his feet. With each step he takes, he fears he won't be able to pull himself free. He pictures a cold, skeletal hand of a long-ago lady of the lake - or mud – grabbing his ankles in her bony hands and yanking him beneath the opaque ground to hell and whatever else might lie under the earth. Soon he'll have enough power to not concern himself with such childish worries.

Eli pauses to pull his foot free from a tangle of hidden roots. Panting with exertion, he craves a rest.

"Don't stop."

The yellow eyes aren't far away. Soon they'll meet. And then...what exactly? All good things, he's sure of it.

Eli snaps a look over his shoulder. What is Silver doing now? It is his last thought about the life he's leaving behind. He can only press on.

Only a flicker of guilt remains over the deaths of Erica and Delta. The closer he gets to the yellow eyes, the less he feels. He yearns to forget all that has transpired, to be free of societal shackles. It won't be long.

Eli faces forward. Toward the mist, the dark, and the

taller trees. That's where he'll find the yellow eyes. And salvation.

Shivering and teeth chattering like a manic wind-up toy, Eli continues through the woods. It occurs to him he has the ability to stop the rain and raise the temperature of the summer night. That's better. His skin is dry for the first time in hours. His internal cravings increase. His thirst for power. Silver's power. He can't wait to see the look on her face when he takes it.

"Oh!"

Eli comes to an abrupt stop and takes in the scene before him.

So that's how it is.

Eli examines the creature. His eyes widen trying to take in the sheer size of it, its dimensions, the wiggling and writhing at its edges, *within* it. It's the most magnificent creature in all of existence. Countless animals flank its sides. All of them black and all standing still, as if muzzled. Wolves and bears, panthers and jaguars, spiders and scorpions, bats and raccoons. So many. So many eyes staring at him.

The moon appears from behind the dissipating clouds. The yellow eyed creature stretches one long, arm, its claws scraping gently at Eli's cheek, caressing. So close and so sharp are those formidable claws, he's sure his two-day stubble is now smoother than newborn skin.

Smells fill his nostrils. Sweat and exertion, the outdoors and animals, the acrid, bitter odor of manure. Then he catches a whiff of its breath. The stench nearly knocks him out. It's more than the stink of death and decay on those dripping fangs. There's something solid within it, and it envelops

Eli lovingly, as though it's no more malevolent than Autumn's early morning mists.

Eli looks into the yellow eyes and is filled with knowledge. Terrible knowledge. But it's too late. He's been manipulated.

The creature plucks him from the earth with one, powerful arm, the claws now digging into his skin, and pulls him toward its...*mouth*? Eli accepts the moment of his death, rebirth, whatever it might be called. There is no other path open to him.

After a few mind-spiraling moments, Eli fills out his new shape. The power surges through him.

It's time.

CHAPTER THIRTY-ONE
SILVER

THE MISSION TEAM, comprising of Francesca, Matt, Lyla, Sawyer, Carter, Mason, and Jacob, sit around the conference table with the baby, my father, Claus, and Francesca. We've been here for hours, trying to anticipate when an attack might come, and how.

"Patrick stays with me," Jacob says for the third time.

"Don't you think he'll be safer here? We could leave him with the nurses. He'll be well taken care of during your absence," Francesca says.

Jacob's dark eyes turn to steel. "If the monster manages to get through us. Through Silver. Then it doesn't matter where Patrick is, he'll be taken too. He might as well stay with me."

"But won't he be safer if we hide him somewhere?" Lyla asks.

Jacob gestures wildly with his hands, jiggling the baby. "And then who will be left to look after him? If we all die..." Matt shoots him a warning look. "Sorry, Matt, it has to be said. If we all die, there's no hope for Patrick anyway."

Scooping her hair into a ponytail, as though readying herself for battle, Lyla's gaze skirts the room. "Maybe Patrick will be able to protect us with his blue bubble."

I had the same thought. On our last mission, when Paige was pregnant, every time she was in danger and the blue forcefield formed around her and carried her out of harm's way, I wondered if it could do the same for the rest of us. But we can't pin all our hopes on a baby. "I haven't seen him produce the blue bubble since he was born. He might not be capable of it anymore. We don't know what he's capable of. It's a huge risk to rely on powers he may or may not have, or he may or may not chose to produce at the right moment. He's just a baby."

"Didn't you take his powers when you touched him?" Jacob asks me.

"I did, but I don't have anything like a forcefield."

"Maybe he lost the ability after he was born," Matt says.

"Maybe," I say. "I'm not going to pretend to know how these abilities work anymore."

"Silver?" Mason walks around the table to me, his eyes slitted to a squint, a finger pointing above my head. "What's with the cloud?"

"What cloud?" I ask.

"The one hovering above your head." Carter adds a second pointing finger.

I look up. A small, gray raincloud floats above my head, around my head, rising and falling gently between my head and the ceiling. "I think it's my new weather ability. I can control the weather." That's what I recently discovered when I went to practice my abilities. After I rested and pushed all thoughts of the color blue and time traveling miracles from my mind, I managed a few bursts of thunder and a couple lightning bolts. I stopped experimenting when I created a whirlwind and found myself sucked to its center.

Mason pokes a finger into my personal cloud and it rises toward the ceiling, as if insulted. Matt approaches, looking up, watching the cloud as it drifts back to me.

"Are you controlling it now?" he asks.

"Sort of. I didn't realize it was still with me. But I think, like my destroyer ability, it's tied to my emotions."

"It could be useful. Did you find anything else? Besides the obvious..." Matt trails off.

Rain falls from the gray cloud and sprinkles Mason and Matt. Everyone jumps as a clap of thunder slices through the air, the decibels rattling the water glasses on the table. I finish the display with a streak of lightning which erupts from the cloud and snakes its way to a water jug resting on a corner table, melting the vessel into a misshapen mess of rippling, folded glass.

Carter raises a ginger eyebrow. "Whoa!"

"That'll do for now," Francesca says, a hint of disproval in her tone. "While we're still inside."

The cloud evaporates, the only signs of its existence a damp Matt and Mason.

"I wonder if Eli is the cause of the storm, the rain." Matt removes his damp sweatshirt. "If his abilities are tied to his emotions too, then it's no wonder the severity of the storm we've had. He's a mess."

"But the storm's over. And it's still raining." Sawyer says.

"I'm not sure whether that's good news or bad news," Carter adds.

"Me neither." I suspect it's bad. If his emotions are now under control, and if he means to side with the yellow-eyed monster, then that is very bad news for us.

"We need a plan of attack." Francesca drums an irregular rhythm on the table. "Silver, have you or Adam had any more dreams that might help clarify what it is we're going to be facing?"

I sigh. "No, I'm afraid not."

"What *can* we expect?" Sawyer asks. He touches the molten shape of the water jug and winces as his finger hisses.

"Animals. Lots of them, a tidal wave of them. Big, snarling, growling animals." I think back to my dream. "And insects. Thousands of them. Like Hell's army. Worse than the mountain—"

"Worse than a two-headed, fire-breathing dragon?" Carter asks.

I nod. "The yellow eyes control them all. It'll be there with them. It's huge. It has no dimensions but seems to build itself from the animals it travels with. But it does have claws, sharp ones, and teeth."

Sawyer sticks his burned finger in his glass of water. "Joy. A walk in the park then."

"You alone could deal with that, Sawyer," Lyla says. She is always stoic before a battle. It's only after, or during, when the fear comes. "Throw the animals and insects with your mind away from us and then burn them." She clicks her fingers. "Easy. Just like the scorpions and spiders." She refers to our battle on the mountain with Earl and his genetically altered beasts.

"It has power too," I add quietly. "It has abilities. I'm worried it might be stronger than me."

Lyla blanches and covers it with a cough. Sawyer gulps. Everyone else stays quiet.

Dad stands behind my chair and puts his hands on my shoulders. "No need for the doom and gloom. You guys can do this. You've done it twice before." He punches an arm into the air. "You can. You're amazing. Give yourselves some credit."

"Knowledge is power." Matt stands. "Like Rufus said, we *can* do this. We thought our odds were bad before and we still won." He is flaming the fire, one my father started, a fire of confidence and determination and belief in ourselves. It spreads, catching quickly in the smiles and nods of my friends. "We *can* do this. There is no alternative. We've triumphed before, twice, and we'll do it again. We'll fight this yellow-eyed beast, and we'll win. We'll find Eli and make him pay for the deaths of our friends. This is who we are. It's what we do." He circles his palms, encompassing us all. "We will stand and fight, and we will win!"

"Hooraah!" Mason stands and clenches both biceps in a muscleman pose. He pops his biceps in a little jig and the rest of the group fall about laughing.

"I can do better!" Carter places the misshaped water jug in the crevice of his elbow, flexes his bicep and reduces the jug to a pile of glass shards which slip off his impenetrable, bulk skin and rains on the carpet. "A-ha!"

Feeling energized, I toss another rain cloud in the bulks' direction and soak them both.

"No fair!" Mason says.

"Okay, okay, dial it back a notch." Francesca rises. "So, Patrick stays with Jacob at all times. When it comes to it, the rest of you protect him. For now, get to the weapons room and train, the fight will be here soon and we need to be ready. Silver, discover what you can about your new abilities. The pool room is a good place for you. We've got a few hours before nightfall, and then I want everyone to get a good night's sleep. You'll need it."

"I'm going to bury my bombs," Matt says.

We pat backs and sock shoulders as we file out of the room. Dad catches me on my way to the pool.

"Are all the soldiers now bulked up?" I ask.

Absentmindedly, he nods. "Silver, I want to fight with you."

I stop walking. "What are you talking about?"

"But I can't."

We lock eyes. When it comes time, Mom and Dad won't be there. They have no combat skills. I pat his chest, where his faulty heart continues to beat. "You need to look after Mom."

He folds me in a hug, but I feel his tears on my cheeks.

CHAPTER THIRTY-TWO
SILVER

ADAM and I erupt from the dream at the same moment. He screams at the top of his lungs and wakes half the sleeping inhabitants of the bunker. I clamp a hand over my mouth and stifle my own whimpers.

Matt flies to my side. "Is it time?"

Koko shushes Adam and rocks him in her arms. Someone turns the lights on. Everyone knows what Adam's screams mean.

"It's time," I whisper, blinking away the images that formed during my vision. The same vision in the cornfield with the black wave of evilness. A crowd gathers around my bunk. "It's here, and it's coming. Now."

I slide out of bed and pull on my combat boots. Matt's parents hover nearby, with worried eyes and drawn faces and hands twitching nervously at their sides. Dad is beside me, handing me items I need, tucking my knife into my belt.

"What about Eli?" Matt asks, pulling on his own clothes.

"It *is* Eli." I pause, recalling the newer details of this latest

314

vision. "The yellow-eyed monster and Eli are the same thing." I can't explain any better. I don't know how to decipher the terrifying images of my dream, when the monster and Eli appeared to meld together, a tangle of limbs and hair and claws and skin. They merged their powers to become something even more frightening.

"Silver!" The shout comes from the far side of the room. "Silver!"

The dormitory door slams. "Silver!"

My mother appears, in her pajamas, fully conscious, shouting my name and searching wildly.

"Silver!" She shouts again. Grabbing my arms, she shakes me, rattling my teeth. "He's here! Eli! He's here, and he's coming for you. For all of us." Her wild eyes roam the room, taking in the people, the soldiers in various states of preparation, the bunk beds. She spots my father and tears run down her cheeks. He wraps her in his arms. My own tears brim, but we don't have time for reunions.

"What's going on?" Mom asks.

"It's okay." I take her hand, never so grateful for a returning squeeze. I haven't spoken to my mother in over three years. "It's okay...Mom. *Oh, Mom.*" I am no longer strong. I don't want to leave the bunker. I want to stay with her.

"Eli..." she whispers.

"We know," I say.

"He's Earl's brother," she says.

"I know."

Pain is reflected in her pupils. "I wanted to tell you. I was stuck somewhere, in a deserted fairground, I was strapped to

315

a ride and I couldn't undo the belt and then it started to move, faster and faster, and I was screaming and I couldn't get off and then Eli was there, and Earl, and these scary yellow eyes and they were chasing me but they couldn't get onto the ride and I couldn't make it stop until, finally, it did." Her words come out in one long rush.

Dad pats her hand as I wipe at my tears, but my eyes refuse to stay dry. "It's okay. You're here now. You're okay."

"Earl murdered Eli when they were teenagers. He murdered him but Eli never really left. Earl used to talk to him. Anytime he looked in a mirror he'd talk with his dead brother. I'm the only person who knew. And now he's here, and he wants to hurt you."

"I won't let Eli hurt Silver," Matt says, his own eyes glistening.

Nodding, my mother sinks into the bunk. Resting her head on the pillow, she closes her eyes. Dad tucks the blanket around her. I kiss her forehead and stroke her hair once more. Dad hugs me and tells me to be brave. I want to spend more time with her, I want to make this moment last longer. I want her to be alive when I come back. What if I don't come back?

"You have to go now, Silver." Dad squeezes me hard. "Promise me you'll come back."

I stare at him. "I promise." What else can I say? I give him one more hug and walk away. I can't prolong the agony of goodbyes.

I leave the living quarters with Matt and the rest of the mission team. We meet the soldiers at the entrance to the presidential compound.

Matt plants the Stetson on my head. "I thought you might want it. I thought it would help."

"It does." I tug the hat into a firmer position. Erica and Sean are with me. All those we lost.

The doors swing open and we march into the night. The loud, clunking security system engages behind us. The civilians will remain here and in the other underground sanctuaries dotted beneath the old city. Safe.

We drive to the farmlands. That's where it all happens in my dream. The red barn looms out of the darkness as we park. We are a force of one hundred. One hundred against a beast that has never existed before. The two stealth helicopters in Francesca's command hover above our heads. They move on a little way, toward the city, scouting the immediate area.

Matt jumps from the jeep and shoulders a backpack of grenades. He wears a belt of twenty of them and has two automatic pistols holstered at his side. His larger bombs are already buried along the borders of the fields. The bulks, towering above the rest of us with their impenetrable muscle, choose automatic machine guns. Jacob slips out of his vehicle with a gurgling Patrick strapped to his chest.

Looking at the line of my friends, my heart clenches against the loss of those who aren't here. I stumble under a wave of grief. I'll have to face my future without them. Without Paige. Maybe it won't be so long until I see her again.

Although Lyla has no offensive abilities, she refused to be left behind. She is armed with a gun and a knife. I finger the familiar hilt of my own knife. My abilities offer a stronger defense, but I can't bear to be without it. It brings me confidence. I think of when my father taught me how to throw it. So long ago now, on our flight through the forest.

Unarmed, Sawyer's hands twitch at his sides as though his fingers rest on triggers. He draws in a breath, then turns to Lyla and places his arms across her shoulders. They exchange a volley of whispers which ends in a passionate kiss.

"Matt..." I call to him as my heart stutters. Blood rushes in my ears and drowns out other sounds. "Matt!" I need him.

"Here." He entwines his fingers in mine.

The soldiers begin to sing. A familiar song of freedom. My song.

> *Young, like a new star shining*
> *Bold, like a lone wolf stalking*
> *Lost, like a child wandering*
> *Scared, like the whole world's falling*
> *But I am free. And I won't back down.*
> *We are the young, we are the fools,*
> *We're the ones to cast down your idols and rules.*
> *When all the world surrounds us with our backs up to the*
> *wall,*
> *Still, our lips scream freedom,*
> *Still, they will hear our call.*

As dawn crests the old skyline, I scan the land in front of us. Fields of corn and wheat and potatoes and green beans and strawberries grow in various stages of development. Breathing deeply, I suck in the cool, morning air.

"It's beautiful," I say to Matt as I hold his hand.

"It is."

"I..." I want to tell him how much I love him. I want him to know how sorry I am, about Eli, about messing around with my abilities, but most of all, that I didn't trust him enough with my problems. I want him to know, in case we don't make it back. And that maybe, as I look at the smiling Patrick, a child wouldn't be so bad.

"I know," he says. "Me too."

The baby giggles.

The fields turn black.

The corn, the wheat, the green beans, the potatoes, and the strawberries no longer exist. Darkness takes their place. A thick blackness rolls on as far as I can see. The dream is here.

"Remember, stay away from your blue bubble. You need to live, Silver," Matt says, his free hand releasing a pistol from his side.

I look at him. "I may not be able to. It may be all we have." I've been trying to prepare myself for the end, but cower at the grisly images of my potential death. I can't think that way. Can only take one minute at a time.

As we look across the field at the woods and the old city beyond, a black line appears above the last remaining skyscrapers I didn't demolish with my destroyer ability. It's the black wave. I know what it contains. Matt spots it too and he calls for the soldiers and our friends to prepare.

I square my shoulders. "And so it begins."

There are hideouts in the old city in front of us and at the compound behind us. No civilians will survive this. Bricks and mortar and locked doors are not enough to protect against the power of this beast. I grit my teeth against the oncoming wave of death.

"Sawyer," Matt calls, as the soldiers take their position in front of us.

"Yeah?"

"Love you like a brother man," Matt says, without turning around.

"You too."

"Let's put this beast back where it belongs," Matt shouts into the rising sun.

"Hooraah!" Sawyer, Mason, and Carter reply, fireballs and weapons raised, respectively.

We advance into the black, infested fields. The soldiers kneel in front of us, facing the wave. The wave comes, demolishing buildings as it advances, the black line growing larger with every mile. As it approaches the woods bordering the farmland, I can make out the animals within its crest.

"It's a freaking tsunami!" Lyla says, as Sawyer shoves her behind him.

"It'll run out of power at some point," Mason says. "It has to."

The two stealth helicopters fly to the advancing black line. The line grows taller and the helicopters fire. Nothing stops the advancing mass. One of the helicopters fires a missile into the black wave. A hole appears in the wave and the missile passes through, causing no harm to the creatures within it. The hole fills with roaring, clawing, snapping animals and the missile lands in the forest behind. An almighty boom sounds as the missile strikes wood and earth and an enormous fireball ignites. But the fire doesn't spread thanks to the storm.

"Silver?" Matt says,

"Yeah?"

"You got this, right?" There is a tremor in his voice I've never heard on our previous missions.

"We've got this." It is a lie.

The wave creeps closer. It takes the woods and the remains of the smoking fireball. It swallows the fields. Within the wave I focus on the snapping mouths of a starving wolf pack. An enormous grizzly bear stands on its hind legs and roars louder than thunder. As the crest rolls over the grizzly, it's replaced by a stampede of wild-eyed stallions, contained within the wave, but looking for escape. Their hooves slam against rock and other animals within the wave and I can imagine too well what those hooves will feel like against my body.

"Hold the line!" Carter yells to the soldiers kneeling in the field. We have one chance at this, and our timing must be perfect.

The second helicopter flies into the black line, machine guns firing. Without warning, a thick black projection extends from the wave and grabs the tail of the helicopter, oblivious to the whirling tail rotor.

"Oh, shit!" Matt says.

I probe with my mind, sure Sawyer is doing the same thing, but the grip on the helicopter is too strong for me to remove. It swings the helicopter around in one slow loop, as if it's trying to propel a giant hula-hoop. The helicopter nose-dives the earth and slams into the fields. Another fireball erupts as the gas tanks blow. A gust of wind brings ash and smoke and heat and fiery sparks toward us, as well as the faint reek of charred flesh.

The soldiers in the field fire, ripping holes into the waves. They hold the line, but it won't be long before they're engulfed.

"Get ready!" Mason calls.

The wave rolls closer. Eli appears within the wave, shirtless, as I last saw him, but that's where the comparison ends. His skin is peeling, his once lustrous hair crawling with worms and centipedes, his eyes a maddened yellow. He roars at the sky, at us, but I can't make out his words.

He is replaced by the yellow eyes. The same yellow eyes I see in my dreams. Their familiarity unnerves me. Each moon-sized eye glows a vibrant, sickly yellow. The yellow of trodden insect guts. They loom at us.

With the appearance of the yellow eyes the wave pauses and hovers at the edge of the field, seeming to size us up. The yellow eyes survey our group, searching. They lock onto the baby cradled behind me. The wave moves again, slower this time, a cat toying with a mouse.

The soldiers continue to fire, punching holes in the wave, but I'm worried we're going to run out of ammo before the wave is close enough to stop.

"Silver, do something," Matt says, as he grabs for a grenade at his belt.

The black lightning dances over my hands. I am filled with power. It surges through my veins. This is what it's all come to. President Bear. Earl. And now this.

Skittering toward us, scorpions advance with pinching

claws and stinging, twitching tails. Hissing black cobras slither and bare venomous fangs. Centipedes as long as my arm dash forward, tripping over their numerous legs, only to right themselves and spit angrily at each other. Spiders scamper over all the other insects, weaving pathways of silk, tying other creatures in their toughened string, biting others with enlarged beaks who get in their way.

Raising an arm to the sky, I swirl my sparking hand in a circle. The wind gusts, causing leaves and twigs to flutter into the sky. Circling my hand faster, the whirlwind begins. The Stetson flies off my head and my hair stands on end as I call to the wind to do my biding. I point in the direction of the wave and the whirlwind grows, changes direction, and spins toward the wave.

"Yes!" Sawyer shouts, fire flickering at his fingertips.

As the whirlwind approaches, it sucks the smaller insects from the black wave into the middle of the spinning force.

"That's it!" Matt calls. "That's my Silver!"

A horse whinnies as the wind yanks its mane away from its neck and it gallops back into the center of the wave. Invisible hands pluck a black, growling wolf cub from the wave. It snaps at the wind as if it's possible to bite it.

The wave continues forward and the whirlwind, now heavy with insects and animals, faces the oncoming wall of black. They meet. The wave consumes the whirlwind easily, as though it's a single puff of air.

"Noooo!" The strangled cry rips out of my throat.

The wave grows. Taller, wider, thicker. Animals snap and growl and scuttle in a vicious fury as they fall over each other.

"Do you think any of them are infected?" Sawyer's voice trembles, but he holds his flaming hands prone.

"Does it matter?" Carter asks.

"I guess not."

Gathering the moisture in the air, each droplet and puddle and river created by the storm, I bring them together. I mix them into a thick mist and cloak us all. I add peep holes. We can see the wave, the monster, but it, I hope, can no longer see us. The wave stops. The yellow eyes appear again, searching.

"Good one!" Mason claps, then puts his hands back on his rifle.

But is it good enough? My skin flushes hot and my entire body trembles, but I can't show my friends how scared I am. I don't have a choice but to face this. I want to see my parents again. I want to grow old. I want to be with Matt. I have to win.

The wave vibrates with seething creatures. The monster hesitates. The mist won't hide us for long. But it doesn't need eyes to find us. It traveled this far using other senses. Reaching us quicker than expected, the wave overturns the first line of soldiers.

Furious winds rip through the fields. I don't know if it's me or the wave. Thunderous noise fills my eardrums, threatening to burst them. I hear the wind and the animals and the soldiers screaming.

Matt shoulders his grenade launcher and fires. Pockets of insects blow into the air and rain over us. But there are more to take their place. The holes Matt punches into the wave are quickly filled. Sawyer throws groups of the animals with his telekinesis into the sky. But they are immediately snatched back by the long, clawed arms to be buried back into the body of the wave. His fireballs erupt in the sky, igniting parts of the wave, scorching several of the threatening creatures. But the wave doesn't stop. Mason and Carter join the next line of soldiers.

I don't know if I expected to win. Maybe the outcome of the last two missions gave me false confidence. Despite all the powers I have, it's not enough.

I don't cry. I don't despair. I'm more accepting than I thought I'd be.

But I won't give up either. I won't. I can't. It's not who I am.

Raising my palms to the sky, I call to the dark power. Black lightning whizzes around me. My fingers twitch. Directing my palms at the wave, the black streaks shoot out of my hands, blowing large sections of the writhing mass apart with each burst of power.

"That's it, Silver! Keep going!" Matt yells. Face streaked with dirt, he loads grenade after grenade.

"We might win this thing yet!" Sawyer yells.

I never saw the end of the vision. In my dream, I never escaped the claws of my prison. It ends in blackness every time.

A grizzly's head explodes. Three wolves are ripped limb from limb. A mass of seething insects disappears with the next black streak. Large holes appear in the wave now. We are making progress. Maybe my dream is wrong.

A few of Matt's bombs are triggered, throwing animal parts into the air and sending a shockwave under our feet.

Stumbling under the pressure as bomb after bomb explodes, animal parts land on us and the ground turns red.

Grotesquely, Eli's head appears on the crest of the wave. Bigger than human, bigger than life, as though he's an inflated version of himself. He thrusts his oversized head back and spews his manic laugh. It cuts off. He levels his gaze at us, at me, and narrows his eyes. "Now, now, Silver, we can't have that."

He surrounds the wave with his shimmering forcefield.

The balance tips in the wrong direction. Matt's grenades bounce off the black wave. Sawyer's fireballs ricochet so violently he has to stop throwing them. My black streaks make holes, small holes. Far too small to make a dent.

The yellow eyes appear again and remain, watching us all, towering above us, making us look at the sky. We take a collective step back.

Another line of soldiers flies into the air and are engulfed by the black wave. Mason and Carter with them.

"No!" Matt screams at the oncoming wall of death. "No! No! No!"

"Oh, *yes!*" Eli replies seductively from within the wave. "Oh, yes!" He laughs again. A gut-wrenching, spine-tingling, bowel-loosening laugh.

"I'm scared!" Lyla cowers behind Sawyer. "I'm sorry, I'm scared!"

"We're all scared," I say. "You don't have to be here, Lyla."

"There's nowhere else to go." She's right. The wave is fifty yards in front of us. It will destroy everything in its path, us and the civilians hiding in the bunkers.

We take another step back. There are a handful of bulk soldiers left. They fire their weapons from behind me, perhaps thinking I can save them. I can't let them all die.

I try to make the wave disappear, like I did with the farmhouse and the trees, but the wave is too big, too powerful, and I can't get past the forcefield.

I step forward. Into the fray. Into the cacophonous tornado of deadly animals. I push against the wind it creates, forcing myself to hold against its deadly force. Holding my palms high, I shoot continuous black streaks, one aimed at the forcefield and the other at the blackness within. It's up to me now, no one else has enough power.

"Silver! What are you doing?" Matt yells, as I take another step closer to the wave. My hair whips my face and is yanked toward the slithering wall of doom, as if attracted by static electricity. My feet slip. I feel the pull like a rip current. Subtle but forceful. I'm in danger of being sucked into the wave.

"If I can touch it..." Maybe I can gain the forcefield ability. I didn't acquire it when I touched Eli in the past, but maybe it will be different now. I can't think of another way to protect us, not without evoking my blue time bubble, and that's likely to take us right back to the beginning of the battle, not change anything significant. With all the abilities I possess, as big as my destroyer power has grown, it's not enough.

Screams ripple from behind. I whip around ready to face another enemy. I'm greeted with the sight of a hundred woman and children flying through the air. Civilians from the closest underground sanctuary.

One of the creature's long, black arms stretches over our heads, into the hideout, digging into the earth. It scoops out all the people as if they're nothing more than grains of sand. They drop to the ground, their screams cutting off abruptly. It's like Koko's plaza all over again. But so much worse.

Leaning forward, I sweep my hand against the sickening wave of horror. My fingers brush the seething mass and a hellhound chomps on my wrist. As I wrench my wrist free, a powerful jolt shudders through me, punching a fist of pain into my chest. Is my heart still beating? Stunned, I gasp for breath, unable to move. I have gained every power the creature possesses. Somewhere inside me is Eli's forcefield ability.

Shaking off the temporary paralysis, I rub at the pain in my wrist. Ignoring the teeth marks and ribbon of blood running down my fingers, I dash the few feet back to the group, to Matt. They stand there, arms hanging by their sides, weapons useless. The wave engulfs the last of the soldiers with a series of protests and screams. The last of the bombs go off, punching holes in the wave. But they're temporary.

It's Matt, Sawyer, Lyla, Jacob and Patrick, and me. That's it. I look at the baby. *If there's ever a time, Patrick...*

Nothing. Not even a faint blue light.

I square my shoulders.

It's time for the last stand.

It's time for the final reckoning.

Glancing at Matt, his piercing blue eyes wear an expression I've never seen before. Defeat. I grab his hand, hard, and make him look at me. "It's not over yet," I scream above the noise of the growling, snapping, scuttling creatures.

Raising one palm to meet the wave, I close my eyes and

suck in a steadying breath. I have one shot at this. A tingling sensation bubbles deep in my chest. It grows quickly, churning inside me. Opening my eyes, I make out the shimmering edges of my own forcefield. I gesture for the others to gather close to me. An instant later, the black wave smacks against my forcefield, producing a deafening noise bigger than a bomb. My ears ring and the reverberations echo in my chest.

"Lyla!" Sawyer screams. Her hair floats outside the confines of my forcefield. Animals grab and bite at it, drawing her away.

The forcefields connect and the rest is a battle of strength. I slip on the red, wet ground. Releasing Matt's hand, I conjure the black streaks of power and aim them at the wave. Animals disappear and ash floats around us, covering us as though we're witnessing Earth's largest volcano. Some of the animals in the wave are flung outside its confines. A black horse, with wild eyes, tumbles over my head. A horde of skittering cockroaches sizzles when I hit them with my lightning.

The crest of the wave arcs over us, descending, ready to swallow us. Swarming over my forcefield, it crashes to the ground behind us. We are surrounded. Wolves and bears snap at me. Panthers and jaguars claw and bite. Snakes wriggle and hiss. Everything seethes with angry life. I try not to focus on any one part, the images are too terrifying.

We stand in the middle of a dark, black wave of terror, within a private bubble of protection with indeterminate strength.

The wave tugs at Lyla's hair. She floats above the ground,

half in and half out of the forcefield. While she unsheathes her knife, she is wrenched upwards and manages to slash a snarling wolverine across its face. Screaming, Sawyer grabs her ankle and is pulled after her. As Lyla rises higher into the black wave, her gills appear along her ribs. Maybe she thinks she can swim through the wave to whatever is on the other side. A cascade of fireballs follows Sawyer, burning holes through insect, reptile, and mammal. But it isn't enough. They're sucked away, into the wave, soundlessly.

"Lyla! Sawyer!" Matt yells.

Jacob stands rooted, cradling Patrick in his arms. The baby is oblivious to the events and smiles at the enormous black wave.

"I can't..." My destroyer power continues to make dents, but the wave is so big, so strong. I fall to my knees. Jacob cradles Patrick to him and whispers in his ear. The baby whimpers.

"Do what you can," Matt says, as he wraps his arms around my waist and buries his chin in my shoulder, ready to face the end with me. "I love you."

I love you too.

My strength wanes. The wave, the creature, is stronger than me. The yellow eyes wink at me and its wide slash of a mouth opens into a terrifying grin. The claws on its disease-covered arms stretch down and I know I'm about to be imprisoned in a jail of claws and teeth.

My power fades. I've never tried to use so much before. The forcefield winks out. With a final shimmering surge in the surrounding black, I collapse onto Matt.

There is one thing left to try.

Snapping mouths surround us. Violent spittle sprays and wide jaws gnash. I call on the color blue, on the shape of an amorphous bubble that might change our odds. Evoking it in my mind, I use the last of my strength to control it.

Before I'm torn in two, my blue bubble appears. It radiates from my core, shimmering and sparkling. I stare at it, transfixed. It throbs with strength and power.

"No!" I hear Eli shout.

"No!" The yellow-eyed monster screams from somewhere within the wave.

The animals fight back. They kick and buck and bite and claw and roar and scratch and sting. I cover my ears against the medley of animal sounds and the roaring of the yellow eyes. I push with all my strength. There is a great pressure in my head, as though it might explode, but I don't stop. Blood runs from my nose, my ears, my gums. Even my pores turn dark with blood. But I don't stop. I can't ever stop. If I stop now, it's all over.

Matt holds me. Jacob cradles the baby, who also shines with a blue light. It's exactly the same color as my bubble.

The pain in my head reaches an unbearable level. I fall backward, even though Matt's arms are around me. As my knees give way, the blue light explodes, like a thousand stars lighting the sky.

I shudder as a new vision accosts me, pushing consciousness away. I cling to it, unwilling to let go, but I have no choice. In all probability, I'll die now. Maybe it isn't so bad.

CHAPTER THIRTY-THREE
SILVER

"WAKE UP, SILVER!" Matt's voice reaches me, disturbing my dream. "Wake up, Silver!"

I open my eyes.

"Where the hell are we?" His eyes are frantic, darting around the room.

Shaking my grogginess away, I rub at a throbbing headache pulsing at the bottom of my skull. With slitted eyes, I examine my surroundings.

I'm on my bed. In my room.

Matt sits beside me, every muscle tense. "How did we get here?"

Frowning, I try to clear my muddy thoughts, but can't remember what I was last doing. Inspecting myself for clues, I see I'm wearing a pretty dress and strappy sandals. The dress is blue with a repeating pattern of a small white bird in flight, maybe a dove. There's a sticky lip balm on my lips. I'm wearing a *dress*. I can't remember the last time I wore a dress. Or strappy sandals.

Looking at Matt, his eyes shine a little brighter than usual, a sign he is tired, and his rugged five o'clock shadow bears more than one day's growth. An unidentifiable, soft blue light illuminates the room. I clutch for the pendant at my neck and am reassured to find it nestled against my collarbone. I frown. I thought I lost it. But I can't remember when.

"Are you okay? You're bleeding?" Matt points to my nose and hands me a tissue.

I wipe at my nose and the tissue darkens, but there isn't a lot of blood.

Tense, I brace myself for...what exactly?

A sheer blue scarf covers the bedside lamp. It was a birthday present from my mother. I always admired the scarves she wore and when I turned thirteen she said I was old enough to have my own.

I clench my teeth. There's something familiar about the particular blue light that illuminates the room. Blinking rapidly, I try to adjust to the light, and when that doesn't work, I rub my eyes. It feels like there's a ton of sand in my eyeballs. Was I at the beach?

"I think I was dreaming," I say.

"Me too." Matt holds my hand.

"I think you were there, in my dream." I swing my legs to the floor. Something seems off, but I can't put my finger on it. Is it the dream, which I now can't remember, or something else? I look at the blue light again. On the table beside the lamp is a framed picture. My mother. We were on vacation in the mountains and she had her back to the sun, her face in shadow, but I can still make out her magnificent smile. I thought I lost that picture. I haven't seen it for...

"Knock, knock." A voice sounds at the closed bedroom door, followed by a gentle rapping of knuckles on wood.

"Come in?" Confused, I can't place the voice.

The door opens and my mother pokes her head into the room. She smiles at us. "It's time, you two."

I look blankly at my mother. Isn't she dead? Isn't everyone dead?

"You guys must have been tired." Concern crosses her face. "Are you okay?" She steps into the room, coming forward, a hand held out to touch me.

"Fine!" I answer shrilly, wriggling away from her hand. Surely she's not really here. I'm seeing things. "We'll be out in a minute."

"You're sure?" Mom asks.

No longer trusting my voice, I nod.

"Don't be long, everyone's waiting." Mom backs toward the door and closes it softly behind her.

"What the hell's going on?" I wring my hands at Matt.

"Shhh!" He pushes himself off the bed and walks to the door, putting an ear to the crack. "There's people out there. A lot of people."

Lowering my voice, I twist my hands into the folds of my dress. "My mother is supposed to be catatonic. Or dead. I can't remember... I don't know..."

"I know." Matt purses his lips. "What's the last thing you remember?" He sits on the bed and looks at me with beautiful, blue eyes that are filled with trepidation.

"I don't know. I remember rain. A storm. A blue light," I say, as I glance at my bedside lamp again. It's unnerving, that weird blue light. I pull the scarf off the lamp and the room is bathed in a more normal, artificial glow.

Matt lets out a breath as though he too is relieved.

"Yeah, me too." Taking my hand, Matt frowns. "And animals. Black animals."

"Oh my God!" The dream comes back to me. "The wave of beasts and the yellow-eyed monster..." I wrap my arms around my waist as I remember the terror. "But I thought I was dreaming. How did you have the same dream?"

"It wasn't a dream. It was real."

"Eli," I whisper, remembering it all. It comes back to me like an electric shock.

"Eli and the yellow-eyed monster." Matt shakes his head repeatedly.

"And Erica and Delta and Einstein," I say. "Mason, Carter, Sawyer, Lyla," I stutter over her name.

"Yeah," Matt says, still shaking his head. Shoulders slumping, he picks up the blue scarf from the floor and winds it around his fingers. "And Earl and the altereds and the hellcats."

"And my mother is okay." I smile.

"And your mother is okay." Standing, he turns in a slow circle, pausing to look out the window. "We're in your old room. In your apartment building from *before* the resistance." He pulls open the drawers of my bedside table, looks under the bed, opens the closet. "What the hell is going on?"

"But I blew up the city with my destroyer power," I say, my headache pulsing. "This building doesn't exist."

"Exactly," Matt says, as though I solved a tough riddle.

"Then how...?

"I have no freaking idea!" His hands fly high. He looks terrified, then understanding flickers in his eyes. "You're blue bubble. The time thing."

"It worked?"

"Come on you two." My mother's voice at the door again.

My chest tightens. My mother is here. Alive. Present. Okay. "Coming!"

"Who else is out there?" I ask Matt.

"I don't know." He rubs the back of his neck. "What happened?"

Closing my eyes, I think back to my dream that wasn't a dream. "There was a wave of animals and the yellow-eyed monster and Eli and they were overpowering us and everyone was killed apart from you and me and Jacob and the baby." I flick my eyes open. "Jacob and the baby."

"Where are they?" Matt asks.

"I don't know!"

"Are we even alive?"

"Yes," I say. "Yes, I'm sure of that. The wave crested over us and my forcefield gave in and my destroyer power stopped working, but the blue bubble came. It belongs to both me and Patrick." Glancing at my fingers, I see they are sparking with tiny electrical bolts. I blow a small breath at my hands and the mini lightning disappears.

"Still got the power then."

"Yes," I say, sitting on my hands. "I thought we were going to die."

His eyes glisten. He pulls my hands out and holds them. "Me too. I wrapped myself around you."

I smile at the tender memory. We braced ourselves for

death, united. "Yes, and then I got another vision...something about Joe."

"Joe's dead."

"Is he?"

We stare at each other, no longer sure of events. How can we be here, alive?

"But where are we now?"

Standing for the first time since I woke, I walk to my dresser on jelly legs and pass a brush through my hair. Looking into the mirror, at my silvery-blue eyes, I slap color into my pale cheeks. I touch up my lip balm. "Let's go find out."

I take Matt's hand and lead him to the closed bedroom door. I run my fingers through Matt's wavy hair in an effort to tame the kinks, and button a hole that's come loose on his dress shirt. Leaning my forehead against his, I kiss him. I hold his jaw in my hands and kiss his cheeks, his nose, his ears, the crook of his neck where he always smells so good.

"I'm afraid," he says, holding me. "My sister..." He looks at the closed door.

"I know." But I have a good feeling about this. Somehow, we won the battle against the yellow-eyed monster and Eli. Somehow, we triumphed, against the odds, and have managed to bring the dead back to life at the same time.

We look at each other one last time before we place a hand on the door and turn the knob together. The door opens onto an empty corridor. Muffled voices and the clinking of glasses and laughter come from further along. It sounds like a party. Matt and I edge closer to the noise, toward the open plan living and kitchen area of my luxury apartment.

Rounding the corner, we pause and watch. There is a sea of smiling, laughing faces. It fills me with hope.

"There you are," my mother says from behind us, startling us both. "I was beginning to think I'd have to call the army to come and dig you out of your love pit." Mom smiles. Her face is filled with love and warmth and all the things I so dearly missed.

"Oh, Mom!" I hug her hard.

"Silver! What's the matter?" She pushes me away and holds me by my arms to examine my face.

"I'm so happy. It's so good to see you!" Joyful tears blur my vision.

"You were only gone for a weekend."

Something wet swallows my right hand and I turn to find a furry face nuzzling into my side.

"Einstein!" Matt bends to one knee and ruffles the dog behind his ears. "Do you think...?" Matt glances at the laughter and clinking glasses.

"Woof, woof," Einstein barks softly.

"He says, 'yes, go and see,'" I interpret.

Matt takes my hand and we enter the living area.

"Happy birthday!" Paige leaps on me, all sparkling, emerald eyes and dark hair flowing as though she came with her own personal wind-machine. She laughs and spins me in a circle. Paige is here. Alive.

"Thank you," I stutter. "How old am I?"

She laughs and pecks my cheek. "What's gotten into to you? It's not every day a girl turns eighteen. Now you can vote!"

"I'm sorry," I say, remembering our last conversation.

"What for, silly?" Paige presses a champagne flute into my hand and clinks her own against it. "Here. You obviously need it."

Paige is alive.

My best friend is alive.

All I can do is stand and stare at her.

She shuts my mouth with her hand. "You don't want to catch any bugs."

After wiping my cheeks, I wrap my arms around her. "It's so good to see you."

"It's only been two days! Does a romantic weekend away turn your brain to mush?" She disentangles herself from my arms and points to my champagne glass. "Drink."

"I thought you were more of a whisky person," I say.

She looks at me blankly before she's swallowed by the crowd and other well-wishers take her prominent position. Does she not remember?

Matt squeezes my hand. He is speechless, his gaze darting over the room.

Koko is next. "Happy birthday!" She presses a small, wrapped gift into my hands.

Then Adam. Matt's parents, his youngest sister Megan. Lyla pops up in the middle of them with Sawyer in tow.

"Thank God!" Matt mutters as he wraps his sister in a bear hug.

"You're such a softie." She socks him on the arm. "Go away for a romantic weekend and get all homesick?"

Matt's parents embrace me warmly before they, too, are swept along with the tide of people.

During a brief moment of respite, Matt whispers in my

ear. "I can't believe..."

"I know. It's a miracle."

"Do you remember, during one of our arguments, when I told you to stop playing with your abilities unless you could bring the dead back to life and restore our world to its former glory?" Matt turns in a slow circle, fidgeting with the glass in his hands. "I was being sarcastic..."

A burst of laughter from the other side of the room snaps his attention away. I startle. They are soldiers and friends I recognize. Bulks. But they don't look like bulks now.

"It wasn't just me. It was the baby too."

Matt and I look up at the same moment. Jacob approaches with Patrick strapped to his chest. He pushes his way to us through the crowd as he pats Patrick on the back.

"Thank God you guys are here. What the actual *fuck* is going on? Excuse my language, little guy," he says to the baby, then looks back at us. "One minute we're fighting the yellow eyes and the next we're.... I don't know what the hell we're doing. Is it your birthday, Silver?"

"I have no idea," I reply. "You remember?"

"Of course I freakin' remember. But why doesn't anyone else?"

Patrick smiles and emits a soft blue light.

"Where did you wake up?" Matt asks.

"Over there." Jacob points to a leather armchair. "In the middle of the party. I was still wearing the sling but there was no Patrick in it and I was freaking out..."

"We're still freaking out," Matt says.

"And then I looked up and saw Paige, holding a sleeping Patrick and stroking his cheek and singing him a lullaby."

Jacob's eyes turn watery. "I just stood there and stared, and she came over and gave me the baby and... I'm so glad to have her back."

"He gave me the power," I whisper, looking at the baby.

Jacob kisses the top of Patrick's head. "And then you did this." Jacob raises his glass to the room to include all the once-dead people, now alive, now resurrected and chatting and smiling in my apartment. My old apartment from the time before.

That's when I see Erica, sitting in Sean's lap, wearing his Stetson. He has his arm wrapped around her and whispers in her ear. She grins and throws her head back, allowing him to smother her neck with kisses.

My heart lurches. Erica is alive. Sean is alive.

I look for others and spot Luis, William, Kyle, dear, sweet Kyle, and Delta.

Circling the room, I look for one person in particular. I hope, I pray it's possible.

"He's not here," Matt says. I wince against his words. He knew who I was looking for. Joe. A bulk. A fighter. He was one of the kindest people I ever met and he was my friend. He saved my life. Matt pushes my hair away from my face and kisses my nose. "I'm sorry."

I glance at the kitchen to see my father refilling empty glasses and my mother beside him chuckle at some joke he just told, her eyes full of love for him and his for her.

"How is this possible?" Jacob asks.

"I don't know, but I'm not going to question it." Matt accepts a second glass of bubbling champagne from a waiter. "And pray I don't wake up."

"It's the time power," I say. "I don't know how it works, and man, it almost killed me trying to use it, but it seems to have saved everyone, and wiped the slate clean at the same time."

"I think," Jacob gestures to the bulks, "the bulks are no longer bulks. They're still army though." He points at Sean's army-issued dress trousers. "Do you still have powers?"

Nodding, I allow my healing light to glow and sparkle across my palm.

"I thought so," Jacob says. "We're the only ones left who remember. We were the last ones standing and so we've kept whatever abilities we had."

I look at the bulks. The ex-bulks. Sean's muscles are impressive, but they're merely well-defined human muscles. He is not exceptionally tall, neither does he possess armored skin. None of them do.

"They could have it turned off," I whisper.

"Look at Erica." Matt nods in her direction. "Her wings were stuck, permanently exposed."

She must feel our eyes boring into her back for she turns, and seeing us, waves cheerily. Sean throws her into the air and she laughs. She may not be a fairy anymore, but she still looks like one. She has a pointed chin and button nose. Somehow, her hair is still lavender with glistening silver flecks. Maybe she dyed it.

"You're right," I say. "So it stands to reason no one else has maintained their powers."

"Welcome to the new, unadjusted society. How we always wanted it to be." Jacob grins and strokes Patrick's perfect head. "We've been returned to the time before. How did you do it, Silver?"

"I have no idea."

The tinkling of a spoon on glass quickly hushes the room. All eyes swivel to my father and the words he's about to impart.

"Well, this is quite a celebration we're having," Dad says.

"Hear, hear!" Mason calls, standing next to Carter. An image of them tumbling into the black wave fills my mind.

"We're here to celebrate Silver's birthday," Dad says. The room erupts in applause and more shouts of 'Happy birthday!'

Heat rises up my neck as everyone stares at me.

"I promised you a party," Dad mouths to me.

I remember the conversation as we ran through the woods to the cave. He forgot my sixteenth birthday and promised to make up for it.

My mother appears in front of me holding a pink princess cake with eighteen glowing candles, expecting me to make a wish and blow them out.

"Don't catch on fire!" Sawyer yells.

"Haven't quite grown out of the princess phase have you, Silver?" Sean teases. But he doesn't know that's what my mother does. It was our thing, ever since I rejected her efforts of the perfect princess cake three times for my fifth birthday. Every year since she's made me a pink, princess cake. I cherish each one.

Squeezing my eyes tight, my wish is that this reality is here to stay. Then I blow the candles out in one with a little help from an ability.

Mom retreats to the kitchen to slice the cake and hands it out on paper plates.

"But things are different," Matt says, as normal conversation resumes around us. "It's before, and the future, all at the same time, as if nothing ever happened." He takes fast sips from his champagne flute.

"As if genetic modification never existed." I clamp a hand over my mouth. It's too good to be true.

"Is that even possible?" Matt asks. "And how do we all know each other? Most of us met during the resistance...and yet everyone's here."

"I don't know," Jacob replies. "We could spend years trying to figure it all out and drive ourselves crazy in the process. I suspect we'll never know. I think we should accept it and marvel a little every day at the wonder of it all. Well, that's what I'm going to do anyway."

Another tinkling of glass quiets the room again. Dad clears his throat. Most of the crowd hold a piece of cake in their hands. Megan licks the frosting off her fingers. She is still in a wheelchair, how she always was. Mom hands me my own piece. It is the largest slice and contains a huge chunk of the princess's dress.

I look at Dad, a strange trepidation filling my veins.

"This is actually a double celebration," Dad's voice rises above the crowd, but before he can continue, a hard knock sounds on the wide front door.

One, two, three.

Knocks suggesting the person on the other side of the door is not used to being kept waiting.

"Ah!" Dad says. "Right on time!" Swiftly, he moves to the

door and throws it open to reveal Francesca with an army of bodyguards. "Please welcome President Montoya!"

Francesca enters the room, shakes hands with some, exchanges words with others. It takes her ten minutes to reach the center of the room, me. She whispers a 'Happy birthday, Silver' in my ear before joining my father at the front of the room.

I scan the handful of bodyguards who entered with her. My heart stutters in my chest when my gaze falls on one. It is Joe. With his gentle honey-colored eyes, hair the hue of corn, and the cleft in the middle of his chin. Joe. Alive. Here. I forget to breathe.

"What a relief," Matt says. "For a minute I thought it was going to be—"

"President Bear," Jacob finishes.

"It's Joe," I whisper.

Matt and Jacob both look at our old friend. Will he know me in this life? As he walks around the room with Francesca, I notice a limp in his right leg as if he never took the nanite to heal it.

"Dim the lights," Dad says. "And turn the TV on please."

A massive screen on the other side of the room drops from the ceiling on its mechanical hinges and Dad thumbs a remote. We're greeted by a familiar news reporter from the time before, one I remember reporting on the deadly virus that swept across the country, before she turned and ran for cover. She was one of the last standing. Now, she sits at her news desk, her face made up and hair coiffed as if she's due for the red carpet.

"As our closest family and friends are here, we thought it

the perfect time to share with you our greatest achievement." Dad gestures for my mother to join him. Francesca smiles proudly at the pair.

Apprehension grips my stomach. Something is going to happen, and it isn't going to be good.

"Well, we're very proud and excited to announce our first success in the genetic modification trials." Dad claps his hands in child-like glee and turns to my mother. He plants a big kiss on her lips before he turns back to his audience and regains a more authoritative composure.

Smiles slipping, Matt, Jacob and I look at each other. My heart still skitters. I don't know whether to look at Joe, my parents, or the screen. With trembling hands, I put the cake and the present Koko handed me on a table before I drop them. A panic attack builds, twitching at the back of my knees and tightening my chest. My heart won't beat in a steady rhythm. Matt grips my hand, his palm slick.

The chatter and the laughter and the double declarations of congratulations swirl around us. Patrick giggles, burps, then emits his pale blue light. Jacob reaches for my free hand. His, too, is clammy.

The three of us stand together and brace ourselves. It was too good to be true. It always is. The three of us squeeze each other's hands and wait. The next few moments will define our places in this new, unadjusted world.

"But I'll let the news reports tell you the rest." Dad points at the screen and the happy crowd grows silent.

"...in the wake of the completion of the all-species genome project over a year ago," the reporter speaks seriously into the camera, but she can't hide the smile at the corners of her mouth. "The first successful trial of limb regeneration has been achieved by using genetic manipulation..."

The camera pans to a hospital room where an overjoyed patient smiles so widely I think his lips might split from the effort. If this occurred during the time before, I would have assumed he'd opted for a permanent smile nanite. The patient lies on a hospital bed, clutching one of his legs, obviously the regenerated one. He was a soldier. Stepped on a mine. He was lucky. Luckier still to have a new limb regrown from a mixture of his own and lizard DNA.

The camera moves to encompass the smiling doctors.

"It was the DNA of a lizard."

The voice chills me to the core. It's one I recognize. A voice I thought belonged to a dead man buried in the depths of hell. Looking at the screen, magnified cold eyes stare back at me. They glint with intelligence and knowing and something else I struggled to put my finger on in the past. But now I know better. It's evil shining from those eyes. And those eyes belong to Earl.

"It was simple." Hovering next to the patient, Earl speaks to the camera, to us. "Once we identified the correct DNA sequence responsible for the regeneration, we adapted it to human DNA. A little complicated as we needed to regenerate new bone..." He shrugs as though it wasn't complicated at all, not for him, "...with the help of nano-technology we did it and we achieved these amazing results. It won't be long until this therapy is available, in hospitals countrywide, in clinics, in general practitioners' offices from coast to coast, maybe even from the drug store in the form of a pill..."

A nanite pill. God no.

The film cuts back to the news reporter but my father aims the remote at the TV and it winks off.

There's a thundering round of applause that goes on and on. I can't think straight. I can't feel anything. I want to close my eyes and go to sleep, wake in a different reality. I can't do this again.

"Shit," Matt says, his face bleached of color.

"What do we do?" Jacob asks, equally pale.

"And," my father says, the triumph in his eyes hard to take, "in this room we have a volunteer for one of our regeneration trials!"

I scan the room, looking for a disabled soldier. But I know who it is. Joe approaches my father and raises a hand so he can be identified.

"Meet Joe Rucker," Dad says. "He tore his ACL while playing football and he's taken a job in the presidential security detail. But we'd like to fix his knee for him."

"Hurrah!" Sean yells, a shout that is taken up by everyone else in the room.

I can't deny Joe wanting to get his knee fixed. He deserves it. I want him to have it. But at what cost?

Joe's gaze scans the crowd and comes to settle on me. There's a flicker of recognition, but I don't think we've met properly in this world yet. Everything we shared before is gone. I smile and turn away.

"This is...This is..." Matt gathers our small group into a tighter circle. "What do we do?"

"When do you get to regenerating me a new ear?" One of Francesca's bodyguards remarks as he points to a half torn off ear.

"I can think of something else you can regenerate," Sean calls. "Or generate further, if you know what I mean." He twirls his hat around and waggles his eyebrows suggestively at Erica. Erica blushes and swats his pursed, waiting lips away.

"We have to do something," I say. "We can't let this happen again. We have to put a stop to it. We have to warn them."

"Congratulations, Drs. Melody. This is quite a day, quite an achievement." Francesca says. "To celebrate this momentous occasion further, we'll be holding a ball in your honor at the president's mansion." She smiles at my parents and shakes their hands again.

"Do I get an invite?" Sean calls.

A soldier pipes up. "Of course you can go, all the officers get to go." I do a double take. The soldier who spoke is Hal. It's all I can do not to run across the room and launch myself into his arms. The image of his death still haunts me.

"Will they listen?" Matt asks.

"My parents will," I reply. "If we tell them everything, from the beginning."

"What about Earl?" Jacob asks.

"That's what worries me," I reply.

Matt surveys the celebratory crowd. "We'll have a fight on our hands."

"But that's what we're here for." I remember Matt's words and allow the black lightning to dance briefly across my palms. My meaning is clear. "It's who we are. It's what we do. We will fight, if we have to, and we will win."

Feeling eyes on me, I look up and catch Hal's gaze. Did

he see me use my powers?

"We'll take Earl down before it comes to that, again," Matt says.

"We will. It will be simpler this time," I say. "I suspect the blood of only one person will be spilt." I'll do it unflinchingly.

Francesca leaves the party with her entourage, although Joe stays behind to talk more about his upcoming experimental procedure. The guests eat hors d'oeuvres and drink champagne into the small hours of the night. The music blares and people dance on the kitchen tiles. Hal lifts me into his arms and swirls me around in a circle during a particularly lively number. He passes me off to Joe. They are friends in this life too.

Joe wraps his arms around me. He smells the same and I lean into him, drinking him in. He asks me questions, which I can barely reply to. I can't find my voice. I wish my dress had a pocket full of acorns to soothe me.

Jacob, Matt and I watch the party. We talk with our now living friends. It is bittersweet. I'm afraid this new reality will shatter.

Telling me he has an early start the next day, Hal tries to leave. I persuade him to stay. He'll be needed.

"We need to gather the team," Matt says. "Before they all leave."

Jacob wakes a sleeping Paige from where she's curled in an armchair. Matt asks Carter and Mason to gather William and Luis. I approach Erica and Sean as he's shrugging into his officer's jacket.

"Don't go." I lay a hand on her shoulder. "We need you to stay."

"Ooo, an after party!" Erica squeals. "I'm honored, Silver."

"Sure thing." Sean slips off his jacket again and removes the champagne glass from Erica's hand with a can-you-believe-what-I-gotta-put-up-with expression written on his face, but he smiles as though it isn't so much to put up with.

Matt finds Delta, Adam and Koko. Matt's family remain. Firmly attached to Lyla's side, Sawyer is settled in for the night.

I approach Kyle. "Don't go anywhere yet."

He grins at me, as if he might sweep my legs out right here. "You think you can take me down again? You only won by one point. I won't let it happen again."

I look at my old friend. He doesn't have a speed ability anymore, but we must train together still.

"Not going to fight in this dress," I say. Impulsively, I hug him. His death is one which hit me hard. But he's here now, and I don't need to think about that anymore.

After most of the guests leave, Matt turns the music off. Gathered in the living room are my parents, Matt's family, Jacob, Paige and Patrick, Delta, Koko, Adam, Claus, Sean and Erica, Hal, Joe, Luis, William, Carter, Mason, Sawyer, and Kyle. They are my family. All of them are here now. I can't wish for anything more.

"Please sit," Matt says from the front of the room. Jacob and I stand with him, Patrick now asleep in Paige's lap. "You'll need to sit for what we have to tell you."

Sean looks at me, a cocky smile propped on his lips. "Are you pregnant?"

"Sean..." Erica lays a cautioning hand on his arm.

I look at my friends as they sit on the uncomfortable but fashionable leather corner sofa barely big enough for them all. They wait, concern creeping into their faces and the alcohol vanishing from their bloodstreams as they react to the tension in the room.

We tell them, all of it, what their roles were and how they died. It takes the rest of the night. Mom rises halfway through to gather refreshments and make sandwiches. We get through it, the whole story and we put forward our case. I even sing them the freedom song. Giving them a showy demonstration of my powers to emphasize the point, I feel uneasy when I catch an impressed look flash across Kyle's face.

We wait. Jacob, Matt and I stand in a line, watching our family and friends digest our information. We wait to see which way the world will turn.

And so it will begin again. Or it won't. If we've said enough, shown enough, to convince our friends and family not to make the same mistakes.

It will begin again, or it won't.

The End

If you enjoyed *The Reckoning*, you can leave a review here:
https://geni.us/TheReckoning

Read on for a sneak peek of
The Mermaid Chronicles, Secrets of the Deep...

THANK YOU!

I hope you enjoyed reading The Reckoning, the third book in The Unadjusteds trilogy. If you did, leaving a review is the best possible present for an author! You can do it here:

https://geni.us/TheReckoning

If you're interested in my other books, you can read the first chapter of all of them on my website at

www.marisanoelle.com

or buy from any bookshop. Please sign up to my mailing list to get the latest news, free stories, novellas, and chapters from all my other books. Every month I hold a competition and three lucky readers get an **e-book completely free**!

You will automatically receive the first three chapters of The Shadow Keepers!!!

Read on for the first chapter of *Secrets of the Deep*...

ACKNOWLEDGMENTS

Books cannot come into existence without a tremendous amount of support from other people. It really does take a team. With that in mind, there are two teams of people I want to thank. Firstly, my writing group, The Rebel Alliance —I couldn't have done this without your support. You've had my back for several years now and you've encouraged me at every step. Secondly, Team Swag—you've been there while I negotiate the publishing waters. We hold each other's hands and share our knowledge. What a fantastic group of writers and friends.

Fay—the cover is gorgeous, and I couldn't be more pleased!

My husband, Neil—Thank you for being my rock, my Steady Eddie. You stole my heart in a night and continue to keep it every day. I love you.

My kids: Riley, Lucas and Quinn—you have been so supportive and proud of me, as long as I don't turn up at your school fairs with a stack of books. You have encouraged me to keep going and stay strong. You are always my first port of call when I get stuck on a plot problem, and you always help!

My parents: Larry & Rita—thank you for your support and encouragement. For being the best parents anyone could ask for. Special thanks to Mom for being my eagle-eyed proofreader, unless there's a typo, then blame her.

My early supporters who have given me advice and feedback along the way: Sasha Newell, Michelle Oliver, Nikki, Adrian, Darcy & Hetty Kane, Rhia Mitchell, and Sarada McDermott.

The amazing writing community on Twitter. I've made a lot of friends there and you have all made my journey less lonely and the rejections easier to deal with. You know who you are. Thank you.

Booktok! What a fantastic community I've fallen into. You've made me buy crowns (several), and you've supported my journey, not just by engaging with me, but by buying my books too. I have found beta and ARC readers here and I know it is my new home.

My A-level English teacher, Michael Fox, who taught me to first think for myself and then to defend my ideas.

I'm saving this last one for the most special group of all: my readers. I wouldn't be here without you, and I hope you stick around to discover some of my other books.

(www.marisanoelle.com)

Read on for a sneak peak of *Secrets of the Deep...*

ABOUT THE AUTHOR

Marisa Noelle is the writer of middle grade & young adult novels in the genres of science-fiction, fantasy, horror & mental health including *The Shadow Keepers*, *The Unraveling of Luna Forester* (First place Incipere Awards, WriteBlend Finalist, BBYNA Semi-Finalist, Bookshelf Finalist), *The Unadjusteds Trilogy* (*The Unadjusteds*, *The Rise of the Altereds*, & *The Reckoning*), and *The Mermaid Chronicles* (*Secrets of the Deep*, *Quest for Atlantis*, *Fight for Freedom*, *Ghost Pirates* & *Vendetta*).

Marisa is a mentor for the Write Mentor program that helps aspiring MG & YA authors. With dual citizenship, Marisa has lived on both sides of the Atlantic and uses settings in both the USA and UK as inspiration for her novels. When she's not writing or reading or watching movies, she enjoys swimming. Ocean, lake, or pool, she's not fussy, as long as she can pretend she's a mermaid. Despite being an avid bookworm from the time she could hold a book, being an author came as a bit of a surprise to her as she was a bit of a science geek at school. She lives in Woking, UK with her husband, three children and dog (Copper).

Marisa loves to hear from her readers. You can find and connect with her at the links below.

Twitter & Instagram: **@MarisaNoelle77**

Tiktok: **@MarisaNoelle12**

Website: **www.MarisaNoelle.com**

Read on for the first chapter of *Secrets of the Deep*...

 twitter.com/MarisaNoelle77

SECRETS OF THE DEEP

CORDELIA BLUE IS AFRAID OF WATER.
CORDELIA IS ALSO A MERMAID.

Determined to face her fear, Cordelia enters the ocean for the first time since her twin brother was killed and learns she is from the oldest bloodline of mermaids. Entrusted with a magical relic, it us up to her alone to break an ancient curse and free the mermaids from the water.

But the selachii—mysterious shark shapeshifters—also have their eyes on the relic. As tensions increase between the mermaids and selachii, Cordelia doesn't know who to trust. Forced to choose between love and race, she doubts every decision and the intentions of those around her.

Trusting her head will lead to a path of betrayal, but she might just get her family back. If she chooses her heart, the mermaids may stay cursed to remain in the ocean forever.

Find out more at www.marisanoelle.com

Turn over for chapter 1...

SECRETS OF THE DEEP
CHAPTER ONE

Shark Attack in San Francisco, 2 killed.

ANOTHER ONE?

"Oh, Cordelia!" Dad spotted me hovering in the hall. The remote rested in his hand, teetering on two fingers. It overbalanced and crashed to the wood floor.

I switched my gaze to the TV, which portrayed a sunny beach oddly devoid of families and surfers. Instead, ambulance crews and police dotted the length of the coastline, and a thick yellow tape prevented people from entering the water. They held hands to their foreheads to shield their vision from the sun and conferred in huddled groups. The tickertape scrolled by endlessly at the bottom of the screen:

Shark Attack in San Francisco, 2 killed.

A memory stabbed deep. My mother and brother...

The boat crested a gentle wave, gliding along a sparkling ocean, and twisted my stomach like I was riding a roller-coaster. The bow peered at the valley. It stalled there until something large shunted the boat forty-five degrees. I stumbled against the seating and stretched for the grabrail. With my heart hammering against my ribs, I pulled myself up and looked over the starboard side. The sea remained sparkling and calm, revealing no clue as to what had collided with us. I glanced at Dylan. He shrugged. Mom pulled her lifejacket tighter.

Shark Attack in San Francisco, 2 killed.

My heart thumped in my chest as the news report ticked on and all the memories from five years ago slammed into me like a cartoon anvil. That made ten fatalities from shark attacks along the US Pacific coast this year alone. What the hell was going on? Although sharks were territorial and often defended their patches of ocean, this behavior was unprecedented. What crazy experiments was Dad conducting at the Navy lab? His explanations were starting to wear a bit thin.

I sucked in a breath. Dad turned toward me. He bent, retrieved the remote and thumbed the power button. The screen went blank. We looked at each other. Neither of us could speak.

"Breakfast is ready." He ushered me to the table. After sitting, he busied his hands with moving the jug of maple syrup and the plate of bacon and a thousand other unnecessary things. "Here." He placed a mountain of waffles in front me and proceeded to drown the whole thing in a gallon of maple syrup.

I pointed to the blank TV screen. "Are you going to ignore what we both saw?"

His shoulders sagged. "I didn't want you to see that."

"Too late," I said, putting the cap back on the maple syrup.

"You know shark attacks are rare, right?" He held a forkful of waffle poised before his lips. "What happened to your mother, to Dylan—it's extremely rare."

"You've told me before, Dad. It was Sod's law. Wrong place, wrong time. A crappy, unfortunate accident." I couldn't meet his eyes. If I looked into those compassionate blues, tears might fall. "Or so you say. But the shark that took Mom and Dylan wasn't an ordinary shark. You must know that."

He frowned and somehow managed to pull his whole face into the gesture, stubble and all. "What else could it be?"

"I don't know! You're the shark expert!" I chucked my knife and fork onto my plate. The clatter startled both of us. I took a breath, calming the building anxiety. "The fact that ten people were killed by sharks this year alone tells me something else is going on."

Dad chewed on his waffle and swallowed carefully, then rammed in another bite. I wasn't about to let him off the hook.

"How do *you* explain what happened?" I picked up my knife and pointed it at the TV, then pierced a mouthful of waffle.

"It is unusual," he said, running fingers glistening with syrup through his short beard. "I think illegal feeding, combined with the rise in pollutants and a decrease in prey, has made sharks bolder. I don't know. That's just a guess. You're not the only one thinking about it. I'm going to talk to the others at the lab when I get in."

"You guys work for the Navy. You're a marine biologist. Surely you have a better idea than '*I guess?*'" I jabbed my knife in little stabbing motions to emphasize my point.

He shoved his plate aside to lean over the table. "Cordy, have a little faith in me. I'm working on it. I don't share everything with you. You still won't get into a bath. And don't think I don't know you had a nightmare last night. I don't want to add to that."

I brushed his comments aside. "I don't know how you can work with sharks. Walk into a lab every day, look at those sadistic smiles, and not think about Mom and Dylan. How do you do that?"

He splayed his hands on the table. "You know why. For your mother."

I blanched. "Mom hated the water."

"She had anxiety."

"I know that."

Dad's voice lowered as he said, "A hormone in sharks' brains is showing promising signs of regulating anxiety. How can I *not?*"

A renegade tear slipped down my cheek. Dad yanked his plate back and poured more maple syrup onto his drowning waffles. He took his time cutting his last few bites.

My knee bounced under the table. "Do you think it was the same shark that attacked Mom and Dylan?"

Dad coughed and spluttered. He slapped his chest a couple times to ease the food down. "Cordy—"

"It could be." I pressed my hands onto my knee to make it stop jiggling. "Who knows what your experiments are doing to them."

"Not *that*."

"Then we have two killer sharks swimming up and down the coast of California. Don't you think that's a little odd?" I snatched a piece of bacon and swirled it in a puddle of syrup.

"What I think," he said, after swigging the last of his coffee, "is that we should change the subject. This isn't getting us anywhere."

"You're avoiding."

"I'm not avoiding."

Behind my head, the kitchen clock ticked a full sixty seconds. The hum of the refrigerator purred and clicked. A calendar hung next to it. The picture for September depicted an ocean scene with a boat uncomfortably similar to *The Big Blue*—our old boat.

Dad swiveled his baseball cap around on his head a full three-sixty degrees and fiddled with the peak, pulling it lower on his brow. "I wanted to talk to you about your birthday."

"You're changing the subject."

"Not entirely."

I blotted my sticky lips with a paper towel. "I don't do birthdays.

You know that."

He gave me one of his thin sympathy smiles. "I think it's about time you did." Lifting my plate, he placed it on top of his. Then he folded his hands on the table and waited me out.

I half stood, tucking my legs around the stool. "I don't want to be late for school."

"You don't have to be there for a while yet."

I eased myself back into my chair and focused on the suddenly interesting condensation pattern my juice glass had made on the wood table.

"You're going to be eighteen."

Not looking at Dad, I ran my fingers up and down the side of the glass. "I'm aware."

"Cordelia."

I remained fixated on the tabletop.

"Cordy." His voice softened. "It's been almost five years."

"I'm aware of that too." I met his eyes, surprised to find them watery. "I think about them every freaking day."

He took the glass out of my hand. "So, what do we do now?"

I lifted a shoulder. "I guess we keep on keeping on."

Dad reached for my hand. "I don't think that's enough. I want you to be happy."

I wiped the dampness away from my eyes. "I want to be happy too. But I can't. Not without them. Not while other people are being killed by some serial killer shark."

Dad brought his coffee cup to his lips, must have realized it was empty, and put it back down. He blew out an extended breath, which ruffled the sparse hairs of his moustache. "What do you think Dylan would want you to do?"

I recalled the worst day of my life. The day he and my mother died. The day he tried to steal a bottle of beer from the cooler. At thirteen. "Something outrageous."

"Will you at least think about it? It doesn't have to be a

big deal. You could do something small with Trent and Maya."

"Maybe."

Dad pressed his palms against the table. "You deserve it. We...I...you...need to move on. We need to celebrate the happier times in our lives. You need to stop being chained to the past." He stood, gathered the dishes and carried them to the kitchen sink. He rinsed them and loaded the dishwasher, the clang of the plates fraying my already unraveling nerves.

I traced the condensation pattern with my finger, spreading it across the table. "Maybe."

He stared at me, seeming to assess my sincerity, my willingness to cooperate. "Okay. Good." Stooping, he kissed the top of my head. "I've gotta get to work. You'll be okay?"

I nodded.

"See you for dinner. I'll bring back some fish from the market."

"See you for dinner," I echoed.

Dad grabbed his work satchel, keys, and cellphone and then left the house. The door caught on a breeze and slammed behind him. Above my head, the kitchen clock continued to tick, and the refrigerator clanked and whirred. The calendar picture called at me, mockingly. But I couldn't sit there all day trying to avoid thoughts I could never escape. Rising from the table, I glanced briefly at the TV, picturing the widening jaws of the great white shark from my past. I shook my head, trying to dispel the image. Not daring to glance at the spare room or think whose room it used to be, I walked past the framed family prints dotting the hallway. I refused to take in the wide smiles and arms around shoulders of a life long ago and stepped into my room. Today was the first day of my last year of high school. A milestone, if I cared enough to think that way. Maya would be all over it.

I hovered in my doorway, my hand grasping the cool of the brass door handle. Inside, the scrunched pillows, askew lampshade, and twisted sheets spilling onto the floor revealed the extent of last night's nightmare. I wished, for the millionth time, that everything was different.

Tasting salty tears at the back of my throat, I struggled against the graininess of tiredness and drooping eyelids. A morning breeze blew through the open window and billowed my curtains, making humanoid shapes of the woven fabric.

I straightened the lamp shade. Underneath sat a framed photograph of my family: mother, father, daughter, and son, like many other families. The picture was framed simply and elegantly in a band of thin silver, and it glinted under the soft lighting of the lamp.

The four of us sat on the beach wearing shorts and T-shirts and backward baseball caps. Our smiles were wide and twinkling, the great American toothpaste commercial. Our arms were thrown around each other. Dylan had planted bunny ears above my head. It had been taken five years ago, almost exactly. Right before the attack.

A dorsal fin appeared on the crest of a foaming wave. My heart rate ratcheted up a notch. Twenty feet away, the fin hovered on the crest. The dark shadow beneath the waves snaked one way, then the other. Jaws burst through the surface. Jaws bigger than I'd seen in any movie or documentary. Impossible jaws.

Three lines of serrated teeth. Two rolling black eyes. Intelligent eyes. Eyes that portrayed a murderous purpose. My pulse thundered in my ears, and my hands turned slick.

"Holy..." Dylan muttered. His thirteenth birthday badge glittered in the sunlight.

"Chris," Mom yelled, pointing at the advancing shape. She leaped across the deck, slipped over a rope, and went sprawling, bumping her head against the fixed seating. Dad let go of the wheel and ran to help her.

"It's a great white," I said, tensing against the guardrail.

"And it's huge."

To carry on reading, click here:

https://geni.us/SecretsoftheDeep